THIS WORLD IS OURS

THIS WORLD IS OURS

THE GEISHA WHO RAN AWAY VOLUME THREE

INDIA MILLAR

Red Empress Publishing
www.RedEmpressPublishing.com

Copyright © India Millar 2018
www.IndiaMillar.co.uk

Cover Design by Cherith Vaughan

ALSO BY INDIA MILLAR

Secrets from the Hidden House

The Geisha with the Green Eyes

The Geisha Who Could Feel No Pain

The Dragon Geisha

The Geisha Who Ran Away

The Song of the Wild Geese

The Red Thread of Fate

This World is Ours

Warrior Woman of the Samurai

Firefly

Mantis

Chameleon

Spider

Dragonfly

Scorpion

Cricket

Moth

Haiku Collections

Dreams from the Hidden House

Song of the Samurai

This book is humbly dedicated to Benzaiten, the Japanese goddess of good luck for both writers and geisha. May both she and you enjoy the words herein!

PREFACE

"Living only for the moment, giving all our time to the
pleasures of the moon, the snow, cherry blossoms, and
maple leaves. Singing songs, drinking
sake, caressing each other, just drifting, drifting. Never
giving a care
if we had no money, never sad in our hearts. Only like a
plant moving
on the river's current; this is what is called
The Floating World."

Tales of the Floating World
Asai Ryoi, 1661

PROLOGUE

*I*f there is one certainty in this world, it must be the fact that a bride's first meeting with her new parents-in-law causes deep concern.

It was certainly so for me. The fact that I had been married once before made no difference at all to my worries now. My first mother-in-law had truly been the stuff of nightmares for a young bride. She was a Southern lady. A devout Catholic, steeped in the traditions of her Virginia home. So shocked was she to discover that her beloved only son had brought home a Japanese geisha for his wife that she had a heart attack moments after she first met me. Or rather, she pretended to have a heart attack. No matter, the message was exactly the same. I understood perfectly. I was not welcome in her life. Nor, from her point of view, would I ever be welcome in her son's life.

But that is my past. That meeting now only has a place in my memories. All that is of any concern is my life now. The shuddering breath I take at this moment. The moment before the door to the low, unremarkable white house is about to swing open and my new husband's parents will be waiting to greet me.

Wish me luck. For although I am no longer a geisha, my past life and all that happened in it cannot be changed. And my new mother and father are missionaries for the Free Church of Scotland. They are living here in distant China to convert those remaining wayward heathens who stubbornly refuse to accept the joys of Christ the Redeemer, choosing instead to cling to the gods of their ancestors.

As I do.

As the door widens, I pray to Baizenten, Goddess of Geisha, to bring me good fortune, for I think that I may need it.

ONE

My future is mine
To take. You may help me, but
You will not hinder!

*O*ur journey from the terrible war zone in the Turkish Crimea to Shanghai was long and appallingly difficult. If it hadn't been for my instinct telling me that at the end of it we would surely be close to finding my dear, lost daughter, the daughter I had been forced to abandon only hours after her birth but who was with me in my thoughts every single day, I would have lost heart. Given up and asked my husband Callum to turn around and take us both back to our beloved Scotland. But how could I, when a letter from my father-in-law had assured us that Kazhua was not only still alive, but was famous throughout Edo as the most talented and beautiful geisha of her generation? Or at least that had been so, many months ago when his letter had been written.

"We shall find her. I promise you," Callum said. I nodded, tears brimming in my eyes. My first husband,

Simon, had died in Edo when he had gone back to find my beloved Kazhua. That memory haunted me. I could not turn back from my search for my lost daughter, yet so many years had passed since I had seen her, I could barely believe the moment for us to be united was here at last. I prayed anxiously to Baizenten that we would find her, and that we would finally be allowed to live together in happiness as the family that neither of us had ever known.

Surely, if we were to be reunited finally, this was the time! As soon as the Crimean war ended, Callum resigned his commission as a captain in the British army. He was no longer simply Captain Niaish, but was once more the Marquess of Kyle, master of huge estates in the Highlands of Scotland. But he assured me that there was no urgent need for us to return to Scotland at once. He pointed out that Turkey was so much nearer to Japan than Scotland. Now that we had no need to remain in the Crimea, it seemed to us both that fate was surely urging us to go east.

First, to China, where I could finally meet Callum's parents in Shanghai. And I felt sure that that in itself was a good omen. Shanghai was the nearest point on the Chinese mainland to Japan. We could slip into Japan unnoticed from there and search for Kazhua. I was elated. I had no idea at all of how far away Shanghai was from Turkey. I was far too eager to set off to ask.

It would have been far better had I been prepared for the journey. Callum had tried to tell me that it would be better to go by ship. Much as I hate sea journeys, he had almost persuaded me when his conscience got the better of him—as usual—and he added that although the journey would be far more comfortable by ship, it would also take longer. We would have to use local vessels, and not only change ships many times, but would also have to wait in port until a ship that was heading in our direction was willing to take passengers. Because of that, most of the stages couldn't be booked until we arrived in the next port, so it could mean waiting idly for long periods.

"How long would it take?" I demanded.

Callum shrugged. "How long's a piece of string?" He smiled winningly. "It could take a lot longer than traveling overland. I really don't know. But it would be safer, and far more comfortable for you."

I took no time at all to think about it. At least if we were traveling by horseback, we could make progress each day. Our journey was in our own hands.

"I'll learn to ride," I said firmly.

I had never ridden a horse before, and for a long time I was so stiff and sore I could think of nothing else but my pain. But as the days turned into weeks, my body began to adapt to the rhythm of my mount, and as my physical discomfort lessened, my mind became more and more dull. Each day was exactly the same as the last. We rode on dirt tracks, our horses kicking up dust that choked us unless we kept scarves tied over our mouths constantly. Even then, the dust got into our eyes and left them sore and weeping. We passed through a village perhaps every other day. Just as each day was the same, so was each village. They were all poor places, barely able to provide us with water and rice. When dried meat or fish was on offer, we took all of it. And paid an extortionate price for the poor stuff. Often, we could find no firewood and could not boil water to cook rice, so we were forced to gnaw on nothing but cold, dried meat or fish.

The sight of a golden eagle, hovering close in search of its pray, was a topic of conversation that lasted us for days. Apart from that, Callum, too, was almost silent. It was as if we no longer had any words between us. And this terrible journey had killed not just our conversation, but also it seemed our desire for each other. The countryside between villages was deserted. If we had had the inclination, we could have climbed off our horses and made love at the side of the road. We did not. At night, we ate our poor meal in silence and then wrapped ourselves in blankets, not even close enough to touch.

On yet another dreary, dusty morning, a mosquito bit me spitefully on my temple. I scratched the bite and it irritated me. The mosquito escaped my slap, so I snapped at Callum instead.

"Where is everybody in this terrible country?" I demanded sullenly. "We haven't gone through a single large town, and all the villages are half dead. Has there been a plague or something?"

Even as I said it, I flinched, wondering if there really was danger to us from the plague. I had seen it when I was a child in Japan, and I knew only too well how deadly an outbreak could be. Callum's listless answer was far from reassuring.

"A plague of a sort has blighted the whole of China these many years past." I put my hand in front of my mouth with horror, and he shook his head. "It's not the sort of illness you can catch, don't worry about that. Most of it is directly due to my fellow countrymen, I'm very sorry to say. Have you ever heard of the East India Company?"

It was the longest conversation I could recall us having since we had entered China. I stopped scratching my bite and shrugged. I didn't need to think, the name meant nothing at all to me.

"No," I said simply. In spite of my lack of interest,

Callum carried on talking. He sounded angry, and I turned to look at him in surprise.

"The East India Company caused all this devastation." He waved his hand at the almost derelict village we were passing. An old man stuck his head out of a hut that was more holes than walls and watched us totally without interest. "Until very recently, they had half the world's trade in the palm of their hand. They even had their own army." I shook my head; this was nonsense. If they were so powerful, I would have known about them. Callum glanced at me and added, "You wouldn't have heard of them in Japan. Not even the East India Company could maintain a presence there even though they tried, centuries ago. And for that Japan can give thanks."

He paused, staring at the ruined village as though it disturbed him. So, he was still interested in something! But not me. I was angry. What did I care about the East India Company? And how dare Callum find it so fascinating when he had barely taken any notice of me since we began this terrible journey? I cleared my throat. It had been so long since I had spoken more than a few words, my voice was rusty with disuse.

"How could a single company do this to a country as big as China?" I demanded.

"Opium." Callum turned in his saddle and stared at me intently. I almost laughed at the anti-climax. Opium was nothing. Most people in Japan used it. I had even taken it myself, once, but I didn't like the effect it had on me so I had not tried a second time.

"Everybody uses opium," I protested. "It's no different from drinking sake. What's so wrong with that?"

Callum reined in his horse and jumped down. He held his arms out for me and I slid off my own mount clumsily.

We had already been riding for hours, to take advantage of the cool of the morning, and I was very stiff. I was also scornful. What was there in this ruined village that was so interesting? I held back, but he grabbed my hand and pulled me toward the houses.

It was not as deserted as I had thought. There were people in many of the tumble-down shacks. They stared at us listlessly, showing no surprise at these two strange foreigners who were intruding so very rudely into their lives. Callum pulled me from one dwelling to another, saying nothing but simply inclining his head as if to say, "Look." Finally, I had had enough.

"Callum, stop it. Why are you showing me these poor people? They all look on the verge of starvation. Give them some money for food and let's get away from here."

I was puzzled and impatient. I could see nothing in this wreck of a place that might be interesting to Callum. He walked me away without a word and helped me back on my horse silently. Normally the most generous of men, I was bewildered that he had not given a single one of the villagers the charity they so clearly needed.

"What was all that about?" I nagged. Callum urged his horse into a canter, and I followed on my own mount. Increasingly angry, I grabbed his reins and tugged hard, forcing him to stop. "Stop ignoring me and tell me."

He slumped in his saddle. It was as if his defenses had suddenly been lowered and all at once I saw the pain our long journey had inflicted on my husband. The scar that ran through his eye was inflamed with all the dust we kicked up. His hair and beard were thick with the same dust; through it I could see he looked deathly tired. My anger died in a surge of remorse. Callum had agreed to this terrible journey for one reason and one reason only: to please me. And all I had done was sulk and bicker and turn my face from him. I cursed myself silently for the bloody-minded bitch I knew I had been.

"Callum, I'm sorry," I cried out loud. I suppose I should have explained what I was sorry for, but it didn't seem to matter. He smiled ruefully and shook his head slightly. I knew he understood.

"I think we're far enough away from the village to camp in safety. It's approaching dusk. Do you want to stop for the night?"

"Yes, please." We tethered the horses and unpacked our blankets and food. The horses nibbled at sparse grass. There was no wood for a fire, so yet again hard, dried meat and tepid water was our evening meal. I could think of nothing but the dreadfully emaciated village people and my food stuck in my throat and threatened to choke me. Callum put down his plate with food still on it and I knew he felt the same.

"Please, tell me what's happened here. I don't under-stand," I said quietly. I put my hand on his arm and he did not turn me away. He paused, obviously gathering his thoughts, and then closed his eyes wearily.

"I'm sorry I had to show you that. But you had to see the problem for yourself or you would have thought I was exaggerating. Anyway, as I said earlier, it's all down to The East India Company. The biggest company the world has ever known. They're on their way out now, thank God. The British Government has taken down their monopoly on trade with the East, and they're too used to having every-thing their own way to be able to cope with serious compe-tition." I was still bewildered, but if it were important enough for Callum to want to explain to me, I would listen. "The point is, for the last hundred years or so, they've single-handedly imported enough opium into China to enslave millions upon millions of people. According to Da, and he should know, at the moment there are at least twelve million opium addicts in China. And many millions more who are happy to spend every spare cent they have on the drug. Da hates the opium trade passionately, and I suppose he's passed that hatred on to me."

He opened his eyes and looked at me. I felt intensely stupid, but I still didn't understand.

"I'm sorry, I don't see the point. What's that got to do with all these ruined villages?"

"The people here have sold everything they have to buy opium. It's the same throughout the country," he explained seriously. "I saw it firsthand when I lived here with my parents, and it's very terrible. Once the drug takes hold, they care about nothing else. They sell their furniture and all their other belongings just so they can have their pipe of opium. When they have nothing left, they beg in the streets. When that fails, they sell their children. The girls go to any brothel that wants them, the boys to be worked to death. And when they have no children to sell, then the man of the house sells his wife into prostitution."

I had noticed without thinking about it that the village we had just left had contained only men. There were neither children nor women. Now I knew why.

"But why doesn't the Chinese government do something about it?" I demanded. "Surely, they must know what's going on?"

"They do. But many of the officials are corrupt, and they earn a fortune from the opium trade. And even the honest ones have been powerless in the face of the huge organization of the East India Company. In any event, everybody knows the Company has the might of the British Empire behind it. Who really wants to fight that?"

"And you say it's like this throughout China?" I asked in disbelief.

Callum shrugged. "More or less. It's the peasants who suffer the most, as always. The rich can usually find enough to pay for their pleasures." He paused, raising his head to listen. I stared around and pressed on his arm in warning as I saw a figure duck behind a bush, too close for comfort. Callum spoke without changing his conversational tone. "I've seen him."

He rose and stretched, rolling his shoulders as if to ease the stiffness. He walked casually over to our horses. I screamed as the figure darted from behind the bush and ran swiftly toward me. In spite of the fact that the young man running toward me was little more than a walking skeleton, he terrified me. His expression was entirely blank. It seemed to me that there was no thought behind his actions. Before I could stand, Callum swiveled round from his horse, his precious minié rifle pointing and ready to fire. The man stopped, hopping from foot to foot in his anxiety, and then his need got the better of his fear and he lunged for me, his eyes fixed on the jade and gold bracelet around my wrist. Callum immediately fired a warning shot that blasted the dust at his feet. That did it. The man howled and turned to run away from us. Callum loosed another shot and the man fell face down on the earth, his arms and legs spread-eagled. I thought Callum had actually killed him, and I was torn between relief and horror.

Callum walked across and poked him, hard, with his rifle. He spoke to the man in rapid Mandarin, and I gave thanks to the gods when the man replied. After a moment, Callum leaned down to him, and when he stood, he had something that glinted in his hand in the last of the sunlight. He spoke again and I guessed he was telling the prostrate figure that he could go. A second later, the man scrambled to all fours and stumbled off in a strange, crouching shamble that seemed more dog-like than human.

I had no idea I was shaking until Callum came and sat next to me and put his arms around me. I was trembling so hard I almost jittered out of his embrace.

"It's all right," he said reassuringly. "It was as I expected. He was going to try and rob us to buy opium. He said he wouldn't have hurt us, but I took this off him." He opened his hand and showed me a tiny, wickedly sharp dagger. "I don't doubt he would have used it."

I swallowed and looked at his calm face in amazement. "Are we safe here? Should we go on? What if he—or somebody else—comes back in the night and tries again?"

"We'll be safer here tonight than near another village," he assured me. "He—and I imagine nobody else in this place—had ever seen a foreign devil before. And the fact that I spoke fluent Mandarin terrified him out of the few wits he had left. I told him my minié rifle was possessed by a spirit I had put in it to guard it, and as a result it had the power to call out to me in the darkness if anybody approached. He believed me, I promise you." I stared at him, wanting to believe but still not sure. "It might have been no bad thing. News about us will travel from village to village. In a week's time, the locals will be convinced that I'm a *yaoguai*, a terrible demon. And that you're a fox spirit, bound to serve me."

I laughed, although shakily. "We have fox spirits in Japan," I said. "I was always terrified of them when I was a child. I was sure they were snuffling around my futon in the night, ready to take over my soul. I was so sure about it, I woke one of my brothers up once to tell him. As it turned out, it was a real fox trying to get at our ducks, so Father was very pleased with me. Funnily enough, the fox spirits never woke me up again."

"We live and learn," Callum said seriously.

I laughed, rather creakily at first, and then properly. My head was resting on Callum's shoulder, so I couldn't see his expression, but I realized after a while that he wasn't laughing with me and my own laughter ground to a halt.

"I'm sorry, Tara-chan," he said. "If I had known how bad and how dangerous this journey was going to be, I would never have considered it. But now we've come so far, we will get to Edo, and we will find Kazhua. I promise you. It will all be worth it."

Any desire to laugh fled. Simon, my first husband, had also promised that we would find Kazhua. And he had died trying. Foreboding writhed in my belly, as though worms were unwinding there.

"Don't speak of it. Not now. Not until we're closer." My voice shook as I wondered if Callum understood or if he thought I no longer cared.

"We will find her," he repeated stubbornly. "The past is gone. It can have no influence on us unless we let it. We will find her, I promise you."

He did understand then. I remained still, listening to his heartbeat. After a long, comfortable silence, I raised my hand and found his scar. I stroked his closed eyelid very gently.

"I worry about your scar," I said seriously. "There is a certain kind of woman who likes her man to look as if he has seen the wicked side of life."

"Really? Speaking from personal experience, are you?"

His sudden lightness delighted me. I felt my own spirits

rise in response. I laughed and tried to pull away from him, but Callum was having none of it. His grip tightened around my shoulders and he ducked his head and bit gently at the side of my neck.

"Ah, my pretty fox spirit. Are you going to growl at me? Show me your teeth and scratch me with your claws? Or just possess me and turn me mad for your beauty?"

"I thought I had already done all that," I said, all the time praying that this pleasure between us was going to last. Callum laughed and I felt intensely guilty as I realized that this was the first time I had heard him laugh, *really* laugh, since we had left his comrades in the Crimea.

"And so you have." Callum turned my face toward him with his finger, and I stared at his face with as much curiosity as if he had been a stranger to me.

"Ah, but you have changed from the first time I saw you." Tears stung my eyes and made me blink as I remembered my first meeting with him. Simon, my first husband, had hated him on sight and had forbidden me to allow him into the plantation house if I was alone. But I had been intensely attracted by Callum's combination of black hair and blue eyes and the laughter that always seemed to lurk behind even his most serious expression. Now, there were threads of silver in that black hair and his beard. The scar that puckered his eye would be a constant reminder of the Crimea. But more than that, his lightness of heart had gone. Had I driven it away? I hoped not.

"For better or worse?" Callum asked. I sensed he wanted an honest answer, and I thought about the question carefully.

"Neither," I said finally. "You're just different."

Callum's rifle fell over with a thud and we both jumped. Then we laughed in relief. I stared across at the horses and realized that the last of the light had gone while we had been talking.

"Are we really safe here?" I asked.

"I'm sure we are. Hasn't the spirit I imprisoned in my rifle just spoken to reassure us?"

"Idiot." Still, it was comforting, in an odd kind of way. I sat quietly, wondering how much this terrible journey had really robbed us of. How much that was special to us remained? I intended to find out. "Make love to me, Callum. Now."

It was a command, not an appeal. Suddenly, I was ravenous for him, much as a starving man might long for food. Or an opium addict for his pipe, I thought wryly.

"Your wish is my command, my lady."

I sat, neither hindering nor helping him. I found my self-imposed passivity immensely exciting. I could feel the blood pounding in my neck, hear my own heartbeat in the silence of the night.

Callum seemed to understand. He reached out and tugged the combs from my hair, allowing my hair to cascade down my back. I shook it free, reveling in the sensation of abandon that always came when it was loosed. Callum lifted it in his hands, feeling the texture and heaviness of it.

"I am so glad you decided not to cut it." His voice was throaty. I said nothing, just watched his face. "I know you were forced to pleasure Lord Suliman with your hair, but that has been washed away, long ago."

He leaned forward and buried his face in my hair, rubbing it against his mouth and nipping and tugging it with his teeth. When I had escaped from the harem in Chisaray Palace, I had been determined to cut it short, as if by doing so I could also erase the memory of Lord Suliman taking me into his bed. Callum had talked me into leaving it long. He had said persuasively that cutting it could never change what had happened to me. He had been right, and now I was pleased I had left it untouched. Less for my own sake, rather because I knew Callum loved it long.

"Make me live again, Callum."

Such a short sentence to try and tell him what I wanted! I would not instruct him in my needs. He should know, without words. And he did.

He grabbed my hair and pushed it back behind my shoulders. Without speaking, he leaned toward me and unbuttoned my coat. The row of buttons ran from my throat to my ankles. During our journey the weather had turned cold, and I was glad of the warmth of my thick, woolen coat both night and day. Now, even though the night was very cold, I ached to lose the barrier between us. I was about to help Callum with the unyielding buttons, but he raised his hand and put his finger to my lip.

"No," he said firmly. "This is my task, and I will not allow as much as a button to come between us."

The buttons finally dealt with, he pushed the coat away and sat back, staring at me. My dress was plain and dusty. I looked down at it sadly, wishing Callum's efforts had revealed something far more splendid.

"Ah, but you are beautiful, wife," he said. His voice was very loud in the absolute silence around us. "May I?" he added almost shyly, reaching for the bindings on my dress. I held my arms out in invitation.

It was only when I was completely naked that Callum touched me. And then it was with his tongue and his lips, not his hands. He ran his mouth down from my throat to my breasts, lingering tenderly on each nipple. The bitter night air had made them erect. I drew in a deep breath of both pleasure and hurt, and Callum spoke without raising his head from my body.

"I know. There is a very fine line between pleasure and pain. Is that good for you?"

He didn't bother to wait for my answer. His dry tongue rasped down my belly and tickled my black moss. I gasped and arched against him, wanting to take my pleasure—a pleasure that was truly verging on pain such was my need—now. But Callum was having none of it. He plucked at my black moss with his teeth. Not hard. Just hard enough to tease.

"Callum," I whispered.

"Who else, my love?" He spoke very tenderly. Almost in contradiction to his gentle words, I felt his tree of flesh pressing very hard into my thigh. Ah! I sighed with pleasure for all that was to come.

Perhaps Callum was tired of his own teasing. In any event, he lowered his mouth to the very entrance to my sex, flicking his tongue in and out as quickly as a snake tastes the air. I moaned with pleasure, rearing up to meet him, trying to force him further into me. I heard him chuckle, then he was rubbing his lips inside me. His beard, soft as it was, prickled. I shouted my pleasure out loud, my fists beating the ground at my side. I could feel my *yonaki* building deep in my belly. It had been so very long since we had enjoyed each other! Callum must have sensed my excitement as he took his mouth away from me and sat back on his heels, watching me. The moon was almost full, and I could see his face quite clearly. Oddly, one side—the side where his poor scar ran—was in blackness while the other side shone clear and silver. The Callum I could see was the Callum I had loved before the cruel war had changed him.

And I loved him all over again, as he had been, and as he was now.

"Not yet, wife." He was smiling. I wanted to grab him, to force him to push his tree into me, to make me yell with delight. Yet at the same time, I appreciated that pleasure postponed—at least for a moment—is always far greater than pleasure that is snatched and taken without thought. I closed my fists tightly, allowing the small pain of my nails digging into my palms to distract me from my need.

He ran his finger down the entrance to my sex, lingering for a moment on my love pearl. I gasped, closing my eyes with pleasure. Then his touch had gone and the cold, cold night air made me shudder. I opened my eyes and saw he had stood up. He had already shed his greatcoat and was tugging his shirt over his head, without worrying about undoing his own buttons. I watched him greedily as he shucked his trousers off. He stood in front of me, his hands on his hips, watching me as I ran my eyes down his body. I had not seen him naked since the start of our journey, and I mewed with distress as I saw how lean he had become. His ribs jutted so I could count each one, and even his deep, muscular chest was diminished. I held out my arms to him now, desire melting into the instinctive need to give and take the comfort of bodily contact.

Callum kneeled at my side, the movement so smooth it seemed effortless, even though I knew full well that he must be as stiff and saddle sore as I was. He leaned down and I heard his knees crack as he moved and I was desperately moved by the trivial pain I knew it must have caused him. He took my nipple in his mouth, rolling it around his tongue and teeth as if he was about to eat it. The delicacy of it was too much for me. I reached up and grabbed his head, mashing it against my breast with a force that knocked the air from my lungs. I felt him moan softly as he released my nipple to allow him to slide on top of me, covering me with his body. His tree of flesh prodded into my belly. I wanted to wriggle down, to invite him into my private places, but frustratingly, I was captured and bound by his body. He moved slowly, rubbing his tree on my flesh, its silken feel exquisitely teasing. I bit his neck. Hard. Tasted dust. Smelled the long miles on his skin.

Callum pulled away from me almost lazily. I felt his hand sliding down between us. His knuckles bit into me when he wrapped his fingers around his tree. He raised himself on one arm and loomed over me, blocking out the moonlight. Still teasing, he manipulated his tree until it was just at the entrance of my sex. I waited, holding my breath until he slid into me. Slowly. A little toward me, a little away again. I was ready to scream out loud with frustration when he finally gave in to his own need and pushed himself deep into me.

I wrapped my legs around his waist immediately, keeping him safe. Now, the roles were reversed. Now, it was I who called the game. I moved toward him fractionally, relishing his hardness inside me. Drew away again. Allowed him a little further inside, but only as far as I wanted. My vaginal muscles were honed and strong, and weeks upon weeks of gripping my horse's flanks with my thighs had made them stronger still. I heard Callum gasp with surprise as he tried to insert himself still further and could not. I watched his face in the moonlight, saw the need written plainly on it. Need that was as great as my own. I relented in a flash and relaxed, allowing him to slide into me effortlessly.

Now, I rose up to meet him. I took all he had to give me greedily, driving my hips up to him and searching for that last fraction that would satisfy me. Staring at Callum's face, I understood that he was very close to bursting his fruit. I relaxed and allowed my own *yonaki* to build inside me, its heat starting small and growing quickly into a fire that consumed everything before it. I knew Callum felt my mounting pleasure. He began to move faster, finally throwing back his head and howling at the moon as he burst his fruit. I had thought my own *yonaki* had dimmed, but at the feel of his seed shooting in my body, I roused again and the pleasurable echoes throbbed through my entire being.

We lay together afterward as comfortable and content as if we were lying on a futon instead of the hard ground. Callum held me in his arms. I could feel his pulse begin to slow, his breathing to become even. I don't think there is a word in English for the small death that comes to a man after bursting his fruit. In Japanese, it is called *kenjataimu*, and every Japanese woman knows it is the one moment where a man is capable of great clarity of thought. No matter how perplexed and worried a man's mind might be, during the time of *kenjataimu*, he is able to think clearly and concisely. He is free of sexual desire. If a man speaks to you during *kenjataimu*, then listen to him. His words are coming from both heart and brain. A rare combination for most men.

"My love." I had thought Callum had slipped into sleep. His voice startled me. "You are my life. Without you, there is nothing but dust."

I waited to see if he was going to say anything else, but he was silent. It was enough. I slipped into a contented sleep at his side, and my dreams were very sweet.

TWO

The round smoothness of
A pebble beneath my foot.
Your face in my hand

I have always been rather proud of my feet. They are small and beautifully shaped. Don't just take my word for it. When I was a geisha in Edo's Floating World, they were much admired by my patrons in the Green Tea House. So much so that one patron wrote a haiku to them, comparing my toes to sea-washed seashells. It was not a very good haiku, but at the time it delighted me greatly.

When I married Callum and moved to Scotland with him, I found it very difficult to buy shoes that fit me. Even the smallest size on offer was too big and far too wide. Eventually, I had to have my shoes made for me, as it seemed that nobody could sell me anything that was small enough or narrow enough for me to wear in comfort. Indoors, I clung determinedly to my beloved wooden *geta*, but even I could not wear the high, open sandals outside in the Scottish cold and damp.

Alas, as the proverb says, "pride goes before a fall." Here in Shanghai, I soon found that my feet were considered large and horribly ugly. And not just that, suddenly they were important. In fact, they were so important that I noticed everybody I met looked at my feet before they even raised their eyes to my face or spoke to me. And when they did, they made it clear that they regarded me with thinly veiled contempt. Suddenly, I understood what the *burakumin*—the lowest caste of people in Japan, "untouchables" who butchered animals for meat and emptied the cesspools of the better off citizens—must feel like every day. It was a deeply uncomfortable thought.

"What is wrong with my feet?" I asked Callum. He rubbed his nose in a familiar gesture of worry, and I knew at once I wasn't going to like his answer.

"There is nothing at all wrong with your feet," Callum's mother, Catriona, broke in. "You have very elegant feet. It's the abominable habit of binding women's feet that's wrong."

She was obviously angry. I could see that Alexander, my father-in-law, was made anxious by her tone. He raised his hands in a supplicating gesture, but Catriona was not to be placated.

"Don't you try and shush me, husband," she snapped. "Foot binding is an insult to the poor girls it's inflicted on. Do you know what they do to them?" Understanding the question was aimed at me, I shook my head quickly. "They wait until the poor children are around four years old, sometimes as old as nine, and then they mutilate their feet. And to make matters even worse, it's often the child's own mother who tortures them. They soak the girls' feet in herbs and hot water, and then curl their toes right under their foot, and bash them so hard the toes are actually broken. If it's thought the nails are ugly, they shove bits of tiles in the sides, so they infect and fall off eventually." I curled my own toes in sympathy. "And not content with that, they then bind the feet tightly, so the entire shape of the foot is altered and it's kept tiny. Once bound, they stay bound forever. Can you imagine that? Can you imagine what pain it causes to literally walk on your toes all your life?" I swallowed nausea. I had heard of the process when I was a child in Japan, but I had never actually seen a bound foot. "Not only do the feet stay very small, they're bent out of shape entirely. The most favored shape and size is called the Lotus Foot. I've seen so-called Lotus Feet, and I can tell you they are hideous. They look like nothing more than a child's drawing of a shoe with a heel. And of course, the poor girl can never walk properly afterward. And why do they do it? Because some fool of an emperor hundreds of years ago liked tiny feet. Or so they say," she added darkly.

"Catriona, please," Alexander pleaded, obviously embarrassed. But she was in full flow and not about to be distracted.

"I've heard it's still done to show that the family is so rich the women don't have to work for a living. That's rubbish, of course. Lots of the peasant women have bound feet and they have to work in the fields all day, no matter how much it hurts their poor feet. No, it's all down to sex." I blinked in surprise. Catriona's face was flushed with anger, her lips pinched into straight lines. I glanced at Callum and my father-in-law and—if Catriona hadn't been so very serious—I would have laughed out loud at their embarrassed expressions. "Because the girls can't walk properly with mutilated feet, it means they have to move with their hips tipped forward all the time. That throws them off balance, of course, and means that they have to keep their vaginal muscles tightly clenched to try and compensate. Great fun for the menfolk, but just an additional nuisance for the poor girls."

Alexander stared miserably at the floor. "Catriona, dear. I know you feel strongly about it, but it's nothing to do with our mission here. And the locals get very angry when you try and stop some ma from doing what she thinks is the best thing for her daughter." He smiled briefly at me. "It's very difficult for a girl with unbound feet to find a husband, so it's very rare to find a girl with natural feet. That's why they can't understand why a lovely girl like you has normal feet, Tara."

I understood at once. What girl child would dare refuse to have her feet bound if it meant she would live her life as an old maid, dependent on the charity of her family?

Catriona was obviously not appeased. She was sewing, turning the cuffs on one of Alexander's shirts to make it wear for longer. She took her anger out on the sleeve, jabbing her needle into the cloth viciously. In spite of her indignation, I found her homely money-saving device curiously moving. After all, there was no need for her to practice the minor economy. Callum was Marquess of Kyle. He owned estates that were so large that a man on a good horse could not ride across them in a week. His lands were fertile, his herds productive. It was said in Kyle that even the salmon flocked to his rivers in preference to his neighbors. He was a very rich man. When he had been in the British army, fighting in the Crimea, his men had called him "Romany Cal." Not just a reference to his deep blue eyes and black hair; those could, I suppose, make him look a little like a gypsy. But really the nickname was in honor of his supposed good luck. As one of the men under his command had explained to me, "You always get told a good fortune from a Romany. And your man is always lucky." But Callum should never have inherited the title. Truly, it belonged to his father. But that good man had refused to accept it, insisting that he had been chosen by God to do His work as a missionary, and a mere title and great wealth would not distract him from that purpose.

So Callum had inherited the title and the vast estates that went with it while his parents remained impoverished missionaries here in Shanghai. The thought made me very uneasy. It felt wrong to me. The more so as I watched his mother glance around for a pair of scissors, and finding none, break the thread with her teeth. The scissors were close at her side, but she had not seen them. I could tell from the way fine lines were forming at the bridge of her nose that she should wear spectacles, and I also guessed that she did not wear them because she felt the family's money could be better spent elsewhere and not from vanity.

I felt a sudden surge of love for Catriona, for her care not just for her own family but also for the poor girls with their bound feet who meant nothing to her. And to think that only a few weeks before I had been terrified of meeting my new parents. My eyes grew misty as I remembered standing in front of their modest door, my hand clasped firmly in Callum's fingers as we waited for our knock to be answered.

"Where are we?" I asked, more for something to say than because I really wanted to know.

"Dream Flower Street," Callum said.

I stared around at the packed street, pulsing with people and carts and stray dogs slinking furtively past in expectation of a kick. The noise was deafening, the smell of so many unwashed bodies nauseating. *This* was Dream Flower Street? I almost laughed in disbelief.

"You're shaking," he said softly, tightening his grip. "Don't worry. My parents know all about you. They'll love you, just as I do."

I wished I could share his certainty. My first mother-in-law had hated me. She had always regarded me as what Virginia society called me behind my back— a high yellow negro. She never forgave me for marrying her only son. I left her well provided for when I ran away from the family's plantation with Callum after my first husband died, but I still doubted if she ever gave me a fond thought. As if he had read my mind, Callum put his arm around me and squeezed me tightly. I leaned against him and jumped as the door swung open.

"Welcome! Callum, what are you thinking of, knocking on your own door like a stranger. Come away in, the both of you."

I smiled. The Scottish brogue was loud. If I had not gotten used to it in the time I had spent in the Highlands, I doubt I would have understood a word. And to hear it here, in the middle of Shanghai, was amazing.

"Da, it is very good to see you." Callum sounded oddly formal. Suddenly, I realized that in spite of his reassuring words he, too, was nervous.

I peered around as the door was shut behind us. The inside of the house was very dark after the bright sunshine, and my eyes were slow to adjust. I was disorientated as well. I had expected to find that Shanghai—being the closest Chinese city to Japan—would be much like my beloved Edo. But it was not. Certainly, it was as thronged with people, all seeming to be talking at the top of their voices at the same time. But the streets were laid out differently, and where I had been expecting single-story houses built of wood, with silk or paper door screens and windows, a surprising number of these houses were two and even three stories high, and many were constructed of stone. They seemed to my bewildered eyes to look more like European homes than Japanese. The people who thronged the streets did look more Japanese than European, but at the same time they were different enough to be disturbing. Oddly, the resonating Scottish tones of Callum's father were more homely to me than the rabble outside.

"Well, dear. As my great hulk of a son seems to be tongue-tied, I must guess that you are my new daughter." Callum's father mocked him gently, and I began to relax a little. "Welcome to our home, Tara dear. I'm delighted to see you here at long last."

Out of both habit and respect, I bowed deeply.

"Och, away with all that formality. I'm Alexander. But I would be very happy if you would call me Da."

Tears made my vision shimmer. I could remember my own father, of course. But it was very many years since I had last seen him, and I remembered him as a withdrawn, rather fierce sort of man. Certainly, he had never spoken kindly to me. Of course not. I was merely a worthless girl child. A useless mouth to feed. I had been only eleven years old when Auntie came to take me away to the Green Tea House, where I was to become a maiko, and finally a geisha. My mother had told me firmly that if I went with Auntie, then the whole family would eat well for a long time, so I was proud to go with her. But on that day, Father had been hard at work in the fields, together with all my brothers, so I had never had the chance to say goodbye to him. Suddenly, I felt the loss of my family all over again and my heart ached. I had no words, and simply stepped forward to my new father and leaned against him, sagging with joy and relief when he put his arms around me and embraced me warmly.

Callum was a tall man with a muscular build to match his height. He towered head and shoulders above me. Because of that, I had assumed that his father would also be tall. But he was not. He was taller than me, certainly. But that wasn't difficult! I had seen at once that he was below middling height, and comfortably built. In a few years' time, I guessed he would become fat if he wasn't careful not to eat too much rice. Perhaps Callum had inherited his great-grandfather's height? The thought fled as I buried my head gratefully into my father-in-law's shoulder.

"Put the poor girl down, Alex."

My fears arose anew. The woman's accent was as richly Scottish as Alexander's, but I thought she sounded abrupt and not at all welcoming. My impression was reinforced at once as Alexander hurriedly took his arms away from me and stood back, as if he regretted his warm greeting.

"Just welcoming our lovely daughter, my dear Catriona. And isn't she a beauty?" he added happily. My eyes widened with surprise as I stared at my new mother-in-law.

Callum's mother was very tall for a woman. Tall and as slender as a bamboo. Even in the darkness of the hall, her hair glowed so blonde that it was almost as if it shone with its own light. She was as out of place here in dark Shanghai as I had been in Virginia. The thought gave me courage, and I managed a shy smile. She studied me carefully for a moment, and then nodded as if I had passed some unknown test.

"Tara. It is very good to see you. I'm Catriona." She smiled warmly, but I noticed she did not invite me to call her Ma. "And you, my son. What do you have to say for yourself?"

She turned her attention to Callum and her face changed at once. Genuine delight lifted her expression. Her eyes were deep blue, just the same color as Callum's. His black hair came from his father, I realized, and I wondered at the perfection of the combination. Suddenly, she sounded horrified.

"My God! What has happened to your eye!" She leaned forward and stroked Callum's eye gently, her fingertip tracing the terrible scar that puckered the skin from his eyebrow down through his eyelid to his cheekbone. "Can you see? What happened to you?"

Irrationally, I expected that she would blame me for poor Callum's wound, and I shrank back toward Alexander.

"Shrapnel," Callum said briefly. "I was too close to an exploding shell in the Crimean war. But it doesn't matter. I can see perfectly well. And I rather thought it gave me a certain roguish charm," he added hopefully.

There was silence for a moment, and then Alexander began to laugh. He sounded rather short of breath, almost like a pair of bagpipes that had run out of wind, and the thought made me laugh with him. Callum's mother glanced from Alexander to me, and her stern expression faded.

"Fool of a son that you are." She pretended to tap his face in anger and shook her head fondly. I stopped laughing and held my breath as I saw the beauty she must have been before time and self-imposed hardship had worn away all the softness in her features. "Tara-chan. What on earth persuaded you to marry this great oaf of a son of mine?"

She held her hand out to me. I took it gladly and she held it and stared at me for a moment before she nodded, apparently satisfied.

"Come away ben, both of you."

I followed her down the gloomy passage, smiling as I remembered the Highland greeting. Strange as it was to hear it here in China, it was a comforting reminder of the place I had come to think of as home.

Callum and I sat side by side on a Western-style sofa. I was surprised. I had anticipated kneeling on the floor. I waited almost fearfully for the questions to begin, and rehearsed my responses carefully in my mind. Even to me, my history hardly sounded reputable. I was sold to a tea house at eleven. Trained to be a geisha and auctioned to the highest bidder—a man old enough to be my grandfather—for my *mizuage* ceremony, the ritual deflowering that all maiko must endure before they can become geisha. I was made pregnant by my *gaijin* lover, but I was forced to leave my beloved daughter behind me in Edo on the day she was born when I fled to America with my lover. *There was a reason for all of it!* I thought wildly. *None of it was my fault!*

"Tara, dear. Are you thirsty? Would you like some tea? Or perhaps we could offer you some mijui? It's very similar to sake."

My new da was smiling at me anxiously. I glanced around the shabby room uncertainly. I was confused. Callum was a very rich man, yet his parents appeared to live in something close to poverty. Callum had explained to me long ago that he had inherited the title of Marquess of Kyle, together with huge estates in the Highlands of Scotland, by a series of unfortunate accidents. His eldest uncle had died very soon after inheriting the title from Callum's grandfather. His second uncle should then have become Marquess of Kyle, but he had died suddenly a few weeks before his elder brother. The title should then have passed to the third brother, Callum's father, but he was already here in China, working as a missionary, and he had firmly refused the honor. Neither did Callum love the life of an aristocrat. In fact, he had been happier serving as an officer in the British army in the Crimea than he was as Lord Kyle. But my dear husband had a tender conscience, and he had agreed to take on the title reluctantly.

"You care more for the families who work on the estate than you do for yourself," I teased him. For once, Callum wasn't in a playful mood.

"I have to," he explained earnestly. He waved his hand at our opulent drawing room. "I've got everything. Good food. A whole castle to call my own. So much land even I don't know every bit of it. I'm never cold or worried where the next meal is coming from. But my tenants don't have a fraction of this, and they depend on the Kyle estate for the little they do have. Most of their families have served us for centuries. The Marquess of Kyle owes it to them to take care of them. And apparently that is now me," he added glumly.

I took him in my arms and held him very tightly. I sensed his frustration. Callum hated being Lord Kyle. He wanted to be free to live his own life. When I had first met him, he had simply been Callum Niaish. I had been drawn to him instinctively, but Virginian society was pleased to accept him as a slave trader, and I had been a slave myself for too long to countenance such cruelty. I wanted to hate him, but no matter how I tried, I could not. And then, after my husband died, I discovered Callum was actually working with the Underground Railroad and was freeing slaves, not buying them. We ran away from Virginia ourselves when Callum's disguise was undone, just as the local plantation owners were about to set their blood-hounds on him.

By a twist of fate, once we left Virginia and returned to

Scotland, Callum himself became the slave. The Kyle estates took him over, body and soul. He worked harder than any of his tenants, and when I told him so, he simply shrugged.

"It's not mine," he explained. "Me, my uncle, my grand-father. All of us, stretching back down the years. We all just look after things for the next generation. It's just the way it is. I'm responsible for it, whether I want to be or not."

I saw the hopeful look on his face when he spoke of the next generation and I closed my own eyes in pain. I told myself constantly it was no more than superstitious rubbish, but I didn't even convince myself. I knew my dear daughter, Kazhua, was still alive. And equally did I know that until I found her again there would be no more children for me.

I realized Alexander was still waiting for my reply. I cleared my throat, worried that if I accepted his offer of mijui, they would go hungry as a result. Callum decided for me.

"Mijui, please. For both of us." He grinned slyly. "Although I have to tell you, Da, that I have something rather special in my bags for you. A bottle of Edradour whisky. I've hoarded it for you all the long way down from the Crimea. And believe me, there were days when I longed to break the seal and take a dram for myself!"

I was amazed when it was Catriona who replied.

"Glory be! I have to say I've missed a wee dram now and then."

Callum laughed and I joined in uncertainly. But at least the ice was broken. The mijui arrived and I sipped it happily. It was served warm, very like sake. For the first time, I began to feel as if Edo was no longer an impossible dream for me.

THREE

Peace is in the air
I breathe. Be careful! It will
Shatter at a shout

I had hoped for a futon, laid on the floor. But my hopes were all for nothing. Our bed was Western style, made with a deep, feather mattress and stacked with sheets and blankets. Callum caught my rueful expression and shrugged.

"Don't worry. You'll get a futon as soon as we get to Edo. And then it will be my turn to moan that I'm not comfortable."

"I'm not moaning," I said indignantly. I threw a shoe at him. He ducked and the shoe hit a vase, shattering it. I put my hand in front of my mouth in horror. "Oh no! Was it very valuable?"

"I doubt it. I imagine it was something Ma picked up at the market. She hates wasting money."

This was my chance to ask the questions that had been confusing me. I seized the moment eagerly.

"Callum, I don't understand. You're a very rich man, yet your parents seem to live in poverty. Couldn't you give them some money?"

Callum leaned his chin on his hand and stared at me. I thought that I had offended him, until I realized his lips were twitching with amusement. I threw the other shoe at him, but he caught it and then grabbed for my robe, pinning me tightly.

"So impatient, little one!" He grinned. His scar puckered when he smiled, giving his expression a wicked, piratical look. I found it deeply attractive, and Callum knew it. "All questions will be answered in the fullness of time. But just at this moment, I really don't think I feel like talking at all."

I didn't reply. I couldn't. Suddenly, I was short of breath. I lay down on the bed and patted it invitingly. Callum slid beside me and lay full length teasingly, not quite touching me. I poked his ribs. In response, he buried his face in my neck and nibbled my flesh.

"Ah. But that is delightful." In my pleasure, I had spoken more loudly than I had intended, and my words seemed to be a shout in the quiet of the room, which was situated behind a courtyard, well away from the eternal noise and bustle of Dream Flower Street. I put my hand over my mouth in an instinctive gesture.

"The walls are very thick. Nobody will hear us," Callum said reassuringly. All the same, I noticed he spoke very quietly.

"That may be so. But it doesn't alter the fact that your parents are here, does it?"

I sounded so worried, so like a very young girl who knows she was doing something naughty that I expected Callum to laugh. He did not. His mouth screwed up into a button and he shrugged.

"I know. Here we are, a respectable married couple, and still it doesn't seem right to be thinking about making love when Ma and Da are close by. Even though I know that there is very little that either of them hasn't encountered in their time as missionaries."

I nodded seriously. Although I guessed that I had seen far more of life than Callum's parents, still I also felt absurdly guilty.

"Oh, come here, husband," I said. All the same, I whispered the words.

Callum wrapped his arms around me and kissed me deeply. A moment later, and our urgency had dealt with any concerns about correctness. The bed was too fat and thick for my liking. I sank into it and floundered as I tried not to slip from Callum's embrace. He solved the problem easily enough by putting one arm around my hips and the other around my shoulders, holding me so tightly that I couldn't move. Not that I wanted to.

Neither of us bothered removing our clothes. Callum's hand slipped into the bodice of my dress and cradled my breast.

"Just the perfect size," he said teasingly. "Look, it could have been made to be taken in my hand."

I bit his ear, quite hard, to make sure he understood that I had a choice in the matter, and then relaxed, enjoying the feel of the callouses on his palm. Ridges that months holding on to a horse's reins had left behind. My own hands were equally roughened. I slid them beneath his shirt and rubbed them firmly up and down his back. Callum squirmed, rolling his shoulders as I teased.

There was little time for mere amusement. I was filled with the need for him and was impatient for my fulfillment. I had a single moment to reflect that I was being selfish, then I sensed the matching urgency in Callum's movements and understood I had no need to worry.

I wriggled out of his embrace and threw my arms and legs wide, my skirt and petticoats rising up apparently of their own will. Callum's breath caught as he stared at me.

"You are so very beautiful, wife," he said, his voice sawing throatily.

I opened my hands wide in invitation. Perhaps Callum caught my urgency. Perhaps his own need was equal to mine. No matter. He shucked down his trousers and kicked them off on to the floor and slid on top of me, his tree of flesh flirting with my black moss. I was so slippery, I felt my own juices overflow and lubricate my private places and my thighs. Callum hesitated, and I linked my arms behind his back, dragging him as close to me as I could manage. I heard a strange, animal-like grunt and laughed as I realized that the sound had come from my own throat.

Callum needed no further urging. His tree slid into me without him appearing to guide it. I rose up to meet him, fighting that damned mattress as best I could.

I had been right about Callum's need matching my own. Callum's rhythm was immediately too fast. Even in the depths of my own heat, I guessed that he would burst his fruit far too soon for me. In spite of the fact that he was far taller and heavier than me, I found the strength to lever myself up. I elbowed my way from beneath him and used the softness of the mattress as a tool to roll him on his back, all the time tightening my internal muscles to make sure his tree did not slide out of me.

"Tara?" I heard desire thicken his voice, and I laughed with pleasure.

"My turn," I whispered. I lowered my head and bit his nipple, my teeth catching on his chest hairs. I heard him moan deep in his throat and guessed it was far more from pleasure than pain. The soft bed fought me every inch of the way, and I found I had to jam my feet against the wooden bed frame to get the purchase I needed. I put my hands firmly on Callum's shoulders, and then pried myself away from him, as far as I dared without allowing him to pop out of me. In spite of the humid heat of the bedroom, my sex felt cold where he was detached from me. But not for long.

I slid down his tree, a fraction at a time. The anticipation was delectable and agonizing at the same time. I stared at Callum's face and saw his expression was contorted with desire. He was sweating. I leaned forward and licked the salt off his lips, relishing his flavor. Finally, I allowed myself to slide down the final, thick part of his tree. I rubbed the lips of my sex against his black moss, loving the coarse feel of him against my tenderness. I felt my *yonaki* beginning to build, but at the same time Callum began to speed up, his hips bucking against me. Very deliberately, I tightened my vaginal muscles and kept him still. Or at least, as still as I wanted him to be. He quivered slightly, and the sensation was delightful. Finally, I could take no more and I relaxed. Callum responded immediately, driving into me with such force that I had a second to wonder if he was trying to put his *kintama* inside me as well as his tree of flesh before my *yonaki* surged through me. Callum burst his fruit at the same time, and finally we slowed together.

The shadows were shortening when we roused ourselves sufficiently to speak.

"My God. I wonder what you would have been capable of if you had bound feet," Callum said. His voice was so serious that I looked at him in astonishment. When I saw the laughter in his blue eyes, I made to slap him, but he was too quick for me and caught my hand, imprisoning it in a tight grip.

"Idiot." I snuggled against him. "Your mother is very passionate about foot binding, isn't she?"

"My mother is very passionate about many things," Callum said fondly, the love and respect he felt for his mother clear in his voice. "If it weren't for her keeping Da on the straight and narrow road of service to the Church, I wouldn't be Lord Kyle."

"Really? I was astonished. "I thought it was your da who refused to give up his missionary work and take the title."

Callum rubbed his hands over his face and shrugged.

"He did. But only because Ma told him it was the right thing to do." He saw the amazement on my face and smiled. "You don't know my ma! Once she sets her mind on a thing, then she doesn't know how to let go. Her family was not at all happy about her marrying Da in the first place, but she had made her mind up that he was the man for her and they had to give in, eventually. She was of much higher rank than him, and she was expected to make a far better catch for her husband than a mere younger son."

"No!" I said in disbelief. "But your da would have been a marquess when he inherited the title. And rich. What was wrong with that?"

"You're forgetting," Callum pointed out. "Da was never expected to inherit the title. He was third in line to inherit. Even if he had been the eldest son, it still wouldn't have been good enough for Ma's family. She's the daughter of a Scottish Duke. She had a very successful season in London when she came out as a young woman. So successful that she caught the eye of an English Duke. According to Da, she had him wound around her finger and he proposed to her twice. But she didn't like him, and even the lure of marrying into the royal family couldn't change her mind. She and Da had been friends since they were children. She had decided years before that he was the man for her, and that was all there was to it. She threatened her parents that she would elope to Gretna Green with Da if they didn't agree to them marrying, and they gave in at last to avoid the scandal."

"Stop." My head was reeling. "I don't understand any of this. What have the seasons got to do with anything? And what's unusual about Catriona coming out? She goes out all the time. Everybody does."

Callum laughed until he ran out of breath. I stared at him indignantly, wondering what I had said to cause him so much amusement.

"I'm sorry, Tara. You looked so puzzled, I had to laugh." I raised my eyebrows and looked at him stonily and he went on quickly. "In England—and of course, Scotland—young ladies of good birth are presented at the Royal Court. Once they have been formally introduced to the king or queen, they are said to have 'come out' and their 'season' begins. For the next few months, they attend balls and dances, go to all sorts of society events. It's never actually said, but the purpose of the whole thing is for the young woman to be introduced to as many eligible young men as she possibly can. By the end of the society season, most of the young women will be engaged to be married. Those sad few who have not snared a husband tend to be regarded with great sympathy, as it's assumed they will never find a suitable husband and will linger on as old maids."

"Ah. I understand," I said. "It's even worse for ladies of high rank in Japan. Their husband is chosen for them by their family, and they dare not refuse. Occasionally a very brave girl does say no to her parents' choice, but if she does she will probably find herself sold to a tea house. Or worse.

Although in Japan these women are given a chance to redeem themselves. When their father thinks they have learned their lesson, they are taken back into the family as if nothing happened. At which point they are more than happy to marry whoever their father chooses for them." I shuddered as I remembered my own *danna*, Lord Dai. Even after so many years, I could not forget his wrinkled hands on my body and the smell of his pipe breath on my face. Auntie had been delighted when he won me for my *mizuage*; he was a noble, and very rich. She was astonished when I refused him. I understood only too well how much courage it must have taken Catriona to refuse her royal suitor. "Was her family very angry?"

"Furious," he said cheerfully. "It would have been even worse if they had eloped. That really would have ruined her reputation. Not that she would have cared greatly. She had set her heart on Da, and that was it for her."

I smiled, remembering Catriona's anger over foot binding. Clearly, she had not mellowed greatly over the years.

"That still doesn't explain why it was Catriona's doing that your father isn't Lord Kyle," I pointed out.

"I think I told you before that as the youngest son, Da was expected to go into the Church?" I nodded. "Well, Da is nothing less than determined himself. He could easily have risen high in the Church, but he decided if he was going to serve his God, then it was going to be a worthwhile service. That was why he decided to be a missionary. But even Da must have been tempted when the news came that both his brothers were dead and he was next in line to inherit Kyle. He loves the estate as much as I do, and I can imagine how the lure of the Highlands called to him."

Even in our secluded room, I could hear the pounding

pulse of the crowded streets all around us. Day and night, there was no rest from the sound. And the stink.

"I don't blame him," I said. "So why did he stay here?"

"He wrote to me and explained." Callum sighed. "He told me he knew I didn't want to settle down, but the responsibility was mine. Ma had given him an ultimatum. She told him that he had chosen his path in life and should stick to it. That his work in China was far more important than taking the easy option and going back to Kyle. I suppose he might have tried to talk her round, but Ma was having none of it. She told him if he went back to Scotland, then he would go alone. She was staying in China, where she had been sent to do God's work."

"So of course he stayed as well," I said.

"He did. I think he really wanted to be persuaded all along. They both love China, and I can't imagine that his conscience would ever have allowed him to be really happy back in Glen Kyle."

I sat quietly, wondering if Callum knew how very like his mother he was. Just like her, he had obeyed the call of duty, allowing his own wishes and desires to be trampled underfoot. Then I remembered how we had got onto the subject, and I repeated my original question.

"I understand that. But why don't you give them some money? It's not right, your parents being poor when you have so much."

"Of course it's not." Callum frowned and I realized I had touched on a sore point. "I would love to give them money. Lots of it. I've suggested it time and time again. But Da always says no. He feels it would be hypocritical for them to be well off when they're living and working in the midst of such dreadful poverty."

I leaned against him and we were both quiet, each

caught in the web of our own thoughts. Unexpectedly, I was washed by a surge of nostalgia. Not for the lush green of Kyle, which I loved. Nor for the heat and brightness of Virginia. Suddenly, I was physically sick with longing to be back in Japan, the home I had not seen for so many years I had lost count of them. Sick for longing for Japan, and my dear Kazhua.

FOUR

As a tsunami
Strikes, the beach is laid bare. So
Is my heart with you

"Must you go so soon?" Alexander looked as if he might cry. "You've only been here a few weeks. Barely time to recover from your journey. Surely, a few weeks more would take no harm?"

It was clear he was upset. His Scottish accent had deepened so that I had to listen carefully to understand what he was saying. I felt so guilty, I was almost persuaded. But Catriona was having none of it.

"Och, Alex," she chided her husband fondly. "Do you think they wouldn't stay if they could? Don't be so selfish. You've seen your son, but it's years since Tara's had so much as a sight of her daughter."

Alexander's face crumpled into guilty lines. He held his arms out to me and I rushed across, burying my face in his chest. In the short time I had known him, I had learned to love my new father and I was sorry to leave him so soon. But

Catriona was right. Now that I was so close, Kazhua was almost a physical presence. I felt that she was with me constantly, just as she had been when she had been safe in my own body. I dreamed of her at night, although I was deeply frustrated that in the morning I could never recollect her dear face. She was all I could think of and nothing else seemed at all important, apart from dear Callum.

I took myself out of Alexander's arms reluctantly and turned toward Catriona. I had quickly come to like and respect my new mother-in-law, although I could not find the same easy familiarity with her as I had with Alexander. She looked at me intently for a moment and then smiled.

"Away with you both." Was there pain in those lovely eyes at the loss of her newly-restored son? I thought there was. "Tara, go find Kazhua. Bring my granddaughter back to me." She blinked quickly and I knew I had been right. She was fighting tears. Then I realized what she had actually said, and I felt tears come to my own eyes. I walked across to her quickly, and we embraced tightly. She spoke softly, so softly that I knew her words were intended for me alone. "Take care, Tara. I want you both back safely. I always longed for a daughter, and now that I have you I don't want to lose you."

Her arms were taken away from me and she stood back, once again brisk and efficient. But I saw the affection in her eyes, and it made me very happy.

In spite of his reluctance, Alexander made the arrangements for our journey quickly. We stood awkwardly on the dock at Shanghai, making our farewells. Callum covered his self-consciousness by embracing his old nursemaid, his amah, Sara. She had been delighted to see him again, and she was crying now, wailing her distress at losing him so quickly. A few people turned to look at us with amusement and Catriona spoke to Sara briskly. She stopped crying at once and stood looking sadly down at her feet.

"You have a long journey in front of you both," Alexander said seriously. I hid a smile. I had already traveled halfway across the world. This journey was nothing in comparison. "The sea trip will take you perhaps a week, depending on the weather. You'll land at Satsuma Domain on Kyushu Island." The Japanese words made me more homesick than ever. I mentally urged Alexander to hurry, but he was clearly determined to explain what lay in front of us very carefully. "From Satsuma Domain to Edo on Honshu Island is an even longer distance than the sea journey. Japan has no railways yet, so you must travel by carriage, and of course ferry from Kyushu to Honshu."

Alexander paused to gather his thoughts. I was beginning to fidget.

"Enough, husband," Catriona said firmly. "Tara knows what to expect in Japan. She doesn't need a lecture from you. Come away. Let our children board their ship. The sooner they go, the sooner they will be back. Oh, before I forget. A little present for you, dear."

Catriona pushed a bulky package wrapped in white paper toward me. Before I could thank her, she had taken Alexander's arm and was tugging him to their carriage. Alexander turned to look back one last time and I mentally urged him to let us go on our way. Had I known how long it would be before I saw both him and Catriona again, I would have run after them and embraced them both. But I do not have second sight and was eager to begin our journey, so I waved at them and turned to hurry up the gangplank with Callum holding my elbow to make sure I didn't trip on the uneven boards.

Our cabin was comfortable enough, but I was not. I kept

thinking of Catriona's parting words. When I had last seen Japan, I had been barely more than a young girl. Already, I had spent more time away from my own country than I had spent living in it. Would I still know my homeland? How much might it have changed? I was suddenly deeply anxious.

"We're off." Our vessel shuddered as it cast off from the dock. I was sitting on our berth, but Callum was still standing and he was almost thrown off balance by the unexpected movement. He sat down next to me abruptly, laughing at his own clumsiness. His laughter faded quickly as he saw the worry in my face. "Tara-chan, what is it? You look upset."

"Callum, I'm frightened." That wasn't quite the right word. I was worried. Anxious. Was I actually fearful? My stomach clenched and I realized that I was. "What if everything goes wrong? It's been so long since I left home. Perhaps everything has changed. Even the Floating World might have gone." I clutched at his sleeve, willing him to understand. "Even if we find Kazhua, what if she doesn't know me?" There, it was out. The real fear. Had Kazhua ever gotten the letter I left for her? Did she even know I was her mother? And if she did, would she care? After all, I had abandoned her on the day of her birth, ran away with her father, my lover. How could she be expected to know that my heart had never forgotten her, that I had regretted leaving her every day of my life? "Oh, Callum," I wailed. "Should I leave well alone? If she hates me, wouldn't it be better to leave my dreams intact?"

I would have said more, but Callum stopped my words with his lips, kissing me gently.

"No," he said firmly. "No matter what, you have to find out. If you don't, you are going to spend the rest of your life wondering and worrying. I think you're forgetting one thing. Kazhua is your daughter. She will understand. I know she will."

I leaned against him, feeling the stress drain out of my body. He was right, of course. I had to know. I had come so very far. I would not turn away now. He kissed me again, on my closed eyelids, and I managed a smile.

Our journey was nearly over before I remembered the package Catriona had given to me. For one terrible second, I thought I had somehow lost it, then Callum reminded me I had stowed it under our berth for safety. I went on my knees and pulled it out, picking at the silk that fastened it, but the threads would not give way. Callum smiled at me.

"You're going to break your nails on it. Here, give it to me."

I squeezed the parcel tentatively. It gave beneath my fingers, but there was also something very hard in there. Callum produced his pocket knife and snipped the silk bindings apart. The paper followed and I sighed with pleasure as I saw the contents.

"Callum, look!" I held the beautiful kimono against myself. There was an obi, as well. And undergarments. And a pair of wooden *geta*. I searched in the wrapping for a note, but there was nothing. The undergarments were cream, so delicate they were almost white in color. The kimono itself was a very dark blue, ornamented with sprigs that had been embroidered to look like slender twigs. The embroidery was a subtle shade of tea rose pink, exactly the same color as my skin. She had even added a set of bright combs to pin my hair in place.

"Trust Ma to think of the practicalities," Callum said indulgently.

I knew he was wrong. The gift had been thought about

very carefully and given in love. Dear Catriona! I smoothed the silk with my fingertips, and without warning a memory came to me from long ago in my past. Lord Dai had given me a kimono and underwear to celebrate my *mizuage*. I could hear his gloating voice in my head, telling me how beautiful I looked in my new and very expensive garments. The colors he had chosen were exactly the same as Catriona's gift, except in reverse. On his kimono, the background color was tea rose, and the embroidered sprigs dark blue. My mouth was very dry as I couldn't help but wonder if this was an ill-omen. Then I remembered thinking that Catriona ought to wear spectacles, but couldn't—or wouldn't—afford to buy them for herself. Yet she had chosen to spend a huge amount on my new clothes! What an ungrateful creature I was. Of course it was just pure coincidence. Nothing more.

"I'll think of Catriona every time I wear them," I said.

Callum was obviously pleased. "I think it would be a very good idea to wear them as soon as we reach Kyushu," he said. "Even if foreigners are as common in Edo now as Sara says they are, I would be very surprised if many of them have lingered in Satsuma Domain. It's bound to cause interest for people to see a Japanese woman with a *gaijin* in Satsuma, never mind about a Japanese woman dressed in Western clothes."

He was right, of course. How truly clever Catriona had been!

Callum cleared his throat. He was looking down at the deck, avoiding my glance, and was obviously very ill at ease. I stared at him, wondering what was wrong.

"In view of that, I wonder if you would mind greatly not being my wife while we're in Japan?" I was incredulous and lost for words. My mouth opened and closed a couple of times as Callum went on hurriedly. "I mean, could you pretend to be my mistress? Da mentioned it before we left, and I've thought it over on the voyage and I think he's right. We want to attract as little attention to ourselves as possible."

I frowned and considered his words carefully. Of course we didn't want to draw attention to ourselves. I understood that. It may have been many years since I fled from Japan, but in doing so I had caused huge loss of face to some very important people. And Japanese memories are very long. I was sure that Simon had been murdered when he returned to Edo as revenge for him stealing me away from Lord Dai. And if he had been remembered and punished with death, how much more likely was it that I would also be recollected? And no doubt punished in my turn. I shivered.

"I understand that we have to be discreet. But wouldn't it be safer if people knew we were married?" I demanded finally.

"No. Not at all," Callum said abruptly. "Sara told Da that there are a few foreigners in Edo who have taken Japanese mistresses. He thinks it probably amuses them to find out if all the tales about oriental women are true." I glared at him, and he shrugged. "I'm sorry, but it's the truth. Da says that so many of the British in Shanghai have done the same thing with Chinese women that nobody blinks an eye about it now. But neither in Shanghai or Edo have any of the foreigners actually married a Japanese girl. If they had, everybody would know about it. And everybody would be gossiping about it as well. If we turned up and let it be known that we were married, it would be all over Edo immediately. Everybody would be interested, and it could jog memories that are best left forgotten. It's better if when we reach Edo, I let it be known that you were a high-class courtesan in Kyushu. That I took a fancy to you and took you for my mistress. I doubt anybody will think that surprising."

"So I'm supposed to trail behind you, with my eyes downcast, am I? Should I look at you adoringly from time to time, to enhance the illusion?"

"That would be excellent," Callum said gravely. I threw a pillow at him and he caught it adroitly, laughing. "And don't forget, you speak only a little English."

I thought about that. English had been my main language for so long, I had long ago ceased to even think in Japanese.

"That will be difficult," I admitted. "But you're right, of course. It would be deeply suspicious if I spoke English well, especially with my mongrel accent. And you, husband, must forget that you speak fluent Japanese. That really would arouse suspicion. You must pretend you know only the few words I have managed to teach you."

I took a deep breath, suddenly aware that there were far more difficulties in going back to Edo than I had ever considered.

"Should I wear geisha makeup, do you think?"

"No. I don't think so. I don't suppose the geisha in Satsuma Domain wear their makeup at all like Edo geisha, and we're not going to have time to get you used to putting your makeup on differently. Besides, it might revive some unwanted memories if you do. It's lucky you're already well used to being called Tara. The name Terue might also have recalled the geisha who ran away."

I wandered over to the tiny mirror that hung on our cabin wall and peered into it. The mirror was sadly dusty, and my reflection was hazy. I pulled my tongue out at myself, sure I could see wrinkles that had not been there only a few months ago. In a second, Callum was behind me, his hands on my shoulders.

"If you think the mirror shows you as anything but the *bijyo* that you are, then it lies and I will break it into a thousand pieces for its falsehood."

He spoke in Japanese and I smiled, my worries put aside. In Japanese, *bijyo* means a beautiful woman. Cruel to their women as they can be, it is a paradox that Japanese men see beauty in women of any age. Indeed, the bloom of a more mature woman is often far more appreciated than a young girl who lacks sophistication.

"Well, I'm glad to see that you appreciate your new mistress!" I smiled at him.

Callum put his finger on my reflection and ran it down the image of my nose. He was smiling, and I found my nervousness soothed, at least a little.

FIVE

It's better to be
Able to bend like the tall
Bamboo. Rigor breaks.

I cannot put into words how much I had looked
forward to being back in Japan. Although I loved
Scotland dearly, Japan was the place where I had been
born, where my earliest memories came from. There had
been times when I had been so deeply miserable in Virginia
that I would wake up from a dream where I was walking the
streets of the Floating World again and my face would be
wet with tears of longing to be back there.

Now that I was finally in Japan, Satsuma Domain was so
very different from what I had anticipated I almost cried
again, but this time with disappointment.

"It's so quiet!" I muttered to Callum. "And so terribly
provincial. I know it's a long way from Edo, but it's not like
being in Japan at all."

As we had anticipated, Callum caused a stir as soon as
we landed. He towered a good head taller than the tallest

Japanese man, and his strange clothes and blue eyes were obviously the subject of much interest to the good folk of Kagoshima. Had we been in the Edo I remembered, people would have drawn their robes disdainfully aside, in case they became contaminated by this foreign barbarian in their midst. They would have stared blatantly and chattered amongst themselves about the *gaijin,* speculating endlessly as to whether the tales they had heard that all male *gaijin* had tails were true.

Here in Kagoshima, people were polite. They bowed to us as we passed. What gossip there was went on behind our backs. Even the merchants didn't try and fleece us.

But curiosity soon won the day. I found myself approached by women whenever Callum was not close to me and I was plied with questions about him. Were his eyes really that color or did he dye them? Why was he so tall? And—of course—did he really have a tail, and if he did, where did he hide it? The question I had dreaded—why had I chosen this *gaijin* as my lover?—was, to my relief, never asked. They were far too polite! But even so, I did notice a certain degree of disappointment when I denied he had a tail. Curious, I responded with my own questions.

"Is he the first *gaijin* you've seen?"

The geisha I was speaking to tittered and hid her face behind her fan.

"Oh, no! As we're so close to China, we've seen quite a few *gaijin* who have come across from Shanghai. They don't stay with us long, generally. Some of them are interested in our exquisite porcelain and want to buy it, but most of them just step off the ship and immediately leave for Edo. I've never been to Edo," she added wistfully. "Do you know it well? Is it as exciting as people say it is?"

"Yes. I haven't been in Edo for a while, but I doubt it will have changed greatly. It's very big and busy. Very lively." She looked at me with longing eyes, and I spoke quickly before she asked me questions I could no longer answer about Edo. "But if you've seen *gaijin* before, why are you so interested in Callum-san?"

She giggled and glanced over my shoulder to make sure Callum was well away. For a moment, I worried that he might have given himself away by speaking in Japanese when the townsfolk could hear him, then I realized she was simply being polite.

"None of the other *gaijin* looked like him," she said simply. "They have always been old and fat. And smelly." She wrinkled her nose in disgust. "And very rude. We had all decided that if they were demons, then they must be very low ranking ones and we had no need to fear them. But Callum-san is nothing like them. People are beginning to wonder if the first *gaijin* were sent just to take a look at us and report back. And now a higher-ranking demon has arrived at last."

"And that worries you?" I hid a smile. Her face was so serious, if I didn't remember thinking much the same thing about Simon when I first saw him, I would have found it difficult not to laugh out loud at her superstitious fear.

She bit her lip and then shook her head, looking at me slyly from beneath lowered eyelids.

"Many of the men are worried. But if other *gaijin* look like he does, and are so polite and clean, we women would welcome them. Tell me, does he give you great pleasure?"

Fortunately, Callum turned and called to me at that moment, and I hurried away, leaving her none the wiser.

I told Callum about my conversation with her and he smiled.

"I already know," he said smugly. "Don't forget, nobody

knows I can speak Japanese, so they all speak freely in front of me. It appears that the subject of my tail occupies many minds."

"Does it now?" I smiled, but my good humor faded quickly. Now that I had gotten over the initial amazement of being back on Japanese ground—no matter that Kagoshima seemed almost as foreign to me as Shanghai had been—I was longing to move on. To get back to the Floating World at last. "How long before we begin the journey to Edo?" I demanded.

"As soon as I can arrange transport," Callum reassured me. "Or rather, as soon as you can arrange it. Don't forget, I don't speak much Japanese!"

*W*e were sitting in the bath in our *ryokan*. Normally, I would have expected at least a couple of the inn's other guests to be relaxing with us at this time of day, but it appeared nobody dared enter the water with a *gaijin*. I was delighted, both by the privacy and the bath itself. It had been so very long since I had been able to enjoy a proper Japanese bath. The experience was so delightful, I could almost forgive Kagoshima for being such a dreadful disappointment.

"Ah, but this brings back memories!" Even though we were alone, I kept my voice very quiet, as I thought it better to speak in English. "When I was a geisha in the Green Tea House, we girls would wallow in the bath for hours, gossiping. I'm sure I haven't really felt clean since I last had a proper Japanese bath."

"It's very different to the bathhouses I got used to in China," Callum said.

I looked at him in surprise, wondering if he was teasing. "Is it? I always thought they stole the idea from Japan and that bathhouses in both countries were very similar."

"Oh no." Callum looked so serious, I believed him. "This would never happen in Shanghai. It would be scandalous for men and women to bathe together in public in China." He grinned slyly. I paused, waiting for more, and then looked at the laughter in his eyes and slapped the water so hard it lapped under his chin. He went on, "Do you know what this reminds me of? Our huge bathtub at home."

I smiled in spite of my determination to be annoyed with him. Our bath in Scotland had been made especially for his great-grandfather, a huge man who needed an outsized bath and furniture so he could be comfortable. Even with both of us in it, there was plenty of room to splash about and amuse ourselves. I caught my breath as I recollected our favorite form of amusement in that gigantic tub.

"I wonder how private we are here," Callum mused innocently.

"Nobody will interrupt us," I said promptly. "They wouldn't dare. Don't forget, everybody here still translates *gaijin* as 'foreign barbarian' or even worse, 'foreign devil.' They wouldn't dare risk making you angry by catching you naked, not even if it meant finding out whether you really do have a tail tucked away somewhere. Why do you ask, *master*?" I added slyly.

"Oh, it just occurred to me that it would be interesting to make love in all this lovely, hot water. I've never tried it before."

"Neither have I." In spite of a surge of pure lust, I was unsure. The bath was a place to find cleanliness. I knew that it probably had been used for lovemaking many times, but it still seemed to be oddly wrong to me to spoil such wonderful cleanliness. In spite of my doubts, I looked at Callum hopefully, willing to be persuaded.

"Just a thought." His grin widened. My gaze traveled down from his head and shoulders—the only parts of his body above the water—past his chest and stomach. Although his outline was slightly hazy beneath the hot, mineral-rich water, I could see, very clearly indeed, that his tree of flesh was all too ready to try the experiment. My resistance melted like snow falling from spring blossoms.

"Come here, *master.*"

I held my arms wide, welcoming him to my body. Callum surged the few steps necessary to reach me, his passage causing a tide of steaming water to slip up to my neck. It had a silky feel to it, more like very fine oil than water, and it was very slightly perfumed, probably by the natural minerals in it. I inhaled deeply, appreciating the smell. Closing my eyes to enjoy it, I decided it was a mixture of forest that has basked in the sun all day and sea spray.

Callum had taken advantage of my closed eyes. I jumped with surprise as his hands found my breasts, cupping them delicately. Perhaps it was the effect of the strangely unctuous bathing water, but I could not feel the callouses on his palms at all.

"You called? I am here to obey your every whim." Callum raised his eyebrows at me and leered in a mime of lust. I allowed my hand to slide down his belly and discovered that there was nothing false about it. My mind was made up in a split second. Very well, if Callum had declared himself at my disposal, then so it would be.

I put my hand on his chest and pushed him away. I saw the surprise in his expression as I leaned back against the wall of the bath and opened my arms wide.

"I am not yet quite clean. Wash me." His eyes sparkled as he raised his hand, slightly cupped as if he was holding a sponge. "No. Not like that. With your tongue."

Callum drew a quick breath and licked his lips. He made to run his finger down my face, but I slapped it away.

"I have told you what I want," I said crisply. "Now!"

His eyes seemed to deepen in color from bright, sparkling blue to almost black. Staring at him, I realized it was not a trick of the light. His pupils were so large, they dominated his eyes entirely. Had I been playing this game with any man but Callum, I would have been afraid. Even so, I felt a distinct shiver of anticipation travel down my spine. It was delightful.

He did not speak. He simply leaned forward and brushed my nipple with his tongue. Before I could do more than sigh with pleasure, he ducked his head and took a mouthful of the hot water, allowing it to trickle from his lips between my breasts. Watching my face intently, as if seeking approval, he finally lowered his head again and trailed his tongue against my wet skin, rubbing his face between my breasts.

"Yes?" he asked throatily. I guessed he was asking if I enjoyed that. I nodded. I thought I heard a noise outside the bathhouse and raised my head quickly. There was nothing except the sound of the mineral springs, running very slowly into the bath, replenishing it constantly as our movements caused the water to ebb out. The fine hair on my arms prickled erect and I understood that the thrill of somebody catching us making love in the bath was adding to my excitement.

I wanted to reach out to Callum, to spread my body against him. To arch my breasts against him. To feel him pressing on me. And above all, to feel his tree piercing me.

All subtlety was forgotten in my need. Yet I overruled my body. I would not hurry this. Anticipation would surely make the moment when we found each other all the better! I stayed still, taking deep, slow breaths. Callum's tongue had moved to my neck. He was licking the front of it slowly and carefully, stopping now and then to pluck at my flesh with his teeth and nibble the sensitive area just behind my shoulder blades. I shuddered with pleasure.

"Lower," I said urgently.

Callum paused for a second, and then his tongue trailed down between my breasts. He did not hesitate at the water line, but simply moved down, his lips smoothing over my belly and finally finding my black moss. Alas, at that point he ran out of breath and was forced to surface, panting for air.

"Enough?" he asked. I smiled. Instead of replying, I turned my back on him slowly, pretending it was the depth of water that was forcing me to move so languidly. I put out my arms on each side of the bath to support myself, and thrust myself toward him, so very slightly it might have been a trick of my rippling reflection rather than an actual movement.

Callum was obviously not fooled. He slid across me, his entire body moving against me with the delicacy of a fine silken gown. I sighed and put my head back with pleasure. His body was hotter still than the water around us. I waited, and then felt his hand smoothing the peach split of my behind. So delicate was the sensation that I wondered for a moment if it was just the water lapping around me, then the pressure of his touch increased slightly and I moaned out loud with desire.

"Now, Callum. Now!" I spoke far louder than I had intended. My voice bounced around the bathhouse walls, coming back to me with a diminishing echo. Callum buried his head in the back of my neck. He bit, just hard enough to hurt, and I arched instinctively, relishing the pain. At the same moment, I felt his tree of flesh probing for me.

He slid into me so quickly and easily, I blinked in surprise. It was the water, of course, lubricating both of us as if we had been oiled, inside and out. And with his tree also came a gush of the hot, slightly salty water. The sensation was sensuous beyond belief. I felt full to bursting and so near my *yonaki* that I almost screamed with delight. Callum moved in and out of me rhythmically, with every outward stroke allowing more scented water to enter me. Every time he closed to me, the water pushed further in. I felt as if he was some divine machine, filling my sex until I wanted to shriek out loud with the sensation. Yet still my *yonaki* hovered, almost ready to burst but never quite spilling over.

Quite suddenly, I knew exactly what I wanted. I slithered and wriggled away from beneath Callum. I felt rather than heard his moan of protest as his tree slid out of me. I waited for a beat, and then turned my back to him. His tree probed for me instantly, but that was no longer quite what I wanted. I went up on tiptoe, using the bath side for leverage. I slid against him, positioning myself carefully and then shoved. Hard.

Callum's tree slid into my back passage as easily as it had moved into my sex. The sensation was deeply agreeable—for both of us. Callum's tree fit me tightly. There was no discomfort at all, but much pleasure, edged with just a fraction of pain. The hot water swelled around us as Callum thrust against me. I put my head back and shouted happily. I could hear Callum laughing, and then my pleasure was complete as he reached down and ran his hand into my black moss, his fingers rubbing silkily against my love pearl.

My *yonaki* could wait no longer. It exploded deep inside, sending ripples through my sex and my belly that were so like the ripples around us that for a few, wonderful moments I was as elemental as the water itself.

I came around slowly. My whole body felt languid and satisfied. Callum had slid away from me and his head was thrown back. He seemed to be staring carefully at the ceiling.

"Did you enjoy that?" I asked innocently. He cleared his throat, but his voice was still husky when he spoke.

"Oh, I don't know. Perhaps we could try it again so I could be sure?"

I glanced down at his wilted tree and laughed out loud. I was almost tempted to reach down and see if I could bring it back to life, but I was so satiated I knew I needed no more. For the moment, at least.

"There will be plenty of bathhouses in Edo, husband," I said. Callum grinned and lay back, his chin barely above the level of the hot water. Wreathed in steam as he was, I had to admit that he looked singularly demonic.

Suddenly, I felt intensely guilty. I had forgotten all about Kazhua in the depth of my desire. I spoke quickly in response to my stinging conscience.

"Callum, listen to me. How are we going to set about finding Kazhua when we get to Edo?"

"Ah. I've given that a lot of thought." I blinked in surprise. He had not spoken to me about Kazhua, and I had assumed he had barely considered her in his joy at being reunited with his parents. My guilt was a pain in my gut. "We can't just march into the Floating World and start asking probing questions about a geisha with green eyes and red hair. After all, I'm just a *gaijin* who's never set foot in Japan before, and you're a courtesan from the provinces. We're supposed to know nothing at all about the Floating World."

He was right, of course. But my thoughts seemed to hit a stone wall at that point, and no way forward had suggested itself to me. I had consoled myself with the knowledge that shortly we would be back in the Floating World. Once there, I prayed that the gods would be kind to us and show us the way to find Kazhua.

"So? What have your thoughts shown you?" I demanded eagerly.

"We need to behave as the good people of the Floating World would expect. I shall play the ignorant *gaijin*, who wants to see all the sights. And of course, that has to include a visit or two to a geisha house."

I wrinkled my nose in distaste. "You mean you want to visit some tea houses," I corrected. Callum shrugged and I realized he was already playing the innocent foreigner. "That might not be as easy as you think. The really good establishments will demand an introduction from an existing patron. Especially so if you want to be entertained by the best geisha. What good is that going to do, anyway?"

"Actually, I was thinking of trying to get an introduction to your own Green Tea House. Logically, that's a good place to start, isn't it? I thought if I managed to get inside the place where Kazhua was last known to be, if she's still there, I might be lucky enough to catch a glimpse of her."

"It's a start," I agreed. "The problem is, if she really does have that important yakuza at her feet, he might well have insisted that she keep herself for him alone. If that's the case, she's not going to be found in any tea house."

"I've thought about all that." Callum grinned widely. I

watched his expression and saw the light of excitement in his eyes. "If I can get an introduction to the Green Tea House, I'm going to pretend to be an ignorant *gaijin* who speaks no Japanese. No doubt the geisha will gossip happily in front of me. Even if Kazhua's not there, I may pick up something useful. If it doesn't work and I draw a blank, then it's your turn."

I pointed a silent finger at myself and raised an eyebrow in question.

"You can move about the Floating World. Look and listen. Keep your hair up in the Kagoshima style and pretend to be just as much a stranger to Edo as I am. Ask about the kabuki. Say you're keen to see a performance, that you've heard about the great Danjuro and can't wait to see him act. You're supposed to be a great courtesan. You could even hint that you might be interested in more than just his acting talents. See what the gossip is then."

Callum smiled at me happily. It all sounded easy, the way he had described it. But we would have to be so very careful. Edo—and in particular the Floating World—could be a dangerous place. I knew that Auntie would never forget the loss of face I had caused her when I ran away with Simon. If Lord Dai were still alive, he would spend each day nursing his hatred of me. Even if neither of them connected me with the geisha I had once been, gossip in the Floating World flew like leaves in autumn. If either of them —or the unknown yakuza—discovered that a *gaijin* and his Japanese mistress were asking probing questions about Kazhua, then it was likely that neither of us would ever leave Edo.

Just as poor Simon had never been allowed to leave.

I reached across and gripped Callum's arm. "Don't take anything for granted," I said. "We must take great care not to arouse suspicion. If we don't, then we could well be signing our own death warrants."

The smile faded from Callum's face. "I promised you when we left the Crimea that nobody was ever going to hurt you again. And I intend to keep my promise."

And with that, I was content.

SIX

Wise men say that it's
Unwise to wish for what one
Can't have. They are wrong.

When I was a very small child, my mother, when she had time, would tell me stories of the old days, when she herself had been a child. Her family had been very poor, she said. Catching my look of astonishment, she had smiled fondly at me and shook her head.

"Much poorer than we are now," she insisted. "At least we have food most of the time and a proper roof over our heads. My father drank a great deal of sake, and was very fond of visiting a particular courtesan, and of course his needs came first, so we were hungry more often than not. When the wind took the thatch from the roof, we were wet and cold until the reeds were ready to be cut, and then we all—except for father, of course—went and cut them and repaired the roof. Even my brothers often went barefoot. No, we are very lucky. If you find a man as good and considerate as your father for a husband, then you should be very thankful."

I thought about that, and stayed silent. My father often went for weeks without even speaking to me. Although, as I was his only girl child and, hence, worthless unless he decided to sell me as a slave, it was only to be expected. Father did not inspire love in me, only fear.

I had not thought about father in many years. Now, as we traveled the length of Japan to reach Edo, memories of him came back very strongly. And I found myself deeply thankful that I had not remained in my poor village, no doubt to be given in marriage to any man who had a fancy for me. Or—if there had arisen a very bad year when the rice failed and my brothers and father went hungry—I would probably have been sold to a rich man as his slave. Or perhaps it would be more accurate to say I would have been sold to a man who had more money than my parents, which would not have been difficult.

"Penny for your thoughts," Callum teased.

I turned back from our carriage window and smiled at him. The carriage was very basic, being pulled by oxen rather than horses. But even that was better than I had expected. When I had left Japan, rich people traveled in palanquins, carried carefully by at least four men. I had traveled in them occasionally, when I had been summoned to attend to a special patron. They were very slow, and not at all comfortable. Poor people had gone on foot, or—if they were a little better off—on a stinking cart, pulled by a donkey that was also used to transport crops and anything else too heavy to be carried on a human back. Admittedly, our oxen were very slow after the horse-drawn carriages I had become accustomed to in Scotland and Virginia, and almost stationary compared to steam trains, but the poor beasts seemed content to travel at a steady amble for hour after hour. Horseback would have been much quicker, but it was unknown for a lady to ride a horse in Japan, and had I attempted it I would have caused so much gossip Edo would have been waiting for my arrival with huge interest. Exactly the sort of interest I was desperate to avoid.

So I sat and swayed to the rhythm of our carriage, and mentally urged the poor beasts onward with every step they took. The Floating World and my daughter were waiting for me. At long last, I was keeping my promise to my dear Kazhua. And to myself. Surely the oxen could go faster. They must. But I wasted my efforts. Nothing made any difference to their slow plod.

"You were miles away," Callum said gently.

"Not so much miles away as years away. I was thinking back to when I was a child," I explained. "If somebody had told me then all that would happen in my life, I would have laughed out loud. And," I added very reluctantly, as my thoughts seemed disloyal even to me, "I couldn't help but compare this to life outside Japan. All this must seem very old-fashioned to you." I waved my hand around, indicating not just our lumbering carriage but the countryside around us.

"Not as much as you might think," Callum said thoughtfully. "Don't forget, I spent a lot of time in China, and you know how dreadful the backcountry is, where it's been ravaged by opium addiction."

I nodded seriously. I would never forget the horror of our journey from the Crimea to Shanghai.

We were silent for a while. The comfortable silence that can only lie between two people who know each other well enough to need no words. I was surprised to find I was becoming reassured by the steady rhythm of our oxen's hooves, trudging down the miles. If so very little had changed in the rest of Japan, perhaps it might be the same in Edo. Could the Floating World be just as I had left it, apart, of course, from the odd *gaijin* about the place?

For some reason, my memory went back to my mother again. When I was a young girl and I had whined about some trivial thing, she had always said the same thing. "Be careful what you wish for. You may get it." Her adult words had passed straight over my head, but as we approached Edo, I understood. At first sight, everything seemed exactly as I had left it. People were everywhere, talking loudly. Bargaining over everything from fish to jade. Carts thronged the narrow streets, occasionally running over a stray foot when the owner was either too slow or too hemmed in to move away briskly enough, then the air was torn by curses. Even the houses were exactly as I remembered them. Nearly all made of wood, with silk or paper screens for windows and doors. Nor had the fashions changed greatly. My kimono and *geta* would blend in perfectly. Automatically, I scoured the crowd for one face. For a geisha with green eyes and red hair. But she was not there. There were geisha, certainly. Lots of them, tottering on high *geta*. But they all had black hair and dark brown eyes. I cursed my stupidity in hoping for the impossible.

The more I looked, the more anxious I became. Even though I had longed for Edo to be the same as when I last saw it, now that I thought that it had barely changed at all, I was alarmed. If nothing had changed, then how many people would still remember me? Although I am by nature a modest woman, I have to admit that I was once the most sought after and well-known geisha in the whole of Edo. The common people turned and stared at me in awe when I walked the streets, my maid at my heels. Rich and important men had bid a fortune to take my virginity at my *mizuage* ceremony. The man who finally won me—Lord Dai —was a fabulously wealthy nobleman. And not only did he pay a high price for me, he risked everything by cheating to get me. A sudden shiver of panic made my stomach clench. Had his terrible secret become common knowledge while I had been away from Edo? If it had, he would have become a laughing stock. His reputation ruined. Unable to show his face in society again. If that had happened, he would, undoubtedly, have blamed me for it. And no matter how long he waited, he would still want his vengeance on me. Suddenly, I understood that my mother's words had been very wise. I leaned against Callum, hiding my head in his sleeve.

"What is it? We're here at last. Doesn't that make you happy?"

"Yes." I took a deep breath. "But now that I am here, I'm worried. Simon was murdered when he came back here, because of me. I don't want the same thing to happen to you, husband!"

"It's not going to happen," he said simply. "Trust me, Tara. We're here to find Kazhua. And we will do that, I promise you."

I smiled tightly. It all seemed so easy when he said it. But the worry refused to leave me. Callum was not Japanese. He could not be expected to understand the terrible consequences involved in losing face. And even if Lord Dai's secret was still unknown, could any man forget that his bride had run away with her *gaijin* lover while he had been busy making plans for his own marriage? And I had no doubt that my auntie from the Green Tea House would never forget my betrayal either. And apart from the danger to both Callum and me, if Kazhua was still here in the Floating World, what danger might I be putting her in? I clenched my teeth to stop myself from shrieking out loud.

"We are here. Neither you nor I am going to back down now." Callum's voice was calm. "Could you live with yourself if you did?"

I nodded silently. He was right, of course. I raised my head and stared out of the glassless carriage window. A stray breeze carried the scent of geranium to me, lifting from the crowd that surged around us. Japanese people rarely wear scent. Very high ranking courtesans might rub a little scented oil onto their skin, but that was enough. The scent I could smell now came from the clothes of the crowd. Clothes were folded away with crushed *jako* seeds—a type of musk geranium—strewn amongst them, both to preserve their freshness and to deter moths. I inhaled deeply, and the years rolled away. Poor as we had been when I was young, even my mother had used *jako* seeds when she put freshly laundered clothes away. Although she, of course, grew the geraniums and gathered the seeds. We would never have had enough money to actually buy such fripperies.

Nostalgia made me close my eyes in almost as much pain as pleasure. Callum put his hand on my arm. I opened my eyes to look at his face and I smiled. He was right. I was home. Back within touching distance of my daughter. All the longing and dreams of those many years came back to me on the subtle perfume of geranium seeds. How could I ever have doubted that I was doing the right thing. The only thing.

"Are you all right?" Callum asked quietly.

I nodded. "Yes. I just realized suddenly that I was back. That I'm really here, back in Edo. Nothing seems to have changed at all. I can't believe it." I paused, marshaling my thoughts. "Kazhua will have changed, though. She was only hours old when I had to leave her. But I'll know her, Callum. Even if she didn't have such distinctive eyes and hair, I would know my own daughter when I found her. But why should she know me? I'm going to be a complete stranger to her. After all, she's managed without me all these years, so why should she care?"

My voice became shrill with panic as the old fears threatened to overwhelm me. Callum wrapped his arms around me and held me very tightly. I felt as if he was willing me to believe in his own certainty and I relaxed slightly.

"We will find her, Tara-chan," Callum said gently. "If she is here in Japan, then we will find her. I can't lie to you, I hope and pray that she will have been told about you, and that she will have longed to be reunited with you just as much as you have with her. But I don't know."

I wanted him to reassure me. To tell me my fears were groundless. That by some miracle everything would be all right. Not to be brutally honest. I stared out of the carriage window, suddenly reluctant to see the geisha with the green eyes.

SEVEN

The wind sighs through the
Pines in my garden like a
Lover's sweet whisper

*I*f Edo did not seem to have changed much from the great city I remembered, the Floating World within it had, and I found I was perplexed. Did I like this place that was at once so familiar and yet so subtly different? Did the changes have any meaning to me? I felt disorientated by the oddity of it, and I was deeply unsettled.

Callum insisted that he explore on his own to, as he put it, "get the lay of the land." I was surprised, and rather annoyed. Surely, it would be better if I went with him. We had decided that he should speak no more than a few words of Japanese. How was he going to find out anything, arrange anything, if he couldn't ask the simplest of questions? Callum shook his head at my doubts.

"It's not that I want to leave you out of anything, Tara," he said. "It's just that if the locals think I don't understand them, I'm more likely to pick up on any gossip. They might not be so keen to speak freely in front of me if they know you're listening."

He was right, I supposed.

"If that's what you want." I shrugged. "Where are you going to start?"

"Our innkeeper has been only too keen to help a poor *gaijin* who wants to see the sights of Edo." Callum paused and grinned at me.

I raised my eyes to the heavens. "You want to be careful, husband," I said tartly. "His English is terrible. He breaks off and goes into Japanese halfway through a sentence. If you didn't speak Japanese well, you would find it very difficult to understand him."

"Ah," Callum said smugly. "I realized that. I played the innocent and made him repeat himself until I pretended to understand him. In any event, he has directed me to a certain *ryokan* on Kyô Street where he says many important *gaijin* gather. I thought that would be a good place to start."

"And why should meeting with *gaijin* help?" I was puzzled. "Wouldn't it be better for us to go out together? Do some shopping? Try and pick up on the gossip?"

"No. You're forgetting, Tara. You come from Kagoshima. Edo and the Floating World are as strange to you as they are to me. What could be more natural than one *gaijin* wanting to seek out the company of his fellow foreigners? Without his woman beside him, of course. Besides, if some of the *gaijin* have been here for a while, they might have picked up some information."

He was right, of course. I felt quite deflated.

"What shall I do then?" I asked. Although I had already decided that if Callum said "stay here and wait for me" that

I would give him a piece of my mind. Even that small satisfaction was denied to me.

"Why don't you do a little sightseeing? Take Chiyô with you and go for a walk. Do some shopping. Everything a newly arrived lady from Kagoshima would do."

I barely waited until Callum had gone before I shouted for Chiyô. I smiled at her and asked innocently, "Even in Kagoshima, we have heard of the famous Floating World. I would like to see as much of it as I can. Where should we go, Chiyô?"

My newly-acquired maid puffed up with pride. "I have spent my whole life in the Floating World, o-sama. It is a very interesting place. There are many shops, selling fine jade and decorations. Or perhaps you would like a new kimono?" she said eagerly. I pretended to consider her words carefully. I might pick up some gossip from the merchants' shops, but I was doubtful. The more so as I knew that Chiyô would select her shops very carefully. I would only be taken to those merchants who would give her flower money if I spent freely with them, and I doubted they would want to chat. They would be too busy trying to relieve me of my money.

"That would be lovely." I smiled. "But I would also like to see some of the culture of the Floating World. Perhaps take a look at the kabuki? We have a very good kabuki theater in Kagoshima, but I'm sure it can't compare to the one here in Edo. And after so much shopping and sightseeing, I will definitely be in need of some refreshment. You might know of a suitable tea house?"

Chiyô's eyes opened wide, and her expression was suddenly sly. I realized at once that she thought I was already tired of my *gaijin* lover and—as a free courtesan—

was in search of another *danna*. I didn't disillusion her. Surely, I was more likely to find a trace of Kazhua here in the flower and willow world than anywhere else. I pressed a coin in Chiyô's hand.

"I'm sure we understand each other very well," I murmured.

The coin vanished into her obi so quickly I barely saw it go.

I soon found that my first impressions had been right. This Floating World was subtly different from the Floating World of my memories. I was relieved to find that I no longer knew every turn, and soon I stopped worrying that I might give myself away with my familiarity. Much had changed—some streets I thought I remembered seemed to be composed entirely of new dwellings. Of course, as everything was built of wood, fire was a constant hazard and whole streets burned sometimes, with new houses being built as soon as the ashes cooled.

"That's going to be the new kabuki theater, o-sama," Chiyô said cheerfully, nodding at a half-built structure. "They say the new building's going to be even finer than the old one. Such a shame it's not going to be finished for a long time, so you're not going to be able to see a performance."

I stopped to stare at the builders going about their work. One of them turned and gave me an insolent up-and-down look. I frowned at him haughtily, and he laughed and said something to a fellow carpenter.

"What happened to the old kabuki?" I asked. I had been to the kabuki theater many times with patrons, although I preferred the bunraku puppet theater. But it was not nostalgia that made me stand and watch so anxiously. I remembered the letter from Callum's da that had set us out on our quest to find Kazhua. He had written that there was word of a geisha in the Floating World who had green eyes and hair as red as a fox spirit. A geisha who was rumored to be so beautiful and so talented that she had both the most feared yakuza in Edo and the lead actor in the best kabuki in Edo at her feet. And now that kabuki theater had gone. An instinctive fear made me suddenly cold.

"Oh, there was a terrible fire. It burned to the ground in a single night. They say—" She lowered her voice conspiratorially. "—that Danjuro, the lead actor, died in the fire. My, but he was a good-looking man! I don't suppose the new kabuki will be the same without him."

"Really? How awful. How on earth did that happen?" I managed to keep my voice steady. Worry, jagged as lightning, danced through my head. I wanted to know more, but couldn't find the words to ask. I had no need to bother. Chiyô was eager to impart the latest gossip.

"It was thought that he dashed back inside when the fire started, to try and rescue some of his things." The tone of her voice invited comment. I obliged.

"Do you think that's what happened?"

"No!" Chiyô said scornfully. She glanced around carefully before she went on, her voice lowered to a whisper. I had to lean toward her to hear what she was saying. "Everybody knows that Danjuro and Akira shared the same woman. They were both mad about her."

"Who's Akira?" I asked innocently.

Chiyô stared at me in amazement, then forgot her manners and laughed.

"Oh. I forgot you're not from Edo. Do you know, o-sama, your accent is so good, I quite forget you're from the provinces!"

I smiled tightly. Much as I wanted to know more, I was angry with myself for forgetting such an obvious thing. In the future, I would take care to try and mimic the provincial dialect I had found so dreary in Satsuma province.

"It's rather a long story." Chiyô smacked her lips as if they were suddenly dry. I took the hint.

"That looks like a nice tea house. Shall we take tea, and perhaps something to eat?"

Chiyô needed no urging. I allowed her to lead me into the tea house—which was indeed a very elegant one—and I ordered tea and daifuku cakes for both of us. A couple of men at an adjacent table stared at me with blatant interest and I glared at them. Pretending to be a high-class courtesan when I was with Callum was one thing, but it obviously had its drawbacks when I was alone.

"Now, Chiyô, do tell me all the gossip about the kabuki. It's such a shame the playhouse has burned down. I have heard so much about Danjuro," I lied. "I was really looking forward to seeing him perform."

"You would have enjoyed it." Chiyô rolled her eyes and nibbled her sweetmeat happily. "He was the most wonderful actor. And so handsome! He could have had his pick of any woman in the Floating World. But until *she* came along, he was only interested in the theater. Most of the old kabuki troupe has gone out of Edo now that Danjuro's gone. I don't suppose the new lot will be nearly as good. Mind you, Akira-san is putting up the money for the new theater, and he'll only want the best."

I sensed the men at the next table tensing at the mention of Akira's name. They both looked like prosperous merchants to me, and I thought that they must have good businesses to be able to take time off during the day to visit a tea house. Now, they seemed to find it necessary to drink their tea very quickly. They called for their bill and rose to leave, although they still found time to give me a few lingering looks as they went out.

"You were going to tell me about Akira," I murmured. I ached to ask about the mysterious "she," but I would wait a little longer. If I asked about this woman who could be Kazhua too quickly, I might give myself away.

"You've never heard of him?" Chiyô said incredulously. "I thought everybody in Japan knew about Akira-san."

"Kagoshima is a long way from Edo," I said firmly. "Who is he?"

"He's a yakuza."

I almost laughed at her serious face. Yakuza—gangsters —were nothing. The Floating World had been full of them when I left. Many of them traded in opium and charged the merchants and tea houses and brothels money to ensure that rival yakuza did not bother them. Oddly, I remembered that it had been said that Auntie's tea houses were the only ones in the whole of the Floating World that did not pay one yakuza or another "tea money," the yakuza equivalent of Chiyô's much less corrupt "flower money."

Many yakuza were very rich indeed, but they had no status. We geisha—together with the kabuki and bunraku actors—were always referred to by the contemptuous name of "riverbed beggars" by the true nobility. Yakuza were even lower class than we were, barely ranking above the *burakumin*, the caste of untouchables who performed tasks like emptying cesspits and slaughtering animals for meat. I was not at all surprised that Kazhua had had the good taste to prefer her kabuki actor.

"He's not just any yakuza." Chiyô seemed offended by my amusement. I schooled my face to be serious. "With you coming from Kagoshima, o-sama, you wouldn't understand. Akira-san's father was head of the most important yakuza gang in Edo. When he died, Akira-san took over. He's a very ruthless man. There were a lot of battles in the early days. Many yakuza died. Some of the smaller clans joined with Akira-san in the end. Now, he owns tea houses and brothels and shops all over Edo. It's said that those who still own their own shops are pleased to pay him tea money. And he protects all the important courtesans, as well." She paused and added tactfully. "I'm surprised he hasn't asked you to pay him a visit yet."

"You forget," I said firmly. "I have Callum-san to protect me."

"Of course," she said courteously. "But Callum-san is just a *gaijin*. And Akira-san is very rich and very important. And very much feared. They say that his enemies have a habit of disappearing. Or worse," she added darkly.

I made my face worried, even as I wanted to laugh. Clearly, this upstart yakuza took himself very seriously indeed!

"So, tell me about Akira and Danjuro and this mysterious geisha." I realized, too late, that I had given myself away yet again. Chiyô had never mentioned that the woman Akira and Danjuro were supposed to share was a geisha. I needn't have worried. She was so keen to bring me up to date with all the gossip, she hadn't noticed my slip.

"Ah! Midori No Me, you mean." That was the name Alexander had mentioned in his letter. The name meant "Green Eyes" in Japanese. It had to be my Kazhua. I was suddenly angry. I had named her Kazhua. Green Leaf. Who had dared to call her by such a derogatory name?

"What an odd name!" I said lightly. "A Japanese girl would never have green eyes, would she?"

"She had," Chiyô said smugly "Green eyes and red hair. A lot of people thought she was actually a fox spirit who had cast a spell on both Danjuro and Akira. Others said that her father had been a *gaijin*, but I can't believe that. We'd rarely even seen *gaijin* in Edo until a year or two ago. No. I think it's more likely that she really was a fox spirit, out to amuse herself."

"She sounds very strange," I agreed. "Did you ever see her yourself?"

"Oh no." Chiyô sounded amused. "She was far too well protected for me to ever see her. But everybody says she was the most beautiful geisha that Edo has ever seen."

"What happened to her?" I had to know! Had we really traveled all this way, only to find my daughter was gone from the Floating World? Gone—or far worse.

"Nobody knows for sure." Chiyô shrugged. "It was the gossip of the Floating World a while ago. Akira-san had taken her for his concubine. It was rumored that he was so mad about her, he was going to marry her. But everybody knew that she had been having an affair with Danjuro, and that Akira was insanely jealous of Danjuro as a result."

She sipped her tea and looked around her over the rim of the tea bowl. I realized with a shiver of apprehension that Chiyô was obviously terrified somebody might overhear her and wasn't going to speak until she was sure we could not be overheard.

"So what do you think happened to her?" I said again.

"The kabuki burned," she repeated with a slow nod. "Supposedly with Danjuro in it. And nobody has seen sight or sound of Midori No Me since the kabuki burned down. She's just vanished. At first, everybody thought Akira-san had set fire to the theater himself, and that he murdered Danjuro and left his body there as an example to anybody else who wanted to cross him. Apart from anything else, Danjuro owned most of the kabuki and he refused to allow Akira to buy into it. Now that he's gone, Akira is building the new theater himself, and he'll own all of it.

"Anyway, at first, everybody thought Akira had started the fire himself to get rid of his rival. With Danjuro supposedly dead, it was thought that he was keeping Midori No Me a prisoner until she forgot Danjuro and agreed to marry him. Then when nothing was seen of her at all for months, a rumor started that Akira had done away with her as well. But now people are saying that Danjuro didn't die at all, that the body they found in the ruins was somebody else entirely. The gossip is that Midori No Me hasn't been seen because she ran away with Danjuro and they're both going to stay well away from Edo until Akira finds another woman to take her place and they can come back safely."

"Goodness," I said shakily. "It sounds just like a kabuki plot! So, who was the poor soul who died in the fire if it wasn't Danjuro?"

"Nobody knows. But it's a coincidence that a man who adored the kabuki and was said to have wanted to take Danjuro as his lover hasn't been seen since the fire. I wouldn't put it past Akira-san to have murdered him as well, just to show the Floating World how much power he has," Chiyô said. She glanced into her tea bowl and finding it empty, put it down reluctantly. "Would you like to carry on shopping, now?"

"That's a good idea," I agreed. My head was so full of her hints and gossip, I needed to get out into the fresh air. Or at least, as fresh as the air ever got in the Floating World. I was deeply amused to find that the men at the next table had paid our bill. One of them had also left a little note, giving his name and saying he would be back at the tea house at the same time tomorrow.

Chiyô watched in disbelief as I crumpled the note up and threw it away. She was obviously amazed.

"Is it really true what they say about *gaijin* men having tails?" she asked breathily.

I said nothing, just smiled mysteriously.

EIGHT

Even the fiercest
Man can be tamed by the touch
Of his beloved

*C*allum looked so smug, I knew at once he had not wasted his day.

"Did you enjoy your shopping with Chiyô?" he asked innocently.

"I did. And what about you? What have you been up to?" I demanded. "Where have you been until this hour? And how do you come to smell of whisky, here in Edo?" I sniffed suspiciously. "Cheap whisky, at that."

He threw his arms up in mock anger and caught me around the waist before I could get away.

"Sit quietly, woman, and I will tell you all I know."

"Yes, master," I muttered subserviently, my head dipped in mock fear.

Callum grinned widely. "That's better. I think I could get used to a nice little wife who does as she's told."

I smiled and then pulled his nose, hard enough to hurt.

Callum gave my cheek a mock slap and then his face became serious.

"I visited the *ryokan* our innkeeper directed me to. It's just inside the Floating World, and as he said, it's very popular with *gaijin*. In fact, the proprietor is obviously doing so well out of us stupid foreigners that hardly any Japanese go there now. I wasn't hopeful of finding any information, but I was very lucky indeed. I went in and ordered a drink and I was astonished when I was given a large shot of scotch instead of sake. I was coughing after my first sip when a chap came up and spoke to the innkeeper in fluent Japanese. It was a good job my eyes were still streaming or I would have given away that I understood him.

"'Not that rubbish, Goro,' he said. 'I think this gentleman is used to something better. The good stuff, if you please.' I wiped my eyes to give myself a moment to think, and by the time I had put my handkerchief away, the stranger was pushing a much smaller glass toward me. 'Judging by your accent, I would guess you're Scottish, sir,' he said. 'Now this certainly is not going to be up to your usual standards, but at least it won't result in you waking up in a back alley in the Floating World wondering where you spent the night and your money.'

"'Thank you.' I sipped cautiously. He was right. It wasn't the best whisky I had ever tasted, but it was far better than my first glass. 'Your good health.'

"'And yours,' he replied. We drank in silence for a moment or two.

"'I think you must be the *gaijin* who has caused much gossip by bringing a courtesan from Kagoshima who is said to be so radiantly beautiful she outshines even the lovely Edo ladies,' my new friend said conversationally. I stared at him in amazement.

"'And how did you know that?'

"'Not a lot happens in Edo that I don't find out about.' He smiled and gave me his card. It was written in Japanese and I was about to give it back with barely more than a glance, protesting it meant nothing to me, when he gestured to me to turn it over. His name and business were written on the back in English. 'Christian Mountjoy. Negotiant.'

"'Negotiant? You're some sort of wine merchant?' I said in surprise. He shook his head, smiling.

"'Not at all. I'm afraid my business doesn't translate from the Japanese very well. I buy. I sell. Anything and everything that I can make a profit from. Porcelain, jade, silk. Opium.' He must have seen my frown when he said opium. He shrugged. 'You don't approve? If I didn't supply it to the gentlemen of London town, somebody else most certainly would.'

"'It's not up to me to approve or not. But I have traveled a good deal in China and I've seen the damage opium can do.' I realized how stuffy I sounded and managed a smile to soften my words. 'I didn't realize it was popular as far away as London.'

"'It most certainly is. Especially amongst that class of gentleman who has much money and no idea how to spend it.' He clapped his hand to his mouth in obvious amusement. 'I do hope I haven't offended you, sir? That you do not yourself belong to the class of rich idiot who— or at least I sincerely hope—will one day make me rich myself?'

"His eyes were gleaming and I had to laugh. He was the sort of instantly likable chap that isn't met with often. Already I felt as though I had known him for years.

"'I may be well off, but I hope I'm not an idiot.' I held out my hand and he took it in a warm, firm handshake. 'Callum Niaish. Delighted to meet you, Mr. Mountjoy.'

"'Christian, please. Or if you prefer, just Mountjoy. Nobody calls me Mr. Mountjoy unless I'm about to do business with them. And I doubt, somehow, that I have anything that would be of interest to you.'"

"That's all very well," I interrupted. "I'm sure this man's very agreeable, but did he know anything about Kazhua?"

"Turned out, he did," Callum said smugly. "He's been here a couple of years and he says he loves the Floating World. He claims to have visited every tea house and brothel in the place. I said I was looking forward to visiting a few myself and asked if he had any recommendations."

"Callum!" I said indignantly. "If you're supposed to have the most beautiful woman in Edo with you what do you want with a brothel?"

"That's what Mountjoy said." Callum grinned widely. "I muttered something about looking for something a bit different and he nodded, as if he understood perfectly.

"'It's a great pity you didn't get here last year,' he said. 'If you have a fancy for something different, you need to visit a very special tea house. It's called the Hidden House, and it's the most exclusive place in the Floating World. Mind you, you've missed the greatest gem of them all. Not that either you or I would have been allowed anywhere near her and lived to tell the tale, but if any woman was worth dying for, it was her. But I can still show you a few ladies who will make your eyes pop, and no mistake.'"

Callum paused, smiling at me. I put my hands on his shoulders and shook him so hard that when we went to the bathhouse later, I found I had bruised his skin.

"Kazhua? Was he talking about my Kazhua?"

"I believe so." Callum was suddenly very serious. "He

called her Midori No Me and said she was the mistress of the greatest yakuza in Edo. A man called Akira. Mountjoy told me he's so ruthless everybody is terrified of him. Except Midori No Me. He wanted to marry her, but she refused him in favor of her lover, an actor in the kabuki."

"That was Danjuro," I interrupted. "Chiyô said it had been thought that Akira had murdered him, and then burned the kabuki to cover up his crime. And that he murdered Midori No Me as well out of jealousy that she preferred Danjuro to him. But she says the gossip is now that all that was nonsense, and that both Danjuro and Kazhua—I mean Midori No Me—escaped together and fled from Edo safely."

"That's what Mountjoy said. In fact, he believes the gossip about them both being dead was started by Akira himself to save face. He couldn't stand the whole of Edo knowing that his woman had run away with his rival. Mountjoy's sure they're both alive, and I believe him. He says he knows Akira quite well. I suppose it's only natural, as their business interests must overlap in a few areas. He said that Akira used to talk about her constantly, until both she and Danjuro disappeared; he hasn't mentioned her since. I believe him. I think he knows what he's talking about."

There it was again, you see. Fate. Callum had met this man by accident. Against all the odds, a *gaijin* who knew Akira well. Oh, but everything was fitting together just as it should! A sudden thought subdued my pleasure.

"So they're no longer here in Edo. In that case, how are we ever going to track Kazhua down if someone like Akira can't find her?"

I stared at Callum, torn between delight that Kazhua

was still alive and despair that she had slipped away from me.

"Because it's Akira she's hiding from, not us. Don't forget, I'm just an innocent *gaijin*. I can bumble about and play the stupid foreign idiot who's interested in all the gossip. I can ask questions that nobody who knows Akira would dare to ask. That's how I got Mountjoy talking. He obviously found my total ignorance about how the Floating World works deeply amusing." Callum paused and I sensed he was delicately probing for the right words. "Tara, I did find out one thing from Mountjoy that you need to know about."

Callum was staring at me intently, and I found I was becoming nervous.

"What?" I demanded. "It doesn't sound as if it's good news, but tell me anyway."

"You left Kazhua in the Hidden House, didn't you? And Big promised to care for her for you. That's right, isn't it?"

"Yes. You know it is," I said impatiently. "I've told you all about it. And Big must have kept his promise if she was trained to be a geisha."

"That's only half of it, my love," Callum said flatly. "Kazhua did become a geisha. But not in the Green Tea House. She was raised in the Hidden House. She was a maiko there. Had her *mizuage* there and worked there as a geisha entertaining the men who had a taste for something a little different in a woman. She stayed there until Akira took her away as his concubine. When Mountjoy said I had missed the greatest gem of them all, he meant out of the geisha in the Hidden House. And he was talking about Kazhua. It couldn't have been anybody else."

For a merciful moment, my mind was filled with sweet images of my own dear friends from the Hidden House.

Beautiful women, with souls as pure as sparkling water. Then memories crowded in of Simon rescuing me from the advances of some of the geishas' clients. Men who had come to the Hidden House to be entertained by the bodies of the flawed gems who lived there rather than to listen to them dance or sing. Men exactly like all of the other men my dear friends were obliged to take into their bodies every day of their lives.

Callum had his hands tightly on my shoulders. His voice, near as he was to me, seemed to be coming from far away.

"Tara. Are you all right? You're rigid."

I turned my head to stare at him. It took a great effort. I felt as if my body had been turned to wood.

"Big promised me that he would look after my baby." Callum flinched back from the sound of my voice. "I hope he is still here in the Floating World. If he is, I am going to kill him for what he did to my lovely Kazhua."

"Tara. No." Callum shook me slightly, and I felt as if a spell had been lifted from me. I sighed deeply and my taut muscles slumped.

"I will kill him," I repeated. "If he doesn't remember me, before he dies I will tell him who I am so that he understands why he deserves death. Do you have any idea what the Hidden House is, Callum?"

"I know what you told me about it. And Mountjoy said it's more or less a very high-class brothel. Very exclusive, a place only the richest men can afford. He said the geisha were incredibly beautiful, and very talented, but that they were all a bit different from normal women. He said that if I really wanted something a bit out of the ordinary, I might enjoy a visit there when I had grown bored with everything else the Floating World had to offer. He said there's nothing else like it anywhere in Edo. I would have to have a sponsor to get me in the Hidden House, but he would be delighted to help me out there as he knew it well."

"Is that what he said?" I laughed harshly. "Well, it's a good enough way to describe the Hidden House, I suppose. The geisha there were called 'flawed gems' in my day. One girl had webbed fingers and toes. Another was an albino with white hair and eyes so light they were almost colorless. But that's not the point. Normal geisha would never be expected to have sex with their patrons. If any man were crude enough to suggest it, he would have been thrown out of any tea house immediately. But the Hidden House was different. It wasn't just a brothel. Not even a very high-class one. As your friend said, it was available only to the very rich and the very well connected. A man had to be introduced by an existing patron, and even then, if Auntie didn't think he was rich and important enough, she would refuse to allow him in."

"Surely, that must have made things a little better for Kazhua?" Callum looked at me hopefully. "If the geisha were so very sought after, she must have been well taken care of?"

"You think so?" I spoke very softy. "The Floating World is crammed full with courtesans, and every street corner has a brothel. But the Hidden House was like none of those. It was—still is by the sound of it—a very special place. Men went there to taste the delights of the flawed geisha. Oh, why am I bothering to dress it up? They went there to visit the freaks. None of the geisha were normal, and because of that the men could pay to do anything they liked with them. Abuse them. Hurt them. The geisha there told me that Big and his lover Bigger were employed in the Hidden House to keep the patrons in order. But I think that meant they would stop a patron from actually killing a geisha, but almost anything else was permitted. Those poor girls were forced to accept anything their patrons wanted to do to them. Each and every day. And because the patrons viewed them as freaks, what they wanted were things that were too extreme even to be found in the ordinary brothels."

Callum's face was white to his lips. "I'm sorry. I didn't know," he said softly.

"Of course you didn't," I said. "But that is why I'm going to kill Big if I possibly can. He took my trust. He took my baby. And he allowed her to grow up in that hellish place. When she was still just a child, he knew that she would be forced to welcome strange men into her body every day. Men who would use her and abuse her and walk away laughing, boasting to their friends what the Geisha with the Green Eyes had allowed them to do to her. I wonder even more now if she ever got my letter. If she ever knew how much I loved her." My voice cracked and I almost shouted at Callum when I went on. "If I had known, I would never have left her! I would have stayed and taken the consequences. Even if both of us had been executed, it would have been a merciful end. Better than facing such degradation every day of her poor life."

My tears came then, and I could not hold them back. I collapsed into Callum's arms and he held me tightly, stroking my hair and whispering soothing nonsense to me. When I had no tears left, he spoke my name over and over again until I listened to him.

"You didn't know," he said firmly. "You trusted Big. You had no option. And it wouldn't have been better if you had both died. That's nonsense. You both survived, and now you have the chance to find each other. And never forget, she must have grown into an exceptional young woman. She had the courage to defy Akira, and the determination to take what she wanted out of life. She wouldn't have run away with Danjuro if that wasn't the way of it. And everybody says she was the most beautiful geisha in Edo. And above all, she is still alive, Tara. We are going to find her eventually, and then you will get the chance to wipe away all these years and get to know your daughter."

"If she wants to know me," I retorted. "Even if Big did give her my letter, she must think I've forgotten about her after all this time. And if she didn't get my letter, then I don't suppose anybody else will ever have said a word about me. Nobody would have dared even mention my name. She'll have forgotten she ever had a mother by now, if she ever cared in the first place."

"I doubt it." Callum smiled gently. "I think she is far too much like you to do that. She survived the Hidden House. She refused to give way to Akira. And she took what she wanted, no matter how dangerous it was. If all of that isn't proof that she is your daughter, I don't know what else you need. If it had been you who had been left behind, would you ever have stopped wondering about your mother?"

I shook my head reluctantly. "No. I would have always wanted to know about her." A small smile stretched my lips. "And Kazhua would always have known that she was very special. At the very least, she must have realized that her father was a *gaijin*. There were so few of them in Edo at the time, she must have known that he was a very important man to have been allowed into the Hidden House. Even leaving aside the amount of money she must have earned, I can understand why Auntie kept my poor Kazhua imprisoned in the Hidden House. She would have done it to punish Kazhua for being my daughter. And at the same time, she would have gloated over the fact that if I had known, I would have been devastated. Did I tell you that Simon was Auntie's lover, before he met me?"

Callum looked so shocked, I almost laughed.

"No. I don't believe you mentioned it," he said faintly. "Do you think keeping Kazhua in the Hidden House was her way of getting revenge on all of you? On you and Kazhua and Simon as well?"

"Oh, yes. She probably made Big hand Kazhua over to her straight away." I shuddered. "I hope Simon never found out. It would have been very terrible for him to go to his death with that on his conscience."

"We'll never know for sure. But he didn't mention it in his diary or you would have known. So I think the answer must be that he didn't know."

I nodded sadly, wishing that I, also, didn't know.

NINE

Inside the earth is
Fire. Fire lies in you also
But the flames are cold

J stared at Callum in disbelief, hardly able to credit that I had heard him correctly.

"I can't come to the tea house with you! It would be scandalous. Men go to places like the Green Tea House to enjoy the company of geisha, usually before they move on to visit courtesans for other sorts of pleasure. Besides, it would be too dangerous. If Auntie sees me, she would remember me, I know she would. And even if we're fortunate and she isn't there, I'm sure that Big would know me, even now."

Of course Big would remember me. He had wanted to be my lover. The blow to his pride must have been devastating when I had run away with Simon. But I had thought him my friend, fool that I was. I wondered how I could have been so innocent, and even more did I wonder how I had ever entrusted my lovely Kazhua to him.

Callum caught my agitated hands and held them tightly.

"Don't worry about Auntie or Big. Mountjoy took great amusement in explaining the role an auntie plays in a tea house to me. He said I would have enjoyed meeting *your* Auntie, as she's a remarkably witty and attractive woman." I stared at him in disbelief, but he shrugged. "Anyway, he said it was a shame I would miss her as she's gone off to the provinces somewhere and taken Big with her for protection. She's looking for a couple of new maiko for the tea house and could be gone for ages."

"I hope so," I said. The news was reassuring. I remembered from my own time in the Green Tea House that Auntie occasionally disappeared for long periods of time on what she sneeringly called "fishing trips." "But what if Bigger's still there? He hated me. He would still recognize me, even now."

"Mountjoy mentioned that there was only one man who was allowed to work in both the Green Tea House and the Hidden House, and he was called Big. He seemed to find the nickname very amusing. Bigger must have moved on." A sudden thought chilled me. Bigger had loved the kabuki. When it burned, a man's body had been found in the ashes, no doubt too badly disfigured to identify. And now it seemed Bigger had vanished without a trace. Another coincidence? I wondered whether to share my thoughts with Callum, but I had no chance as he carried on speaking. "Don't worry about Bigger. If Mountjoy says he's not there, then he's not a problem. I think it's important that we both meet Akira. If anybody knows all about Kazhua, it's him."

I couldn't shake my fears, but reluctantly, I knew Callum was right.

"Do you really think me going back to the Green Tea House might help?" I asked finally.

"I do. We've been here over a month and have not found anything concrete. I think this is probably the only chance we have of meeting Akira. Mountjoy says he's sure that he's going to be there this evening. He suggested I go, as he seems to think I would find it amusing to meet a real yakuza. And given what we do know, I'm sure Akira is the key to finding out what really happened to Kazhua. You need to be there, as I'm equally sure that you would pick up on hints that I would miss. It'll give you a chance to meet Mountjoy as well. I'd be interested to find out what you make of him."

I hesitated. "You're right. I need to see Akira. I'm coming with you."

If Akira had truly loved my daughter, then I wanted to meet him.

In spite of my brave words, I worried so much about my return to the Green Tea House that I was almost physically sick with anticipation. Although Callum assured me repeatedly that neither Auntie or Big would be present, I still wondered if it were at all possible that one of the geisha I had known would still be there. I racked my brains for their names and finally remembered. Tamayu, who had terrified me. Saki, who had taken me under her wing and supervised my passage from maiko to geisha. And Ren, who had been a maiko with me and who had had her *mizuage* not long before I did. From what I remembered of Tamayu, I guessed she would have persuaded one of her patrons to buy her out long ago. Saki had spoken fondly of retiring and buying a little house with a garden for herself. But Ren, she would be my age now, or just a little older. It was entirely possible that she could still be a geisha at the Green Tea House.

Throughout the walk to Willow Road, I trotted at the heels of the men, and with every step, I willed them to walk quickly before my fears could grow so huge that they overwhelmed me and forced me to turn and take myself back to the safety of our *ryokan*. When we finally arrived at the Green Tea House, Mountjoy opened the door without even knocking, which astonished me. Surely even an ignorant *gaijin* would knock and wait to be admitted. Sheer terror froze me. My mouth became dry. I could only take the shallowest of breaths, and even those hurt the space between my breasts. I was cold, even though the evening was hot and quite humid. I thought it was impossible that my companions could not hear my heart beating, the sound so loud in my own ears that I could barely hear anything else. I tried to speak, to explain to them that I suddenly felt ill, that I must go back to the *ryokan*. Callum glanced back at me and smiled encouragingly. I took courage from his belief in me and somehow I was able to walk into the entrance hall calmly, looking around with subtle interest.

Callum was also glancing around, but far more obviously than I was, whistling softly under his breath and pretending to be nothing more than a stupid, poorly mannered *gaijin*. I knew the act was as much to reassure me as to fool anybody who might be watching us. Mountjoy caught him by the elbow as he made to leave the hallway.

"Hang on a moment. We have to take our shoes off and leave them here before we go any further."

"Sorry, I'd forgotten that bit of nonsense." Callum looked amused, but did as he was told. He smiled at me, and I found I could breathe again. Some of my fears fled. Surely I would be safe with Callum at my side. He kicked his shoes off, leaving them leaning against each other. Mountjoy followed suit, more carefully. My own *geta* were shed in a second. "Lead on, old chap," Callum said chirpily and followed Mountjoy through the open door into the main room. As was only proper, I followed both men a respectful distance behind.

The Green Tea House's layout was exactly as I remembered it. I could have walked the short distance from the hall to the main room blindfolded. And even worse, as soon as I stepped through the front door and inhaled the familiar perfume of subtly scented lamp oil and incense, I was a geisha again. I saw Callum staring at me in perplexity, and I knew that I was walking differently from how I normally did, that my whole way of carrying myself had changed. My head was held deferentially down. I was taking small, shuffling steps, looking neither left nor right. Someone in the reception room was playing a samisen. I listened to the flow of the notes and ached to take it out of their hands and play it myself. That was the smallest of distractions.

With every hobbled step I took, I was certain that Auntie and Big were expecting me. That this was no more than the calm that is sometimes found before a terrible storm. Once we were firmly inside the tea house, a door would slide open and they would walk out and claim me for their own for the final time. My senses were preternaturally alert. I could hear a bat skim outside the open window, shrilling as it caught an insect. Somewhere close, someone had imprisoned a cricket in a cage. I heard its forlorn song for freedom quite clearly. And above all else, I sensed Kazhua. Just as I could hear the trapped cricket, I knew she had been close to where I stood now. The Hidden House was only a few seconds' walk across the courtyard garden, and I fancied I could hear the rustle of her silken kimono, her quiet laughter as she responded to a patron's joke. And also did I feel her pain as that same patron claimed her body, later on when the evening was passing into night. Not always the same man, but always the same pain of body and spirit. Time after time, until she had taken her karma into her own hands and escaped from her prison.

She had been here, almost within touching distance of where I was standing now. For a moment, I closed my eyes and cried out to the faint echo of her soul. *I am here, daughter. I told you I would come back, and now I am here.* But there was no reply.

"Akira-san, I am honored to be in your presence once more. As you can see, I have brought a new friend with me. This gentleman is Callum-san. He is new to the Floating World and already he has heard so much about your Green Tea House that he wished greatly to see it."

Mountjoy's cheerful greeting jerked me back to the present. I took a deep breath as my panic began to recede. I understood that Auntie and Big were really not here. If they had been, Big would have been ready to greet us at the door. And Auntie would certainly have been present to take a look at this mad *gaijin* who brought his own courtesan to be entertained by the geisha of the Green Tea House.

Mountjoy had not introduced me, of course. I saw Callum frown and glance at me and I gave the tiniest shake of my head. *Don't worry. This is etiquette. I am only a woman, a courtesan at that. I do not belong here. I am invisible.* I willed him to play the game and above all not to show that he had understood Mountjoy's rapid Japanese.

"Mountjoy-san, it is good to see you again."

I kept my head down, resisting the impulse to look at Akira. He spoke courteously, far more so than I would have expected from a yakuza, and his voice was deep and attractive. This man had been my daughter's lover. I longed to take a good look at him, but it would have been incredibly rude. Instead, I simply kept my gaze on the *tatami* matting, a timid smile expressing my deep pleasure at being here. And at the same time, I gave thanks to Baizenten for the rigorous training that had made me the most sought-after geisha in Edo. Truly, Auntie had taught all her girls very well. I remembered the normally placid Saki protesting that she could not attend a particularly expensive occasion. She had just started her monthly bleed and had the most terrible stomach cramps. And although she did not say it, I knew she was afraid that if she had to sit on her heels for hours, her flood would stain her kimono.

"So?" Auntie had snapped. "You think your patron is going to care about women's problems? Pad yourself well so you don't bring disgrace on both of us. Sit and smile and make your patron feel like the shogun himself. When everybody has gone, you may whine all you please. But not before."

And Saki had done as Auntie commanded. She had smiled at her patron and played and danced for him as if nothing in the world could have delighted her more than his presence. When he had gone, she had swallowed a draught from the apothecary and had slept until the next afternoon.

In just the same disciplined way, I chained my worries and smiled constantly, showing my delight at being here only in quick, darting glances at each man when they spoke, as would any expensive courtesan.

"Callum-san, I am delighted to meet with you. Please, do sit down. Here, next to me."

Akira spoke in English—very good English—and my impression of a dutiful courtesan crumpled for a second. I jumped and stared him full in the face in my shock. Fortunately, he was concentrating on Callum and I was sure that he hadn't noticed. Then he spoke again, in Japanese, and I was no longer sure.

"And this beautiful creature must be Tara-san. I have never been as far as Kagoshima, but if the women there are as lovely as she is, then perhaps I will make the pilgrimage. Tara-san, sit here where I can see you. I always thought that my tea house held the most beautiful women in the whole of Japan. Now I realize my error."

He pointed to the floor beside Mountjoy and I darted across. I knew my face was flaming, and I was grateful for the light makeup I had decided to apply at the last moment.

"Akira-san, I am most honored." I spoke breathily, my voice high-pitched. And it was no act. I barely had breath enough to get the words out. Akira nodded at me graciously, then turned to speak to Callum.

I understood at once why Kazhua had found him attractive. He was probably about my age, perhaps a little older. A handsome man with skin the color of polished hardwood and light grey eyes. A few Japanese people have the fortune to have grey eyes. It is said of such people that their spirit is elementally water, and that this is lucky as well as beautiful. But it was not just his looks that made Akira so attractive, nor his clothes. He was very well dressed, in rich robes that were clearly expensive. Yet his attraction went beyond his appearance and his clothes. He emanated an aura of power. Had he worn his hair loose and uncombed and dressed in beggar's rags, he would still have turned any woman's head. And any man with sense would have given him a wide berth.

And yet, I didn't need to wonder if I liked him. I knew I did not. He had loved my daughter to distraction if the rumors were true. For that, at least, I should have liked him. But somehow, I could not. He worried me. Even if I had not known he was the head of the most feared yakuza gang in Edo, I would have found him terrifying. Instinctively, I knew that Kazhua had never returned his love. Of course she hadn't. Would she have risked all to run away with her actor if she had cared for this creature?

"Akira-san! You speak English. My, but I wish I could speak Japanese as well as you speak my language!"

Callum, bless him, playing the ignorant *gaijin* again. His voice was far too loud, and he looked straight at Akira when he spoke. Akira's smile never slipped at the blatant rudeness, but I saw the coldness sparkle in his eyes and I worried. This was not a man one would wish to offend. Yet he shrugged and answered Callum depreciatingly, and I took the chance to unfurl my fan and peer around the room from behind it.

In the flickering lamplight, I saw my memory of it was false. It was the same room where I myself sat and entertained patrons with my wit, my dancing, my playing. Yet it was subtly different. It took me a moment or two to understand the changes. The roof and wall struts had been newly lacquered; they reflected the light with their gleaming surface. The scroll in the *tokonoma*—the alcove where Akira had taken his seat as guest of honor—was new and beautifully executed. In my day, the walls had been bare of decoration. Now, there were a number of exquisite woodcuts. A pillar held a bowl decorated in subtle earth tones, another a vase with a single sprig of blossom. I saw Callum glancing around in obvious appreciation and willed him not to comment on anything. If he did, politeness would force Akira to insist he took the object of admiration as a memento of the evening, and Callum would be expected to accept it with pleasure. I shivered at the thought. I was deeply reluctant to have anything that had any connection to Akira near me. Perhaps Callum felt the same as he did not mention anything.

There were four geisha present. All very young women, and strangers to me. One of the girls was playing the samisen very quietly. I ached to take it from her and to draw music from it with my own fingers. As soon as we sat down, two of the geisha rose and one kneeled beside Callum and the other beside Mountjoy. The remaining geisha hovered at the side of the sake flask, waiting for one of the men to signal to her to pour for them. Each of the geisha looked through me as if I wasn't there.

But all too clearly, I was not invisible to Akira. He broke off his conversation with Mountjoy and turned to look at me. He nodded at the girl who was playing. She stopped immediately, her hands suspended awkwardly above the strings.

"I'm sure Tara-chan must be bored with all this chatter between us men." I fluttered my fan and closed my eyes, smiling shyly and shaking my head in polite denial. "Perhaps you would like to play for us, Tara-chan?" He nodded at the geisha who had been playing. "Ren, bring your samisen to Tara-chan. She will play for us."

Ren. A common enough name, but I shivered as I stared at this woman, seeking any resemblance to the Ren I had known. There was none, but still I wondered if it was an omen.

I took the samisen from her with great joy, and not a little nervousness. It had been many years since I had coaxed music from a samisen, and I prayed that I had not forgotten the art. I had not; I knew as soon as my fingers touched the strings that the gift of music was still within me.

There was silence when I stopped, and for a moment I

thought I had deceived myself and I had played very badly. Then Akira began to clap, the traditional *ippon tejime*. Three claps, followed by another three, and then another three and a final, single clap. He was smiling broadly and was obviously pleased.

"Tara-chan, you are as talented as you are beautiful. Perhaps on another occasion, I might persuade you to dance for us?"

I mumbled my gratitude for his kind words and accepted a cup of sake gratefully. It gave me something to look at other than Akira.

At exactly the right moment dictated by politeness, Mountjoy bowed deeply to Akira and murmured that it was time that we took our leave of him.

"Our thanks for a superlative evening's entertainment, Akira-san," he murmured unctuously. A thought occurred to me. Who had paid for the obviously expensive evening. Mountjoy? Or had Akira treated us all? I guessed instinctively that it was Akira, and my suspicions deepened tenfold. "But the evening draws on, and it is time I took my guests away from your generous company."

It was Akira then. I watched him from lowered eyelids and saw his smile, as wide and ruthless as a shark's grin.

"The delight is entirely mine, Mountjoy-san. Of course, Tara-san will wish to go back to your *ryokan*. But could I tempt you two gentlemen to taste the very special pleasures of my other house?"

His other house? I was startled. Both the Green Tea House and the Hidden House had belonged to Auntie. What had caused the change? And then my brain caught up with my surprise and I felt close to vomiting with shock. Akira was inviting both men to visit the Hidden House. The prison where my poor daughter had been kept to be despoiled by so very many men. Even though I was almost certain she was no longer there, I could not stop myself agonizing that the unthinkable might be about to happen. What if she was there? If she were, then surely Akira would offer her delights to his honored guest, Callum. By a supreme effort, I kept my face blank but turned tortured eyes to Callum. He rose to the occasion magnificently.

"That is most kind, Akira-san." I noticed his Scottish accent had become more pronounced. A large amount of sake had been pressed on to him by his attentive geisha, but for a man who was used to drinking Scotch, it would have had little effect. He was play-acting. "But I think perhaps it's time I got Tara here back to her bed." He closed one eye in a deliberate, leering wink. Japanese people do not wink. It is considered the grossest of gestures. I glanced at Akira and was amazed to see his smile had not faltered.

"Of course, Callum-san. If our positions were reversed, I would be equally eager to return to the pleasures of my own bed."

All the men smiled. Callum nodded foolishly. In other circumstances, I would have thought sourly "all men together," but there was something curious in the atmosphere that was at odds with the joking words. I hid behind my fan and glanced from one to the other. Callum was smiling happily, his expression good-natured, his mouth hanging slightly ajar. Mountjoy, too, was smiling. But his smile was tight, and his gaze was fixed on Akira. Akira himself was also smiling, but there was no humor at all in those cold, grey eyes.

I thought I could feel the weight of the air pressing on my shoulders. I found it difficult to breathe. Was I imagining it? I glanced at the other geisha and understood instantly that I was not. All geisha are trained to anticipate anything their patron might want. More often than not, they would read a man's wants in his body language. The sake would be in his cup before he needed to ask. His brow would be mopped even before he knew he was hot. Now, the geisha with the samisen plinked out a wrong note and looked deeply embarrassed. The girl who had poured sake all evening hovered with her hand over the flask, not quite touching it. The other two glanced at each other and raised their eyebrows, virtually a sign of panic in a geisha.

Akira got gracefully to his feet. Mountjoy followed, and a second later Callum also rose, but less gracefully. Yet more out of place behavior. I would have expected Akira to have remained seated whilst his guests were shown out by one of the geisha. He took Callum's hand in a firm grip and shook it, Western style.

"It has been a pleasure to meet you, Callum-san." He was standing so close to Callum it was practically an insult. I heard the nearest geisha take a deep, nervous breath. "And of course, an equal pleasure to make the acquaintance of Tara-chan. I hope our paths will collide again. Very soon."

Callum murmured something pleasant, and then Akira was standing back. As if a physical chain had been broken, we all moved to the door. I was in the rear, of course, and if Akira had taken a dagger and stuck the point between my shoulder blades it could not have felt as piercing as his gaze.

"My God, Callum. I think you had better keep a close eye on Tara." Mountjoy waited until we were at the end of the street before he spoke. His voice was over-loud and hearty. "I haven't seen Akira so interested in a woman since Midori No Me disappeared."

Bluff and double bluff, I wondered? Was he speaking jokingly but really meant it? Or was I endowing this apparently blunt merchant with far too much subtlety?

Callum ran his fingers through his hair and grinned. His scar gave his face a rakish, devil-may-care look, and I decided I was looking for something that was clearly not there. Mountjoy was obviously just responding to what Callum appeared to be—a rich idiot, out to enjoy all the Floating World could offer in the way of amusement.

"What say?" Callum glanced at him as though he had not heard his words. Mountjoy grinned and nudged him with his elbow.

"To be honest, when you turned up with Tara in tow, I thought the whole evening was going to be a frost. I couldn't believe Akira wouldn't be shocked at the idea of taking a courtesan to a geisha house. Coals to Newcastle, what!"

I had never heard the expression before, but I guessed its meaning. I smiled sweetly at Mountjoy, pretending not to have understood him. Just for a second, his face carried a shrewd expression totally at odds with the foolish, worse-for-drink character he was showing us. I stowed the thought away, deciding I would speak to Callum about it later, when we were alone.

"Ah. Hard lines for poor old Akira then. Tara's not for sale." Callum slurred his words slightly. "Not to Akira. Not to anybody. She's mine. All mine!" He spoke far too loudly for politeness. "Anyway, how on earth does Akira come to speak such good English? That threw me good and proper!"

"It surprised me, as well," Mountjoy admitted. "I'd heard he spoke excellent English, but I've never heard him speak anything but Japanese, so I had forgotten about it. I believe good old Akira didn't trust his translators, so he made Midori No Me learn English to talk to the *gaijin* he traded with. And then he made her teach him English so he could be sure she wasn't cheating him either. Trusting sort of chap!"

Mountjoy chattered on until we reached our *ryokan*. He said good night to me politely and winked at Callum.

"Sleep well!" he murmured.

Callum sank onto our futon and stretched. "I'll never get used to kneeling for hours at a time," he complained.

I heard his knees crack and I leaned over and massaged them. After a moment, Callum groaned with pleasure and lay back. He shuffled about for a few moments and I watched in amusement as he threw back the *kakebuton*—the quilt—and then managed to almost wrap himself in the *ketto,* the under sheet.

I wanted to talk about the evening and, above all, about Akira. But he sounded so exhausted, I relented. We would talk in the morning. It would give me time to get my own thoughts ordered. I felt sleep beginning to steal upon me almost as soon as my body met the futon. I had taken only a couple of cups of sake, but I felt as if I had downed two flasks. Callum had drunk a great deal more than I had. Was Akira's sake stronger than usual, or had there been another ingredient in it? Something, perhaps, designed to loosen our tongues?

That was the last thought I had before sleep claimed me.

TEN

A mountain stream is
Always beautiful. Alas,
It is always cold!

*M*y sleep was not pleasant.

I thought that I began to dream immediately. Of course, it may not have been so. Just as Callum always insisted he was not asleep when I dug my elbow in his ribs to stop him snoring, I may have been deceived by the passage of time.

In any event, my dreams were deeply unsettling. They were of that peculiarly vivid kind, where one is quite sure that one is awake, and not dreaming at all. That, I think, made things far worse. I was back on Willow Road, but not in the Green Tea House. I was in the Hidden House.

I flitted down the corridor noiselessly. The lamps had been extinguished for the night, but there was a half-moon to give brightness and I did not stumble. I knew that the geisha in the Hidden House entertained late into the night.

It was deathly silent, so I thought that morning must be preparing to intrude on the darkness.

Only my own light breathing disturbed the silence until I heard a noise coming toward me. An even rhythm of bare feet, pattering down the corridor. A man's stride, firm and assured.

Big was walking quietly toward me. He stopped almost close enough to touch me, turning from side to side and glancing around. He seemed puzzled. I could not stop myself. I took the single step that took me in front of him. Still he didn't see me. His eyes turned this way and that, obviously seeking something he could not find.

"I am here, Big. Terue. I have come back. Do you remember me?"

I spoke clearly, but he appeared not to hear me. His handsome face creased into a frown and I saw there were deep wrinkles at each side of his eyes. His mouth was down-turned and sulky. He was no longer a young man, and not as beautiful as he had been when I had seen him last. I rejoiced in that knowledge.

"Can't you hear me? See me?"

Big rubbed his ears as if he was being annoyed by a mosquito. I could take no more. I darted forward and pounded my clenched fists on his chest as hard as I could. But he clearly felt nothing.

He muttered something I couldn't make out, and then turned and left. There came a soft current of air from the closing of the door, and it felt as violent as if somebody had dashed cold water in my face.

"Tara. Tara, wake up. You've been having a nightmare. It's me, Callum."

I stopped pounding my fists on the suddenly substantial body at the side of me, and let my breath go in a hiss.

"Are you awake now?"

For a hazy moment, I had no idea where I was. "I was in the Hidden House. I saw Big!" I blurted.

"Just a dream." Callum rocked me back and forth as if I was a distressed child. "You're awake now. Don't worry."

"But it was so very real!" I was still only half convinced. Callum lifted my hand to his lips and kissed each fingertip very gently.

"See? You're here. With me." He rubbed his hands over his face. "If we ever enjoy Akira's hospitality again, remind me not to drink so much sake. I was so deeply asleep I thought I was dreaming myself when I heard you shouting."

"What was I saying?" I asked curiously.

"You were yelling 'I'll kill you' over and over again."

"Ah. The last thing I remember in my dream was Big standing in front of me. I wanted to kill him for what he'd done to Kazhua."

I suddenly felt bewildered and lost. I held my arms out to Callum like a child demanding comfort.

"Just a bad dream," he soothed softly. He slid his arms around me and held me against his body. After the humid heat of the day, the night felt chilled and I was grateful for the heat of his body. Suddenly, cuddles were not enough.

"Please." Just one word, but I heard the longing in my voice clearly. To my deep relief, Callum clearly understood.

He kissed my cheek and then moved his mouth down to my lips. I was deeply aroused instantly. I bit his lips, hard, and he jerked back in surprise. I took myself out of his arms and flung myself back on the futon, my arms and legs splayed wide in invitation. I stared at him in the moonlight, watching the play of shadow and light across his face. I almost screamed in frustration as he simply stared at me in obvious surprise. I grabbed his hand and forced it down to my black moss. His eyes widened as his fingers immediately found my slippery wetness.

He needed no further enticing. I could hear the even pattern of his breathing become ragged. He slid his first finger up and down the entrance to my sex and I thrust against him, instantly wanting more. Callum took his hand away and licked his finger deliberately and then smiled. His expression seemed almost wolfish in the silver light. I shivered, although whether in anticipation or fear I could not decide myself.

"Callum." I whispered his name. He paused for a second, then nodded as if he had made his mind up. He moved across me fluidly, balancing on his hands. It seemed to me as if his tree of flesh had a sense of purpose all of its own. Without any need for guidance, it slid down my black moss and nuzzled at my entrance like an animal searching for the entrance to its burrow. At any other time, the comparison would have made me giggle, but not tonight. Tonight, I needed Callum in a way that was alien to me. There was no love in it at all. Nothing but naked desire.

In the moment it took before his tree pierced me, I had a sudden, shocking thought. This was Callum, my husband. The man I loved. Yet at that very moment, I would not have cared who was about to take me, as long as they could satisfy the overwhelming need that raged through my body. Would I have accepted Akira if by some strange alchemy it had been him with me and not Callum? Before the red mist of longing took me utterly, I acknowledged the answer. And I did not like it.

Callum slid into me as if I had been oiled. I thrust up against him frantically, trying to force the very last fraction of him inside me. I raised my head and bit hard at Callum's shoulder. I tasted his blood on my lips and I bared my teeth with ferocious delight. Glancing at his face, I saw his lips drawn back in a feral grimace. His face was so distorted, I barely recognized him. He leaned down and bit at my lips as if he was intent on paying me back for the hurt I had inflicted on him. As soon as he took his mouth away, I laughed out loud, rejoicing in the pain I had given and taken.

He rolled against my belly, turning and twisting sensuously. I grabbed his arms and used them to lever myself up. I rubbed against him in my turn like a cat in heat. My *yonaki* began to build, deep in my belly. I kept my eyes wide open, intent on watching Callum's expression. His pupils were huge, his mouth hanging ajar. A thread of spittle, silver in the moonlight, flicked the side of his lips. I licked it away with the very tip of my tongue and laughed as I heard him groan.

I knew he was close to bursting his fruit. Too soon! I slid away from him very slightly. And then back. It was only when I could stand it no longer that I allowed him to dictate the rhythm. He thrust at me as if I was flesh without soul, and I suddenly understood that we were still deeply in tune with each other. Just as I was using Callum, so was he using my body to find his own satisfaction. At that moment, we were no more than two animals, rutting mindlessly.

And it was glorious.

Callum burst his fruit a second after my own *yonaki* made my body shudder. My toes clenched beneath my feet and my back arched. I opened my mouth wide, but no sound came out. My *yonaki* was all the more intense as I watched Callum's face intently all the time and understood that his need mirrored mine.

My *yonaki* seemed to leave echoes that made my whole body tremble. I lay beside Callum and he drew the *kakeb-*

uton tenderly across me. Neither of us spoke for a long time. So long that I thought he had fallen asleep and I was startled when he spoke.

"No more bad dreams, Tara," he said softly. "There's no need for them. Not now. Not ever."

"I haven't the power to control my dreams," I protested, although I understood perfectly that was not what he meant.

He sat up and stretched. "It's nearly dawn. The birds have started to sing. Noisy creatures! We would have been getting up soon anyway. Do you want to talk about last night?"

"You mean what happened at the Green Tea House?"

"Well, I was thinking of that. But if you would rather talk about what came after...?"

"Idiot," I retorted. "I can't really explain it, but all the time we spent at the Green Tea House just felt wrong to me."

"I felt the same." Callum nodded. "Akira was obviously interested in you, which wasn't in the least surprising. I expected him to be angry that you were there in the first place, but he wasn't, and I got the impression he expected you. And I thought the geisha seemed on edge as well."

He had picked up on it then. I was relieved. I had begun to think I had imagined it.

"Exactly," I agreed. "In fact, I felt as if Akira knew all about us. Did you notice he didn't ask a single question about what we were doing in the Floating World, where we had come from, nothing at all? I would have expected him to be full of questions. It would have been done very politely and subtly, of course, but he didn't ask anything at all." Something occurred to me suddenly, and I gasped with surprise. "He knew I came from Kagoshima! Do you remember him saying he had never been there?"

"Perhaps Mountjoy mentioned it to him," Callum said uneasily.

"Perhaps. I don't like Akira. Chiyô's obviously terrified of him." I frowned. "And I don't trust him. And I'm not at all sure I trust your friend Mountjoy. I think he's sly."

"Oh, he's all right. He's just trying to be friends with everybody."

"Maybe. Oh, never mind. Where do we go from here? We know Kazhua's disappeared, and so has Danjuro. The kabuki's burned down, so there's no clue there. All we've got so far is gossip, nothing solid to go on at all. Akira was our last hope."

I felt deeply depressed. The quest that had started so full of joy and hope seemed to have dwindled to a futile dream.

"We've found out more than you're giving us credit for," Callum said. "We know that both Kazhua and her lover have fled Edo. If they have left Japan, logically they would have made for Shanghai. It's the nearest point to Japan in a foreign country. We know she hasn't been there or my parents would have heard about it. So I'm certain she must still be in Japan somewhere, and not between Edo and Kagoshima, or we would have heard talk about it."

I started to laugh.

"Why is everything so easy when you talk about it, Callum?" I demanded. "There's an awful lot more to Japan than the distance between Edo and Kagoshima. They might even be hiding in the far islands, where nobody from the civilized parts of Japan would even think about visiting."

"So, we keep looking." Callum smiled. "We stay in Edo. Keep asking innocent questions. Somebody must know what happened to them. If we spread enough tea money about, we'll get our answer."

"We need to be careful," I said firmly. "The more questions we ask, the more we're going to arouse suspicion. And there's always the chance that Auntie and Big will arrive back. I have no wish to meet either of them."

"Understood. But last night Akira apologized for Auntie not being there. He assured me that I would have found her a fascinating woman." Callum smiled at my incredulous expression. "He said that she was expected to be gone for a good while. She has a number of villages to visit, a long way from Edo"

"Don't you think that's odd? Why should he bother telling you that?"

Callum looked as uneasy as I felt. "I never thought of that." He frowned. "I think perhaps it might be better if we both kept as far away from Akira as we possibly can."

"Amen to that!" I agreed instantly.

ELEVEN

The cry of seagulls
Is a forlorn echo of
Your voice in my ears

*T*here is a Japanese proverb that says, roughly translated, that karma and shadows follow one everywhere. I recalled that uneasily a few hours later. Mountjoy came knocking on our door soon after breakfast. He seemed amazed that Callum wasn't expecting him.

"You must have taken more sake than I thought, old chap!" He winked roguishly. I stared into space, smiling politely as I pretended not to understand a word he was saying. "Don't you remember us agreeing to meet up this morning? We're going to take a look at the *real* Floating World. See the ladies hiding behind the lattices." His meaning was clear. He intended to show Callum some of the famous lattice brothels. The places Auntie had always threatened her geisha with when she was particularly annoyed with us.

"Really?" Callum ran his hands through his hair,

glancing at me under cover of the gesture. I nodded very slightly. Let them run about the Floating World together. I was sure Mountjoy knew far more than he was saying. Perhaps he might let something slip. It was worth a try. Besides, if Callum found something to interest him in the poor drabs behind the lattices, then he was not the man I knew he was. "To be honest, I don't remember. But it sounds great fun. Could you explain to Tara that she's to stay here until I get back?"

A nice touch, that. I glanced from man to man innocently, and nodded happily when Mountjoy translated.

"Of course, Mountjoy-san," I murmured dutifully. In Japanese, of course. I dismissed the thought that he was laughing at me as nothing but my imagination. As the men left, I realized that I, too, did not remember Mountjoy making any arrangements to see Callum today.

I had no time at all to think about that. Or anything else. I had barely begun to plan my own day when there was a tap at the door and Chiyô slid the screen back. I was surprised. Our maid was normally very polite and never intruded into our room without waiting for me to call out. I was even more surprised when she immediately almost jumped aside as a man lounged into the room.

"Tara-san." His words were polite, but his bearing was not. He slouched against the wall, picking his teeth idly with a wooden tooth-pick.

"Who are you?" I remained sitting, staring at him angrily. This was beyond rude. Even if I was supposed to be no more than a courtesan, neither he nor anybody else had the right to force their way into my bedroom and make themselves at home. "I did not invite you in. Get out."

"Akira-san has sent me to take you to him."

I was white-hot with anger. If he had told me the

shogun himself had asked for me, I would have told him to go away.

"Really? Then Akira-*san*—" I drawled the title insolently. "—had better come and ask for my presence himself. I do not care to be summoned by servants. Get out!"

Chiyô put her hand before her mouth. I heard her breath hiss. It sounded like the whimper of a kitten. Akira's man was obviously taken aback by my response. He seemed to me to resemble a bunraku puppet, given life by the master puppeteer but having no words except those uttered by the narrator. He had delivered his message and had obviously expected to be obeyed without question. Now that I had sent him about his business, he didn't know what to do.

"Get out," I repeated, pointing at the door.

"You'll be very sorry." He tried for a sneer, but looked more like a sulky child when I stared him down. "Nobody refuses Akira-san. Especially not a cheap whore like you."

"Really? Well, this particular whore does as she likes, not as she's told. You may tell Akira that, with my blessings."

Chiyô almost leaped back as he shouldered his way past her. My heart was pounding, although whether with anger or fear I didn't quite know myself. Chiyô was staring at me with eyes as huge and fearful as a trapped rabbit.

"I'm sorry, Chiyô," I apologized. "Did that great bully frighten you?"

"He's Akira-san's man, o-sama," she whispered. "Akira-san sent him for you and you refused. Nobody refuses Akira-san. Nobody."

"I just did." I was annoyed. A hired thug had forced himself into my room. And now my own maid was telling me I should be afraid of a damned yakuza. I was having none of it. "Come, Chiyô. Callum-san has gone sightseeing with his friend. I have the whole day to myself. I think I will go to the bunraku. Would you come with me, show me the way?" I had no need at all to be escorted to the bunraku. The narrator of the bunraku puppet theater had been my great admirer a lifetime ago and I knew I could find the theater with my eyes closed. But still, it was good to get into the character of an innocent from the provinces. "But before we go, help me put my hair up, please. And you may help me with my kimono."

I could feel poor Chiyô's hands trembling as she brushed out my hair. It had hung very long when we left the Crimea, and now it had grown so much I could sit on it. I wondered idly if I should have it trimmed. Then I remembered seeing enchanting woodcarvings that showed illustrations of ladies from the olden times who always seemed to wear their hair loose. Hair that actually touched their heels. Perhaps I would not let mine grow that long, but to my knees? The idea made me smile. When I had been a prisoner in Lord Suliman's harem, he had made me pleasure him by wrapping my hair around his tree of flesh and using it to bring him to the point of bursting his fruit. As soon as I escaped, I had intended to cut my hair short, but I had never done it. Now, I was pleased I had reconsidered.

"My apologies, Tara-san."

Chiyô yelped and dropped the comb she had been about to insert into my pinned-up hair.

"Akira-san." I did not move. Did not even turn my head. Nor was I surprised. "Such a pleasure. I am sorry I could not accept your earlier invitation. I was made most unhappy by having your servant force his way into my room uninvited, demanding my presence."

Chiyô moaned. I glanced at her and saw she had turned the color of spoiled tofu. I felt sorry for her, but at the same time I was annoyed. I could understand her being afraid, given Akira's reputation, but did she have to show it so obviously?

"Chiyô. I believe I am ready to go out. You may leave me now."

Akira watched her go. I saw he was hiding a smile as Chiyô brushed the door frame in her effort to get past him without so much as touching his robe. He turned and walked the few steps it took to bring him to my side. Stooping, he took my comb delicately in his fingertips and stood back inspecting my hair critically.

"About here, I think." He pushed the comb into my hair. I bowed my head in thanks. "You have remarkably beautiful hair, Tara-kun." I stiffened at his use of the word "kun." It was a word that might properly be used by men when addressing female inferiors. As well as that, it implied some sort of familiarity.

"Thank you, Akira-san." I spoke formally and dragged out the syllables of "Akira-san" very deliberately. He understood, I knew instinctively. His tongue showed pinkly between his rather full lips and I guessed he was trying not to laugh.

"It was not a compliment, merely the truth. In fact, I have only known one other woman with hair as thick and lustrous as yours. Although her hair was red. Red as a fox spirit."

The air between us seemed to coagulate. I stared carefully over Akira's shoulder, certain that if I met his eyes he would read the shock in my expression.

"Red hair? Surely that is very unusual? Was she a *gaijin* woman?"

I cursed myself. In my attempt to appear merely vaguely curious, I had forgotten my manners and had not addressed him correctly. Had he noticed? He seemed not to have, but I wasn't sure.

"Some said she truly was a fox spirit. And that the gods had sent her to punish me for I have been a very wicked man, Tara-*san*." He grinned at me, his face alight with amusement. I put my head on one side and regarded him with cool interest.

"Really? Well, it is good that you are showing regret, Akira-san. May I ask if your fox spirit punished you adequately?"

"Oh, I think so." His eyes were sparkling. Odd that I should have thought them as cold as a dead fish last night. He held out his hand. "Have you any plans that you cannot set aside? I rather thought that you might like to see my home. It is immodest of me to say so, but I have been told many times that it is the most beautiful house in the whole of Edo. That, of course, is no more than idle gossip. It is very rare that I choose to ask people into my home."

The flattery trickled like honey in his voice. I simpered, lowering my eyes and doing my best to look flustered.

"That is most kind, Akira-san. But I had already decided that Chiyô could show me around the Floating World and we would go to the bunraku. Of course, I would dearly have liked to have seen a kabuki performance. I was most disappointed when I found that the theater had burned down."

I held my breath. Had I gone too far? I glanced at Akira. He was tapping his finger on his lips, his expression unreadable.

"Such a shame," he agreed smoothly. "I myself was a great patron of the theater. So much so that I have paid for the new kabuki to be built. If you are staying in Edo for some time, perhaps you might be able to see a performance? I have chosen my actors very carefully. You may have heard that Danjuro, the old lead actor, died in the fire. Such a great talent, to die in such a tragic way. I was bereft."

He fell silent, and I swallowed the lump that was suddenly stuck in my throat. Was it possible that even Akira could talk with such apparent sympathy about a man he was said to have murdered? The man who had been my daughter's lover? Then I reminded myself that Akira had also been Kazhua's lover and my thoughts whirled. His hand was still outstretched toward me, and my body moved independently of my brain. I took his hand and he pulled me to my feet with no effort at all.

"Indeed. A terrible tragedy," I agreed. "Much as I would love to see a kabuki performance, I do not think that Callum-san will wish to remain in Edo that long."

Akira bowed me politely out of the door. His excessive courtesy made my scalp prickle. It would have been normal for a Japanese man to have barged out, leaving me to follow behind him.

"What a shame." His voice was close to my ear. "And where will you go from here?"

I stumbled and pretended that I had caught my *geta* in the *tatami*. Careful! I reminded myself that while ever I was with Akira, I must think about every word before it passed my lips.

"I really don't know. Callum-san speaks only a few words of Japanese, and those very badly. Like all the *gaijin*!" I tittered, to take the sting out of my words. "And of course, I do not speak English, so it is difficult to communicate with him."

"I'm sure it must be," Akira said drily. "That being so, how did you get together?"

He paused to put on his shoes and I took the time to

gather my thoughts. It was much easier to think when those grey eyes were not looking directly at me.

"Oh, things were arranged by my auntie. In Kagoshima," I said innocently. "Callum-san was introduced to Auntie's house by a fellow *gaijin*. He was very taken with me at once. His friend said that he wanted me to go to Edo with him, and I was delighted. I have always wanted to see Edo. And Callum-san is a very nice man. For a *gaijin*, that is," I added quickly.

The noise of the street blasted my ears as soon as the door opened. Strangely, it seemed to become much quieter as soon as Akira came out. Also did I notice that the crowds parted in front of us. Peasants, merchants, and even the odd noble moved away to give us passage. I immediately thought of the way the sea leaves the beach moments before a deadly tsunami strikes. The comparison made me shudder. Was I underestimating him? I thought that perhaps I was, and reminded myself yet again to be careful. Every word, every expression, must be thought about.

And yet, I was pleased he had come for me. With a reputation as fearful as Akira's, I would have expected another visit from his servant. And much less courtesy on the second occasion. But it had not happened. Instead, the great man himself had knocked on my door. Was it amusement at my defiance? Or something far more sinister?

I decided I didn't care. I had Akira on his own. If anybody in Edo knew what had happened to Kazhua, then it was him. And I would risk anything to find out what I needed to know. I thought fleetingly that taking a risk with Akira would probably be very enjoyable. Had Kazhua once thought the same thing? The idea made me shiver. I could not trust this man. Had the gossip I had first heard been true, that he had been responsible for both her death and that of her lover, then I would have been overjoyed to slide a sharp dagger between his ribs.

To avoid looking at Akira, I kept my eyes fixed on the road. There was an excuse for it; the cobbles were uneven and I could easily have fallen. Akira slowed his step, apparently concerned for me. I was confused and glanced at him slyly as we walked.

It seemed that everybody in the Floating World knew him. Most men drew back and bowed their heads as he passed. Several well-dressed merchants smiled fawningly at him, their faces expressing rapture when he nodded at them. Even a samurai, immediately recognizable with his two short swords and top-knot, gave Akira an admiring glance as he swaggered past. I wondered if a samurai was exempt from the strict rules against carrying weapons into the Floating World. Or had he simply bribed the gatekeeper?

"You no doubt have honorable samurai in Kagoshima?" Akira asked casually.

"Oh, yes," I said quickly, pleased to find a safe topic of conversation. "We often had samurai visit our tea house in Kagoshima."

"Is that so? Obviously, your provincial samurai are a different breed to those from Edo. Here, the tradition of *wakashudo* is still very much treasured."

I knew instantly I had made a bad mistake. When I was a geisha we had sometimes been honored to receive samurai in the Green Tea House. But it had been notable that they had always declined Auntie's suggestions that they might wish her to recommend a courtesan for them. Auntie never really expected to have her offer taken up, she was just being polite. Everybody knew of the samurai tradition of *wakashudo*, the way of the youth. Most samurai married, although unusually late in life. Of course they did; they wanted a male heir for the family. But at the same time, they almost invariably kept a beautiful youth as their lover. Their true love. The wife was just an unfortunate necessity. And it had been only too obvious that the samurai we had passed a moment ago had looked at Akira with interest rather than me.

"Really? As you say, perhaps things are different in the provinces. And Kagoshima is a very long way from Edo." I smiled, I hoped innocently. But Akira was not finished. He turned and glanced at me and smiled. His teeth were very white and even, except for his canines which were rather long and pointed. They gave his smile a wolfish look.

"You've never heard the old poem?" He frowned slightly, as if recalling it was an effort. I didn't believe him for a moment.

> "I cannot believe that you
> Are far away
> For I can
> Never forget you
> And thus your face
> Is always before me."

"I believe that was written hundreds of years ago by a samurai to his younger lover. Or was it the other way around? No matter. The sentiment is the same."

"Of course," I said. Akira's voice had been very tender when he quoted the poem. I stared at him in surprise and then agreed smoothly and very quickly, gathering my scattered wits as I remembered to play the world-weary courtesan. "It doesn't really matter who love touches, does it? As long as both people are happy with the arrangement."

"Of course." Was Akira mocking me? I rather thought he was. "We are nearly there. Do be careful not to trip."

I had lost my bearings in listening to him. I understood with a flare of surprise that I had no idea where I was. How was this possible? I thought I had walked each and every street in the Floating World when I was a geisha. I had enjoyed rambling about the crowded streets and had spent every moment of every fine day that I was free exploring each area of the famous flower and willow world. But I did not know the corner we were standing on. Even the elegant little tea house opposite was unknown to me. I paused and stared around me in unfeigned surprise.

"Where are we? It's so peaceful. Not at all like everywhere else I've seen."

"This area is not visited by many people." Akira strode forward into a short cul-de-sac. "I own the tea house you were admiring just now." He paused and then smiled his wolfish grin. "In fact, I own all of the properties in the whole of the streets that form this crossroad. My men are very careful to make sure that only people I wish to be here are allowed into the area."

I stared at him in genuine amazement. Property in Edo was expensive. Property in the Floating World was far more expensive still. And Akira owned not just a house and a number of tea houses, but whole *streets?* My respect for him rose.

"You must be very rich, Akira-san." I hoped I had injected just the right note of greed into my voice.

"Oh, I manage to get by. I daresay I'm not anywhere near as wealthy as your *gaijin*. All the other *gaijin* in Edo are here to trade. They're as much riverbed beggars as the rest of us. But your Callum-san seems to be just here to take a holiday and enjoy himself. Now that is true wealth, being able to do exactly what you like with your time without having to worry about earning money."

He was probing. And none too subtly either. I was absurdly pleased. He hadn't seen through my pretense then. If he had, he would never have asked such blunt questions. I almost expected him to fish into the purse that hung by means of a beautifully carved *netsuke* from his obi and offer me flower money in exchange for my information. But he did not.

"Oh. Do you really think he is very rich?" I sounded deeply hopeful. Akira glanced at me and I told myself sharply not to overdo the act. "He did buy me some lovely jewelry and a new kimono in Kagoshima. But that wasn't so unusual," I added modestly.

"Jade, was it?" I looked at Akira enquiringly. "Did he buy you jade for your present? I seem to remember that Satsuma Province is famous for its jade carving."

"No. Callum-san purchased gold for me," I lied cheerfully. "And I'm afraid you're misinformed, Akira-san. Satsuma Province is very well known for the exquisite porcelain produced there. I'm sure I saw a beautiful Satsuma moriage ware bowl in the Green Tea House."

"Ah, yes." Akira flashed me a look of what I thought was genuine surprise. "So there is. I had quite forgotten it was there. Please, do go in."

He pushed open a huge, solid door. The wood was silvered with age and very smooth. Most doors in Japan are flimsy sliding screens made of slats of wood filled in with silk or paper. This door was Western style, and it reminded me instantly of the door that led from the Green Tea House garden into the Hidden House. The thought made me nervous.

"I promise you, my house holds no fear for you." Akira put a strange emphasis on the word "you."

"I am honored to be invited into your home," I said formally.

"My home is pleased to greet you. Again."

As I stepped over the threshold and slipped off my *geta*, I wondered uncomfortably if he really had breathed the word "again" very softly or if it was only my overwrought imagination playing tricks with me.

TWELVE

They say that women
Are the weaker sex. How comes
It that we give birth?

"*Y*our house is truly beautiful, Akira-san." I had no need to try and inject wonder into my voice. I spoke the simple truth. Even the hall was an example of good, and very expensive, taste. The woodwork had obviously been taken from a far older building. It gleamed with the gentle sheen that only very old wood gains. There was no *tatami* matting, just wood-block flooring so finely wrought that not even a sheet of rice paper could have been inserted into the grooves.

"I am delighted that it is to your taste. Please, come in."

Akira's words recalled Libby Kelso calling out to me—a world and years ago—"Come ben!" when she welcomed me to her simple Highland croft. Yet how different was this sumptuous place! Akira sounded genuinely pleased that I was admiring his home, so I raised my eyes and looked around boldly.

After a second, I became puzzled. My gaze flitted over exquisite scrolls. A single pillar bearing a vase, unadorned by flowers. Screens that were glazed with the finest silk rather than paper. Surely, none of this was new to me! Hope rose in a tide of joy. Was I seeing all this through Kazhua's eyes? Was her spirit still here, whispering to me? I almost laughed out loud at my own incredulity. Of course, I had seen this before. Or something very like it. Akira had re-decorated Auntie's Green Tea House to reflect his own taste. That was why it looked so very familiar.

Akira slid open a door at the end of the corridor and I stepped through. The whole house was percolated with a strange scent. Not flowers, although there were flowers in this room. Nor incense. This perfume was headier than either. I breathed deeply and the aroma seemed to linger on my tongue. I tasted it and found it exotic. Did I like it? I wasn't entirely sure.

"You will take tea." Akira clapped his hands without waiting for me to answer. A maid came in at once. "Are you hungry? Would you like some daifuku cakes? Or perhaps some bean curd jam?"

We had eaten dinner very early yesterday, and I had had no appetite for breakfast this morning. My hunger awoke at his words.

"Yes, please," I said simply.

Akira nodded at the maid. It seemed to me that she was gone barely a second before she was back with a tray containing plates of food and a steaming kettle along with all the paraphernalia needed to make tea.

"Thank you," I said politely. "Please leave the tray next to me. I will prepare the tea."

She glanced at Akira. He must have nodded as she put the tray down and left silently. I took the steaming kettle and poured water on the green tea powder, whisking it carefully before I handed the brimming cup to Akira with a bow. I sat back on my heels and waited for him to taste it before I made myself a cup. It had been a very long time since I had performed the tea ceremony. I examined my performance critically. Had I done everything right? I thought so. My own tea was delicious.

The steam from my cup mingled with the teasing aroma. I inhaled both and felt myself very content. Akira smiled at me. I returned his smile and allowed myself to stare around the room.

Kazhua had been here. She had walked these same floorboards. No doubt admired the *tokonoma*, backed by a scroll and a vase of flowers with a sparsely beautiful *ikebana* flower arrangement. Perhaps she had arranged the flowers herself at one time; Auntie would surely have instructed her in the art. I put my head on one side, trying to feel her presence. Had she been happy here? Had she stayed because she wanted to, or had Akira made her his prisoner? Alas, the empty air divulged no whisper. I saw that Akira was watching me and I returned his glance firmly. I decided that surely Kazhua must have enjoyed living in this lovely house. And Akira was, undoubtedly, an attractive man. It must have been pleasant for her, I thought, having such a rich, powerful man dangling on her every whim.

I smiled at the thought, and Akira smiled with me.

"You perform the tea ceremony with great grace and skill." I inclined my head in acknowledgment. "I doubt if any geisha in Edo could do it better. In fact, if I didn't know that you came from Kagoshima, I would have taken you for a native of the Floating World. Your accent is not at all provincial."

"You are most kind, Akira-san," I murmured.

I tried to gather my scattered wits. What was the matter with me? I was here to find out about Kazhua, not to eat and drink and be flattered by Akira. But it was all far too much trouble. I sipped my tea and simply waited for him to speak again. Instead, he threw his head back and laughed with what appeared to be very real amusement. A thread of silvery saliva ran from one of those sharp incisors to his bottom tooth. For a moment, I fancied myself a morsel of food, caught between his strong, white teeth and I shuddered.

"Tara-chan, you are truly beautiful. And very mysterious. I can't make you out at all. I wonder, would it amuse me to try and steal you from your *gaijin*?"

"I don't know. Would it? I had heard rumors that your heart had already been stolen, never to be returned." I put my head to one side and stared at Akira quite rudely. His pupils were so huge that they dominated his eyes, almost drowning out the glittering grey that surrounded him. His face was very calm, neither amused nor angry.

"Is that so? And do you really believe that I would allow my most intimate business to be known by the whole of the Floating World, Tara-chan?"

I thought about that for a moment. The way Akira put it, it did seem like nonsense. Did that mean that the search for Kazhua that had led me here was no more sensible than chasing leaves in the wind? I frowned. I was angry with Akira for giving me hope and then snatching it away.

"I suppose not," I said sulkily.

"And if I told you that it was true?"

He was mocking me. I glared at him, and it seemed to me that the glitter in those grey eyes intensified.

"Have you been smoking opium?" I demanded abruptly. My terrible manners seemed to amuse him still further.

"I have. Would you like some? My enemies, of which I have many, would tell you that the opium I keep for myself is made only from white poppies, grown at very high altitudes. They say it is grown in fields kept especially for me, and that it casts a spell that cannot be compared to any opium available elsewhere. That is all nonsense, of course. But it is the very best opium. I reserve the last of the seed-head crop for myself. That way, the residue is very strong and very fragrant."

So that was the fragrance I had been enjoying. Truly, it did not smell like any opium I had ever encountered before. I closed my eyes and inhaled deeply, I thought for a mere second or two, but I must have been wrong. When I opened them again, Akira had a little tray in front of him. It contained a burner with an open flame and a bone pipe with a long, slender silver stem. He was holding a knob of deep, black opium over the flame. Already, it was beginning to look sticky and to smolder. He smiled at me and pushed the opium firmly into the pipe, holding the bowl back over the flame until it was to his satisfaction.

"Would you like to try it?" Akira held the glowing pipe out to me.

I shook my head firmly. "I took opium once. I did not enjoy it."

"Ah, but I have told you. This is different. Come, Tara-chan. If we are to be friends, surely you will do me the honor of sharing a single pipe with me?"

He was at my side. How that happened, I had no idea. I had not seen him move. His hand moved very slowly as he pushed the pipe between my parted lips.

"Just breathe the smoke in." I took a cautious breath. The smoke was very hot and very intense. It caught in my throat and I coughed. Akira patted my back very gently, and for some reason, I found that funny. I laughed, and he promptly put the stem of the pipe back between my lips. I had to breathe. I had no choice but to inhale.

In the days when I had been a geisha, I had prepared opium pipes many times for my patrons. They had always tried to entice me to take some of the drug. Their descriptions of the effect it had on them differed widely. Some said I would find it very relaxing. Others went further, and promised it would give me dreams more beautiful than any I could ever find in sleep. Some, probably more truthful, said simply that they could not describe the sensations it induced. I had never been tempted. I had taken opium only once, and very briefly. But I had not liked the sensation it had given me at all. I had felt deprived of my own will, uncaring what I did or what was done to me. I had never been tempted to try the drug again.

This was nothing at all like the opium I had taken. Akira had spoken honestly when he said his opium was very special. I stared around me in fascination. All the beautiful objects that filled his home glowed. I was sure that an unfelt breeze swayed the ikebana display. Its perfume seemed to steal across the room to me, winding itself in my senses. I could hear colors and see sounds that could not have been in that room. Sighs—of pleasure or pain? I had no idea which. The sea, sliding across a beach far, far away.

"So beautiful!" I whispered.

Akira took a deep pull on the pipe. And then another. "Do I really know you, Tara-chan?" he asked softly. "I know the Tara-chan who is kept by the tall, clumsy *gaijin*. I know you enough to be intrigued. But apart from that, why do I feel that I have known you for a long time? That the little I know of you hides many things that you will not let me see? It's very odd, but although you come from the back of beyond, far away from the Floating World, your accent is pure Edo."

I shrugged. "I have the unfortunate habit of speaking like the people around me, Akira-san," I said innocently. "The girl I shared a room with in Kagoshima came from Kyoto, and everybody told me I sounded just like her."

"Really? That explains it then." Akira arched his brows. Did he believe me? I had no idea. "In any event, listen to me now, Tara-chan. Nobody defies me. Ever. They are all far too afraid of me to dare. Are you afraid of me, little one? I suggest that you think carefully before you answer and tell me the truth."

I barely gave it a second's thought. "No," I said simply.

He stood, towering over me and almost blocking out the light. "In the whole of my life, only one ever dared to flout me. And that was a woman. The only one who has ever dared to disobey my wishes. There were those who said she was not a woman at all, but a fox spirit. Were they right, I wonder? For sure, she had green eyes and hair almost as red as a vixen's coat. Are you her, come back to torment me in a different body? Has my fox spirit possessed you, just as she possessed my Kazhua? If you are inhabited by Kazhua's fox spirit, then jealousy must have drawn you back to me. Ah, but that pleases me greatly."

He was talking about my daughter. There could not be two geisha in the Floating World with red hair and green eyes. Surely, the coincidence that Akira had chosen to call her by the name I had given to her was the final proof. Even in my befuddled state, I felt a deep well of pure happiness.

I had found her at last!

"What happened to her? To your fox spirit?" My voice was slurred. I focused desperately on the ivory netsuke that hung from Akira's obi. It had been styled into the shape of a fox's head—of course!—and as I stared at it I was sure it winked at me in return. I couldn't help it, I threw my head back and laughed out loud.

"She laughed at me as well," Akira whispered. "No matter what I did to her, she still laughed. She would not break, would not bend to my wishes. To my needs. I would have given my life for her, but she didn't want it. She didn't want me at all. If I hadn't loved her so much, I would have killed her. There still are days when I wish I had."

I stared at him. The opium was still fast hold of all my senses, but I had heard one thing very clearly. *No matter what I did to her.* How dare Akira say he loved my daughter in the same breath as he uttered those terrible words?

"If she really was a fox spirit, surely it was foolish to try and hurt her?" I forced my thick tongue to speak carefully. "She could have taken the most terrible revenge on you."

"She did. She left me for a riverbed beggar of an actor. Perhaps he was protected by her spell as well. I tried to kill him, but he wouldn't die. Get to your feet." Akira's tone was suddenly harsh. I scrambled to my feet and swayed. His hand grabbed my arm and he tugged me after him.

"Where are we going?" I asked helplessly. His grip was so tight, my arm felt as if it was bound with iron.

"I don't know what to make of you, Tara-chan. You worry me. Did we meet in a past life? Is that it? Or are you really my lovely Kazhua come back to me?"

My lips were too dry to form words. Instead of trying to speak, I turned my head and bit his wrist as hard as I could. I tasted blood, but it worried Akira not at all. He threw his head back and laughed.

"Here." A screen door slid open at his touch and he tugged me into a large, airy room. The scent of *jako* seeds was gentle on the air. "Is any of this familiar to you? Do you know where you are? Tell me now."

I stared around. My head was spinning to the extent that I was not sure if it was me who was whirling or if it was the room that was whirling around me. I took a deep breath and then another. I closed my eyes and wished immediately I had not as the dizziness threatened to knock me off my feet. Still, when I opened my eyes again I found it had helped a little. At least I could focus.

"What do you see?" Akira's mouth was very close to my ear. I could smell his breath, heavy with the scent of opium poppies.

"It is very beautiful," I said seriously.

Akira moved away from me and I swayed, grabbing the wall for support.

"What is in these drawers?" He had moved across the room and placed his hand on a Western-style chest of drawers made of some very fine, almost white, wood. "Do you know?"

I put my head on one side, considering. "Underclothes?" I guessed. "Perhaps an obi or two?"

He was staring at me, as if he was trying to read my face. "Is that what you think? Or are you lying? She lied to me constantly. She told me that she didn't love me. That she would never love me. She was lying, wasn't she?" His voice was suddenly deeply pitiful. My befuddled mind balanced the thoughts that this wicked man had hurt my child with the sudden shocking knowledge that in her own way she had hurt him equally as much.

"I don't know," I said simply. "I don't know what happened here. What passed between you."

Akira's arms hung limply by his side. He fingered the

drawer behind him and pulled it out with his fingertips. I watched his face and saw a sudden look of cunning there.

"Look!" He held up his hands, palm upward. They were full of delicate combs, the bands glittering with gold and the prongs bright red. Lord Dai had bought me a set of combs similar to these. They were fabulously expensive and I had taken them from him with many expressions of gratitude. But I had never worn them. Each prong was a kingfisher's beak, and I couldn't bear the thought that a once-living part of such a beautiful bird would touch my scalp. "Do you like them? I gave Kazhua a set of combs for each day of the week. She loved them and wore them always."

He was lying. If I hadn't been able to see it in his face, I knew my daughter would never have been happy to think so many kingfishers had been slaughtered for nothing more than an expensive trinket. I kept a stone face.

"They are very beautiful," I said neutrally. "I have never seen such fine examples before. I'm surprised she didn't take them with her, if she liked them so much."

The combs trickled through his fingers and fell back into the drawer like so many blossoms of blood.

"She took nothing I gave her. Nothing but the clothes she stood up in."

I shared his pain. Suddenly, I understood that this man who appeared to have the entire Floating World at his command had lost the one thing that had meant everything to him. Just as I had.

"I'm sorry, Akira-san. I do not know your Kazhua." And that was true enough. The Kazhua I knew and loved was not *his* Kazhua. "Perhaps you will be happier when you take another woman into your life."

I spoke quickly, knowing that if I paused, my words would become jumbled. The opium fumes in my brain were clearing a little, but I was still floating on a cloud of euphoria that made everything seem unreal.

"Perhaps I will." Akira was staring at me. I felt his gaze pin me with as much mercy as a moth plucked by a bat. "I sense my pretty combs did not appeal to you, Tara-san. Perhaps I have something else hidden away that you might like?"

The air was thick with anticipation and I was suddenly sure that he was talking about his tree of flesh. The conceit of the man, to think that all he had to do was wave it at me to make me happy. In her better moods, Auntie had been fond of warning us geisha to beware of the patrons, no matter how sweet they were to our faces. Trust none of them, she instructed. They will all lie to you. Believe those lies, and you are as foolish as they are. Lie with them for the lie, and we had no place in her house. We had laughed behind her back at her old woman's wisdom. Little did I know at the time that Simon, my husband, had been her lover before he met me. And that it was Auntie who had taught him the tricks of pleasing a woman.

"I thank you for your hospitality, Akira-san." My voice trembled. I knew it was with anger, but I hoped he thought it was the opium. "But I think it is time I left now. Callum-san will probably have returned, and will be worried if I am not there to meet him."

"Callum-san does not worry me in the least." Akira fingered the neck of his robe. "When you get back, you may tell him where you have been or not, whatever pleases you. He's not going to understand a word you say, but I daresay it may salve your conscience to tell him anyway. It doesn't matter. Only one other woman has ever seen what I am about to show to you. I assure you, you will find it worth keeping Callum-san waiting."

I was about to snap at him, to tell him what I thought of his smug arrogance, when I suddenly realized he could not be talking about his tree. Surely, many women would have given pleasure to the great yakuza. Many women must have seen his tree and enjoyed it. I remembered the samurai who looked at him in admiration and thought that perhaps many men, also, had seen his hidden jewel. It was something else then. I was intrigued despite myself and I watched him silently as he tugged at the elaborate knot in his obi. It defied him and he cursed, tearing at the expensive silk with his fingernails. I leaned forward, almost ready to help, but changed my mind and stayed still. Whatever Akira had in mind, I would not give him the satisfaction of showing I was in the least interested in what he had to offer me.

He gave a grunt of satisfaction as the obi finally parted and his robe fell open. As he shrugged it from his body, the netsuke that hung from his obi made a noise almost like the chiming of a tiny bell as it hit the floor. I barely registered the noise, my whole senses were reeling as I looked at Akira's naked body.

He stood for a moment with his hands on his hips, then turned slowly until he was once again facing me.

"Well?" he demanded. My mouth opened and closed, but no sound came out. Without any instruction from my brain, my body jerked upright and I walked across and ran my hand across his chest and down his stomach. I felt the skin beneath my palm glowing red hot, like a fine piece of silk that had just been ironed. I walked around Akira, studying him from every angle in mingled amazement and admiration.

His whole body was a superb work of art. I knew, of course, of the yakuza tradition of tattooing much of the body. In Japan, it would be unheard of for any man who was not allied to a yakuza organization to have any sort of tattoo. But this! Every fragment of Akira's body shimmered with color. Only his head and neck and hands, from the wrists down, were unadorned. And in contrast to the rioting, writhing tattoos everywhere else, the naked skin looked as dull as a dead fish's belly.

The tattoos had been inflicted by the hand of a master. What fancy had possessed Akira, I wondered, to make such choices to decorate his body? Flowers opened their blossoms beneath my touch. I leaned forward, sniffing his skin, certain that I could smell their fragrance. A crested crane cradled his chest muscles. Beneath it, a tiger raised its massive paw casually, as if to swipe. So real were the images that I found myself hoping the great cat would miss its target. On his back, I saw a fox, its teeth bared in defiance to the world, its tail dangling artfully so that it disappeared into the cleft of his buttocks. In my heightened state of awareness, I thought the fox tattoo might be newer than the rest. It seemed to me that the colors were just a little brighter, and that possibly it had been executed by a different hand than the rest of the tattoos. A tribute to Kazhua, the fox spirit? Everywhere I looked was color. Birds and flowers and vines and snakes, all seemed to writhe before my astonished gaze until I thought I was truly looking at a jungle filled with creatures that had never seen the soil of Japan.

And as I looked, eyes looked back at me. Inserted cunningly amongst the other artwork, a half-closed eye peered around the tiger's belly. Another rested against a rioting flowering vine. A pair stared insolently from each side of Akira's belly button. The more I looked, the more eyes I saw. I put my finger out and poked one deliberately, hoping that they would close beneath my probing. They did not, but Akira laughed.

"You understand? Even when I sleep, my body does not. People say that I see into their very hearts. And they are correct. My body sees what my true eyes do not. Nothing can be kept from me."

I nodded, but it was more to keep him quiet than in agreement. I licked my lips as I saw that even his tree of flesh was decorated. It was covered in vines, decorated with shy, just opening white flowers. White. In Japan, the color of mourning. Akira's idea of a joke perhaps? Or was it a warning? I trailed my finger down the length of his tree and felt the way that the path of the vines followed his veins. I winced, feeling the pain the tattoos must have caused in my own flesh. Was it the tattoos that made his tree seem to stand so tall and proud, or was Akira really so well favored by nature? I giggled at the thought, and his hand shot out and grabbed my wrist.

"You have seen the pain I have endured, and yet you dare still laugh at me?" he snarled.

I stared at him and the giggle turned to a full-throated laugh. Akira might be feared by everybody in Edo, and I had no doubt with very good cause, but his words had sounded exactly like the dialogue a villain in a kabuki play would utter just before the hero charged on stage and rescued the maiden-in-distress.

His eyes bulged with anger and I saw the pulse in his neck beat fiercely. It was all so shockingly over-done that I laughed until tears ran down my face. When I wiped my streaming eyes with my hands, I saw his rearing tree had wilted. I rather thought that even the colors of his tattoos were diminished.

"I must apologize, Akira-san." I found my manners and

my sense at the same moment. I even managed a reasonably servile cringe, staring at the floor with lowered eyes. "I think it must have been the opium. Please forgive me."

He stooped and picked up his robe, flinging it over his body. He grimaced as he glanced at the obi, forever ruined by his own scrabbling nails. Still, he pulled it tight around his waist. He was massaging his wrists in an odd gesture, as though he felt pain there.

"I do not frighten you." It was a statement, not a question, and I did not reply. He reached out and pushed my chin up so that it was fully in the light. He watched my face curiously. "You have heard my reputation, Tara-chan?" I nodded. "Perhaps people have told you how many of my enemies have disappeared without any trace of their passing. Or have you heard of bodies found in public places, impaled on bamboo stakes or lacking limbs?"

I shuddered. I had heard of this, and at the time thought it nothing but tales to enhance Akira's reputation.

"I have heard such rumors, Akira-san," I said.

"And you have seen the glory of my body, so you know that I do not fear pain myself. And you still laugh at me."

The last of the opium fumes left my head. I felt my mind clear and knew suddenly exactly what danger I had put myself in. I took a deep breath and inhaled the pleasant scent of *jako* seeds. My eyes flew open and I met Akira's gaze calmly. He had not broken my daughter. He would not break me.

"You will not hurt me." I spoke clearly and firmly. He blinked in surprise. For a long moment, we stared at each other. I knew I was safe when Akira shook his head.

"I will not hurt you." He echoed my words. I waited, certain he was going to say something else, but he did not. Instead, he gripped my chin in his fingers, quite gently, and turned my head from side to side, staring at me all the time. My voice was muffled by the effort to move my lips.

"I think I should go now, Akira-san."

He nodded slightly. "Yes. Go back to your *gaijin*. Tell him what happened to you today after all. He will not understand you, of course. But I think it is only fair that he should know. *Mata mite ne,* Tara-chan." *Until we meet again.*

I arched my lips in a small smile. "*Sayounara*, Akira-san," I said with rigorous politeness.

I felt eyes on my back as I walked out, but whether they were Akira's eyes or the tattooed eyes on his body, I had no idea.

THIRTEEN

No matter how hard
We try, neither of us may
Turn back time one bit

*A*s soon as Callum walked back into our *ryokan*, I pounced on him. He had been gone far longer than I had expected and I was nearly frantic with worry. I was so relieved to see him safe and well, I decided that finding out where he had been was more important than telling him about my extraordinary encounter with Akira. For the moment at least.

"Where have you been? It's almost dinner time. You've been gone hours! Don't tell me Mountjoy really did take you to a lattice brothel!"

"No, of course not. I'm sorry I'm so late. I've had a very odd sort of day."

He had had an odd sort of day? It was on my lips to tell him about Akira then and there, but his face was so puzzled, I was instantly curious.

"Why? What happened? And where's Mountjoy? I expected him to come back with you."

"That's one of the odd things. He disappeared." My eyebrows shot up in surprise. Callum shrugged. "As soon as we got out of the door, he said he didn't really feel in the mood to visit a lattice brothel. Would I care to take a river trip? It was by far the best way to see Edo."

"He's right," I agreed. "But that couldn't have taken you all this time!"

"It didn't. We got a boat and meandered our way down the river for perhaps an hour. It moored at rather a nice tea house that had a terrace on the river. In spite of the fact that the boat trip had been Mountjoy's idea, he seemed bored all at once.

"'Come on, old man,' he said. 'Let's get off here and get something to drink and eat. Tell you what. I'll teach you to play mahjong.'

"To say I was surprised was putting it mildly, but what could I do? I could hardly protest. I had no idea where we were, anyway, so I gave in and followed him into the tea house. We had tea and a bite to eat, and then Mountjoy said he was going to teach me to play mahjong. He seemed to find it deeply amusing that I couldn't get the hang of the game at all."

"You couldn't understand it when I tried to teach you how to play," I interrupted.

Callum grinned. "One of these days, I shall get my revenge and try and teach you to play chess," he threatened. "Now, where was I? Oh yes. I had just lost a second game to him when a strange man came in and whispered in his ear. Mountjoy suddenly lost all interest in both me and the game. As soon as we were alone again, he said he had to go. Immediately."

"'Sorry about this, old chap. Something important has come up,' he said. 'I shouldn't be long. Why don't you sit on the terrace for a while, enjoy the sun?'

"And with that, he was gone. I did as he suggested and went and sat on the terrace. Drank some more tea. I think I dozed for a while in the sun. I was rather tired; after all, we didn't get much sleep last night!"

"And whose fault was that? Never mind. What happened then that kept you all this time?"

"Nothing," Callum said simply. I stared at him in disbelief. "It was late afternoon when I woke up. There was still no sign of Mountjoy. By then I was worried about him. He'd been gone for hours and I began to wonder if his important business had caused him some problems. But I couldn't do anything; I'm not supposed to speak Japanese, so I couldn't even ask the tea house owner if there was a message for me. I went out onto the street and I realized at once that I had no idea where I was. I wandered about for a while, hoping I would get my bearings, but it was useless. Eventually, I realized the best thing to do would be to go back on the terrace and hope a riverboat would pull up. One did, eventually, and I just climbed on board and prayed he would take me back to where we started. I was lucky that he did. And that's it. The very odd story of my day. I'm sorry you were worried about me. Did you enjoy your shopping trip with Chiyô?"

I started to laugh. It was no doubt a combination of relief that Callum was home safely and the sudden understanding of how much danger I had been in, but once my laugher started I could not stop. Callum stared at me in surprise as I wiped my streaming eyes with my hand.

"You may have had a strange day, but it wasn't anywhere near as exciting as mine!" I managed to say. "I didn't get to do any shopping at all."

I recounted my experience with Akira. Even though I took care to speak about it as matter-of-factly as I could, when I finished I realized that I had never seen Callum so coldly furious, and I hoped never to see him so again.

"I'm sorry." I shrugged. "I had no option but to go with him. Don't forget, I'm supposed to be a mere courtesan. I sent his man away, but when Akira himself turned up, what was I supposed to do?"

"I'm not blaming you. Did Akira hurt you?"

"No," I said promptly. "He didn't. He spoke about Kazhua all the time. I really believe he loved her. I've thought about it, and I think he only took me to his house because I reminded him of her in some way. But he was disappointed in the end when he found I wasn't really like her at all."

"You must be enough alike for Akira to perceive it." Callum frowned. "You're sure he said nothing about where she is now?"

"Nothing at all that we hadn't already heard. He just said that she had run away from him with Danjuro. They must both still be alive, as he admitted that he had tried to kill Danjuro, but somehow he had recovered."

"At least that confirms what we thought," Callum said grudgingly. "But if Akira comes sniffing around you again, he will wish he had never been born, I promise you."

I smiled fondly at my husband. "Take care, dear one," I said seriously. "Akira has more power here than you could understand. We can't afford to make him angry. He admitted to me that he had murdered many of his enemies, and in particularly nasty ways. He might, I suppose, be reluctant to murder me, but I'm sure he wouldn't hesitate to get rid of a mere *gaijin*."

Callum looked as if he would like to spit with anger. I put my finger up in warning, and finally he shrugged.

"Perhaps we should stay together, then. And you can protect me!"

He was joking, but I nodded anyway.

"Now that is a good idea."

"Are you hungry?" Callum stretched. "I'm starving. It's late for dinner, but never mind. I'll order some food anyway."

*C*allum looked at his miso soup sourly.

"I would prefer a decent helping of roast venison," he said sadly.

"Drink your soup. It's good for you." I wagged a mock-motherly finger at him and we both smiled. Suddenly, Mountjoy jerked the screen door aside and came in without announcing himself. We paused, spoons at our lips, staring at him in shock.

"Well! If it isn't the proverbial bad penny turning up!' Callum said. "What happened to you? I waited for hours before I gave up on you. Decided to pop in for some dinner, have you? Sit down and help yourself." Callum nodded at the table. "What's the matter? Edo on fire, is it?"

I could tell from his voice that he was actually relieved to see Mountjoy. But he did not get the answers he was expecting.

"It might as well be, as far as you're concerned." Mountjoy was fidgeting, his gaze roving around the room anxiously. "Pack your things, Niaish. It's time you got out of here."

"What are you talking about? Why should we leave

Edo? There's lots I haven't seen yet. Tara here hasn't even had the chance to go to the bunraku theater. We haven't been here above a month and I was planning to stay for a lot longer. You're talking nonsense." Callum put his spoon down with exaggerated care. "Spent the afternoon drinking, Mountjoy?"

My eyes swiveled between the two men. I read their body language as well as their words. Although Callum was relaxed, Mountjoy was rigid. He held his hat in his hand and passed the brim repeatedly through his fingers. Normally a very well-groomed man, I noticed he needed a shave. Worry trailed cold ripples down my spine.

But what could I do? I was supposed to speak only Japanese. The two men were speaking in rapid English. I confined myself to looking anxious.

"Niaish, I am not joking. You need to get out of Edo now. In fact, the further away from Japan you can go, the better. There's a cargo ship at harbor ready to sail for the East Indies as soon as it's loaded. It might not be quite as comfortable as you're used to, but it will do."

"What the hell are you talking about?" Callum seemed to have finally caught some of Mountjoy's urgency. "Why should I leave? And do I gather from what you've said that you think I should leave Tara here?"

Mountjoy's expression was almost laughable, his surprise was so obvious.

"Of course you must leave her here. You were seriously thinking of taking her with you?" he asked. "Forget that idea. Get out, I tell you. Now. You've no idea of the danger you're in."

Callum raised his eyebrows and glanced at me. Simon had come back to Japan to find Kazhua and had been murdered here. Callum and I had come back together in search of my daughter, and now Mountjoy was insisting that Callum was in danger. I had to assume he was right. I nodded at Callum.

"I'm hardly likely to leave my wife behind, Mountjoy," he said calmly.

Callum spoke evenly, but he might as well have punched Mountjoy in the stomach for the effect his words had. Mountjoy's face drained of color, leaving his skin a curious green tinge. His jaw sagged. He sat down abruptly on the only Western-style chair in the room.

"Your wife?" He stared wildly from Callum to me and back again. Callum moved across to me and took my hand.

"Tara is indeed my wife, Mountjoy." I noticed his Scottish accent was suddenly very pronounced. "Now, please, tell us why we are in such danger?"

I smiled at Callum, wondering if Mountjoy had noticed that he had said "we" and not "I."

Mountjoy put his face in his hands. When he raised his head, his eyes were wild.

"I have no idea what's going on here, but I promise you I'm deadly serious. I've probably put myself in danger by coming here to warn you. It's Akira." He breathed the name softly, as if somebody other than us might be listening to him. "He intends to take Tara. If you get in his way, Niaish, then he will dispose of you, whether she's your wife or not. For God's sake, what sort of game have you two been playing here?"

I felt my heart jolt, as if I had had one of those terrible dreams where one thinks one is falling from a great height. I stared at him silently.

"He's going to take Tara?" Callum echoed in obvious disbelief. "That can't be true. I had heard rumors that he was about to take a new concubine from the Hidden House."

Chiyô had told me that, her eyes huge with the importance of her gossip.

"Just think, after all this time! I've heard that he's finally taken a fancy to another geisha from the Hidden House." She paused delicately. "Perhaps you might not have places like the Hidden House in Satsuma Province, o-sama?"

"No, we don't. But I've heard of it. Go on."

"Well, apparently this new girl was very close to Midori No Me. I think myself that he's decided to take her as his concubine in the hope that Midori No Me will hear about it and be jealous. Maybe even jealous enough to come back to him."

"And do you think that's likely?"

"Oh no." Chiyô's answer was prompt. "She's not going to toss the magnificent Danjuro. No woman in her right senses would ever do that."

Mountjoy broke in on my remembrances rudely.

"You heard right. He told me a while ago he had decided he was going to take Mineko, one of the geisha from the Hidden House, as his concubine. He likes the girl, and I think it amuses him that she is said to be unable to feel any pain at all. He was no doubt looking forward to seeing if that was true. And apart from that, she was very great friends with Midori No Me, so that's added to the spice of it for him. But all that was before he had the chance to take a good look at Tara here. Now, he's changed his mind. That's why I went dashing off and left you in the tea house. Sorry about that, but when Akira summons you urgently, it's best to go." I shivered, thinking about how I had defied Akira only that morning. "He told me that he's determined he's going to have her. I've never seen him so agitated. He wanted to see me to ask whether I thought he needed to take any action about you, Niaish. Whether you would make a fuss about it. I assured him that you wouldn't." His face twisted. "Of course, that was before I knew the truth. I guessed you would be awkward anyway. That's why I came to tell you to get out of here. Now that I know Tara's your wife, it's essential that you get away. Akira would never stand for a mere *gaijin* stopping him from getting what he wants. If you tried, you would be a dead man."

"I'm afraid Akira is going to be disappointed. I've told you. Tara is my wife. Akira must find his fun elsewhere," Callum said flatly. Mountjoy stared at him, biting his lips. Finally, he shook his head.

"Is there something going on that I don't know about? Come on. Tell me what I'm missing," he demanded. "Why did you both really come here? It's obviously not just for the thrill of exploring the Floating World."

Callum raised his eyebrows at me and I nodded. It was clearly time for the truth.

"Tara was born here in the Floating World. She was a geisha in what is now Akira's Green Tea House. She fell in love with a *gaijin* and ran away with him."

Mountjoy's jaw sagged in horror. "And you brought her back?" he asked incredulously. "Didn't you realize how dangerous that was? What was so important that you would risk her life?"

"Yes. We knew the risks," I said quietly. Mountjoy blinked at me and shook his head. He couldn't have been more obviously shocked if a pet dog had suddenly answered him. I stared him full in the face as I spoke. "But we thought it was worth it. We're here to find my daughter. I had to abandon her in the Hidden House on the day she was born. It's a long story, but until now fate never allowed me to come back and try and find her. I called my daughter Kazhua, Mountjoy-san. But in the Hidden House, she was known as Midori No Me."

Mountjoy stared at me. A procession of expressions passed across his face—shock, disbelief, and finally amusement. I wondered yet again why *gaijin* had to show every thought on their faces. He pointed at me, very impolitely, and shook his head.

"Oh no, *Tara-san*." His voice was mocking as he spoke my name. "You're going to have to do better than that for an explanation if you want my help. Come on, why are you really here?"

I could see Callum was becoming angry. "It's the truth, man," he snapped.

Mountjoy grinned insolently and shook his head. "Is it? The only problem is that I happen to know what happened to Midori No Me's mother. True enough, she ran off with her *gaijin* lover, back to America where he came from. But he came back here, years ago, and never left Edo again. He died here, and I doubt his widow could have found her way to Scotland. And anyway, she was called Terue, not Tara."

I spoke for both Callum and myself.

"You're right. Simon-san was my first husband," I said quietly. "We did go to America together. But when he got the chance, he came back to Edo with the American expedition that first tried to open Japan to the west." I scoured my memory for a name. "Captain James Biddle commanded it. Poor Simon wanted to find our daughter, but he wasn't careful enough. He forgot how long memories are in the Floating World. He was discovered and murdered and he is buried in the Dutch Cemetery close to Edo." I shook my head sadly. "I had hoped to get the chance to visit his grave before we left." I raised my head and stared at Mountjoy proudly. "My birth name was Junko. When Auntie took me to her Green Tea House and I became a geisha, my new name became Terue. After Simon died, I married Callum and became his wife and went to live in Scotland with him. We live in the Highlands, and Terue is difficult for the Scottish tongue to pronounce. So now I am called Tara. When we came here, we both felt it was safer for me to keep my new life name in case Terue raised unwelcome memories."

Mountjoy's mouth was opening and closing, but no sounds came out. Callum and I both watched him, saying nothing further. Finally, he wiped his hands over his face and took a deep breath.

"You really are Terue," he said incredulously. "Even now, people still talk about you in the Floating World. They say you were the most beautiful geisha of your generation. That you refused a nobleman for a mere *gaijin*."

I nodded. "That I did. Lord Dai wanted to marry me, but I hated him. I ran away with Simon instead, and I became his wife. I had to leave my poor Kazhua. She was a newborn, and she would never have survived the dreadful journey. I left her in the Hidden House. Big promised to care for her. But he obviously did not," I added bitterly.

"Oh, I don't know." Mountjoy shrugged. "Auntie could easily have had her exposed. Given the loss of face you caused dear Auntie, I'm surprised she didn't kill her. So perhaps Big did keep his promise in a way." He pushed his head forward like a tortoise peering from its shell and looked at me carefully. "I suppose one never looked beyond Midori's green eyes and red hair. But now I know, I can see that you are her mother. Your skin tones are exactly the same. So is the shape of your head and your mouth. But it's more than that. It's the way you hold yourself. Proudly, as if nothing in the world could ever be allowed to harm you.

She was just the same. Defiant. Determined that no man would bend her to his will. I suppose Akira must have seen the similarities between the two of you as well, but he hasn't consciously made the connection. He just finds you immensely attractive."

"You knew her?" I ignored the rest of his words. They were the twitter of birds at dawn and meant nothing. "You knew my daughter?"

"Not well. Akira guarded her far too carefully for anybody to get to know her well. But I met her several times at his house. She was very special."

"Thank you."

Mountjoy seemed to understand what I was thanking him for. He smiled at me. Then fear wiped away the smile and he looked horrified.

"My God. What am I thinking of? The situation was bad enough when I thought it was just Niaish that had to get away. Now, it's both of you that must go. Now."

He stood and looked wildly around the room, as if he was deciding for us what we needed to pack. Callum stood abruptly and walked across to him. They were so close that they were almost nose to nose.

"Mountjoy, we came here to find Kazhua. We're not leaving until we do that. I don't give a damn about Akira. Things were different in the old days. Now, Edo is full of *gaijin*. He can't just do as he likes with us anymore. Thank you for warning us. We appreciate it, and I promise we'll be very careful. But we are not leaving Edo until we are ready."

Mountjoy turned to look at me. "Tell him, Terue. Or Tara, whatever your name is these days. Make him understand." He raised his eyebrows at me, inviting me to comment.

"No," I said simply. "Callum's right. We came to find Kazhua. Until we find her, we're staying."

"You're both mad," he said bitterly. "Very well. I've probably cut my own throat by telling you about Akira's plans. I might as well tell you the rest. You might as well leave Edo now. Today. You're not going to find Kazhua here."

He paused, staring at me as if willing me to believe him. My mouth was very dry. I had to wet my lips with my tongue before I could speak.

"Is she alive?" My voice was very husky. I almost cried with relief when Mountjoy nodded.

"She is. And safe. Or at least she was the last time I saw her. You know she had another lover? Danjuro, the famous kabuki actor?" I nodded, my eyes fixed on his face as if I could read the truth in his eyes. "Akira tried to murder him, to get him out of the way. He had his men ambush him and inflict the *seppukku* cut on him so it would look as if he had committed suicide when he was found." I felt sick. *Seppukku* involves cutting one's own body open from breastbone to groin. It is hugely painful, and death can take days. Nonetheless, it has always been a popular way to end one's own life as it takes immense courage to inflict the deadly cut. The family of a man who commits suicide by *seppukku* would be very proud.

"But Danjuro didn't die, did he?" I said.

Mountjoy shook his head. "No. He had some very good friends who knew the danger he was in and worried when he wasn't supposed to be where he should have been. They found him and called me in to help."

"You?" I said in such obvious surprise it was insulting.

"Me." Mountjoy seemed not in the least offended. "Do you know, when I was younger, I longed to go on the stage? I was sure I had the talent to become a famous actor." Callum shook his head impatiently. I shrugged. Let Mountjoy tell the story in his own fashion. "My parents were horrified. And as Papa controlled the purse strings, it never happened. But if I do say so myself, I do have a certain talent. I can be all things to all men. Understand?"

Callum clearly did not. His expression was tight with puzzlement and anger. I noticed the scar over his eye was flaring red, a sure sign of anger. But I understood perfectly. I put my hand on Callum's arm to calm him and spoke for both of us.

"You're not just a man about town and a bit of a fool at all, are you?" I asked. Mountjoy bowed his head ironically. "Nor are you a merchant, here to trade. Why are you here?"

"Because—until you two arrived—I found the Floating World great fun. Much more so than most places I've visited. Although I suppose the glitter began to wear off when I saw what my dear friend Akira had done to Danjuro. Who, by the way, was also my friend. You find that odd, I suppose, that I could be friends with two men who were sworn enemies?"

"Not at all," I said. "You found the situation amusing, didn't you? A bit like a kabuki play, but in real life."

"Exactly! Until Danjuro nearly died at Akira's hands, that was. Anyway, we got a discreet doctor for him and spirited him away until he had recovered, which took a long time. I suppose Akira found out he had recovered, but he thought nobody else knew that mattered and he was content to let the Floating World speculate that he had actually had his rival murdered. I tried to persuade Danjuro to move well away once he recovered enough to travel. Kyoto, I suggested, had an excellent kabuki theater. If he changed his name, he would be safe there. But he would have none of it. He insisted that his life might as well have ended if he could no longer be with Midori No Me. Nothing could change his mind. If I do say so myself, if it hadn't been for me, I doubt the damn fool would have survived. As it was, I knew a Japanese merchant who had fled to America from Edo recently, partly for family reasons and partly because he had also crossed Akira and was terrified that he would disappear, like so many others. This man was not only very rich, he had clawed his way up from a *burakumin* family and, probably as a result, he was determined to be seen as a deeply cultured man. He insisted that he loved the kabuki, although anybody could see it bored him half to death. In any event, I got word to him through various contacts that the great Danjuro wished to leave Edo and would be delighted to bring the kabuki to enrich America. The merchant said at once that he would be pleased to welcome the great man to his new country and would help him all he could to establish a new kabuki. The *gaijin* would, he was sure, appreciate some genuine Japanese tradition."

My lips were moving soundlessly, repeating the word "America" over and over again. Mountjoy gave me a sympathetic glance and then carried on speaking.

"Partly because Danjuro was my friend, and partly because it gave me a thrill, I arranged for him to be spirited away. And because the stubborn mule refused to go without Midori No Me, I also arranged for her to be abducted and taken to the harbor where his ship was waiting to sail." He saw my expression and shrugged. "I had to make sure that no blame could ever attach to me. It was the only way."

I barely heard his last words.

"America," I whispered. "She—they—are in America? How long have they been there?"

"Well over a year. Probably more. I lose track. Time does fly when you're having fun, doesn't it?"

One moment I was sitting down, talking quite sensibly. The next, I was standing close to Mountjoy. My fingers were twisted in his jacket and I was shaking him like a puppy playing with a rag toy. I had a glimpse of his surprised face, and then Callum's arms were around me, pulling me away.

"America!" I moaned. "She's in America, Callum. How could fate do this to me? All those years, I was there. If I'd stayed, she might have found me."

Callum's arms were so tight around my ribs I found it difficult to draw breath. I was shaking, my whole body feeling as if I had a sudden fever.

"If you had stayed, we would not be together."

I felt his words reverberating in his chest. I heard the pain in his voice and guilt and sorrow fought with my grief. The knowledge that my lost daughter had followed me, and regret that I had hurt Callum with my thoughtless words, nearly tore me apart.

"I'm sorry," I whispered. "I didn't mean it. It was just the irony of it!"

Callum lowered his head and kissed my hair softly. "I know," he said very gently.

Mountjoy cleared his throat loudly. "Much as I hate to interrupt this tender scene, now will you both take some notice of me?"

"Get on with it," Callum said roughly.

Mountjoy clutched his heart with his open hand in a dramatic pretense at grief. "My dear man! Is that any way to speak to the person who is trying to save both your necks? Always remembering it will be my neck on the block if Akira finds out?"

I pulled myself away from Callum. I felt very weary, as if

it had been many nights since I had last slept. I spoke to Mountjoy civilly, guessing that if I sounded in the least emotional he would seize on my distress greedily, like some vampire spirit searching for nourishment.

"Is everything you say true, Mountjoy-san?"

"It certainly is." He put his head on one side and smiled slyly. "You know, if you had confided in me, I could have saved you all this trouble. If I'd known that you were searching for Midori No Me, I would have told you what happened, and where she was, straight away."

"Would you?" I asked thoughtfully. "Are you sure you wouldn't just have dropped hints, kept us wondering?"

"Now why on earth would I have done that?" Mountjoy's face was hurt.

"Because you would have found it...*fun*," I said.

"You're probably right." He shrugged. "But could I suggest that we've talked long enough, good people? Akira has been forced to leave Edo to take care of a little unfinished business." He spoke cheerfully, but I shuddered as I wondered about the nature of Akira's "business." "But that doesn't mean you're safe until he gets back. He has eyes and ears on every street in the Floating World. You must move very quickly."

"What are we supposed to do?" Callum was staring at Mountjoy as if he still didn't believe him. I spoke for us both. "If we're being watched, we can't just march down to the harbor and board the ship. We would be taken as soon as his spies realized where we were going."

"Tara, really." Callum's voice was indulgent. As if he was humoring me. "Now we know that Kazhua is safely away from here, of course we can go. But I'm damned if I'm going to run away with my tail between my legs."

I exchanged glances with Mountjoy. Suddenly, he was

no longer the amiable jester who had diverted Callum. Now, he was our lifeline.

"There is that, old man." He smiled at Callum cheerfully. "One would hardly like to be seen as running from a mere Japanese, what? And a damn gangster at that. Tell you what, why don't I sit down to dinner with the pair of you and we can chat a bit more about the best way forward?"

Truly, but Mountjoy was a chameleon. Either that or the stage had lost a great talent. I was trembling with the need for action, but no matter what my tumbling thoughts came up with, I knew there was nothing Callum and I could do. On our own, at least.

"The tea is cold." I clapped my hands briskly and Chiyô was there in a second. "Fresh tea, please. And another cup. And tell the kitchen we will need more food shortly."

Mountjoy was very courteous. As soon as he heard Chiyô coming back, he sprang to his feet and opened the door for her. She smiled at him timidly, obviously flustered by this *gaijin* politeness.

"Allow me to take that." He took the tray and turned to speak to Callum at the same moment. It nearly slipped from his hands and he grabbed for it one-handed, the other hand steadying the teapot of boiling water. "Oops. Clumsy creature that I am."

I whisked the green tea powder into the hot water automatically. It gave me something to do, and I was pleased to be distracted. I served Mountjoy first, as was only correct. He might have brought discord into our midst, but he was still our guest. Then I poured for Callum, and finally myself. I was too agitated to drink, but Mountjoy sipped at his tea with apparent enjoyment, and Callum drank his quickly. I refilled his cup and leaned forward to see if Mountjoy's cup was empty. I noticed with surprise that he had barely drunk any tea at all.

"One thing puzzles me, Mountjoy," Callum said. Only one? My mind was so full of questions, it itched. "What are you getting out of all this? If Akira's as dangerous as you make him out to be, aren't you putting yourself in danger by helping us?"

Mountjoy held out his hand, fingers outstretched, and tilted it from side to side. His mouth was pursed, his eyebrows raised.

"I suppose I am. But then again, what's life without a pinch of danger to add some savor? Although I must admit, if I had known the whole story, I might well have simply thrown you to the wolves. Or rather, to Akira!"

He was smiling gently, as if at a joke only he understood. I bent my head to take a sip of my tea and out of the corner of my eye saw Mountjoy shake his head, very slightly. I put the tea down untasted.

"All right, old chap?" Mountjoy's voice was concerned. I watched Callum and saw that he was looking around him as if he was suddenly confused.

"Of course I am." His voice was slightly slurred. "I just feel a bit tired all at once."

I put my hand out to him, but Mountjoy was much quicker. He caught Callum deftly just as he swooped toward the tea things. Between us, we hauled him onto the futon.

"Now, my dear." Mountjoy rubbed his hands together briskly. "I shall tell you exactly what you're going to do. And I understand it may be the first time in many years that you do as you're told, but this time, you will. For his sake, if not your own."

I stared at him and waited silently. His bearing had changed out of all recognition in the last few seconds.

Before, he had adopted the louche slouch that I had noticed seemed to be popular amongst the rich, young men in Edo. Now, he was standing erect, his whole body alert. Like a soldier on duty. Or an actor waiting for his cue? I wondered very briefly which was the real Mountjoy, or had we yet to see that? And then I concentrated on Callum.

"What did you give him? Will it hurt him?" I demanded. "And why did you do it?"

"Chloral hydrate. He'll sleep like a baby for the next twenty-four hours and wake up none the worse for wear. As to why, I rather guessed he might prove difficult, so I came prepared."

"I see. So how do we get out of here unseen?"

Mountjoy looked at me admiringly. "My, but you do cut to the chase. It's all arranged. I'm going to leave now. I'll give your maid some flower money and tell her she can take the rest of the evening for herself. I don't suppose she'll argue, will she?" I thought of the greed I had seen on Chiyô's face when we had been out shopping and shook my head. "Good. I saw Akira's men on the way in. There's two of them, lounging about on the corner of the street and thinking they look inconspicuous. Even if the whole of the Floating World didn't know they were Akira's men, they would still stick out like a pair of elephants."

"So how are we going to get out without them seeing us? I can hardly carry Callum out of the back door."

"Of course not. No point, anyway. Another of Akira's thugs is watching it."

He sounded smug and pleased with himself. I was suddenly wary and very worried. Was this show all part of some devious plan of Akira's? With Callum helpless, what was to stop Mountjoy from simply shouting for the yakuza and inviting them to drag me away? Not a soul in the Floating World would offer to help me. They wouldn't dare.

"In that case, why drug Callum? Surely that's just going to make things far more difficult." As I spoke, I moved over to Callum and bent over him solicitously. I knew he carried a pocket knife in his jacket pocket. I fumbled for it, hoping Mountjoy would think I was simply worried about Callum. It slid into the palm of my hand and closed my fingers around it.

"Trust me, Tara-chan."

"You may well be the last man on earth I would trust," I said bitterly.

"Really? Well, I'm afraid you have no choice." Mountjoy leaned back against the wall. I rather hoped he would come closer to me so I could have a chance to at least try and use my knife. "Listen to me. When I go, I'll pretend to be startled to see Akira's yakuza. They know me as his honored guest. They will be delighted when I invite them to take sake with me at the tea house over the way. I'll make sure they drink a great deal of very good sake. In about an hour, two *burakumin* will come to the back door with the obvious intention of emptying the household rubbish into their cart. It's the normal time for it—nobody wants the neighbors to see their rubbish being taken away during the day. They'll appear to be bewildered when nobody answers their calls and will make a great play of being worried about going to the front entrance. But eventually, they will do. When they call out, answer the door yourself and let them in. Don't worry about the yakuza in the tea house, I'll make sure they don't notice anything. The men will take Callum and put him in their cart." Mountjoy must have seen the disgust on my face as he grinned. "Don't worry. It's a new cart and spotlessly clean. You, my dear Tara, will hop in at the side of him. The men will take their cart with their extra cargo and go straight to the docks in Edo. When you get to the harbor, the *burakumin* will find somewhere discreet and strip off their rags and change into the robes they have in the cart. All at once, they'll be respectable Japanese gentlemen. They'll make a great show of helping Callum board the ship. You'll explain to the captain that your poor, silly *gaijin danna* took far too much sake at his farewell party and you will be grateful if he can be allowed to lie down in your cabin. He's not going to wake up until your ship is well out of Edo."

"You seem to have thought of almost everything." I pretended to rub my fingers thoughtfully on my kimono and slid the short, sharp dagger into my obi. Until we were actually on board that ship, I would not trust him.

"Almost? You feel I have forgotten something?" Mountjoy's face mimed astonishment.

"As Callum asked, why are you doing this for us?" I demanded. He frowned, staring into the air as if he was taking my question quite seriously.

"Because I've enjoyed your company and wouldn't wish to see any harm come to either of you?" He smiled, raising his eyebrows slyly.

"Try again."

"Very well. Let's just say it amuses me to do it." He shrugged. "To be honest, I was getting a little tired of Akira's attitude. He seemed to feel I was just there to be used, like one of his hired thugs. And I do so hate being taken for granted."

It was probably the truth. Or at least as near the truth as I was going to get. But I still had one question.

"And if Akira finds out you helped us? What happens to you then?"

"He isn't going to find out." Mountjoy smiled serenely. "The man at the back door of the *ryokan* will say, honestly, that he never left his post and saw nobody come out. The two idiots he left on guard will swear on all the gods that they never left their post for a single second. They wouldn't dare say anything else or Akira would have them skinned. Probably literally. At heart, you know, Akira is a very superstitious man. With a hint or two from me, he will convince himself that Kazhua was so jealous that she sent some of her fellow *yokai* to spirit you both away from under his nose. Why on earth should he suspect me, his great friend?"

"I think you're taking a risk," I said bluntly. "But in any event, thank you, Mountjoy-san, and *sayounara*."

He paused, with his hand on the door screen and smiled widely at me. "*Sayounara*? So final, Tara-chan?" He used my name so mockingly, I clenched my teeth to stop the angry words that hovered on my tongue. "No, not *sayounara*. Rather, I think, *mata yoroshiku onegaishimasu*." *Until we meet again.*

In spite of all he had done for us, I hoped not.

FOURTEEN

My palm is empty.
Like a seashell, it once held
Life. Now, all is gone

I loved everything I could see of London. Which wasn't a very great deal. Mainly because of the impossible weather; even in full summer, the sunlight could barely penetrate the thick, yellow, sulfurous fog that cast a pall over everything. It made me shiver and cough.

But London itself was wonderful. The wide streets, the amazing array of shops, large and small, where I could shop until my aching feet forced me to stop. And even then, I found that many of the larger shops, which I quickly learned to call "department stores," had a café attached where I could take coffee and dainty little sandwiches. Never tea. I tried it once and discovered to my horror that it was served the color of mahogany, and with milk added. Even the politeness of the waiters pleased me greatly, although it took me a long time to understand their strange accent. Eventually, I worked out that if I put a mental "H" in front of every word that began with a vowel and took an "H" away from where it should be I wouldn't go far wrong. So, "I 'ope that madam is h'enjoying 'er lunch" became translated as "I hope madam is enjoying her lunch." When the Cockney accent was too ripe to translate, I simply nodded and smiled. It seemed to work.

My wardrobe was crowded to overflowing with new clothes. Dresses with skirts so wide and stiff, I feared that a high wind would see me blown helplessly down the street, like a hoop bowled by a child at play. Hats, also, did Callum buy me. I had several that were almost the size of cart-wheels and I peeked out from beneath them at the world, feeling almost as if I was hiding from my new life.

We made friends very quickly. At first, it was a delight to me that, just as in Scotland, nobody seemed to care that I was neither white nor European. Perhaps I should not have been so surprised by that. The streets of London were a mix of faces of all colors and nationalities. I soon understood that I was not being treated in any special way. I was just another foreigner who had had the sense to find refuge in the capital of England. And I was welcomed accordingly.

Truth to tell, Callum caused far more of a stir than I did. Soon after we docked, he found a Scottish tailor, and as soon as his order was ready he insisted on wearing the kilt whenever we went out. Our new male acquaintances smiled at his quirkiness indulgently. The ladies were fascinated. I was certain that if they thought they could get away with it, they would have patted his sporran, just as I had done so long ago in our own home in the Highlands.

We were seen, I guessed, as the perfect couple. The "pretty Japanese lady" and her handsome, rugged Scottish husband. Both with just a touch of mystery about them, an added allure. Both so obviously very much in love. Ah! How romantic! And how our new English friends adored to see us together.

And how very wrong they were.

I knew exactly what had gone wrong. I could pinpoint the exact moment it happened. The minute after Callum regained consciousness and discovered that he was on board a ship well clear of Edo harbor and heading out into the Pacific Ocean.

"Are you all right?" I asked. A stupid question, of course, but I was worried about him.

"I think so. I seem to have a bit of a headache." He sat up too quickly and put his hand to his head. "Ouch! Where the hell are we?"

"On board the *S.S. Louisa*. First stop, the Dutch East Indies." I tried to sound light-hearted, but even to me my voice sounded strained and anxious.

"What?" Callum stared at me and then around our cabin. That didn't take long. Our accommodation was compact, and that was a charitable description. He put his hands on each side of his temples, peering through his fingers at me like a child playing peek-a-boo. "I don't understand. We were in Edo. In the *ryokan*. Mountjoy interrupted our dinner with some nonsense about Akira and us needing to get out of Edo." And then, very slowly, he asked, "Tara, what have you done?"

"Saved our lives," I said briskly. "I'm sure Mountjoy was right. Akira was going to kidnap me and keep me prisoner as his concubine. Just the same as he did with Kazhua. You would have been disposed of."

"You sound like something out of a trashy romance." Callum's voice was so cold, I jerked back from him. "Do you really believe all that rubbish?"

"Yes, I do," I said firmly.

"So, you decided on behalf of both of us that we should run away. Did you arrange it all with Mountjoy in advance? I must say, I didn't suspect anything at all. Well done the pair of you."

"No." I leaned forward in my urgency to convince him. Callum flinched away from me and I stiffened with anxiety. "I had no idea what Mountjoy was planning. Not until he walked in on us that evening."

"So you just sat there and watched him drug me. And said nothing while he managed to get me out of the *ryokan*. And I suppose you thanked him very nicely when he showed you this sweet little cabin and wished us *bon voyage*?"

"It wasn't like that," I said helplessly.

"Really? What did happen, then?" I had no answer for him. Tears of frustration came to my eyes. I blinked them away fiercely, but not before Callum saw. "Don't bother turning on the waterworks for me, Tara. I suppose you did what you thought was best."

Callum's voice was weary. I lunged toward him and wrapped my arms around him.

"That's exactly what I did. You wouldn't believe Mountjoy, but I know what Akira's capable of. That's why I went along with it."

"You honestly thought it was a good idea that we should run away from that damned yakuza trash like a pair of frightened rats? I've never stepped down from danger in my entire life, Tara. And now you've managed to do what a whole army couldn't manage. You've made a coward out of me. What my soldiers would have called a meater. Your great, big, brave husband. Nothing but a meater."

"No!" I almost shouted. "It was nothing to do with you.

It was all my fault. I lost Simon to Japan. I didn't want the same thing to happen to you."

"So you say. Do you know, I'm beginning to think that you and Japan are a very unlucky combination."

Callum turned away and faced the wall. For the rest of the journey, he was coldly polite. We shared the same narrow berth, but we slept in it and nothing more. Or rather, Callum slept. Night after night after night, I lay awake. Listening to him breathe, praying for a kind hand to linger on my body. But there was nothing. During the day, Callum spent his time on deck. I stayed in the cabin, listening and hoping for the sound of the wild geese that had followed me on my first voyage from Japan, with Simon. I knew perfectly well that the sound I had heard then was actually seagulls, but I had been very ill on that journey and I had been convinced that the birds were wild geese, sent by the gods to care for me and to remind me of Japan.

Perhaps we were too far out to sea, but there was no birdsong at all, neither gulls or geese to break the silence in our cabin.

I comforted myself with the thought that once we were back at the castle—home!—things would be different. But even that small relief was denied to me. Our ship landed in France at Le Havre to discharge its cargo. Callum offered me his arm to walk me down the gangplank, and my hopes soared. I was very reluctant to allow him to detach himself from me once we were on dry land, but he moved away from me briskly.

Once on the quayside, he lifted his head and sniffed the air like a terrier scenting a rabbit.

"France. England is a bare twenty miles or so away from

here. Our captain tells me it would be a simple matter to get a boat from here to Portsmouth."

He drummed his fingers against his thigh, staring out over the sea.

"Good. Then we will soon be back home," I said firmly.

"All in good time. But to be honest with you, it may be a while before I can get back to Glen Kyle."

Callum's voice was regretful, but I knew instantly that he was not telling me the truth. He never said "to be honest with you." He hated the phrase, insisting it meant that somebody was about to tell lies. I tensed, waiting for his deception.

"I have very pressing business in London. I should visit my accountant, and my solicitor." I frowned, not understanding. "You would call Mr. Smythe an attorney, I think."

Callum glanced at me and I nodded. My own attorney in Virginia had been as crooked as a bent twig. I glanced at Callum's face and decided not to share that with him.

"Why now?" I demanded bluntly. "You never mentioned this before."

Callum shrugged his shoulders in an exaggerated gesture. "Didn't I? I thought I had mentioned it before we left the Crimea." He was lying to me. Lying did not come easily to my honorable husband, and he was very bad at it.

"No. I don't believe you did say anything about it."

"Oh. Sorry." I might have been a mere acquaintance, the way he spoke. "Well, to be honest—" More lies! "—Smythe wrote to me several times before we left England. There is some legal dispute outstanding about land in Glen Kyle. Some nonsense about leases and such that has been ongoing for years. I'm afraid my late uncle was as negligent about such things as I am. Anyway, whoever was involved in the deal in the first place has died and their estate has decided to go to court on the matter. It may well be that's it's all been settled while I was away, but it's been nagging at me and I need to know the outcome. I fear that it may keep me in London for quite a long time. Do you want to come with me, or would you prefer to go straight back to Glen Kyle and I'll join you later? When I'm free."

His final words chilled me to the bone. When he was free? Had his tongue tripped him, without him even noticing? I thought very carefully before I spoke.

"Of course I want to stay with you," I said. "Especially if you may be some time."

"Do you?" Callum seemed mildly surprised. "Very well. I'll speak to the captain and ask him about making arrangements for our journey."

It didn't matter greatly, I thought. We would only be in London for a few months at the most. Once we had cleared up Callum's bit of business, we could begin to repair our shattered relationship. Once we were back home.

Almost a year later, we were still here. Firmly ensconced in a beautiful apartment on the oh-so-fashionable Eaton Square, in the center of London. I had learned to play the piano. After all, Callum was absent on his business so often, I had plenty of time to spare to myself. The music I made wasn't the same as my samisen, but still it made me glad to be able to produce melodies that were pleasing to the ear. I learned to sing English songs as well, finding that my training as a geisha made it quite easy to pick up the different rhythms and tones of English verses.

Coincidentally, my ability to read English also improved greatly. Our maid brought us a copy of *The Times* newspaper each day. At first, I ignored it. The front page was covered entirely in densely printed advertisements. Although I glanced at them, they seemed so uninteresting I didn't bother looking any further. Until one depressingly foggy, cold day when I was so bored I began to turn the pages of the newspaper and excitement gripped me.

Inside, the newspaper was full of real news. I worked my way through slowly, turning page after page as I searched for any mention of America. There was nothing—the only references to foreign countries were reserved for the British Empire. But my hopes had been raised, and after that I read every page of the newspaper every single day. Very occasionally, America was mentioned and my heart pounded with anticipation. After a while, I came to understand that it was likely that I was always going to be disappointed. Something as trivial as a kabuki theater performing in America would never be mentioned in an English newspaper. In spite of that, I continued my morning reading, feeling that any mention of activities in America somehow kept me connected to Kazhua's world.

If Callum noticed my interest in current events, he never commented on it. But the new friends we had made in London did. They seemed both amazed and amused that I was so aware of what was going on in the world outside England.

"I daresay it's because you've traveled so much. I just can't work up any interest in the goings-on in foreign parts," my neighbor at a ball commented languidly. "You really must have a chat to Lord Albermarle. He's just got back from America, I believe. I'm sure you'd both have a lot to chat about."

My breath hitched in my throat. Somebody who had actually been to America recently?

"That would be delightful," I said. "Perhaps you could introduce me to him?"

Alas, Lord Albermarle was a disappointment. He was a

vacuous young man who was interested in talking about only one thing—himself. He was deeply rude about his stay in America, laughing loudly as he complained he had barely understood a word anybody said all the time he had been there. My mention of the kabuki theater drew nothing but a blank stare. Still, the seed had been sown in my mind and after that I listened eagerly for any mention of somebody who was lately returned from America. I was deeply excited when I was introduced to the famous writer Charles Dickens. And even more deeply disappointed when he informed me loftily that he had only visited America once, more than fifteen years before, and he had hated both America and the Americans.

The encounter with the great man left me deeply dispirited. If Dickens could be so rude about America, no doubt the rest of London society would follow his lead. Yet still hope refused to die completely, and I continued to read *The Times* every day.

Callum complacently accepted the compliments that were showered on me by our friends. In public, he was everything a good husband should be. The ladies envied me; the men looked at Callum and envied him.

But in the privacy of our luxurious apartment, we slept in separate bedrooms. And it broke my heart.

"Callum, you're not ready. Hurry up or we'll be late." I sounded like a nursemaid scolding a tardy child.

"Go without me." Callum was standing at the window, looking out. He did not bother to turn around when he spoke. "I don't fancy listening to that bloody caterwauling tonight. It gives me a headache."

"Then I'll send our apologies and stay at home as well," I said promptly, although I was disappointed. We were going to see *Acis and Galatea* at the Royal Opera House in

Covent Garden. I loved the opera. It reminded me very much of the kabuki theater; the larger-than-life plots and extreme drama were so very similar. And kabuki actors often burst into song. Callum did not share my passion, I knew, although he had never been quite so rude about it before.

"No. Go without me. Tell Angela and Marcus I have a headache. And give them my apologies." I thought that he was about to say more, but he did not. Instead, he looked at me in a curious way, his head on one side.

"I will, if you insist. What are you going to do?"

"I'll go out for a walk, I think. It's a nice evening." He slouched across and surprised me by giving me a light kiss on my forehead. It was the most physical contact we had had in months. "Go on. Enjoy yourself."

"I'll do my best." I smiled. "I believe we're going for supper afterward, so I'll be quite late back."

"Fine."

"Take care, then." Still, I lingered, hoping for a glance. A sweet word. Anything.

"I will. *Mata yoroshiku onegaishimasu,* Tara-chan."

"How very formal!" I smiled, absurdly pleased in spite of my words. At least he had spoken to me in Japanese, in what used to be our language of love. And he had called me Tara-chan!

I went out with a light heart.

I barely heard a note of the opera. When it was finished, I excused myself from supper. My companions exchanged indulgent looks and Angela patted me fondly on the cheek.

"Ah, but what it is to be so very much in love! Fly back to your man, my little lovebird, and make sure he is well."

They watched me go with smiles. My own smile lasted until I was out of the theater and waiting for the porter to find a cab for me. I thought I was alone, and I was startled when a voice came out of the shadows.

"Spare a few pence, missus?"

The soft gaslight shone on a figure hunched against the wall. I made out a woman wrapped in a filthy shawl with a baby clutched to her body. My cab arrived at that moment, and I hesitated. Then she held out the baby to me. I saw the glint of copper curls through the dirt that covered the child and I signaled to my cab driver to wait.

I fumbled in my purse and gave the woman the first coin my fingers encountered.

"Gawd bless you, missus. That'll get me and the young 'un a bed for a week."

She clutched the baby to her chest as if she thought I might steal it from her. With the movement, I caught sight of the muddy green color of its eyes. I was immediately grateful that they were so unlike Kazhua's emerald green eyes.

The cab driver helped me climb into the cab. I glanced back as we pulled away and saw the beggar had got to her feet and was walking away with a surprisingly brisk step, her baby carried almost casually on her hip. In spite of her poverty, I envied her. She had the one thing I longed for above all else. Her own child.

I sat back, lost in my thoughts. The evening traffic was fairly light. We had only one delay, when my cab stopped abruptly. Before I could tap on the roof to ask the cab driver what was the problem, he leaned down and bellowed at me cheerfully.

"Nuffing to worry about, missus. Some daft soul got taken loose in the 'ead. Tried to do 'erself in by jumping in front of a wagon. The bobbies 'ave taken her off, all right and tight."

Just as would have happened in the Floating World, a large crowd had gathered to watch the fun, and it was them rather than the poor lunatic causing the delay.

"Where will they take her?"

The unfortunate woman was being carried on her back, chest high, her ankles and wrists grasped firmly by four policemen. She was kicking and screaming loudly, and I thought perhaps she was drunk rather than insane. Either way, the crowd was loving the drama. They hooted and shouted at the policemen, one or two going so far as to pelt them with lumps of dirty straw from the street. I guessed the straw was less innocent than it looked when one of the policemen jerked back with blood streaming down his face. I suddenly felt sick. The whole thing was horrible. I felt deeply sorry for the woman, and for the policeman who had been injured for doing his job. Even the dirty, hungry-looking crowd made me guilty for all I had and they had not.

"Where will they take her?" I repeated. "Will she be well looked after?"

"Bless your 'eart, missus." My driver sounded deeply surprised. "Don't you worry yourself about 'er. I daresay they'll take 'er to the Bridewell. If she's sober and sensible in the morning, they'll let 'er go. If she's still not right in the 'ead, they'll send 'er off to Bedlam. She'll be right enough there. Not like the old days. I remember me grandma telling me when I was a nipper that it used to be a Sunday treat to go and 'ave a laugh at the lunatics in Bedlam." He laughed loudly himself and—the crowd having begun to disperse— urged his horse on with a click of the tongue.

His explanation did nothing to soothe my worries. I thought for the rest of the journey about the poor woman who had been so desperate—for whatever reason—as to try and end her own life. Although I am normally the least superstitious of women, I could not lose the nagging fear that the encounter had been a bad omen.

I paid my friendly cab driver and went in, nodding a greeting at the hall porter. On the stairs to our apartment, I paused, smoothing my hair carefully and rehearsing what I was going to say to Callum. I changed my mind on the next step, and the next. Finally, I shrugged and decided I would see what kind of mood he was in before I said anything at all.

I knew my plans were dead as soon as my key turned in the lock and I pushed the door open. The apartment was dark. It had a sense of lack, of emptiness. Even though I knew Callum wasn't there, I called his name. The curtains and carpets absorbed my voice and returned it in a frightened whisper, mocking me.

Immediately, I was worried. I turned the gaslights up in the sitting room and stared around. Perhaps he had decided to forget about his walk and had gone out with a friend? Was there a note for me? Nothing. I searched in the bedrooms as well, but there was nothing there either. I was about to go down again and ask the hall porter if Callum had left a message for me, but then I realized the man had seen me come in and had wished me "good evening." If there were a message, he would surely have passed it to me then.

The gas mantles were flaring smokily and emitting an evil smell, as they always did for a few minutes when first lit. The gas had been switched off for a while, then. I wandered around the room, bewildered.

Callum had said he was going out for a walk. A walk that had lasted for more than three hours? Something must have happened to him. Fear rose with a sour taste in my throat. Not now! Not now, when we had surely been on the verge of being happy again. Could fate be so unkind? I had read in novels of heroines wringing their hands in distress and I had always smirked at such a pointless gesture. Now, I did it myself and found an odd comfort in the pressure of my hands, one against the other. Almost as if another person was trying to hold my hand.

I was weary, but I could not sleep. I decided I would wait for half an hour, and then go down and ask the porter to alert the police for me. If Callum had been in an accident and had been taken to a hospital, then they would know where he was. I sat back in a comfortable chair and fidgeted.

"You're back early." Callum's voice sounded odd. Neither angry nor surprised. Just cold. I had fallen into a doze after all. I was furious with myself and took it out on him.

"Where have you been! I was worried to death about you!"

"Really?" Callum tugged off his jacket and threw it on a chair back. He was wearing a suit, not his kilt. And a very informal suit, at that. Something was wrong here. "You can't have been that worried if you nodded off waiting for me. Why are you back so early anyway?"

"I didn't want to eat without you." And that was true enough. "I thought it would be nice if we could have some supper together. Callum, what have you been doing? You can't have been walking about London all this time."

"Can't I? What do you know about it, wife of mine?" His voice was jeering. He had been drinking, I decided. He had fallen in with some cronies and they had been out to some drinking den together. I relaxed, and—because I felt foolish; what if I had contacted the police only to have my husband walk in safe and well!—I snapped at him.

"You're drunk! Why on earth didn't you leave a note for me? I tell you, I was worried sick about you."

He walked over to me and put his hands on the arms of my chair. Held his face so close to mine, I could feel his breath on my cheek. I knew at once I was wrong. There was no alcohol on his breath.

"How sweet of you to worry about me," he said quietly. The hair on the back of my neck prickled in instinctive premonition. I sat very still, very stiff. "But I assure you, you have no need to be concerned for my welfare."

"Callum." I spoke in a whisper. My voice could manage nothing else. "Where have you been? What have you been doing?"

"I've been looking for a whore."

He spoke so casually, I thought he was making a joke in bad taste. That he would wait for a heartbeat and then laugh at my shocked face.

"Don't be silly." My voice shook. "I suppose you've been out with the boys, have you?"

"Not at all. I have been all alone, I promise you. I have spent the entire evening combing the streets of Whitechapel for a whore. There were plenty to choose from, of course. But none of them was the very special one I was seeking."

He broke off and smiled, raising his eyebrows in invitation for me speak. I cleared my throat, wondering if my husband had suddenly gone mad. Finally, I spoke in a quiet, conversational tone. I had read somewhere that it was essential to humor those who had lost their wits.

"And did you find her?"

"No. There was no need. Somehow it had slipped my mind that the very whore I was seeking was at home all the time, waiting for me. The finest whore in the whole of London."

I forgot all about keeping him calm and slapped his face as hard as I could. It must have hurt, as he flinched back. I was bitterly pleased. Somewhere deep in my soul I understood he was just trying to hurt me, but it did nothing to dull the pain his words gave me.

"Get out," I snarled. "Get back on the streets and find your whore. I don't want you here. I don't want you anyway near me."

I kept my eyes wide open, defying the tears that lurked there ready to fall. One kind word, just one, would have been enough to quench my anger.

But the word did not come.

"Ah. The truth at long last. If I walked out tomorrow, went back to Scotland without you, you would be delighted, wouldn't you?" Callum sat back. I thought he looked hurt, then I realized it was only a trick of the flickering gaslight and he was actually smiling. "I wonder why you waited so long to tell me? Did you worry that none of our delightful new friends would be so pleased to accept a woman alone? You're wrong about that. I've seen the way the men look at you. The way they let their glance creep over you when they think I'm not looking. If I were out of the way, there would be a queue of them waiting to offer you *carte blanche* in return for services rendered. An apartment of your own? But of course! Jewels? Most certainly. Anything that would please the lovely little Japanese whore. And of course, it wouldn't be the first time, would it? I remember you confessing to me that you had been about to take a generous offer from some man or other in Virginia in exchange for allowing you to keep the plantation. If I hadn't been so besotted with you then, I would have seen the truth and walked away. I wish I had. Once a whore, always a whore."

I was speechless. I had told Callum the story of the whole of my life before we had married. At the time, he had heard me out and then held me tightly in his arms. I remembered his gentle words.

"That is all in the past. I can't say forget about it because it's hardship that's made you the person that you are. And I love you for it, not in spite of it. But from now on, we face the future together. No matter what."

Now, he was staring at me, a sneer lifting his upper lip. That did it. My self-control snapped. I launched myself at him, scrabbling with my nails at his face. Callum caught my wrists and held them easily. But he forgot I could still move my head. I bit him on his wrist. He yelped and let go, so I took the opportunity to free myself and I kicked him as hard as I possibly could. I was aiming for his *kintama*, but he moved just as I kicked out and I hit the large muscle in his thigh instead. He shouted, obviously more in surprise than in pain, and moved away from me abruptly. The flicker of the gaslight cast odd shadows over his face, but still I could see the pain in his eyes. Pain that I understood was nothing at all to do with the injury I had dealt to his leg. My fury went down a notch. I was still angry, but suddenly I understood what this scene was really about.

I thrust my face so close to his that I was nearly touching it.

"If you knew you had the best there was here at home, Callum Niaish, why did you bother to go out and look for what wasn't there?" He bared his teeth in a snarl of anger and tried to push me away. I was having none of it. I had kept my peace for too long. He had started this quarrel, but by all the gods, I was going to end it. "You're lying. You're lying to me, and to yourself. And we both know it."

He stood and tried to walk away, but I was too quick for him. I darted round and planted myself in front of him. If he wanted to move me, then he would have to pick me up and put me to one side. He was easily strong enough to do that, I knew. I waited for a heartbeat, and when he hesitated, I decided that the time for honesty had arrived.

"Let me past, Tara." He stared over my shoulder. "We have nothing to say to each other."

"I have plenty to say. And it's time it was said. You are going to listen to me, Callum Niaish, whether you like what you hear or not. You're ashamed of yourself. It's not me you're trying to punish, it's yourself." His hand jerked up and I thought he was going to strike me. I watched his face; I would not back down now. His hand fell to his side. "You think of yourself as a coward. As a meater. The dog that will only eat meat because it's frightened of anything that can fight back. My big, brave husband, the meater. If anybody knew how we left Edo, you're convinced they would see you as a coward who ran away from a yakuza, a mere gangster, with your tail between your legs. From the moment you woke up on board the *Louisa*, you've been so ashamed of yourself you won't let your conscience stop torturing you for a minute. Are you trying to drive me away from you? Is that it? If you can manage that, will you feel as if you've been suitably punished?"

He stared at me coldly. "I wouldn't blame you if you did leave me," he said quietly. "You don't have to tell me I'm a coward, Tara. I know it. You're right. I've known it every waking moment since I woke up on the ship. Why did you do it? You should have run away yourself and left me in Edo to take my chances. But you never gave me the choice, did you? I am a coward, you're right. And even worse, I was made into a coward by the woman I loved. That's me, Captain Niaish, the brave soldier who was pleased to hide behind his wife's skirts."

"Getting out of Edo was nothing to do with you." I was so angry, I was almost shouting. "Mountjoy drugged your tea. You were out cold. You had no idea what was going on until it was too late. Can't you understand that and forgive yourself? You're not a coward. I only threw that at you to make you come to your senses."

"Did you really? Strange that you should choose the one word that would hurt me more than anything." He paused suddenly. My fury had ebbed into pity. I began to raise my hand with the intention of touching him, offering comfort, but I saw him flinch away and turned the gesture into a touch of my own hair, pushing a stray lock away that had come adrift in the violence of our quarrel. Callum's shoulders slumped and he shook his head slowly. "You're right, of course. I am a coward. But there's something else. Something you don't know. I need to tell you the whole truth, and it might as well be now." His voice was so soft I had to lean forward to hear him clearly. "I had heard dreadful, unspeakable things about Akira. I had come to realize what he was capable of. I had even begun to think that he must have been involved in Simon's murder. I was frightened of him, but not for myself. All I could think about was what might happen to you."

"I understand that," I said helplessly. "But if you were so worried about me, why didn't you tell me? Explain that you felt we had to leave, for my sake. In Edo, Akira was king. There was nothing you could have done about it if he really had decided he wanted me. He would have swept you into an unmarked grave without thinking twice about it. I would have understood, believe me. Why didn't you talk to me about it?"

"I just couldn't say anything. When we were in Edo, I could see how happy you were to think that we were close to finding Kazhua at last. I thought it would break your heart if I said we had to leave before we got anywhere. You see, the truth is that I *was* terrified of Akira, even if it was on your behalf." I started to protest, but Callum put his hand over my mouth, very gently. "I was in turmoil. Half of me wanted to snatch you away from danger, to walk out of Edo as soon as we could. The other half listened to you talking about Kazhua and saying how you were so sure we were close to finding her at last. So I did nothing at all. Just dithered. If we could have talked it over, agreed that there was no point in staying any longer, that would have been fine. I would have walked out of Edo happily. But before I could bring myself to do that, you made the decision for me."

I felt an absurd desire to apologize. "But I didn't know!" I protested. "I thought I had to get you away, no matter what."

"I know. But that hasn't stopped me worrying at it like a dog with a bone. I tried to tell myself I had had no choice. But when we docked in the East Indies, I almost decided I should say goodbye to you and go back to Edo. To finish our search for Kazhua."

"So why didn't you go back?"

"Because of you, Tara-chan. I knew if I went back I would be walking straight into Akira's arms. And that he would do his best to kill me. I had heard enough to know that he would never tolerate me making a fool of him. He would have to make an example of me. The whole of Edo would have laughed at him if he had lost a woman for a second time to another man, and a stupid *gaijin* at that. I wasn't worried for myself—I've faced death too many times for that. But I thought about Simon going back to Edo and being murdered because he was trying to find Kazhua. I began to think what it would do to you if history repeated itself and I was killed as well. I knew that you would blame yourself and would never be able to forgive yourself. But at the same time, I felt I should go back. I was so torn, I began to think I was going mad. I couldn't live in peace with my conscience telling me I was the world's worst coward, and at the same time I couldn't face inflicting such hurt on you. So I did nothing at all. And if that wasn't the coward's way out, what was?"

My eyes blurred with tears. For Callum, life would never be easy or straightforward. Always, there would be the tug of war between happiness and duty. He had not wanted to be Marquess of Kyle, but he had accepted the title because he felt he must. He had not wanted to fight in the Crimea, but it had been the right thing to do, so he had gone to war for Queen and country and done what was expected of him. And now? Now the balance had been between losing me or losing his own self-respect. And I had won.

That would have given many women great satisfaction. Look at the power I have over my man, they would have gloated. He may hate himself, but look how much he loves me! It gave me no satisfaction at all.

"Fate can be very cruel at times." I stared at the flickering light from the gas mantle, not wanting to look at Callum. "If you had told me what you were thinking, there would have been no need for any of this. I would have understood. Come to that, if Mountjoy had thought to mention that he knew Kazhua was in America, happy with her lover, we would have left Edo in peace anyway."

"Possibly." Callum shrugged wearily. "But I had been

thinking about breaking it to you that we should go for weeks, and I couldn't bring myself to tell you. I kept putting if off. Thinking about your face if I told you we were going to run away and abandon Kazhua. And then when I realized that Mountjoy had made my mind up for me, do you know I was relieved at first? I could blame him—and you. Nothing to do with me, I was as innocent as a lamb. Although before long that made things even worse. I realized I had been so much of a coward, even Mountjoy saw it."

"As if that matters!" I broke in. "You're wrong anyway. Mountjoy only decided to take matters into his own hands because he knew what danger you were in and he knew you would never leave of your own accord."

"Does it matter?" Callum said wearily. "I was a coward. Nothing can undo that. And there's nothing I can do to make that right."

"None of it matters, now." I spoke very gently. "It's not true anyway, but it's all gone by, and time cannot be turned back on itself."

"I thank you for your understanding." He spoke so politely, I might as well have been a stranger. "But I can't undo the way I've behaved since we left Edo. And I can't take back the words I threw at you this evening. I'd walked about for hours, turning things over in my mind and getting no further. I'd expected you would still be out when I got back in. When I found you here and so worried about me that you were going to call the police, I felt ten times worse. I was so guilty, I hated myself. I couldn't hurt myself anymore, so I tried to hurt you instead. I had to turn it around, to make you think that everything was your fault. You were right. I was hoping that you would decide you'd had enough of me and leave me so it would be your choice.

I'm so sorry, Tara-chan. I can't unsay what I said this evening. And I can't take back any of the pain I've caused you. In spite of that, is there any chance at all that you can forgive me?"

I looked at him in silence and then walked over to the gas mantel. I turned the flame down to a pinprick.

"My mother was a very placid woman," I said.

Callum frowned at me, obviously puzzled.

"But she did have a temper, when she was aroused sufficiently. When that happened, my father always said very firmly, 'The quarrels of a married couple and the west wind stop in the evening.' I think, roughly translated for Western ears that means, 'Come to bed. If need be, we will talk in the morning.' Are you coming with me, Callum?"

I held my hand out to him and he rose and walked behind me. I wondered for a moment who was beating a drum so very loudly, then I understood that it was the sound of my own blood, pulsing in my veins.

FIFTEEN

Everything bad
In life is balanced by a
Good. So we are straight

*C*allum was silent as he followed me into the bedroom. I was absurdly nervous. The gaslight in the bedroom was turned very low, and I was grateful for the dimness. I told myself that this was nonsense. Here I was with my own husband. The curtain that had hidden us from each other had finally been torn down. Surely, I should be joyful and full of anticipation. I was, but also was I worried. I sensed that this was make or break for us. What if the fire that had been between us had gone? What if love-making was...pleasant, and nothing more?

Nothing seemed to go right. My hands were clumsy as I pulled back the bedclothes. My fingernail caught in the sheets and I cursed it silently.

"I must tell the chambermaid she forgot to turn down the bed," I said for want of something to say to break the silence.

"She didn't forget. I told her not to bother. She was hanging about and got on my nerves," Callum said.

"Oh." I held my hands in front of my waist, fidgeting with a button.

"You still have your hat on," Callum pointed out courteously. It was too much for my strained nerves to take. My hat was very large and was secured with many long pins. It had taken a few minutes to pin it into place and I had to have my maid's help to get it right.

"Damn the bloody thing!" I shouted. "I don't care about my hat!"

I grabbed it and tugged. It came halfway off, and then stuck. I tugged again and one of the hatpins scratched my hand quite deeply. The cut immediately began to ooze blood. I threw the hat on the floor and stared at my hand. I held it out to Callum, my lips quivering like a wounded child.

"It hurts," I said simply.

"Does it? Shall I mend it for you?" Callum spoke gravely, as if I truly was a child. "Here. Give it to me."

He took my fingers in his hand and tugged them to his lips, licking the blood away softly.

"Better?" I nodded. "And does it hurt anywhere else?"

"I think I may have many hurts," I said seriously. "But nothing that can't be mended, given a little time and attention."

"Really? And would things be made better far more quickly if those hurts were given a lot of time and a lot of attention?"

I had almost forgotten what my husband—my dear, lost husband—sounded like. I had had enough of teasing. I fell against him and wrapped my arms around his waist.

"Callum, I'm sorry," I whispered into his skin.

"You're sorry? No, dear one. You have nothing to be sorry for. If I weren't such a stupid, pig-headed idiot, there would have been no unkindness between us."

I searched for words to answer him with comfort and understanding and found none. But it didn't matter. Callum picked me up in his arms as if I was the weight of a child. He laid me down on the bed and watched me. I bit my lip anxiously. Disposing of the hat had caused enough trouble, but there was surely worse to come.

I had dressed in my finest to go to the opera. A long gown, buttoned all the way down to the waist. Numerous petticoats beneath, to give it shape. A bodice beneath the dress. No traditional corsets for me, my waist was narrow enough to do without, but I was also wearing a pair of newly fashionable silk drawers. And of course, silk stockings and garters. I wanted to tear them all off, to show my nakedness to Callum and hope he still found me alluring. I began to pluck at the buttons on my gown. Callum pulled my fingers away and shook his head.

"How does the rhyme about magpies go?" As he spoke, he pinged open a button. "One for sorrow. Well, that's out of the way. Two for joy." Another button popped open. "Three for a girl. Four for a boy."

His face was so grave, I laughed out loud. Was the old Callum truly found again? Oh, how I hoped so!

"Five for silver, six for gold." I took up the chant, and we both said the next line together.

"Seven for a secret, never to be told."

"There should never have been a secret. You should have shared your thoughts with me." I spoke to the top of his head as he bent it to concentrate on the last of my buttons.

"So I should. And you should have told me how afraid

you were for me. For us."

"Would it have made any difference?" I asked quietly.

"Yes. It would have made all the difference. I was convinced that you thought I should have done more to find Kazhua before we left. That I was useless and I had let you down." I started to protest, but he put his finger on my lips to silence me. "I know now it doesn't make any sense at all, but that's what I thought. Probably because I felt so guilty about it. And—forgive me, Tara—I was beginning to worry that you might have found Akira attractive. More attractive than I am to you."

I laughed out loud at the absurdity of it. And then drew a deep breath as Callum tugged at my petticoats, frowning as they proved difficult.

"Akira? That...that thug? After what he did to my Kazhua? After he made it clear he thought he could just snap his fingers and I would go running to him? And if I did find him attractive, why would I have been so desperate to get both of us out of the Floating World?"

"I know that now. But then, I wasn't thinking straight," he admitted. "I was so torn in those last few weeks in Edo, I was half out of my mind. I wasn't just wild with jealousy over Akira. I even thought Mountjoy was hanging around because of you."

I rolled my eyes in disbelief. "You were jealous of that fop?"

"Is that how you saw him? Mountjoy's no fop, I assure you. He's seen a lot of the world. He talked sometimes, after a few drinks. He's seen things, done things that made our adventures in the Crimea look like children's games."

Mountjoy the chameleon, I thought. Then Callum's fingers found the laces on my bodice and I stopped thinking about Mountjoy entirely.

"I promise you, I wasn't at all attracted to either of them. Well, perhaps just a little to Akira," I teased. He deserved it!

Callum had dealt with my petticoats ruthlessly, dragging them away from me. I felt I must look like a rose in full bloom, lying in all the colors of my silks and satins. My thoughts became less poetical and far more depraved as he tugged the ribbon on my drawers apart with his teeth.

"How much is just a little?" he demanded, his words cluttered by the ribbon.

"Well, he was immensely powerful. And very rich. And he had a wicked reputation. And I suppose he was handsome, in a cold sort of way." He raised his head and looked at me like a scolded puppy. "Oh, Callum! No! I'm teasing. I hated him. Even if I hadn't known how badly he had treated Kazhua, I would never have been truly attracted to him."

I was lying, of course. I doubted there was a woman born who wouldn't find Akira attractive. But even when I had been in the grip of his powerful opium, I knew that rutting with Akira would have been nothing but a physical release. It would have been pure lust, with no love in it for either of us. Akira had a cold ruthlessness that was less than human. I had sensed that he would be almost bestial in his desires. Although the comparison was unfair to the animal. A beast might fight to the death for food or territory. Akira would do it for fun.

I wondered, for a second, whether I should try and explain all that to Callum. I knew there was no point. Callum was as far removed from Akira's animal hungers as the sun from the earth. He would never understand and he would be deeply hurt.

"You're certain?" he asked in the tone of a man looking for reassurance.

"Certain," I said firmly. I was pleased Callum could not

see my face; I'm a terrible liar. "And I don't want to hear another word about Akira. Ever."

"Your wish is my command, lady," Callum said. The ribbons gave way with a snap and he pulled them from the waistband. My drawers joined the rest of the petals that were strewn around me.

"Really? If that is so, why are you hesitating, husband?" I was so deep in anticipation I wanted to wait not one second longer. Perhaps we could not make up for all the lost time in one night, but oh! How I wanted to try!

Callum levered himself from me and stood silently at the side of the bed, his gaze lingering on my nakedness. I wondered for a second if something was wrong, and then I saw his tree of flesh was tenting out the front of his trousers and I was confused.

"Callum? What is it? What's wrong?" I tried to sound amused, but my husky voice gave me away.

"Nothing. Nothing at all. Wait just one moment."

I raised myself on one elbow and watched Callum impatiently as he went to the chest of drawers beneath the window and rummaged around. When he came back, he had something hidden in his hands.

"Lie back," he said. Something in his voice made me excited. I obeyed instantly. His hands felt in the pile of clothing beneath me. I glanced down and saw he was running my pair of silk stockings through his hands. He dangled them in front of me teasingly before he allowed them to slide through his fingers on to the bed. "I'm sorry to keep you waiting, but I felt two would not be enough."

I had no idea what he was talking about. But there was a distinct tremor in his voice and my anticipation rose a notch.

"Enough for what?" I asked curiously. Callum grinned.

In the flicker of the gaslight, his smile was feral. I swallowed a lump of excitement that had lodged in my throat.

"I rather thought we would play a new game. A new beginning, a new game."

He wasn't, I noticed, asking my opinion. He was telling me. I took a deep breath.

"Not fair!" I pouted. "Here I am, totally naked, and you've not so much as taken your tie off. Shall I help you?"

I reached out to his shirt, intending to undo the buttons, but Callum was too quick for me. He grabbed my wrists and held them in one hand. His grip was very firm, but not painful. I wanted him to squeeze them harder, and harder still. Suddenly, the thought of a little pain was delightful.

"No. You will not help me." With his free hand, he plucked one of my stockings from the bed. He put it to his lips and smiled. "Still warm."

My heart was pulsing pleasurably. I made no resistance at all as he wrapped the slippery silk around one wrist, tying off the knot with his teeth. He paused and raised his eyebrows in obvious question. When I said nothing, he passed the stocking above my head, fastening it firmly around the ornate brass bedstead. I tugged experimentally. I could move my arm perhaps an inch, but no more.

"And the other," Callum commanded. He dealt quickly with my other wrist. I was strung to the bedhead, my arms so wide apart they forced my breasts upward, as if they were inviting attention. Clearly, Callum thought so. He kneeled at my side and licked one nipple, and then the other. They rose in response; the slight pain was pleasurable. I moaned out loud when he moved away from me.

"Please." I wasn't even sure myself if the word was a request or a demand. Nor even what I was begging for.

"Soon." Callum nodded at me seriously. He picked up

one of the stockings he had taken from the drawer. Absurdly, I noticed that they were new; there was a neat fold down each.

He took my left ankle in his hand and knotted the stocking around it. Quite tightly; not so tight that it hurt, but I certainly knew it was there. I gave an experimental kick, more to see Callum's response than anything. He caught the sole of my foot in his free hand and bent down, sucking each of my toes in turn, only stopping when I moaned with intense pleasure.

"Less of your nonsense, my girl." He was tying the other end of the stocking to the bottom of the bed as he spoke. "I always thought the purpose of brass bedsteads was to ensure there was nowhere for the bedbugs to live. How very short-sighted of me!"

I heard the hoarseness in his voice and I was delighted. So delighted that I allowed him to fasten my ankles to the bottom of the bed without another word.

When he had finished, he stood back and surveyed me, his hands on his hips.

I was tied as securely as the poor lunatic I had seen earlier had been kept fast by the policemen. Unlike her, I was so deeply excited, I was snatching for breath. At first, I blamed it on the fact that I was roped on my back, but I soon stopped fooling myself. I couldn't breathe simply because I was gasping with anticipation.

Callum tugged each of my knotted stockings carefully. The knots held, and he gave a sigh of satisfaction. I felt as if one more moment and I would explode with need.

Ignoring me, he shook his head almost sorrowfully.

"I don't believe you're quite right." He tapped his lips with his finger seriously. "Ah! I have it."

He leaned over me to reach for something. I managed to

defy my bonds and lifted myself up a few inches. Far enough to bite at his mouth. He paused for a second before he pulled away. He was licking his lips, and I saw I had bitten hard enough to draw a bead of blood to his lower lip.

"Naughty!" Callum gloated. "Now I shall surely have to punish my wife for her wicked ways."

I stared up at him. Did he mean it? I hoped so.

"You can try," I whispered.

Callum slid his hand beneath me, lifting me from the bed as easily as I was weightless. Holding me suspended slightly above the bed, he smacked the exposed cheek of my bottom with his free hand. Then again, and again. It stung, and I was so surprised I shrieked out loud.

Instead of letting me down, Callum leaned across and grabbed the spare pillow in his teeth. He shoved it roughly beneath me so my body was pushed up toward him. He adjusted it and stood back to look, then nodded as if he was quite satisfied.

"Now that's better. I think a little drink is in order, don't you?"

He walked to the dresser and poured a healthy measure of whisky—Edradour, of course—into a cut glass tumbler. I watched him in growing fury. If this was his idea of a joke, then my sense of humor had failed me. Turning, he raised the glass to me in a toast.

"*Sláinte!*" he said cheerfully. He had trussed me up like a chicken ready for the oven, had me screaming with lust, and now he was toasting my health? I was furious. Had he been near enough, I would somehow have managed to kick or bite or scratch him. Anything to pay him back for the frustration he was making me suffer.

"Let me go!" I yelled.

He put his finger to his lips and shushed me. "Softly,

Tara-san. The walls here are no doubt very thick, but we do not wish the other guests to share our amusement."

Amusement? I bared my teeth at him and hissed angrily.

"You are not quite comfortable?" He stared at me, his eyebrows drawn together in a worried expression. "Ah. I know what it is. You think it unfair that I should drink alone. Quite right. We will drink together, wife of my body."

His final words were so tender, I was thrown off balance and lay still. For all that, I watched him cautiously as he moved back to the bed. Keeping the tumbler in his left hand, he reached down to my black moss with his right. I tensed as I felt him part the entrance to my private places, and slide a finger inside, running it up and down delicately.

Better. Much, much better. But not good enough for me to forgive him his behavior of a few moments ago. I lay still, forcing myself to be unresponsive. He smiled at me, and then took a huge gulp of whisky.

I held my breath as he ducked his head to my private parts. His fingers pushed deep inside me, and were quickly followed by his lips. A second later, I felt the whisky jet from his mouth into my sex. It felt very hot and prickled like a living thing. Callum raised his head and took another deliberate mouthful, emptying the glass. I could barely wait as he put his mouth against me again and spat the spirit into me.

My mouth was gaping with pleasure. My sex, also, was gaping wide. Had my bonds allowed me to move, I would have opened my legs still further. I could feel the whisky inside me, making my sex burn.

Callum watched me for a moment and then fastened his lips against my sex. For a moment, he contented himself with running his tongue up and down my slipperiness. I was panting like a dog on a hot day. I pushed myself against him as hard and far as my stocking ropes would allow. The fact that I could barely move, that he had deprived me of all choice, of all liberty, was intensely erotic. I loved the sensation, yet still I fought, determined to get my own way. When I found I could not loosen myself an inch, I shrieked out loud in pleasure.

Callum pushed his tongue inside my sex. Lapped at me, taking little, quick sips of the whisky. I felt my *yonaki* beginning to build and rubbed hard against his lips. Catching my excitement, he pursed his lips and sucked the remaining whisky into his mouth, only to spit it back inside me. He did it again and again and then my *yonaki* was upon me and I screamed with pleasure. Later, I found I had scrabbled so hard against my bonds that my wrists and ankles had been rubbed bright red. At the time, I was aware of it, but the small pain only increased my desire.

I didn't feel Callum untying me. When I descended from the clouds of heavenly delight, my wrists and ankles were free and he was lying full length beside me, watching my face intently.

"You still haven't taken your clothes off," I pointed out lazily. Glancing down at his tree of flesh, I saw to my utter amazement that it was still jutting out the front of his trousers. "You gave me such pleasure, and took nothing for yourself!"

"No. That's not right." Callum smiled slyly. "I took a very great pleasure in watching you, Tara-chan."

Suddenly, I felt absurdly guilty. And—in spite of the depth of my own *yonaki*, which had been very deep indeed —a flicker of lust stirred in my groin.

"Not such great pleasure as all that, I think," I whispered.

I ran my hand down his trousers and picked at each button in turn, as if I was plucking a gentle melody on my piano keys. Callum sighed deep in his throat.

"Take the silly things off." I sat back on my haunches and flicked a disdainful finger at his trousers. "And all the rest."

My turn! I had taken very great pleasure indeed in being forced into bondage by Callum. Now I intended to take as much pleasure in paying him back. Or at least, I hoped so.

He was on his feet in seconds, tearing at the buttons on his trousers and shirt. His undergarment followed quickly. He stood before me wearing nothing but his socks.

"Take *everything* off," I said decisively. He hopped from foot to foot, almost falling over in his eagerness to drag the wretched socks off. I ran my hand over my black moss as I watched him. I was still glowing, both with the heat of the whisky and the last throbbings of my *yonaki*. I felt lazy and deeply lustful at the same time. It was a gratifying combination, and I reveled in it.

"Done!" Callum said triumphantly.

"You think so? Come here." I beckoned to him with one finger. He was by my side before I could lower my hand.

I ran my fingers down his ribs.

"You've gotten fat!" I exclaimed in amusement. Callum looked hang-dog hurt, but I saw from the expression in his eyes that it was only half pretense. "Well, not fat. But you're not as skinny as you were." The words "the last time we actually saw each other naked" hung in the air. I spoke quickly. "Just as well. When we left the Crimea, you were like a walking skeleton."

"Ah. But you may notice the important areas haven't changed."

He grinned and wriggled his hips, making his tree bob

at me. I patted it fondly. Callum sucked in air and the time for joking fled. He slid his hand over my waist and began to move it toward my black moss. I snatched his wrist and held it firm.

"No," I said coolly. "I have played the game like a good girl." I knew, and Callum knew, that our bondage game had been all about me. But I was not going to mention that. Not now. Not when my good man deserved his own treat. "Now, it is my turn. Lie down."

Callum obeyed so quickly that the newly fashionable bed springs beneath our mattress twanged in pain.

"And what a good boy he has been, waiting all this time." I rubbed the tip of my finger over the baldness of his tree of flesh and then rubbed the sticky residue to nothing between my fingers. I felt him wince, whether in pain or pleasure or both, I had no idea. There is often a very fine line between the two. When they meet, the result is ecstasy beyond the imagination of most people. I waited until I felt the fires of my desire begin to build once again before I moved.

I rolled over so that my breasts jutted against his ribs. I rubbed against him like a gentle wave striking the beach. He gasped and reached for my sex, but my hand was there first, holding him an inch away from my black moss.

"Tara, don't tease. Please." He moaned. I thought about it, but not for very long at all.

I wriggled down and took his tree in my mouth. For once, I had no wish to torment him with my nibbling and licking. I took his tree as deep into my mouth as I could and allowed my tongue and teeth to surround his flesh. Callum shrieked almost like a woman and tore his hand away from between us. He found my private places at once, almost scratching at my flesh, his fingers rubbing roughly against my love bud so fiercely I whooped with pleasure. He said something else, but I barely heard his voice through the clouds of pleasure that were taking me over, body and mind.

My *yonaki* was deep and satisfying. It was only when I came down far enough to notice anything outside my own body that I realized that Callum was bursting his seed in my mouth. I closed my lips tightly around his tree, concentrating on taking every last droplet into my body.

Finally spent and satisfied, we flopped back, our arms wrapped tightly around each other. Callum leaned into me and nuzzled my neck, very gently and tenderly.

"I love you, Callum Niaish," I said softly. The nuzzling stopped, and I waited.

"I'm very glad to hear it, wife." Still I waited. I was on the verge of thinking that Callum had not understood what I wanted after all when he spoke again, his voice muffled by my own skin. "It's just as well that you do love me. Because if you didn't, I would have to explain to you very carefully that I love you. That I loved you from the first day I saw you. That I will always love you, and that nothing can change that. And that if, for some inexplicable reason that I can't possibly think of, you decided that you no longer loved me, then I would have to teach you that you did. All over again."

I smiled and curled against him, thinking how very good it was to have his warmth at my side again. I ran my hands between my legs and sighed with the pleasure of being completely satisfied. Never again would I be so foolish as to let anything come between us. Unless it was Callum's tree, of course.

SIXTEEN

There is beauty in
Each seashell. And twice blessed, they
Echo the sea's sound

"*G*et up, Mountjoy."

I darted forward and grabbed Callum's arm, hanging on to him. He could have shaken me off easily, but I knew he was too much of a gentleman to do it.

"Now why on earth should I do something as stupid as that?" Mountjoy muttered thickly. "If I do, you'll only knock me down again."

"No, he won't." I loosed my grip on Callum and went to offer my hand to Mountjoy. He got to his feet groggily, fingering his jaw.

"Nice way to greet an old friend," he complained.

Callum shrugged. "Think yourself lucky. If you had arrived earlier, my temper might not have been as sweet. What the hell are doing here anyway?"

"Oh, just passing by, doncha know? Any chance of some

coffee? And perhaps a bite to eat? I haven't had breakfast this morning and I'm starving."

He looked so woeful, I smiled.

"Sit down. The coffee's hot, and there are muffins and crumpets under the cover. If you don't want those, there's porridge in the dish and scrambled eggs on the burner."

"Thank you, Tara-san. I am most grateful that at least one of you is glad to see me."

Callum stared at Mountjoy in amazement as he poured himself coffee and stacked the plate I pushed toward him with muffins. The butter ran down his fingers and he licked them contentedly. Callum pulled out his own chair and sat down, propping his chin on his fist.

"I seem to be missing something," he said dryly. "Were we expecting you? Last time I saw your face was in a *ryokan* in Edo. And now you pop up here, like the genie out of the bottle."

Callum was beginning to be amused. I could hear it in his voice. I watched him as I poured myself a fresh cup of coffee. A lot of it splashed in the saucer, and I realized how very nervous I had been a few moments before. I remembered all too clearly the long months of anguish that Callum had suffered—that he had been convinced Mountjoy had inflicted on him—and I wondered if Mountjoy knew how lightly he had gotten off with that punch, hard as it had been.

"Sorry to arrive out of the blue, old chap. I had no idea you were both even in London until I bumped into Kelsey at a card game yesterday. He happened to mention your name, and then gave me your address when I told him we were old friends. Which we are, aren't we?"

Mountjoy smiled through a mouthful of muffin. He was so obviously sure that Callum was, after all, pleased to see him that I found it impossible to be angry with him. Besides, my conscience pricked me. He had probably saved our lives, whether Callum liked to face the fact or not. If nothing else, we owed him a welcome for that. I glanced at Callum and was immediately relieved; he was smiling with genuine amusement.

"Kelsey. Yes. I was playing Faro with him a couple of days ago. Never came across a worse card player anywhere. Not that it matters. Dear Lord Kelsey has so much money, he wouldn't notice if he lost each and every game. Which he generally does."

"I noticed that," Mountjoy said cheerfully. "He grumbled about you. Kept on about how he wished he had half your luck."

"Luck has nothing to do with it. He's just a rotten card player."

I stared from Mountjoy to Callum in amazement. A few minutes ago, Callum had knocked him to the floor, and I would have sworn if I hadn't come between the two men, he would have done our visitor much worse damage. Now, they were chatting like old friends who had seen each other only yesterday. Had the conflict been between two women, our fists would never have entered into matters. It would, on the other hand, have taken many weeks of careful skirting around each other before we reached a genuine truce. Men! I would never get to grips with the way their minds worked if I lived to be a hundred.

"Never mind Lord Kelsey," I interrupted. "Mountjoy, what are you doing here? I mean, here in London. I thought your business interests were in Edo?"

"So they were. May I?" Mountjoy looked longingly at the last muffin. I pushed the dish toward him and he grabbed it far too quickly for politeness. Was he thinner than I remembered? I thought he was, and began to wonder if he really was hungry. "Things started to go sour when dear Akira found the birds had flown."

He paused to take a drink of coffee, and Callum and I exchanged looks. Akira again. Would the damned man never cease haunting us?

"Yes?" Callum asked neutrally. "What happened?"

"Well, obviously, he wasn't too pleased to find that Tara here had disappeared. Yet he wasn't as angry as I had expected. In fact, he took it quite philosophically. Almost as if he had been expecting it. He didn't even have any of the men he had left on guard executed, which was surprising. And as I'm here to tell the tale, obviously he didn't blame me either. Or at least so I thought. But it was a funny coincidence that suddenly I began to find none of the merchants wanted to trade with me any longer. And those I owed money to started demanding payment in full. A very valuable shipment of jade and silk I had already sent on its way fell to pirates in the East China Sea. Not only was the cargo lost, but the ship itself was sunk. After that, I was obviously regarded as unlucky and nobody would trade with me, no matter what sort of deal I offered. It's funny, but I had always rather thought of myself as comfortable in Edo, but all at once I realized I was nothing more than a *gaijin*, there on sufferance. So eventually I took the hint and moved on. I spent a while in Java and Sumatra, hoping to get something out of the spice trade, but it was made bluntly clear that there was nothing there for me. I moved on quite quickly when I found a well-grown mamushi in my bed."

I was horrified. Mamushi are amongst the most venomous snakes in Japan and kill without mercy. Their bite leads to an agonizingly painful death.

"I didn't even know they had mamushi in the Dutch East Indies!" I exclaimed.

"Well this one had certainly made itself at home," Mountjoy said drily. "It had curled up right at the foot of my bed. It had been a particularly hot night, I had thrown the bedclothes right back and saw the nasty thing waiting for me."

"Akira?" Callum asked quietly.

Mountjoy shrugged. "Does his influence spread that far? I don't know. I did think at the time that it was an amazing coincidence that the most feared Japanese snake had followed me across an ocean, but I have no proof. Anyway, I took the hint and got the first steamer out. Landed in France and found my way to gay Paree, eventually, and thoroughly enjoyed myself for a good few months."

"Did you?" I asked cynically. His expression was so innocent, a child would have seen through it. "If you enjoyed Paris so much, what are you doing here?"

"Unfortunately, the French police decided to take an interest in my apparently astonishing run of luck in the gambling saloons of Montmartre. You'll find this difficult to believe, but they came to the conclusion that I was cheating. They intimated I should leave Paris immediately, and were corrupt enough to relieve me of my winnings in exchange for not throwing me into jail and leaving me there until the French justice system finally sorted me out. I'm absolutely stony broke." He shrugged. "In fact, I'm boracic lint."

Callum and I both stared at him as if he had suddenly spoken in a foreign language. Mountjoy glanced from Callum to me and laughed.

"Boracic lint. Cockney rhyming slang for 'skint.' Penniless, if you want to be polite about it."

He really was hungry, then. I rang the bell and asked

our maid to bring bacon and eggs and fresh toast. And more coffee. Mountjoy downed it all with no more than a nod of thanks.

Callum was clearly far more uncomfortable with our guest's revelations than I was.

"Sorry to hear that, old chap." He cleared his throat and spoke gruffly. "I can loan you as much as you need. Just to tide you over until you find your feet again."

I smiled. Dear Callum! He knew perfectly well that the "loan" would never be repaid.

"Thanks. But no thanks. My needs are very few," Mountjoy proclaimed theatrically.

"But yes," I contradicted him decisively. "We owe you our lives. How are we supposed to pay you back for that?"

"She's right. Sorry about the jaw," Callum mumbled awkwardly.

Men! I had thought earlier it would take me a hundred years to come to understand them. Now, I knew there would always be something left to confuse me. I was even more perplexed when Mountjoy threw a mock punch at Callum's shoulder, and he reeled back as if the pat had actually hurt him.

"Forget it." Mountjoy waved his hand in a magnanimous gesture. "I daresay I would have reacted in exactly the same way. And also forget any nonsense about me saving your lives. It amused me to help, at the time. I wouldn't have done it otherwise," he added honestly. "And anyway, I'm fairly certain that as of tomorrow, I will no longer be skint." He beamed like an angelic child, and I stared at him suspiciously.

"Got a tip for a certainty at the races, have you?" I demanded. "Or have you found some poor, stupid heiress who's willing to marry you?"

"Neither. But if Callum would kindly advance me just a couple of Victorias, I guarantee that he will have his money back with interest no later than tomorrow night."

A couple of Victorias. He meant two sovereigns. The coins bore Queen Victoria's head on them and were nearly always referred to as Victorias. Londoners meant no disrespect by the term. They were clearly very fond of and proud of their queen. So much for Mountjoy refusing a loan!

"Really? And how does that come about?" I asked suspiciously.

"I'm going to fleece Kelsey for it. And as much more as I can manage."

I stared at Mountjoy, barely able to believe what he was saying. I had always found Lord Kelsey a remarkably charming man. He enjoyed the opera almost as much as I did, and I had met him several times at various performances.

"You can't do that!" I yelped.

"Of course I can." Mountjoy seemed almost hurt by my reaction. "I'm not going to cheat, if that's what you're thinking. I'll play fair and square, I assure you. He's rolling in money. He loses every time he plays, and it doesn't mean a thing to him."

"Mountjoy's right, Tara." Callum's face was serious, but I could tell from his voice he was hiding a smile. "I've seen Kelsey lose a hundred guineas at a sitting, and he just throws his marker in the pot and then comes back next day for more. He never learns."

I stared at him in disbelief. "Since when have you been given to haunting gambling dens?"

"I don't go to gambling dens at all. Just very proper gentlemen's clubs," Callum said defensively. He squirmed beneath my shocked gaze and shrugged sheepishly. "You know I never liked the opera. Even the ballet's not much to my taste. I got into the habit of going to White's or Boodle's instead of sitting about waiting for you to get back home. I had no problem being proposed as a member for both clubs."

"Why? You're no gambler!" I said derisively.

"No, I'm not. But I do enjoy the skill involved in a game of cards. The knack of reading what your opponent has in their hand. Of deciding what they're going to play."

"Kelsey said you were the best Hazard player he had ever come across," Mountjoy said helpfully.

"Hazard is a dice game," I exclaimed. My head was starting to ache. I very much wished Mountjoy had never walked through our door, that I had never found yet another facet of my husband that had previously been unknown to me.

"Dice, cards." Callum shrugged. "It doesn't matter. It's the skill of it that attracts me. Being able to outwit your opponent. And unlike Kelsey, I don't lose."

"Everybody loses sometimes," I said softly. Callum smiled at me and I shook my head, laughing. Mountjoy stared between us in obvious bewilderment.

"So they do," Callum said. "Of course I'll lend you some money, Mountjoy. Pay me back when you can. It doesn't matter. I've no intention of taking any more money off Kelsey anyway. It's becoming embarrassing."

"Oh, surely not!" Mountjoy sounded horrified. "I assured Kelsey that you would come with me tomorrow. It's only a little gaming party at his townhouse. A few friends, you know the sort of thing. Nothing as formal as White's or Boodle's"

"No. You'll have to give Kelsey my apologies. I'm taking Tara to the opera," Callum said.

"No, you're not, Callum. I'm not going to the opera. I'm going with you both to Lord Kelsey's." I stared at Callum, wondering why he seemed so embarrassed.

"Tara dear. I'm sorry. You can't come with us." Callum stumbled to a halt.

"Why not?" I demanded.

"Women—ladies, I mean—just do not go to gambling sessions. It's unheard of," Callum said helplessly. I picked up on his words, and an imp of devilment made me throw them back at him.

"You mean women do go, but ladies don't?"

"Exactly!" My irony had passed Callum by completely. "Occasionally, one of the gentlemen might take a woman with him. Some of them seem to believe a particular female companion will bring them luck. But ladies, no. It really is not done."

"Ah. I see," I said. "You mean it's rather like it was in the Floating World. When it wasn't the done thing to take me to a geisha house?"

They both stared at me silently, their expressions speaking for them. It was too much. I let my laughter go and patted Callum's hand.

"Oh, dear. Your faces! Would Lord Kelsey really be appalled if I went with you?"

"He would," Mountjoy said quickly. "I'm afraid a gentleman's card party can be a pretty louche affair. The men tend to forget their manners and their language, especially when they lose. Most of them drink far too much, and that's not a pretty sight."

"Mountjoy, I was a geisha in the Floating World. Do you really think I would be shocked by seeing men misbehaving?"

"This isn't the Floating World, Tara-chan," Mountjoy

said reprovingly. "There are no rules at card parties like this. It's all boys together, and nobody is going to be reproved for their behavior, no matter how dreadful it is. Even the gentry —what am I saying? Especially the gentry!—go to throw off their manners and amuse themselves. I know you think it would be fun, but I doubt you would like to see them throwing up or calling for the pot to piss in," he said bluntly. "Or worse."

Callum frowned at Mountjoy's choice of words. But I noticed he didn't disagree, and I decided I wasn't that interested in Lord Kelsey's amusements after all.

"Oh, very well. Go on, the both of you. Just make sure it's not you two who are disgracing yourselves."

"You don't need to worry about that." Mountjoy grinned. "I need the money, so I'll be sure to stay sober. And I promise to keep an eye on Callum here."

"Do that," I said sweetly. "If he comes home drunk and with empty pockets, you'll wish you'd never seen the streets of London, Mountjoy."

SEVENTEEN

If the body and
Mind are not balanced, how can
One find harmony?

J was so very happy, I forgot that it is only the gods who are entitled to perfect joy in their lives. And that they take it amiss when mere humans presume to join them. Summer had finally come, and the whole of London seemed to have thrown off the fogs and chills of winter and to be going about business with a smile.

Especially me.

I was convinced that our joyful reunion had made me pregnant. At last! It was irrational, I knew. I had missed only two of my monthly courses. Nothing to get excited about; it had happened before and each time I had been disappointed. But this time I *felt* different. I woke up each morning with a small thrill of excitement, as if my very blood was pulsing a little faster through my veins. I was hungry all the time as well. I said nothing to Callum, wanting to be absolutely sure first. But he obviously saw my happiness and commented on it.

"The sunshine is good for you, sweetheart. You're glowing with health. I'm only sorry we're going to be here in London for a while longer," he said. "I expected the legal business to be sorted out months ago, but it's dragging on forever. It's all Uncle's fault," he added in an uncharacteristic burst of annoyance.

"Your poor uncle!" I teased. "That's not fair. You've said yourself that you hated looking after the legal side of things just as much as he did. Couldn't things be sorted out in Scotland?" I asked hopefully. I still loved the buzz and liveliness of London, but now I had a new life to think of. The very thought of it thrilled me, and the idea of giving birth to a baby in the grime and smoke of London was appalling. And everybody told me that the warm weather would mean an increase in cholera. I had seen the ravages cholera caused in the Crimea. Although I could hardly believe that it could strike with the same dreadful severity here in civilized London, I had no wish to be proven wrong.

"I wish they could." Callum shrugged, obviously annoyed. "That's why I said it was Uncle's fault. The land that's under dispute is in Kyle, right enough. But apparently Uncle didn't bother reading the contract document properly, and it was made subject to English law, not Scottish, so it has to be fought out in the English courts."

"And would you have bothered reading it either?" I teased.

Callum looked glum. "I don't suppose I would have," he admitted. "But in any event, I'm stuck with it. Every time I go to see my solicitor, he tells me the other side has come up with something new, so now he has to examine the fresh evidence and respond to it. And that in turn is going to postpone the court hearing yet again. I wish I could just walk away from it, I really do."

"Why don't you?" I asked, although I knew the answer anyway.

"I can't!" Callum sounded horrified. "It's quite a large piece of land that's in question. It's never been farmed, and according to Mr. Smythe, Uncle was always under the impression that the man who wanted the land was a tremendously wealthy Sassenach—that's an English gentleman to you, Tara—who just wanted to use it to hunt and fish with his friends, which was fine by Uncle. So Uncle leased it to him, or so he thought. He never actually read the contract, of course. Just signed where he was told to put his name. Whatever plans the Sassenach had for the land were never put into place, but now he's died and his heir is claiming that the contract is clear the land was purchased outright, not leased at all. And he says he now wants to evict all the crofters and make it into one, gigantic farm. Put a manager on and run it as a profitable business and to hell with the families who have lived on Kyle land for as long as we have. Can't have that, of course, so I'm now fighting tooth and nail to prove that there was a fundamental mistake and that Uncle only made the deal under the idea that the land was to be leased, not purchased, and always with the intention that it was to be used only for hunting, never for farming. Impossible to prove now that he's dead, of course. But I must try."

I understood at once. My poor Callum's conscience again. I was so certain that I really was pregnant, that this morning it had been on the very tip of my tongue to tell him my news. Now, I was pleased I had not. If I had told him, poor Callum's conscience would have tied itself in knots. Who would have come first, me and our baby, or the tenants who were in trouble? I didn't know the answer. I didn't want to know.

"Never mind," I said cheerfully. "I'm sure right will prevail in the end."

We went for a walk, arm in arm, looking just like every other man and wife on the streets who had an eye for the good weather and each other. We took a light lunch at the Café Royal, and then returned hot and footsore and very happy.

"I think I'll take a nap." I smiled at Callum happily. And why shouldn't I be happy? The long, sad months when we had nothing to say to each other were past, and the pain had begun to be if not forgotten, then more of an unpleasant memory. The sun was shining. I was irrationally sure that the legal problems would be resolved very soon and we could go back to Kyle and get on with our lives as they should be. With a new baby in the cradle, and—who knew?—perhaps more to come. And although I knew it was irrational, I couldn't help my heart leaping with another hope. Surely this good fortune had to be an omen? If I had been gifted with another baby, then perhaps fate would finally relent and send my dear Kazhua back to me as well so my life would be complete. I filled with joy at the thought.

Once back in Scotland, London could be visited as and when we wanted. There would be no reason why we *had* to be here. I even amused myself with the thought of inviting Mountjoy to visit us in the Highlands, wondering all the time how long it would take for him to become completely bored with the country.

Or perhaps—chameleon that he was—he would blend in and become the perfect country gentleman. For the Mountjoy here in London was different again to the Mountjoy who had helped us escape from Edo. He had even changed physically. His hair was longer and curled raffishly on his collar. He had grown a neat mustache and beard. Apart from that, it was a matter of the way he presented himself to the world. In Edo, he had been a prosperous, well-mannered merchant. In London, he was the complete man-about-town, walking with a swagger and a gleam in his eye.

"Paid your tailor, have you?" Callum demanded as he turned up in yet another new suit.

"Certainly have. I'm not one of you fly-boys, here today and gone tomorrow!" Mountjoy said indignantly. "Besides, old chap, money is no object these days." He closed his eye in a deliberate wink.

"And one of these days the likes of Kelsey are going to work out exactly how much you're taking off them," Callum said drily.

Mountjoy grinned. "Don't know why you don't join in the fun yourself, old chap. I know you don't need the money, but a little more's always welcome! And I must admit that you're a far better card player than I am."

"That's precisely because I *don't* need the money," Callum said thoughtfully. "If I did, I might not be so cool about it. As it is, I play because I enjoy the skill of it. And I know when to stop."

I looked at Mountjoy indulgently. I knew his faults, and despite them—or perhaps because he acknowledged his own shortcomings with such unconcern it was endearing—I had come to look upon him as a friend.

Thoughts of Mountjoy slid out of my head as I snuggled down comfortably on our bed. I was drowsing as I heard Callum call out that he was going to the bank and to pay yet another visit to his attorney. I heard the door shut softly behind him, and then nothing more as sleep stole over me gently.

I dreamed I was back in the Floating World. Yet, as if often the way of dreams, it wasn't quite the Floating World I remembered. I was dressed in Western-style clothes. I stared down at myself in confusion and was surprised when nobody seemed to notice. Instead, the crowds simply folded around me and carried me with them. The scent of *jako* seeds rose from them and I inhaled it with pleasure. The pleasure evaporated quickly as I saw they were urging me on toward Akira's house. I tried to pull back, but they wouldn't allow it. Closer and closer, until we came to the crossroads leading to his cul-de-sac. The crowd around me stopped, and a sigh of satisfaction came from many throats.

Akira's house was gone. There was simply an empty plot where the beautiful building had stood. Even the wonderful garden might never have existed. I cried out loud in amazement. I felt almost bereaved by the lack, as if something very precious to me had been lost unexpectedly. I turned my head, waiting for somebody to tell me what had happened. But the crowd had melted away and I stood alone. My sense of mourning was so deep, it was a physical pain in my belly.

And then I woke up. The dream faded slowly. It had been so very real, for a moment I was caught between two worlds and I was unsure where I was. I yawned and stretched, and the pain I had felt in my sleep came back to me. Only this time, it was a real, physical pain. I was off the bed so quickly I nearly tripped over my own skirts. I ran to the bathroom and pulled up my skirts and petticoats frantically. A thread caught and snagged on my nail and I tore at it, whimpering at the small pain as the nail snapped off. I then cried out loud as forced my hand between my thighs and felt the trickle of blood there. I slid to the floor of the bathroom, whimpering and rocking back and forth, praying to all the gods that I was mistaken. That the blood came from my ragged nail even though I knew it did not.

I was grateful beyond anything I had not shared my hopes with Callum. There was no reason for both of us to be disappointed. I smiled at him when he came in and felt my heart break when he yawned and stretched and suggested roguishly that I might like to spend an hour in bed with him.

"Sorry." I shrugged, as if it was the most matter of fact thing in the world. "Wrong time of the month."

"No need for that to stop a bit of fun, is there? I could make it nice for you. You know that."

And he could, of course. Just as I could make it nice for him. I nearly told him in that second. Explained to him just why "fun" was the last thing I wanted, when my precious baby was running out of my body. Instead, I smiled and shrugged my shoulders.

"Thanks, but no thanks. My stomach hurts, and I just want to lie down and be quiet for a while."

Callum was instantly concerned. He drew the curtains in the bedroom and laid beside me, waiting until he thought I had gone to sleep before he dozed off himself. As he often did, he threw his arm across my ribs. Normally, I enjoyed the weight across my body. Today, I moved his arm away, very gently, so as not to waken him. I lay awake and stared into the dim light. Tears ran down my face and wet my hair, but I did not wipe them away. Each one was a pearl, I thought. A pearl for my unborn child to take with him into the next world.

My agonized thoughts slipped from my unknown baby to the child I had lost so long ago. I had been so very sure that this new life inside me had been a sign that I would find Kazhua again. Now, all my joyful hopes for the future left me. I was to have no babe to suckle at my aching breasts, and my dear Kazhua was as far away from me as ever. I cried silently, cursing the fate that had roused my hopes only to snatch them away from me with such cruelty.

Poor Callum understood intuitively that there was something wrong with me. He probed gently, but constantly. I had made my mind up that I would not tell him, and pleaded the heat as an excuse for my sudden lack of energy. And truly, London was vile that summer. The hot air lingered in the streets, captured and compressed by the buildings on each side. I had never gotten accustomed to the fact that even the best parts of London shared their space with factories. Just down from our apartment building was a tannery. The stink of green hides being treated made me want to retch. Almost worse was the fat rendering factory; the miasma from that was almost tangible. It seemed there was no escape. Wherever one went in London, there were horrible smells. Clever Mr. Bazalgette had started work on his massive scheme to give London new sewers, and everybody said that in a couple of years it would be wonderful, but that summer, the work on the project only made things worse. Everywhere we went, there seemed to be enormous holes in the ground and even bigger hills of debris at the side of them. Traffic was diverted and the roads were solidly at a standstill, jammed with carts and carriages and cabs. We were even denied the pleasure of strolling beside the Thames. Not just because of the dreadful fumes that arose from the sluggish river—the water was so contaminated it ran as thick as soup—but also because Mr. Bazalgette had decreed that three new embankments must be made at the side of the Thames, and the on-going work meant that our favorite walks were denied to us.

"Do you think you might fancy a trip to the music hall?" Callum sounded so worried, I knew he was grasping at straws to try and cheer me up. I had not been able to face either the opera or the ballet for over a month. The very thought of those hot, sweaty bodies, the men puffing away on cigars and the ladies drenched in cologne to disguise the stink of their sweat, made me nauseous. I was about to tell him no, I would rather stay at home quietly, when I glanced at his face and saw the depth of concern in his eyes. Suddenly, I wished I had told him about the baby. Our baby. Was it too late now? I decided it was. I knew Callum would not only mourn for our child, but would also be deeply upset for me. I could not bring myself to inflict the double hurt on my poor husband.

"The music hall?" I echoed doubtfully. I had looked forward to seeing a performance what felt a like a lifetime ago. Callum had promised he would take me, but somehow it had never happened.

"The Alhambra," he said eagerly. "I believe they have an excellent bill on this week. It might cheer you up a bit."

I had seen the Alhambra, of course. At least from the outside. It was very difficult to miss. It stood on the east side of Leicester Square, only a few minutes' ride from our apartment. It was a huge, ornate building, built in incredibly bad taste. I had been told it was supposed to resemble the Alhambra Palace in Andalucía, in the south of Spain, but even without seeing the original I knew that it was a terrible, vulgar imitation. It always struck me as looking more like an over-decorated wedding cake than anything else.

Callum obviously mistook my hesitation as interest. He

went on cheerfully, "You'd probably find it dreadful after the opera," he warned. "It's not meant to be serious, just a bit of fun. But they do say a change is as good as a rest."

His voice tailed off hopefully. The scar on his eyes looked sore and inflamed, a sure sign that he was unwell. Was he so worried about me, I wondered, that he was making himself ill? A flare of guilt made me respond far more enthusiastically than I had intended.

"It sounds a lovely idea. I have been a bit down in the dumps. I think it must be the hot weather. And all the dreadful smells."

"There's been a big increase in cholera cases since it got so hot." He put his hand solicitously on my forehead. "You don't feel ill. Should I send for a doctor to take a look at you?"

"I'm fine," I said briskly. "Probably just a bit stale. You might be right. A trip to the Alhambra might be just what I need to take me out of myself." And then again, it might not, I thought cynically.

EIGHTEEN

Everything in my
Life enchants me. How can you
Ever feel boredom?

J fanned myself vigorously. The Alhambra stank just as badly as the Royal Opera House, but in a different way. Here, the smell was of pipe smoke and beer. Sweat unmasked by perfume. And food. Virtually everybody in the audiences seemed to be munching on something, from oranges to saveloys. The combined aromas made me feel quite sick.

"They'll be starting any minute." Callum leaned forward enthusiastically and propped his elbows on the plush edge of the balcony. He was so pleased to have persuaded me to come with him, nothing could have made me tell him how uncomfortable I was. "Look. You can see straight down onto the stage from here. These are the cheapest seats, but I always think you get the best view."

I inched my neck forward and clung onto the balcony edge carefully. I am not very good with heights, and it seemed to me that we were a very long way indeed above the stage. I was struck with a sudden minor attack of vertigo and grabbed Callum's hand to fend off the dizziness. He took my gesture for enthusiasm and returned my grip with a squeeze.

Suddenly, the flare of the limelight around the perimeter of the stage dimmed and then shone even brighter. The sweating orchestra in the pit before the stage broke into music; a drum was beaten in an enthusiastic roll and a trumpet blared out.

"We're off!" Callum said.

The roar of approval from the whole audience was deafening. I flinched back from the noise and was relieved when it died as quickly as it had started.

"My lords! Ladies! And gentlemen!" A man I had not even noticed before was seated at a rostrum at the side of the stage. His words raised a yell of laughter, which he subdued with a brisk bang of an outsize gavel on the table in front of him. "May I welcome you all, my children, to tonight's performance."

"Get on with it, Ikey!" a man just behind me shouted.

"Did your mother never tell you that patience is a virtue?" the man on the rostrum—whom I assumed was Ikey—yelled back. "But I shall keep you all in suspense no longer, my dear friends. Allow me to present for your delectation the most tremendous, the most thrilling, the most dangerous, trapeze act in London today. The Three... Flying...Diamonds!"

The dramatic pause he gave between each word was perfect. I admired his timing and then gasped as the thick, velvet curtain in front of the stage rose smoothly.

From where we were sitting, it looked as though the fragile trapezes slung at each end of the stage were no more substantial than birds' perches. The orchestra launched into a brisk tune, and I was horrified to see a woman, clad in a spangled bodice that stretched just to her thighs and very little else, apparently fling herself unsupported into the air, perhaps forty feet above the stage. I gasped in fear and was amazed when the rest of the audience clapped and cheered.

"Don't worry." Callum had to speak loudly, right against my ear to make himself heard. "They know what they're doing."

And it appeared he was right. The Flying Diamonds threw themselves enthusiastically from perch to perch. Occasionally, they changed trapeze in mid-swing, sometimes twisting themselves around. When the female performer hung upside down by her feet, the applause nearly lifted the roof. I found myself clapping enthusiastically with everybody else. All the same, I was quite relieved when the curtain came down, and even more relieved when all three Diamonds took a curtain call—on the floor of the stage.

Ikey banged his gavel again, shouting for order. The audience shouted back. After a brief bit of repartee, he shouted out the next performer. I had barely a second to wonder how he managed to do this night after night without losing his voice entirely when the curtain rose on a single figure. The beautifully dressed young man sauntered to the front of the stage and tipped his masher's bowler hat to the crowd.

"'Ullo, 'ullo, 'ullo," he called cheerfully.

A great cry of "Evening, Max" answered him, and then he was off. He obviously had the audience in the palm of his hand. I was slightly puzzled. He had a pleasant enough voice—a light, even tenor—and his soft-shoe shuffle routines were well practiced, but I really couldn't see why he was so adored. I would have preferred to have seen the thrills of the Flying Diamonds again, but the audience loved him. When the curtain came down, they stamped and yelled until the slender young man came back for an encore. He stood at the very front of the stage, the limelight sending odd shadows across his face. He raised a single finger and wagged it at the orchestra, and began to sing unaccompanied. Suddenly, I could see what all the fuss was about.

"Come into the garden, Maud,

For the black bat, night has flown.

Come into the garden, Maud,

I am here at the gate alone;

And the woodbine spices are wafted abroad,

And the musk of the rose is blown."

He held his bowler against his chest as he sang, and I could see clearly that he had picked out one very pretty girl in the audience to sing his love song to. She giggled and buried her head in her beau's shoulder, but surfaced every few seconds to glance back at the young man on the stage.

When he had finished his song, he bowed again and again.

"Sorry, folks! Got to be off. If I don't get to the Eagle in the next twenty minutes, you'll surely never see me again as I'll be lynched! Cheerio! Cheerio!"

The audience laughed in response and the noise level fell as Ikey banged his gavel yet again and announced an interval.

"Would you like something to drink?" Callum asked. "Something to eat?"

I found I was both hungry and thirsty. For the first time in months, I wanted to eat something tasty.

"What's he eating?" I gestured at a man who was sitting

at the far end of our row, smacking his lips as he ate out of a newspaper-wrapped parcel. Callum craned round me to take a look.

"Fish and chips, by the smell of it." He stared at me in amazement. "Do you want some?"

"What are they?" I sniffed again. Whatever they were, they were making my stomach rumble with hunger.

"A new fad. Cod deep fried in batter, served with fried, chipped potatoes. And well sprinkled with salt and vinegar."

The dish sounded less than enticing, but still smelled wonderful.

"Do you know, I think I would like to try them."

"There must be a stall outside selling them. I'll be back in a minute."

Callum rose and pushed his way past the good-natured patrons that hedged us in. As soon as he had gone, I felt rather lost. I sat silently, staring at the balcony rail until he came back and pushed a newspaper-clad parcel into my hands. It was hot, and I undid it cautiously.

"You forgot to bring me a knife and fork," I pointed out. The thick fillet of fish was coated in golden batter. The chipped potatoes were equally golden. The aroma of salt and vinegar mingled with the smell of the fish and made my mouth water.

"You eat them with your fingers, straight out of the paper. A knife and fork would spoil it." Callum stole a fat chip from my package and waved his hand in front of his mouth. "Hot," he explained.

My meal was not only hot, I thought it the finest thing I had ever tasted. I ate every scrap, then I glanced at Callum guiltily.

"I didn't save you any! I'm sorry."

"Not to worry." Callum grinned. "I had a bag of chips while I was waiting for your fish to cook. Do you want a drink?"

He produced a bottle of beer from his pocket, rather like a conjurer producing a rabbit from a hat. A bottle opener appeared by more magic from another pocket and he pried the cap off efficiently. I took a cautious sip straight from the bottle. It went so very well with the lingering taste of my fish feast, I drank half of it without taking it from my lips. I suppressed a burp and handed it reluctantly back to Callum, who finished if off.

"Bass Pale Ale." He shook the bottle and sighed when he found it empty. "Finest beer in the entire world."

It was also much stronger than I had thought. I leaned contentedly on Callum's shoulder and dozed through most of the second half. I had almost nodded off completely when the curtain came down for the final time. In the cab on the way home, I found myself humming "Come into the Garden, Maud."

"I enjoyed that," I said happily. "All of it, I mean. Not just that particular young man."

I felt Callum's shoulders shake with laughter. I couldn't be bothered to raise my head and look at him, so just said, "What?" instead.

"You mean Max Marchant, do you?"

"That's right. The man who was on after the Flying Diamonds."

"I'm sorry to disillusion you." Callum smiled indulgently. "But 'he' is a she. Her real name is the far less romantic Daisy Grey, late of Camden Town."

"No!" I sat upright and stared at him in disbelief.

"Cross my heart and hope to die." Callum mimed crossing his heart and grinned at me. "Male impersonators are quite the in thing at the moment, but Daisy is by far the best of them. She takes her craft so seriously that she's rarely seen in a dress. She much prefers the freedom of trousers."

I shook my head at the wonder of it. "And how do you know so much about Miss Grey?" I demanded. Even in the little light inside our cab, I thought Callum looked furtive.

"She's a gambler. And a very good one," he said reluctantly. "She's yet another one who's taken a lot of money off poor old Kelsey."

"What?" I woke up abruptly. "But you said women were never allowed to attend gentlemen's card parties. You wouldn't let me go with you, but it's all right for her!"

"I haven't actually seen her at a card party," he said hastily. Far too hastily, in my opinion. "I've just heard Kelsey mention her. And besides, could you actually describe a male impersonator as a woman? Still less a lady."

"I suppose not," I said reluctantly. It must have been the ale that was befuddling my senses. There was something very wrong with Callum's comment, but I couldn't quite work out what it was.

The steady rhythm of the cab's horses, clipping along at a fine pace on the cobbles, combined with the beer I had drunk and my full stomach. I slept with my head on Callum's shoulder, dreaming of Max Marchant singing to me.

NINETEEN

When you are not here
By my side, the heart of the
Home no longer beats

"You're going to White's again?" I sounded accusing. Callum's face fell, and my conscience pinched like an over-tight shoe. Who was I to question his pleasures? Guilt left a taste like metal in my mouth.

"If you'd rather I didn't go, I'll send a message to say I can't make it. It's just that as I'm the newest member, I feel I should turn up regularly." Callum shrugged.

"Oh, get off with you." I brushed a speck of lint off the lapel of his otherwise immaculate jacket. "I suppose I'm worrying over nothing, but I do get anxious about you gambling so much. I know we're not poor, but I also know you can't afford to lose as much money as you say Lord Kelsey and some of the others do."

"I don't lose money very often," Callum said seriously. "I have a budget. Sometimes I lose a little. And it is very little.

If I get to what I have decided is my cut-off point, then I stop. More often than not, I win. I'm very good at cards, and dice," he added with obvious pride. "And...it gives me something to keep me occupied."

"I thought that was my role," I said innocently.

"So it is, woman." Callum grabbed me around the waist and hugged me. "It's not exactly the gambling I enjoy so much. It's..." He paused, his face intent as he sought for the right words to explain. "It's watching the run of the cards. Keeping an eye on my opponents, trying to work out what they have in their hands, what card they're going to go with. It's a bit like it was in the Crimea, when we were watching the Ruskies and trying to decide what their next move was going to be." He laughed, clearly embarrassed by his flood of words.

"I understand," I said simply.

I knew perfectly well that Callum was bored. True enough, he had welcomed the adventure and excitement of the Crimea. But after the extreme dangers of war, I guessed he would once again welcome the gentler rhythms of life in Glen Kyle. And here in London, he had no responsibility at all. Nothing to get him out of bed in the morning. No reports of crops or livestock to pore over. No tenants to worry about. No disputes to settle. Not even a river to fish in or a brae to walk in. For his sake, I wished that the dispute that was keeping us here was settled, one way or another. I was quite content to linger a little longer, now that there was no baby, and the prospect of finding Kazhua seemed as far away as ever. And especially since my life had suddenly become interesting again.

"Will you miss it, when we finally go home?" I waved my hand around the room. "The hustle and bustle of London, I mean. And your gambling dens, of course!"

He shook his head at once. "It's fun, I suppose. But nothing could take the place of Glen Kyle. I never wanted to be responsible for it, but now I miss it deeply. Perhaps I had to spend time away from there to understand how much it means to me."

I was right, then!

"Any sign of the lawsuit being settled?" I asked.

"It's creeping along," he said glumly. "Apparently all the hard evidence is in place now, and it all comes down to intention and whether there was any mistake there. I'm insisting there was; the Sassenach's heir insists there wasn't." He shrugged. "Da has finally written to the lawyer to confirm that Uncle discussed it with him and that he would never have sold the land, so who knows? Things may be settled at long last. My God, is that the time? I must go or I shall be so late my place in the game will be given to somebody else. Are you sure you don't mind me going?"

I shook my head and made shooing motions with my hands. "Go on, away with you. I don't really mind you going in the least. Christian is going to take me to the Eagle. The new Lion Comique Joe Eggar's top of the bill. He's all the rage, but I haven't seen him yet and am looking forward to it."

"He's Christian now, is he?" Callum teased. "And taking you to the music hall yet again! I think I felt safer when it was the opera with Angela and Marcus."

I smiled at him when he went out, stopping in the doorway to blow me a kiss. The flash of guilt had not come back. And why should it? Callum amused himself in his own way, as did I. Callum was happy. I had no need to be concerned for him. And what else did I have to occupy myself with? Had we found Kazhua, things would have been different. I would have had my daughter, and with her a purpose in life again. If my baby had not miscarried—my thoughts flinched and turned aside in hurt at the recollection—my life would have been full to overflowing with happiness.

But as it was, I had nothing at all. So why shouldn't I amuse myself as I saw fit? It was all perfectly innocent, even if I did choose not to tell Callum what Christian and I actually got up to on our jaunts. He would only worry, or possibly laugh at me, which would make me angry. Better for both of us that he didn't know.

Mountjoy had become "Christian" so gradually, I hadn't even realized the informality had crept in until Callum mentioned it. It didn't matter, he was our friend. In fact, I had rather begun to look upon him as an elder brother. He knew London inside out, from the swell haunts of the rich to the shabbiest music hall. And unlike Callum, who worried for my safety and my soul, Christian was totally unconcerned for either.

The clock on our mantelpiece struck the hour and I hurried off to get changed. And that was my other little secret.

I shucked off my clothes quickly, throwing everything across the back of a chair. No need to put them away. They would be back on my body before Callum came back home. I delved into the dressing drawer at the foot of my wardrobe, throwing aside the top layers quickly, reaching almost to the bottom. I had no need to hide anything; Callum would never look in my clothes drawers. I knew that he would consider it a breach of trust to poke in my things without being invited. Ever the gentleman, bless him! But still I did it. In an odd way, it added to the excitement. I paused, frowning, a fine linen shirt dangling from my fingers.

"Oh, get on with it, woman!" I muttered to myself. My conscience could be appeased later. Now, I was far too excited to worry greatly about the wrongs and rights of things. I hopped from foot to foot as I pulled my trousers on. My fingers were shaking as I did up the buttons on my beautifully ironed shirt, knotting a tie in place expertly. My shoes had decided to be a nuisance. The laces had got themselves tied in knots and made me angry as I fumbled to do them up.

Finally ready, I stared into the mirror and adjusted my rakish cap just so. It was perhaps a little too shapeless, a little too baggy to be truly fashionable. But it had to be big to contain all my hair beneath it, and there was nothing I could do about it. I pulled the peak down over my forehead and grinned with anticipation at my reflection.

Now, I was finally ready. I put my hands in my jacket pockets and slouched about the room impatiently, waiting for Christian. He was late, of course. He nearly always was. I glanced out of the window, watching to see if a cab was about to stop outside our building and let him out. One slowed, and I went on tip-toe to see better, but it did not stop. I drummed my fingers on the windowsill impatiently. I was looking forward to tonight's expedition. Christian had promised me something special. When I had demanded to know what, he had been coy and refused to tell me.

"I think you'll find it amusing," he had said with a wicked grin.

Thinking about the excitement on his face when he said it, I paused for a moment, my own excitement ratcheting down a notch. Had things gone too far? And what, exactly, was "too far?" I didn't bother answering my own question. Too far was anything I would not want Callum to know about. In that case, the answer was a definite "yes." Then a cab did stop outside and I grabbed my cloak and pulled the hood over my head—cap and all—and went down the stairs almost at a run. The hall porter called "good evening" to me and I mumbled something back. The cab door swung open in invitation and I vaulted inside. The movement was so easy in my men's togs, I almost laughed with pleasure.

It had all started so very innocently.

"*M*issed Callum, have I?" Christian picked up an apple from the fruit dish and inspected it critically before taking a bite out of it.

"He's gone to Boodle's."

"Lucky man." Christian pulled a sour face. "I wouldn't be allowed through the door. Not the right sort of class, doncha know? And definitely not enough money. Anyway, what's the silly man thinking of, going off and leaving you to mope about here all on your own?"

"I'm not moping," I said indignantly. "I was all set to go to the ballet."

Christian was still munching his apple. He swallowed before he spoke, checking the core to make sure there was no flesh left on it, and then finding it bare, putting it tidily down on the table.

"Really? Why are you still here then?"

"I couldn't be bothered." I shrugged. "It was *Faust* and I've already seen it once. Besides, I'm getting a bit tired of George and Sara. She chatters non-stop, and he just sits there and leers at me all evening."

"Poor Tara!" Christian mocked. "All dressed up and nowhere to go!"

I looked down at my gown and shrugged.

"Fancy a trip to the Eagle?" Christian asked. "It's one of the best music halls in London. And my old friend Max Marchant's topping the bill."

My attention was caught at once. "You know him? Her, I mean? I saw her when Callum took me to the Alhambra. I had no idea he was a she until Callum told me."

"I know the lady quite well, actually." Christian seemed amused by my interest. "We've met often at the shadier sort of card soirees. The sort the nobs go to for a cheap thrill. She might not be quite what you would call a broadsman, but she's not far short. And the dear thing's the hottest tom act in the halls at the moment."

"I didn't understand a word of that." I was intrigued.

Christian grinned slyly. "Max—or Daisy, to give her the correct moniker—enjoys a game of chance. She is a fine card player, and only just keeps the right side of being a very skillful cheat. I've met her quite often when I've been at card games where the higher-class gentlemen—such as Lord Kelsey—go for the amusement of rubbing shoulders with the lower classes. And if you've seen her act, you know what a tom is."

"No, I don't. Tell me!"

Christian looked distinctly uncomfortable. I stared at him avidly. Christian Mountjoy, embarrassed?

"Tell me," I repeated.

He shrugged. "She's a male impersonator." I was deeply disappointed. I knew that! "She's the best. And the reason she's the best is because she's a tom. A woman who prefers women to men, if you get my meaning."

"So? Honestly, Christian. Nobody would worry about that in the Floating World. Everybody's different. Does it matter?"

"It does here!" He seemed greatly amused by my calm

acceptance. "It's just not done, doncha know? Anyway, do you want to go the Eagle Tavern and see her perform again? I could introduce you to her afterward if you like."

I was so excited, I could barely stammer my thanks. Christian smiled at me indulgently.

The Eagle was lovely. Even better than the Alhambra. At Christian's suggestion, I had changed into a plain gown. I sat in the audience and linked arms with him, swaying from side to side as we belted out the choruses to the songs together. I swigged Bass Pale Ale from the bottle and flushed deeply when it made me burp.

"Get it orff your chest, love." A burly man in the next seat smacked me cheerfully on the back. "You'll feel better for it."

I giggled at his words. I was hot and sticky and slightly tipsy. The world was already a fine place, and I had the treat of being introduced to Max—Daisy—yet to come! I sighed in content.

"Come in do, and put the wood in the hole, for God's sake." The voice was far rougher than it had been on stage. I hesitated and Christian put his hand on my back, urging me forward. He closed the door—I assumed "the wood"— quickly behind us. "Oh, it's you, is it! And who's this you've brought with you to see me?"

I stared, very rudely. It seemed to me that we had caught Max/Daisy in the strangest of transitions. At the moment, she was neither male nor female, but a curious amalgam of both. She was seated in front of a dressing table strewn with sticks of greasepaint and pots of cream. A cigarette smoldered in an old tin lid at her side, and I watched in amazement as she picked it up and took a long drag from it. I had never seen a woman smoking a cigarette before. In fact, until we had gone to the Crimea so Callum could fight for Queen and country, I had never seen anybody smoking a cigarette. The soldiers had acquired the habit there and had brought cigarettes back with them. They were cheaper than cigars, so they were popular with the working class. And also, I knew, increasingly popular amongst gentlemen. It was perfectly acceptable for lower class women to smoke a clay pipe, but for a woman of any class to smoke a cigarette was very daring indeed. My admiration for Christian's "tom" rose another notch.

"Evening, love." She nodded at me through the smoke from her cigarette. "I'll be with you in just a mo. Let me get the old paint off me dial."

Her accent was far thicker than when she was on stage. I watched her slap cream on her face and wipe it off vigorously with an old towel, which she threw to one side. Once her face was naked of greasepaint, she was older than I had thought. Perhaps in her late twenties or a little older. Her face was hard, which made it difficult to tell. There were deep wrinkles on her upper lip, although oddly the skin on the rest of her face was lovely. Was it the cigarette smoke that caused the wrinkles, I wondered? She stubbed the cigarette out and rubbed her hands briskly, turning to look at me fully.

"Daisy, dear. I've brought along a fan to meet you."

Daisy nodded at me. A slow smile spread over her face. "Always pleased to meet a fan." She held her hand out to me. I had expected her to shake hands, and I bit down on a giggle when she took my hand in her fingers and kissed the back of it very elegantly. "Like the music hall, do you?"

"Oh, yes," I said quickly. "I love it."

Max's eyebrows rose in theatrical astonishment. "Cor. Bit of a toff, ain't she Mountjoy?" Before Christian could answer, she rattled on, never letting go of my hand. "Doing a bit of slumming, are we dearie?"

"No," I said firmly. "I really do love the music hall. And especially your act."

"Oh, aye?" She looked me up and down carefully and her rather fierce expression softened. "Not thinking of treading the boards yourself, are you? The public loves a bit of novelty. You'd go down a treat."

"No. That she is not," Christian spoke for me. "Tara is actually Lady Kyle, Max. Her husband's Callum Niaish."

"Oh." Her face fell, then was cheerful again immediately. "Lucky Cal, is it? Top bloke. No point me trying to nick you off the likes of him, is there, love?" She clicked her fingers, her forehead creased in thought. "Now I come to think of it, I heard he had a Japanese wife. Nobody told me you were such a looker, though. Ah well, I better be on me way, chickadees. I'm promised to Margarita's house for a round or two of Hazard. Wish me luck!"

Christian rose and opened the door for her politely. Framed in the doorway, she turned and blew me a kiss, followed by the most salacious wink I have ever received. Although she had removed her stage makeup, she was still clad in her male clothes. Her hair had been cut very short, and If I hadn't known that Max was really Daisy, I would never have guessed. It wasn't just the clothes and the hair, it was the way she walked. Such a swagger. Such confidence.

"Sorry about that," Christian apologized quickly. "It's nothing personal. Max comes on to virtually every pretty girl she meets. It's habit more than anything."

"I wasn't offended." I looked at him in surprise. "In fact, I think she's wonderful."

"You do?" Christian ushered me out of the dressing room and through the stage door. "Really?"

"Really. In fact, I think she's amazing."

Christian was so surprised, he stopped dead. A stage door Johnny, clutching a large bouquet of expensive hothouse roses and lilies and obviously waiting for the object of his passion to emerge from the music hall, bumped into him and glared angrily. Then his gaze moved to me and he cleared his throat and tipped his hat.

"Sorry, miss. I say, didn't I see you on stage this evening?"

"No, I'm afraid not." My voice was low and husky. I put my hand to the base of my throat and glanced at him coyly. I was amusing myself immensely. To my disappointment, Christian jumped in quickly.

"On your way, sunshine. The lady is spoken for."

Both men squared up to each other in the most absurd way for a moment and I almost laughed out loud. Finally, Christian took my arm and hustled me away. A cab was clattering past the end of the alleyway and he hailed it confidently.

"What in God's name were you playing at?" he demanded when we were seated. "You didn't know that damned masher at the stage door from Adam. What were you thinking of, giving him the eye like that?"

I laughed out loud. I was so excited, I could barely keep still in my seat. "Where are we going? To another music hall?"

"I am taking you home," Christian said firmly. I sat back in my seat with a sigh of disappointment. "What on earth has gotten into you, *Lady* Kyle?"

His absurdly formal use of my title made me want to giggle again.

"Max Marchant, that's what." Our cab passed a gas lamp, and in the brief illumination I saw his face was totally bewildered. "Or not exactly Max herself, but the life she leads."

"What? Dashing from hall to hall virtually every night, dealing with all the hecklers who've had a drop too much and think they're as witty as hell? And she doesn't earn as much as you might think either. Fair enough, she enjoys her card games, but if she didn't earn a bob or two from them, she'd be pretty hard up by the time she's paid for her lodgings and cab fares. And all those costume changes don't come cheap either. I'm sorry, Tara, but you don't see the reality of it."

"I suppose I don't," I said doubtfully, then my spirit flared again and I grabbed Christian's arm and shook it. "But she's free to do what she wants, when she wants. That's the thing I envy. She might be a tom, as you say, but she can swagger out of the theater and stroll down the road in her men's clothes and nobody is going to blink an eye at her. She can go to card games. She earns her own keep. She's doing what she wants to do, with nobody to tell her any different."

I was panting by the time I ran out of words. It hadn't made that much sense, even to me, and I was amazed when Mountjoy nodded thoughtfully.

"There is that, of course. But surely it's the same for all the music hall artistes? Those ladies don't have to dress up in men's togs to earn a living for themselves."

"No. But it helps!" I said sharply. "Look at that masher at the stage door tonight. I bet whoever he was waiting for was delighted to see him. He'd buy her supper, I suppose. Probably had a nice, little present tucked away in his pocket for her. And he would no doubt dig deep into his wallet if she was prepared to bestow her favors on him at the end of the night."

I sounded intensely bitter. All at once, I was deeply ashamed of my words. What on earth did I have to complain about? If I wanted anything, I just had to ask Callum either for the money or for him to buy it for me. I was well fed. I had a wardrobe stuffed with beautiful clothes. I wanted for nothing at all. Apart from the never-ending hope that one day I might find Kazhua, I lacked only one thing in my life, and I'd had no idea I was lacking it until tonight.

I wanted to be free. Not free of dear Callum! That idea was absurd. No, I longed for smaller freedoms. I wanted to be able to go to the music hall—or the opera, or the ballet for that matter—on my own, without having some man assume I was on the look-out for company. I wanted to be able to go to places where no lady should be seen. To turn up at a card party and not see the men's faces freeze in horror. Did I want to be a man? Even the thought made me want to laugh out loud. Thank you, but no thank you. I was very happy in my own skin, my own body. But to have the freedoms men took for granted? Ah, now there would be a thing.

I turned to look at Christian, wondering how I was ever going to explain all that to him. He was smiling, a slow, sly smile, and instead of speaking, I waited.

"I think I do know what you mean. Well, just so long as dear Callum never finds out what we've been up to, I daresay something could be arranged. If you're willing to take a chance on me, that is?"

I nodded eagerly, without even asking him what he had in mind.

And so it began.

The next time Callum went to Boodle's—with my blessing, freely given—I told him honestly that Christian was going to take me to Astley's Royal Amphitheater.

"I understand there's a ballerina on the bill who stands on her points on the back of a galloping horse. And trick riders who do stunts you wouldn't believe could be possible."

Callum's face lit up, and for a second, I thought I had gone too far in my enthusiasm and he was going to say he would come with us. But instead he shrugged and hugged me, telling me to make sure Christian took good care of me.

"It's a bit different from the ballet," he cautioned. And then he smiled widely. "Not that it matters. As long as you're enjoying yourself, who cares?"

Who, indeed! That evening, Christian turned up early, with a mysterious, brown-paper-wrapped parcel under his arm. When we went out, I was no longer Lady Kyle. I had given myself a new name. On our evenings out in the future, I was to be Tomo. I knew Christian thought I had chosen the name to reflect Max Marchant's "tom" status, and he was partly right. But also, in Japanese it was a name that could be given equally to a boy or a girl, and it delighted me.

Tomo wore boy's clothes. Tomo left Tara behind him, in Eaton Square.

That first evening at Astley's, the master of ceremonies shouted for volunteers to ride bareback around the ring. Not as scary as it sounds, as everybody was to be roped firmly into a safety harness. I put my hand up at once, and in spite of Christian muttering "no, no, no" at me, I leaped up as soon as I was chosen. And there was better still to come. I was the first to try. My sturdy pony galloped gamely around the ring, and lacking reins, I hung on to his mane for grim death. After a couple of circuits, with the crowd cheering madly, I found myself hoisted bodily into the air, where I dangled from my harness with my trousered legs kicking frantically in thin air.

I laughed like a mad thing all the way home.

"What have I done?" Christian moaned. But I could tell that he was secretly deeply amused.

TWENTY

If I had wings, would
I fly? Or would my spirit
Stay earthbound with you?

I could barely believe that Callum didn't notice the change in me. I no longer asked after the progress of the court case. No longer sighed nostalgically when he handed me reports from Donald, faithful in Glen Kyle. To be sure, I still went to both the ballet and opera occasionally, both with Callum or our friends if he had a prior engagement at one of his clubs. But I no longer found either the performance or our friends particularly engrossing. Yet he seemed not to notice. Or, I wondered, did he see but thought it better not to comment?

Knowing Callum as I did, I guessed that it was the latter. I felt deeply guilty that his only concern was for my happiness. Yet not quite guilty enough to tell Christian that I had had enough of the music halls and "slumming it" in my boy's togs in the East End.

Truth to tell, some nights we never even got as far as

the music hall. Instead, we swanned around the mean streets of Whitechapel and Limehouse, my arm firmly in the crook of Christian's elbow. Although I drank little, the splendid gin palaces of the London working classes became well known to me. I found it fascinating to watch the people who thronged around us, all out for a good time, even if the cost of it was no money for food next day and a sadly aching head. We went to an opium den once, and I watched over Christian's sleeping body while his soul soared on the artificial wings of the drug. Funnily enough, we never did go to a card game, but it didn't matter. I knew I could go if the fancy took me. That was all that mattered.

One thing surprised me above all else. Nobody looked twice at us, a Japanese "boy" arm in arm with an older English gentleman. I mentioned it to Christian, and he laughed.

"Why should they bother? They just assume that you're my lover and that we're both amusing ourselves slumming it in the East End." I was surprised for a moment, until Christian added slyly, "Would anybody have blinked an eye if we had been in the Floating World?"

He was right, of course.

"It's no good, Tomo. I'm going to have to leave you for a minute." My thoughts had been far away and I blinked at Christian in surprise. "I'm desperate for a pee."

He winked at me and nodded at the mouth of a dark alley at the side of us. London had not thought it worthwhile to squander much money on street lighting in Limehouse. There was a single gaslight where I stood, but the alley Christian was indicating was pitch black.

"Take care. If you trip and break your ankle, how am I supposed to get you home?

"No chance," he boasted cheerfully. "I see better in the dark than most people can in broad daylight."

I smiled as he was eaten by the darkness in a second. I felt rather superior; Christian had drunk very little more than I had, but already he needed to pass water! I was sure I could hang on until we arrived home. In any event, the thought of having to duck down in a filthy, dark alley and cope with my trousers to have a pee was a powerful deterrent.

"All on your lonesome, sweetheart?" I jumped and stared in surprise at the man who had spoken to me. I thought he must have seen through my disguise and I was annoyed. "Or are you waiting for somebody in particular, dear boy? If you are, I promise you that you've found him."

Relief made me bold. I smiled cockily, head on one side.

"I'm not on my own. My friend had to pay a visit." I nodded to the alley. "He'll be back in a minute."

"Really?" He either didn't believe me or didn't want to believe me. I couldn't decide which. "He seems to be taking a long time about it. I've had my eye on you for ages and you've been all alone."

He was right. Christian had been far longer than I expected. Surely, he couldn't really have fallen and injured himself?

"I think I'd better go and look for him." I turned to go and found my arm grasped firmly.

"Oh, no. Don't do that. Stay here with me, darling. Just look what I've got here for a good boy!"

He delved into his pocket and produced a Victoria. It winked softly in the light from the gas lamp. A passing man turned to look at it. His gaze flicked from the man to me and he sneered before he passed on. Fear began to tread in my mind with soft, threatening feet. Suddenly, my adventures were far less harmless and much less amusing than they had been a moment ago.

"All yours, dear heart. All I ask in return is a nice suck. Or even better, a poke at your sweet little bum hole. A Victoria for five minutes work, if that. Feel, my pego is as stiff as a poker. Now wouldn't you love that up you?"

He grabbed my hand and splayed it against the front of his trousers. His tree was huge, and hard; it tented the front of his trousers as if he had poked a truncheon down there. I stared at him appalled. We were in a crowded street and here he was, copping a feel! Yet nobody appeared to either notice or care. Only the glimpse of the coin had caused any interest at all.

"I really must find my friend," I gabbled.

"Good idea." The man smirked at me. "You say he went down the alley here? Well, why don't we go and find him?"

He had hold of my arm so firmly, I couldn't get away from him. I looked around wildly, sure that some kind passerby would see my distress and help me. The crowds looked through us both as if we were invisible. Of course they did; my disguise was far too good. To them, I was simply a molly boy, playing hard to get. Somewhere in my mind, the sour thought that I had been playing with fire and was now about to be burned occurred to me.

"Oh, sorry, ducks." A woman almost lurched into us. She put her hands on my shoulders to steady herself. I opened my mouth to beg her to help me, and my "friend" immediately put his palm over it, cutting off my words. I entreated her with my eyes and she bent and peered at me. Suddenly, her face broke into a huge grin. "All yours, love. Good timing, five minutes earlier and you'd have had to queue! Room for another one on top and off we go!"

She cackled loudly and wandered down the alley past us, almost ricocheting from wall to wall she was so drunk.

"Nice to see a gay girl with a sense of humor, isn't it?" The man holding me chuckled as if he was genuinely amused. Even through my terror, I understood the woman's little joke. I had traveled on horse-drawn omnibuses with Christian, always insisting we travel on the open top of the 'bus, where no woman would dream of going, no matter how full it was inside. With wide skirts and masses of petticoats, it would have been impossible for a woman to even climb the stairs. I had reveled in it; now I knew it was forever spoiled for me.

I was being dragged bodily down the filthy alley. I refused to walk, but it made no difference. My heels simply trailed through the accumulated filth on the floor. It wasn't quite as dark down here as I had thought it. In the absence of any light from the street, a half-moon gave some illumination. I howled inside, but it was all I could do to breathe, his hand was clamped so tightly over my mouth and nose.

"Oh, isn't this just lovely? We are going to have such fun, you and I! I do hope you're going to kick and struggle. I love that in a boy. Nothing beats the delight of taking, rather than being offered it on a plate." He giggled happily. I immediately stopped struggling and went limp. But he wasn't fooled. "Oh, my dear one! Such a crafty little tart, ain't you? Feisty as well. Here we are!"

He stopped abruptly, not quite at the end of the alley. I thought wildly that he would have to let go of my arm at some point, if only to unbutton his trousers, and then I would run. I was never given the chance. He kept hold of my arm, but took his hand from my mouth, at the same time swinging me round into his chest. I kicked, as hard as I possibly could and knew I had connected as I heard him grunt. It did no good. If anything, he seemed to relish the pain. He swung me face first against the wall so hard that all my breath was knocked out of my lungs and he leaned against me. I felt him fumbling at my trousers and I closed my eyes in horror.

"Oy. What do you think you're up to with my bum-boy?"

Christian! And not a second too late!

"Yours?" The man was still leaning against me. My face was squashed against rough, slimy bricks. I kept my mouth closed against the foulness. "I think not. I found this dear little boy waiting for a customer at the bottom of the alley. All on his lonesome. He's mine now."

"Let him go. Now. Tomo, are you all right?"

I mumbled "no," but my voice was absorbed by the brick pressing against my lips.

"Tomo? How delightful!" The man sounded breathless and excited. In spite of Christian's growled words, he was still leaning against me. And his pego was still sticking into me like a lump of wood. "If he is yours, sir, may I ask what you were doing down here with a gay girl? Surely, not a good idea to leave a gem like this unprotected! But I think I see the lay of the land. One has to give way to one's baser instincts from time to time, and I daresay you were saving this one for the paying customers. Come now, surely we can reach some arrangement? It's obvious that he's something very special. I've never even seen an oriental sodomite before. I daresay he knows some tricks that I've not come across."

I stared at Christian, mentally urging him to get on with it and make my captor let me go. His face was half in shadow, but I could still see his expression. I shivered as I saw he was smiling.

"Oh, I assure you, he does. You would find him very

surprising indeed. But I really don't think this is an appropriate place to enjoy such a treasure, do you? Perhaps you
might like to come to my—our—lodgings and we could
discuss an appropriate amount?"

I felt the man hesitate, and then he was levering himself
off me.

"Well, I daresay a little wait would only make things
sweeter. Are your lodgings close by, sir?"

"You will not have long to wait long, I promise you." I
was about to make a dash down the alley when Christian
pivoted on the balls of his feet and planted a sweet punch,
straight on the man's chin. He fell with a single grunt. I
watched in disbelief as Christian stooped and went through
his pockets.

"What are you doing!" I shrieked. "Come on, let's get
away before he comes around."

"One moment," Christian said coolly. I heard the chink
of coins as he put his hand in his pocket. He was about to
straighten up when he bent again and fiddled with the
unconscious man's watch chain. "Thought so. A swell toff
like him would be bound to have a sovereign case on his
Albert." He tugged at the watch chain that ran across the
man's waistcoat. A small case came free, and followed the
other coins into Christian's pocket. "All done. Off we go."

I was almost at the end of the alley when I turned back.
My captor was still lying flat on his back.

"You haven't killed him, have you?" I whispered.

"Would you be really concerned if I have?" Christian
sounded surprised. "I haven't, anyway. He'll have a sore jaw
for a day or two. I daresay he'll have fun explaining that to
his wife!"

"How do you know he's married? He can't be, can he?"

"I doubt he would have been wearing this if he wasn't,"

Christian said drily, holding up a thick wedding band for me to see. "Serves him right. He only got what he deserved."

"You stole that?" In spite of what the man had been about to do to me, Christian stealing his wedding ring shocked me. "Why? If you're short of money, just tell me. I'll get some from Callum and pass it on to you."

"Thank you, but no thank you. As the saying goes, 'charity begins at home.' I prefer to find my money myself, with no help from my friends." He put a protective arm around my shoulders. "Are you sure you're all right?"

"I'm fine. No harm done."

I was better than fine. I was deeply excited. My feet felt as if they wanted to dance. I couldn't remember when I had last felt quite so alive. Certainly, not since I had arrived in London! "Just stop for a minute, will you?"

Christian stopped obediently. I turned and slapped him hard across his cheek. A passing man cheered and clapped me loudly. I bowed my head gravely at him, accepting the applause as no more than my due.

"What was that for?" He sounded genuinely shocked.

"For leaving me on my own for all that time. I thought you were just going for a pee, and there you were, frolicking with that whore!"

"Sorry. I really did need a pee." For once, Christian sounded genuinely apologetic. "I'd forgotten that that particular alley was where all the gay girls around here go when they need to relieve themselves. I went down to the bottom and found Polly there squatting over a grating, doing the necessary. She seemed terribly pleased to see me, and I'm afraid I did get distracted for a few minutes."

I began to laugh. After a moment, Christian joined uncertainly.

"Take me, home," I demanded. "You're quite right. I've had enough. For tonight, anyway."

We were silent in the cab. At least for a while. Irrepressible as ever, Christian dug in his pocket and began to examine his stolen treasures. He rubbed his thumb over the engraving on the gold sovereign case appreciatively and then flipped the lid open. I thought he must have found a fine haul of coins when he began to chuckle.

"Look at that." He tilted the case toward me. There was something written on the inside of the lid. It was engraved in a flowing, cursive script and that—together with the dim interior of the cab—made it very difficult to make out. Christian held it close to my eyes, and I started to giggle. The inscription read, *For my dearest Jack. A reminder to think of your loving wife every time you spend! Dora.*

"Oh, dear!" I snapped the case shut and handed it back to him, trying not to let my giggles explode into laughter. "Do you think his poor wife had any idea what it meant?"

"I doubt it." Christian was grinning widely. "It's an expensive case. Solid gold, unless I'm mistaken. Jack is obviously a man of means, and I doubt that—present company excepted!—there are many respectable married women in London that would understand what the slang term 'spend' actually means."

I put my hand in front of my mouth to hide my grin. I hadn't known either until I had started my adventures with Christian. It was a term that had amused me from the start. I had first heard it spoken from behind me in the Adelphi Music Hall. A man who thought he was speaking far more quietly than he was had confided to his companion, "For fuck's sake, Marian. Do you really want to stay to see the end of this? I'm dying to spend."

I had not heard Marian's reply, as the people on either

side of her had shushed him loudly and he had slumped down in his seat, his face crimson. I had thought it rather sweet of him at the time, and had told Christian so. I couldn't understand why the man was so embarrassed about wanting to spend some money on his best girl.

"I don't think he meant that." Christian's face worked with laughter. "To 'spend' is also a slang expression for having an orgasm. To burst one's fruit, as they would say in the Floating World."

I remembered that conversation now and wondered if Jack had laughed as well when he first read the inscription from his doting wife. In any event, it stopped me worrying about him. I sincerely hoped Dora would give him hell when he arrived back home.

Christian was still chuckling when I spoke again. I surprised myself. I had not thought about what I was going to say at all beforehand.

"Why did you rescue us from the Floating World, Christian? I know you got away yourself, but it was very dangerous for you. If Akira had suspected you, he wouldn't have bothered looking for proof. He would just have had you murdered."

"Why do you think I did it?" he asked idly. It wasn't the answer I was expecting, but now that I had finally asked, I decided I would tell the truth. At least one of us should.

"I'm not sure. Probably for love of one of us. But whether it was me or Callum, I've never been able to decide."

He turned his head and stared at me. His expression was unreadable, but I wondered if I had managed to offend him. He spoke before I could apologize.

"You do surprise me sometimes, Tara." I noticed I was "Tara" again, rather than "Tomo." A shame, that. I liked being Tomo. "Well, I'm sorry to let you down, but it wasn't for love of either of you. Oh, I like Callum well enough. I've yet to find anybody who doesn't like him. And you have turned out to be the most diverting companion I've had for a long time. But it wasn't for love, or even liking, that I helped you escape."

"What was it, then?" I asked. He was drumming his fingers on the cab seat. I wondered if he was thinking the question over, looking for a lie. He turned to look at me and smiled, a smile so innocent I was sure he was going to lie.

"I suppose life in Edo was getting rather flat. I was making money without even trying very hard. My friendship with Akira made sure I was well respected. Nobody would dream of trying to cheat anybody who had the great yakuza's friendship. I had exhausted just about every pleasure that the Floating World could offer to me. To be honest, I was getting bored. And then you two bumbled along! You were both far better actors than I realized. I took you at face value; a beautiful Japanese courtesan who had ensnared a rich, rather stupid *gaijin*, and somehow persuaded him to show you Edo. I knew Akira was interested in you, but even I was shocked when he summoned me from my sight-seeing with Callum to tell me he had decided to take you as his concubine. I pointed out that Callum might not be too happy about that, and he just shrugged and grinned.

"'There's plenty of room left in the *gaijin* cemetery, Mountjoy-san,' he said cheerfully. By that time, I was convinced that Akira was going mad. Did you know he kept your daughter's room as it was the day she left him?"

"Yes," I said colorlessly. "He showed it to me. It was like a shrine to Kazhua."

I had surprised Christian yet again. He stared at me in amazement.

"You were in his house?" I nodded. "He never told me that."

"That same morning. He sent a man for me. When I refused to go with him, he came and collected me himself."

"My God," he breathed. "And you lived to tell the tale!"

"Yes. But never mind that. I still don't understand why you helped us escape. You were putting yourself in the most dreadful danger. You might have ended up in the cemetery with Callum. And Simon." I shuddered at the thought.

Mountjoy looked at me curiously. "Don't you know why? Really?" I shook my head. "Very well. I'll explain. I knew that Akira was losing his grip on his empire. He was taking too much opium, brooding rather than getting on with things. He was beginning to lose some of his best men to rival yakuza. And for me, well, it's fair to say I had made a few enemies in my time in Japan. If he was no longer going to be the supreme yakuza in the place, I would have no one to protect me. Besides, I had rather begun to get the impression that Akira regarded me as his tame *gaijin*. And I do so hate to be taken for granted. I thought it over, and decided if I was going to go, then I would go out with a bang." He grinned at me. "There you both were, in need of a knight in shining armor. And there was I, looking for a way to get one over on Akira without causing myself any problems. It was a match made in heaven. I had already made up my mind I would be leaving in a few months. Why not, I thought, leave my mark behind me? Instead of slinking out, why not show the world that Akira was no longer invincible?"

"That was it? You risked your own life to annoy Akira? To amuse yourself?"

"That's putting it rather simplistically. But I suppose, in

essence, that's exactly what I wanted to do. It was lucky I found that snake in my bed or Akira would have had the last laugh after all."

I stared at his face, shadowed and illuminated by turns as we passed the flickering street lights. I started to laugh. Softly at first, and then so loudly I couldn't stop.

"What's so funny?" Christian sounded hurt.

I put my hand on my breastbone and patted the laughter down. "You are," I said simply. "You're just an over-grown schoolboy, looking to play a joke on the world."

"Am I?" He smiled with me, but for a second, I thought there was no amusement in his expression at all.

TWENTY-ONE

I do not know how
The gods' minds work. Some days I
Don't know my own mind

I was back home very early. I slipped in through the entrance hall, my cloak firmly in place over my male togs, and called a quick "good night" to the hall porter. Christian always left my bulky cloak at a house he insisted belonged to a "friend." I was amazed that it hadn't been taken to the nearest pawn shop and exchanged for a few shillings, the friend's lodgings were so tumble-down. Christian grinned when I pointed this out to him and then shrugged.

"They know better than that," he said and would say no more on the subject. It was always there, waiting, so I stopped worrying about it.

I changed quickly, laying my clothes in the drawer and tucking an old sheet carefully on top of them. I glanced at the clock, trying to calculate how long Callum would be. It would, I supposed, depend on how the game went. If he were on a losing streak, he would be home very soon, his budget limit reached quickly. If he was winning a little, losing a little, he could be hours. I had explained his gambling habits to Christian, and he had sat in stunned silence as he examined what was obviously an idea that was entirely foreign to him.

"You mean, he actually sets himself limits? And sticks to them?"

"Rigidly," I assured him. "Why? What's wrong with that?"

"He must be the only gambling man in London who can do it," he said. "I wouldn't have known. He's only won every time I've played with him. He really is an excellent card player. I sometimes think he can read the way the dice are going to fall as well."

"Perhaps he's just lucky," I said cheerfully. Lucky Cal, why not?

"No. No, it's far more than luck." Christian tapped his finger on his teeth. The sound irritated me, and I was delighted when he stopped. "I think it's because he's not a true gambler. Oh, I know he enjoys a game of chance. But he's too cool, too calculating. The rest of us, if we were on a winning streak, we would go on until our luck turned and the house won most—if not all—of it back. But Callum doesn't do that. He wins so much, and then simply stops."

"That's right," I agreed. "He told me he sets a limit on winnings as well as losses."

"Does he?" Christian closed his eyes, as if analyzing something strange beyond belief. "Perhaps I should try it sometime," he added drily.

I laughed and changed the subject. Somehow, I didn't like talking about Callum when I was out on the town with Christian.

I changed into a light, muslin dressing gown as soon as I had hidden my clothes and had fallen asleep, curled up in the armchair, by the time Callum came in.

"Sorry, Tara-chan." I sat up and blinked at him, trying to adjust my eyes to the flare of the gaslight. "I didn't know you were still up."

He stood in front of me, grinning happily. I sniffed; as always when he had been at White's or Boodle's, he reeked of cigars and booze.

"You stink," I told him severely.

"I shall have a bath. At once," he said meekly. But he didn't move. He just stood in front of me, smiling. He was pleased about something. It radiated off him in waves.

"What? Tell me!" I demanded.

Instead of answering, he leaned forward and dug his hands in his overcoat pockets. He held out his bulging fists and dropped their contents on me. Gold Victoria coins showered into my lap and pinged onto the floor. He put his hands back in his pockets and pulled out more. He did it again and then stood back, looking at me like a delighted child.

"Callum! You won all this?" He nodded. "What happened to you setting limits for yourself?"

I was shocked. Glancing at the piles of coins, I thought there must be hundreds of pounds rolling about on my lap and on the floor. I picked one up and examined it curiously. The coin was newly minted and glowed softly in my fingers. It was still warm from his pocket. There was, I reckoned, enough here to buy a townhouse in the best part of London, with enough left over for a modest carriage and pair of horses. I was torn between delight at the sight of so much money and worry that he had thrown aside his principles to win it.

"I'm sorry, Tara-chan." He spoke sheepishly, and I had to laugh at him. Was he the only man on earth who could feel truly sorry for covering his wife in gold? I rather thought he was. "It was all won fair and square."

He hunkered down at my side and put his head on the arm of my chair, tilted up so he could watch my face.

"Tell!" I said again, but smiling this time.

"I was nearly at my limit." His eyes were shining and I stroked his hair softly. "I was about to get up from the table when Sergeant—you've met him, I think?" I nodded, not wanting to interrupt his flow. I had met Sir Andrew several times and wasn't at all sure I liked him. His florid, beefy face did little to hide his equally unlovely personality. He leered at me whenever he thought Callum wasn't looking. "Well, he had been having the worst run of luck ever. He's a good player generally. It was odd. Anyway, he was also a bit worse for drink and insisted, very loudly, that I had to give him a chance to win his money back. Double or nothing on the next game, he said. I didn't want to cause any ill feeling, so I agreed."

"And you won," I interrupted.

"That I did. I had hoped that would be an end to it, but Sergeant grumbled and swore and it eventually became obvious that he thought I had been cheating."

"At White's!" Even I knew this was unthinkable. All the members were gentlemen. If someone were found cheating, he would be drummed out of the club. Not only that, but his social life in London would end forever. He would be shunned everywhere.

"I know." Callum shrugged. "Everybody around the table tried to shut him up, and I realized he was far drunker than I had thought. Even then, I was about to bow out gracefully, but he was having none of it. 'Another hand,' he said. 'And may the best man win.'"

"And you did."

"I certainly did." Callum's face broke into a huge grin. "I called for a new deck of cards and got Sergeant to shuffle them. I even asked a couple of the chaps to stand behind me to keep watch. If Sergeant had been a trifle less drunk, he would have apologized and we would all have shrugged it off. He so obviously thought I was a card sharp, he was insulting. But he didn't want to call it a night, so we carried on, with him watching me like a hawk. And I still won."

"And then you decided to stop," I said as severely as I could.

Callum nodded. "I did. And it's not going to happen again, I assure you. Would you like to come to bed now? I rather feel I deserve a little something rewarding after such an interesting evening."

He rose and stretched and then bent down quickly, hoisting me in his arms and raising me from my bed of gold. I felt absurdly guilty. Here was Callum apologizing to me for winning vast amounts of money, for showering me with gold, when I had spent the evening with Christian, racketing about the worst slums of London. I thought about Jack, deceiving his poor, innocent wife in the nastiest way possible, and Christian stealing his belongings. It had all seemed such a joke at the time, but now I disliked myself intensely. It was I who should be apologizing to Callum! I knew as soon as the thought came to me that tonight would be the last time. I would throw my male togs away the first chance I got. And I would tell Christian that, as soon as I saw him again.

"Are you really angry with me?" Callum murmured the

words into my neck and my remorse constricted until it felt like a tight belt around my gut.

"No, of course I'm not," I said quickly.

"Good. In that case, would madam like to come to bed? Or shall I lay you down on my riches again?"

"Bed," I said promptly. And I added as seriously as I could manage, "Lying on a bed of gold is lovely, but just a little hard!"

We giggled our way into the bedroom. I was suddenly sure I had left the dressing drawer containing my men's clothes ajar and I glanced at it anxiously. It was no more than my guilty conscience as I found it firmly shut. Callum kicked the door closed with his foot and then laughed softly.

"Silly, isn't it? I hardly expect anybody is going to burst in on us, but still I close the door!"

"Burglars?" I suggested. "After your ill-gotten gains?"

"As long as they don't disturb us, they're welcome to it all. I have everything I could ever want or need in this room."

Such sweet words. I didn't get the chance to respond. Callum had reached our bed and rather than lowering me gently, he threw me down on it. I bounced and gasped with mock outrage.

"Now, my beauty. Your master is home. I trust my welcome will be a warm one?"

The popping gaslight threw shadows on his face. For an odd moment, I saw Callum as the world saw him. The scar across his eye gave him a rakish look. That, together with his black hair and blue eyes, made him look more like a gypsy than the gentleman he was. Lucky Cal, I thought breathlessly. Lucky me!

"Why doesn't my master come here beside me and find out?"

Callum threw his head back and pretended to howl like a wolf. Then, very slowly and very deliberately, he unbuttoned his coat and threw it off. The dramatic gesture was spoiled when he got his arm tangled in the sleeve and had to fight with it for a moment. I giggled and he looked enraged.

"Laugh at me, would you, woman? We'll soon see about that!"

He tugged at his shirt and the buttons popped open. His trousers caused him yet more problems; this evening, Callum and buttons obviously were not a match. Fortunately, his silk drawers fastened only with laces at the waist. He yanked them off triumphantly and then hopped around on one leg, trying to kick them off. It was the final straw for me. I started laughing and couldn't stop. Callum stood at the side of the bed, his face injured, his tree of flesh rearing free and proud at me.

"Oh, come here!" I gasped between laughs and reached for his tree to pull him toward me.

"Careful, woman! It's not a handle, you know. Tug too hard and it might come off!"

"Really?" I gave his tree a firm heave. Callum tottered and pretended to lose his balance, falling onto the bed. "It seems to be fairly well joined on to me."

"Keep trying." His voice was hoarse and deep. "I would like to be sure it's not going to come off in your hand."

I smiled at him and lowered my head. My lips nibbled down his chest, pausing to nip and pluck at his nipples. I felt him draw breath; I knew how much I liked this when Callum did it to me. It never failed to delight me when I found it had the same effect on him. At the same time, I rubbed his tree gently, pausing to run my finger over the naked head.

"Ah! Tara. Please."

"Please what?" I asked innocently.

"Please. Harder." Callum's voice had sunk to a rasp. Instead of doing as he asked, I slowed my hand and made my fingers very gentle.

"All in good time," I said softly. I raised my head from where it had reached to his belly and leaned forward to kiss him. Immediately, Callum shoved his hand at the back of my head and forced my mouth hard against his lips. His stubble prickled my skin lusciously. He had been drinking whisky at some point in the evening. I could taste its echo as he slid his tongue in my mouth and began to explore me. At the same time, his free hand loosed the belt on my dressing gown, pushing the thin material to each side of my body. His fingers slid to my breast and grasped it firmly.

"A perfect fit for my hand." He barely took his lips from my mouth to speak, and his voice vibrated in my head. I felt the slow tide of desire begin to build in my body.

"And I wonder what else might be a perfect fit?" I whispered.

Callum didn't answer. Instead, his hand left my breast and roved down past my belly. He flirted with my belly button for a second, scratching it roughly with his nail, and moved on quickly. His fingers found my black moss and began to stroke it, circling gently, almost as if he was caressing a beloved animal. I waited without moving.

"Yes?" Callum raised his head to stare at me. His pupils were huge, so large that his blue eyes appeared almost black. I had no breath to answer him with. The best I could manage was the slightest of nods.

He slid over me, propping himself on his arms. I could

feel his tree nuzzling at the entrance to my sex. With a huge effort, I kept entirely still. Suddenly, I wanted to be spoiled. I wanted Callum to make all the effort, to arouse me and satisfy me without me so much as lifting a finger. I found the idea intensely exciting.

I smiled at him, widening my eyes. I guessed he understood when he smiled back at me.

Very, very slowly, he moved down toward me until his tree brushed my black moss. Callum paused and then— equally slowly—he began to move back up. But this time, the very tip of his tree parted my black moss and rubbed with the gentleness of a breeze against my slippery flesh. I sighed with pleasure and closed my eyes, relaxing happily. For a moment, at least. Then the sweet sensation of his tree rubbing against the lips of my sex changed completely. It became rougher, harder.

"Callum?" I asked.

"Lie still," he whispered. "I promise, this will be good for you."

Something continued to rasp at my sex. I wriggled, trying to make sense of the sensation. It was far from uncomfortable. In fact, it was completely arousing. I wriggled again and something tugged beneath me. I knew at once what Callum was doing. He had taken the delicate material of my dressing gown and folded it into my body. Now, his tree was rubbing it against me. Back and forth. Back and forth. Soft, then hard. It didn't tickle exactly, but it did rouse my tender flesh to a point where I felt I could not bear it for a second longer without screaming with pleasure.

"Do you like that?" His voice vibrated in my ear. "Tell me or I'll stop."

He slowed down, and I spoke immediately.

"Yes. Yes, I like it."

As if he had been waiting, containing himself until he heard my words, Callum drew back very slightly. The pleasing pressure ceased and I moaned out loud with disappointment. But the pause was momentary. Callum sashayed his hips and I felt his tree find my entrance. But strangely, he did not slide into me with his usual fluid ease. He moved slowly. His tree felt different as well. Rough, as if it were wearing gloves. I was bewildered, and then understood that he had wrapped himself in my dressing gown. He was not only pushing his tree inside me, he was pushing the fine muslin of my gown as well.

It scraped, very slightly. As soon as the cloth entered me, it became wet with my juices. Less rough, and at the same time more clinging. I caught my breath, analyzing the new sensation. Callum began to speed up. My tender flesh shivered with pleasure at this strange invasion of my body. I heard a high pitched noise and it took me a moment to realize that it was I who was moaning with intense, complete pleasure.

I tensed my internal muscles as hard as I could, forcing Callum to slow to my rhythm. I let go a fraction, and then tensed again when I heard him grunt. First slow, then fast. Before long, I could wait no longer and threw my legs around his waist, forcing him—and my sodden robe—as far into me as I could suck him. My *yonaki* uncurled deep in my belly, a seething flow of heat that consumed me. I had time to wonder for the smallest part of a moment if Callum could feel my orgasm, and then I knew he could as he released his seed inside me. Our joint heat was too much. I moaned until I had no breath left.

When I felt that the sweetness of Callum's *kenjataimu*

was upon him, I laid my arm over his chest and held him very tightly.

"Thank you," I said softly.

"What for?"

"Everything," I said. And I meant it.

TWENTY-TWO

If you are a world
Away from me, do you gaze
Upon the same moon?

"You don't really mean our games are over, do you? It was only a bit of fun. Nothing Callum would worry about greatly, even if he knew."

Christian looked so hurt, I almost regretted my decision. Then I thought of his use of the word "greatly" and knew I was right.

"I'm sorry, Christian. It has been fun. But no more. That last time was too close for comfort."

He pouted and dug his toe in the rug, ruffling it up. "Callum not here, then?" He glanced around the drawing room as if Callum might suddenly appear out of thin air.

"No. He's gone to see the lawyer again. It looks as if things are beginning to move on his land dispute, finally."

"Oh. I wanted a word with him. With both of you, actually. But you can tell him for me." I looked at him suspiciously. Christian's face was the picture of innocence, but—perhaps because of that—I didn't trust him.

"Tell him what?"

"I'm leaving." He spoke so casually, it took a moment for his words to sink in. "That's what I came to tell you both. I've had enough of London. I'm thinking of going to Vienna, try my luck there."

"Why?" I spoke from the heart. "Christian, you're not in trouble, are you?"

"Who, me?" Again, that too-good-to-believe innocence. I looked at him suspiciously.

"Money? Or somebody's wife?" I asked bluntly.

"Neither." Christian laughed. "I would say I have enough money, but that wouldn't be true. It's downright impossible to have enough. And nobody is searching the streets of London with a pistol in his hand out to avenge his honor. I promise!"

"Why are you going, then?"

His expression clouded for a second and then he shrugged and smiled. "Oh, you know me. I get bored staying in the same place. But never mind that. Are you sure you won't reconsider? I had something planned, a little outing for both of us. You might call it a going away present."

I would miss him. I thought Callum would too.

"Oh. Well, if you put it like that. One last time, and then I give my male togs to the rag and bone man."

"Wonderful!" Christian sounded genuinely pleased, and I was touched. We both looked up as the door opened. "Ah, Callum. Just the man I was looking for."

Callum's face fell when he heard Christian's news.

"You're sure, Mountjoy? If it's a question of money, you know I would be happy to lend you some."

"You might as well say 'give,' old man, and have done with it. You know damn well I would never pay you back. But it's not money. I've already told Tara that. I'm just a gypsy by nature, and I feel it's time I moved on."

We were all silent for a moment. Before things could become uncomfortable, Callum spoke cheerfully.

"Well, I have some good news. It appears that our legal problem has been resolved."

"Wonderful!" I spoke from the heart. "Did your da's letter do the trick?"

Callum was grinning widely. He shook his head.

"Not at all. It appears that Smythe has taken on a trainee attorney. To give him a taste of what he could expect, he gave him all the documentation on our case and told him to read it through. The new man did that, and then pointed out the one thing we had all missed. No money had ever changed hands. Uncle, bless him, never thought to ask for a deposit on the deal. And even though he thought it was a lease agreement, no payments were ever made."

I looked at Christian in confusion. He shrugged and we both stared at Callum enquiringly.

"So?" I asked finally. "What difference does that make?"

"I had no idea either," Callum admitted. "But Smythe explained to me that under English law, there has to be something called 'consideration' for a contract to be valid. In this case, as no money had been paid at all, there was no consideration. And that means the contract isn't valid. Literally not worth the paper it's written on."

I stared at him in disbelief. After all this time, the answer had been there all along!

"You're sure?" I asked.

Callum nodded. "Quite sure. Smythe has a written

agreement from the other side. It's settled. We can go home, Tara. At last."

Home! The word sang in my ears like the sound of hope. I glanced at the window. In spite of the fact that the calendar said it was June, there was no sunlight outside. A dense, stinking, yellow fog pressed against the panes. The "London Peculiar" I had begun to almost take for granted. Suddenly, I longed for the clean air and sweet scents of Kyle. To have grass and heather beneath my feet. Room to walk without being jostled and pushed from all sides.

"At last," I repeated softly.

"See? You're not even going to be here to miss me!" Christian said cheerfully, breaking the enchantment abruptly. "Well, I'm on my way. See you at Seagram's soiree tomorrow?"

Callum nodded. "I'll be there. If only to make sure you don't cheat, Mountjoy!"

I walked Christian to the door. As I opened it for him, he leaned forward and spoke quickly and quietly.

"I'll send a message to Seagram to say I've been detained elsewhere. I'll come and get you at eight. One last fling, my dear!"

Before I could agree or disagree, he had gone, closing the door behind him.

I shrugged to myself. What did it matter? Christian was going to Vienna. And we were going home! I felt it would be terribly mean-spirited to refuse Christian's plans when he had taken the trouble to arrange something that he had obviously planned as a parting gift. I wondered with a flash of excitement what he had in mind for us. A final trip to a music hall? Perhaps to see Max Marchant one last time? Ah well. It could do no harm. And knowing Christian, it would no doubt be extremely diverting. A last, fond memory of London for me to take back to Glen Kyle.

"*A*ll ready? Excellent. I do like to see a punctual woman."

Christian ran his eyes down my boy's clothes and grinned sardonically as he wrapped my cloak around me with a flourish. We walked out quietly, but I had no need to worry about attracting attention this evening. The hall was empty and I could hear voices from behind the baize door that separated the staff from the residents. I always thought of it as the marker between "them" and "us." I had knocked on that door once and opened it cautiously. Our maid had forgotten to leave us fresh towels, and rather than ring for her, as I was passing through the hall I thought I would ask for some to be sent up. My reception had been so incredulously icy that I wished I hadn't bothered. Wryly, I realized it wasn't just the so-called gentry who could be snobs!

Christian paused on the corner, looking for a cab.

"It's very warm this evening," he said. And indeed, it was. Warm and humid with a haze in the air rather than the normal yellow fog. I was beginning to perspire inside my thick cloak already. "Shall I take that off for you?" He slid the cloak off my shoulders and held it loosely over his arm. I breathed a sigh of relief.

"My, but don't you look lovely this evening, Tomo." I smiled at him uncertainly. His voice had an ironic tone that belayed his words. "There's just one thing missing, I think." He patted his pockets in an exaggerated display of looking for something he knew was there all along. "Ah. Here we are. Something beautiful to finish my best boy off."

He held a small, cardboard box in his hand. He flicked the lid off and I said "oh" in pleasure as he held it out for me to see. A corsage for my buttonhole. Two huge carnations, arranged one above the other as if they were still growing on the living plant. Both were ice white with a deep red hearts so dark it looked as if the flowers were bleeding. The stems were tightly wrapped in silver paper.

"Nice, aren't they?" Christian held the corsage up to my face so I could inhale the perfume. I took a deep breath and almost jerked back. The carnations smelled deliciously of spice and sweet blossoms, but beneath that perfume there was something else. A bitter, rather sour smell that seemed to me to bear the corruption of death, as if there was a canker in the living red heart of the blooms.

"Something wrong?" He held the flowers to his own face and sniffed quickly. "I thought you liked carnations?"

He sounded so hurt, I felt absurdly awkward. Perhaps it had been something in the street rather than the carnations that had smelled so wrong. He was holding the corsage out to me, so I took another sniff and smiled. It was the flowers, I was sure of it.

"They're lovely. Thank you."

Christian pushed the silver paper-wrapped stem expertly through the buttonhole in my lapel. It fitted so snugly, it might have been made for it.

"There. Now who's the dandy!"

He raised his hand for a passing cab, and we climbed in and sat down. I was grateful for that as I felt quite giddy and sick. The heat, I thought. I swallowed nausea and wondered if I should tell Christian that tonight's outing was not, after all, a good idea. That I felt ill and should go back to our apartment. But he had already given the cab driver our destination and he was looking so pleased with himself I did not have the heart to ask him to cancel whatever his plans were.

"I almost forgot. For tonight, ladies and gentlemen! For one night only!" I managed a smile at his strident impersonation of the music hall master of ceremonies. "We have something a little different. For you, madam! Or perhaps I should say, master!"

He produced something from his pocket. It glittered in the light and my eyes widened as I saw what it was. An eyeless carnival mask, black silk embossed with sequins.

"What on earth is that for?" I smiled uncertainly.

"For you, dear heart. I told you tonight was going to be very special, and it begins here."

He leaned forward and pushed the mask over my head, tying the laces tightly at the back. I was about to protest when I got another lungful of the scent from my corsage. The scent-beneath-the-scent seemed to be far more powerful in the closed cab and I was suddenly dizzy. The effort of telling Christian I didn't want to be blindfolded was far too much bother. I sat back and gave way to the rhythm of the carriage instead.

"Where are we going?" I asked lazily. "And why the mask?"

"We're going somewhere you're going to find intriguing. And the mask is all part of the fun."

I dozed, I think. In any event, it seemed to be no more than a moment or two before the cab drew to a halt. Christian leaned forward and undid my mask before he helped me out of the carriage. I noticed he still had my cloak folded over his arm and I wondered idly why we hadn't dropped it off at the usual place. Perhaps we were in a different part of London. I glanced around at my surroundings and I no longer wondered. I knew we were.

The cab clopped off briskly, leaving us standing in front of a smart, new villa. It stood alone behind a high-railed front entrance. The brickwork was stuccoed in light cream, the railings picked out in soft, dark grey. Money, I thought at once. And plenty of it.

"This is isn't what I expected!" I smiled at Christian.

"You may well be surprised, Tomo. Shall we say it's in the nature of amateur theatricals?"

He ushered me forward through the gate that swung open on silent, well-oiled hinges. There were four steps up to the front door. Not particularly steep steps, but my feet seemed to be oddly clumsy this evening and I was glad I had Christian to lean against.

"Thank you," I said seriously.

"You're most welcome," Christian replied, equally courteous. We could have been an old married couple, we were so polite! The thought made me chuckle.

Christian rapped briskly on the door. I gazed around me as we waited for an answer. The villa was very secluded. There was a substantial, well-tended garden on the three sides of it I could see, and then no houses at all for at least a hundred yards. I frowned; I had never encountered such solitude in London before and it puzzled me.

A shaft of light showed as the door opened a crack, and then it was thrown wide.

"Mr. Mountjoy. At last. We were beginning to despair of you. And this must be Tomo. Welcome."

Christian's hand was in the small of my back, urging me forward. I looked at him reproachfully; no need to push!

Once inside, I paused in a wide hall, staring around with frank interest. The room was arranged very much like the reception area of a good hotel. A number of deep, comfortable leather armchairs were clustered around a low table. There was even a desk with an open ledger on it. I glanced at the person who had opened the door to us. I had almost passed the figure by, I was so interested in my surroundings, when I glanced back at her.

She was very tall, at least a head higher than I was, almost as tall as Christian, and clad entirely in black silk that gleamed in the gaslight. She wore a skirt suit, beautifully tailored but cut in a very mannish fashion, more like a riding habit than anything. The bodice was tight, the skirt narrow. Her hair was scraped back in a chignon so severe that it seemed to stretch the skin on her face back with it. She smiled, and so tight was the chignon I wondered if it hurt her to move her lips. And she was so very slim. The suit fitted from her shoulder bones down to her hips, with not a bulge or a curve anywhere. Her body looked more like that of an adolescent girl than a grown woman.

"My name is Amy, Tomo. I'm sure we're going to be such good friends. Do come through, dear." Her voice was rather deep and very attractive. I smiled inanely, suddenly shy.

"You go on through." Christian nodded at me. "Amy will take very good care of you. I have a little business to attend to first."

I glanced back at Amy, and then when I turned around again, Christian had vanished. How very rude of him, I thought. Amy crooked her finger at me, beckoning me forward, and I moved automatically. I had no idea what was amusing Amy, but she smiled widely at me.

"Oh, such fun!" She grinned. "Do step this way. Mr. Soames has said he would like you to see a little of our business before he greets you personally."

Business? Mr. Soames? I was mildly puzzled. As the inner door opened, a draught blew the scent of my carnations toward my face and I inhaled deeply. They smelled lovely. Why on earth had I ever thought there was something rotten about their perfume? So delightful did I find it that I raised my lapel to my face and buried my nose in the blossoms, snuffling at them, as much to hide my confusion from Amy as because I had begun to like the smell.

"Now, Tomo dear. What do you think?"

Amy had slid her arm around my waist whilst I had been paying attention to my corsage. She tightened her grip and swiveled me around, at the same time waving her free hand in invitation. I stared. And blinked. And stared again.

The room was huge. So big, I could hardly make out the far wall. It was lit with mellow gas lamps, the flame turned perhaps half way down. I could not, I thought seriously, have read by such a light. But it was certainly enough for me to see what was going on around me. I stared and then gasped, remembering my manners and hiding my mouth behind my hand.

Was this Christian's twisted idea of a joke? Was he really so very angry with me at telling him our adventures were over that he was prepared to inflict this on me? The huge room was filled with figures. I started to count them, then got distracted and had to start all over again. Somebody yelped close to me, and I lost count yet again. Perhaps twenty people, I decided. Men and women, about equal figures of both. Strangely, none of the groups of people were paying any attention at all to their neighbors. Still less did they appear to notice Amy and me. They might as well have been alone and private they were so absorbed in each other.

"Well, dear? Do you like what you see?" Amy had ducked her head so her mouth was close to my ear. Her voice sounded like a cat purring, and it tickled me.

"I don't know," I muttered. "I'm not sure what I'm looking at."

Amy giggled, as though I had said something delightfully funny. "Come. I'll give you a little tour."

She tugged at my arm and moved a few paces into the room. She poked a horizontal body with her foot. When the man didn't respond, she kicked him hard in the small of his back. I winced for him; Amy's foot was shod in a sturdy boot. It must have hurt. I frowned at her reproachfully, but the man seemed not to mind at all.

"I'm sorry, mistress. So very sorry." He crawled toward her, pulling himself along the floor with his hands. I wondered for a moment why he didn't stand, or at least get to his knees, then I saw that his ankles were tightly roped together with cord. I followed the line of the cord absently, and then gawped as I saw it had been wrapped repeatedly around his *kintama* and drawn tight before being tied off in a complex knot. Every movement must have caused him acute pain. His tree appeared not to mind the outrage at all. It reared up like a broom handle and actually wagged as Amy reached down and tugged the cord viciously.

"I'm a naughty boy. Punish me!" the man screamed. A naughty boy? He must have been forty if he was a day. Amy kicked him under the chin and he rolled to his side, howling like a beaten dog.

"Later. Perhaps. If I can be bothered, and if you are very good."

Amy turned and smiled at me sweetly. "Edward really can be too boring. Shall we leave him and find something more amusing for you, sweetheart?"

Her voice was very warm, very concerned. My mind was spinning like a child's top, whipped into life with a piece of leather on a stick. I closed my eyes for a moment, and suddenly my memory fled away from me, back down the years.

When I was a child, Auntie had come to our village and taken me by the hand, just as Amy was doing now. She had led me away from my village, from my family. I had been terrified out of my wits then, but at the same time I had known that it was my duty to go with her. To do as I was told. But I had been just a young girl then. Now, I was a woman, with a will of my own. I no longer cared what Christian thought, whether I upset his joke. I would turn around and walk as quickly as I could out of this terrible room. I would find a cab eventually. Once home, I would take off my male togs and wrap them in a parcel that would go in the dustbin the first chance I got. I deeply regretted that it was so warm and I had no excuse to light a fire and burn them instantly.

Why, then, when Amy turned, tugging at my hand, did I follow her meekly? I willed my hand to tug itself from her grasp, told my feet to run. For all the good it did, my body might have belonged to someone else. Someone who could not even hear my thoughts.

"Now, what do you think of this?" Amy turned and smiled at me.

She had paused close to a trio of bodies. Two were men, sprawled on the floor and totally naked. I looked at their bodies critically and decided that they were not in the least attractive. In fact, they were downright repulsive. Both were late middle-aged and flabby. Veins were prominent on their calves, their hair—what there was of it—was plastered to their scalps with sweat. A woman stood over them, dressed in a tight, silken bodice that ended just below her hips. Her breasts threatened to spill out of the top. Her slender legs were encased in spangled tights. She smiled at Amy, who nodded.

I flinched back as the cat o' nine tails whip in her hand

sang through the air and left red streaks across one of the naked men's back. He hissed with pain and she immediately reached down and grabbed his hair, forcing his head back until I could hear his neck creak.

"Mercy. Mercy, mistress," he bleated.

"You disappoint me, William," she breathed softly. "You must, I think, do something to please me before I can forgive you."

His face was alight with anticipation. His eyes shone, his mouth drooping foolishly. The woman who had whipped him glanced at Amy, who nodded. The other man propped himself on his elbow, looking—not at his companion—but at the woman with the whip. She appeared to think for a moment, and then grinned widely.

"It seems to me that Frederick here is not quite as clean as one might wish. You, William. Take his pego in your mouth. Wash it thoroughly with your tongue. When you have done that, I want you to take his bollocks in your mouth and suck them until I am satisfied they are spotless. When you have done that, I may give you both a little treat."

William didn't hesitate. I felt nausea roll in my stomach as Frederick rolled quickly on his back, his arms and legs flung wide. Yet I could not tear my gaze away as I watched William lower his head and take his partner's tree of flesh in his mouth, sucking at it as hungrily as a babe at the breast. Presumably to encourage him, the woman who towered over them both lashed his buttocks hard with her whip. She rolled her eyes at Amy, who smiled back.

"Come, Tomo. We cannot waste any more time on these foolish creatures. Don't you find that men are intrinsically boring at heart? They have no originality. No spark of innovation."

We meandered onward. I tried to keep my eyes fixed on

Amy, but it was no good. My glance drifted from side to side, poking in the darkest corners. Some of the men were being beaten with whips and what looked like a dog lead. Some were in chains or tightly bound. My mouth dropped open as I saw one man suspended from the ceiling by chains that were wrapped around his chest. My eyes were drawn to the glint of metal at his breast and I saw that his nipples were pierced with thick rings. Thinner chains reached tautly from the rings to the chain he hung from. As I watched, a pretty, sweet-faced young woman spun him around and swatted at his hugely erect tree with a cane every time they faced each other. The chained man was gagged with a strip of rag, but he mewed every time a blow landed. His nipple rings strained with each movement. I stared in horror as I saw the reddened flesh of his aureoles tug and pucker. I was sure that the rings were going to tear through the sore flesh at any moment.

Amy glanced at me and smiled affectionately. "You are very quiet, dear."

I sensed she was laughing at me. I tried to yank my hand from her grip, but yet again my body ignored my instructions. A recollection came to me, unbidden and unwanted, of a soldier in the field hospital where I had nursed at Scutari. He had been injured by a bullet that had severed his spine. Generally polite and cheerful, one day I had found him with tears running down his face.

"I'm sorry, nurse," he had said brusquely, rubbing the tears from his cheeks fiercely. "I hope you don't think any the worse of me. I'm just a bit down today, like."

I had perched on the bed at the side of him and spoke anxiously. He was an excellent patient, and I liked him.

"What is it? Are you in pain? I could bring you some laudanum."

"Would it? I don't think so, miss." He screwed his eyes up bitterly. "I ain't got no pain. I wish I bleeding well did. If I had pain, I would know me legs were still there. But I can't feel nothing at all below me waist. I keep telling me legs to shift. To get a move on. But it don't matter what me brain says, they don't listen to me."

I straightened his bed and chatted to him until he was his usual cheerful self again. At the time, I had felt just a little disapproving that he was wishing pain on himself when I had to deal with men who were screaming in agony. Men who wanted nothing more than for the pain to go away. Now, I understood. Now, I would have given a year of my life to have my own body obey me, even if I felt pain. But it would not.

"I do hope you're not feeling sorry for these foolish creatures." Amy stared around contemptuously. "Each and every one of them pay vast sums to be allowed through our doors, you know. The more we inflict pain on them, the happier they are to come back to us, time after time. I have known rich men run through a fortune here. And then, when the money is all gone and their own families are reduced to nothing, they come back and try to persuade us to take them in for nothing. As if we are some sort of charity."

I swallowed dryly. Something fastened round my ankle. I stared down and saw that a man was slumped at my feet. He was so terribly emaciated, I wondered if he was starving. Amy sneered at him, her lip curling in disgust. It was his hand that was grasped around my ankle. As I watched him, he inched his head toward me and his lips parted far enough to allow him to lick my shoe, pausing after a moment to look longingly up at my face. I thought my lack of response must have distressed him as fat tears began to run down his cheeks. Then his mouth parted, showing dirty, yellow teeth and his tongue stuck out and wagged at me lewdly.

My mind screamed at me to pull away, to take myself as far from this loathsome creature as it was possible to get. Yet I was transfixed and unable to move. Amy had no such problem. She stomped on my tormentor's hand with as much compunction as a gardener might show in crushing a slug with his shoe. She ground the sole of her boot against his bones until he howled and rolled away, his injured hand fixed beneath his armpit.

"Take no notice," she said soothingly. "Come along. Just past the table and we'll be through into Soames' private quarters."

Part of my mind thanked all the gods for that. Another part began to wonder who Soames was. And far more urgently, what had happened to Christian? He could not have known what a dreadful place he had condemned me to. I rolled my eyes around the room—my neck stubbornly refused to turn—just to check that he had not been captured and strung up like the rest of the men in here. I could not see him, and I was grateful for that. Surely, if he had managed to slip out unseen, he would be back to rescue me, and soon. With a few large men, with even larger fists. Or even policemen. I flushed with shame at the thought that Callum would surely find out if the police were to be involved, but anything was better than staying here a moment longer than necessary.

"Ah. Just a moment. This might amuse you."

Amy paused and I had no option but to stop with her. I was like a bunraku puppet, only possessing life when the puppet master moved my body at her command. What was the matter with me? Terror and confusion rose in a lump in my throat and I thought it was going to choke me. I managed to clear my throat, but the effort was terrifyingly huge. I tried to speak, and found I could not.

"Madam." A pretty girl was standing by the table. She stood rigidly to attention as Amy approached her.

"The dice, please." Amy held out her hand and the girl quickly placed a pair of ivory dice in her palm. She turned to me and reached for my hand, holding it out, palm up. "There, Tomo. Time you took something of an active part in our little amusement. Close your hand," she said crisply. "Turn it over and throw the dice on the table."

Why was it I could move when she instructed me to do so? I tried so very hard to defy her, to keep my hand closed, but my treacherous body was having none of it. I opened my hand and threw the dice on the table.

"Double six!" Amy sounded deeply approving. "Who's a lucky boy, then?"

Both women turned to stare at the other side of the table. Amy twitched the thick baize that draped to floor level aside and I saw a naked man, bent over the sort of low wooden bench that might be found in a school. The pretty woman reached under the table and produced a long, whippy cane. Almost casually, she moved over to the man and raised the cane above her shoulders before swishing it down viciously over his bare buttocks. Instantly, a red line appeared on his flesh. By the time she had swung the cane three times more, the lines were oozing blood. He did not appear to be restrained in any way, and I watched bewildered, wondering why he did not get up and run away. Until the last few lashes, he didn't even make any noise. It was only then that he moaned and arched his back and writhed.

"Thank my friend Tomo nicely for allowing you so much punishment," Amy instructed.

The man rolled off the bench onto his stomach and hunched across the floor, the movement looking like the progress of some obscenely elongated caterpillar. He stopped just short of my feet and spoke with his head thrust into the floor.

"Thank you, Tomo. Thank you," he whispered huskily. I bit my tongue, hard, as I saw he had left a trail of his own blood behind him.

"Come along, Tomo. Ignore that wretch. It wouldn't do to keep Soames waiting." Amy took my arm and tugged me forward toward a plain oak door. "I wonder if I might be able to persuade him to leave you with me for a while. It would be such fun!"

The door was perfectly plain. It had neither a handle nor a doorknob. Amy placed her fingers in the exact center of one of the panels and made a curious turning motion. The door swung open at once and she stood back, pushing me through in front of her.

"Ah. At last. What has Amy being thinking of, keeping you all this time? Welcome, Lady Kyle. A thousand times welcome."

TWENTY-THREE

The lightest fruit may
Break a bough that hangs proud on
A very great tree

"*P*lease, do sit down."

He indicated a padded, leather chair at his side. Just as my body obeyed Amy's every command, it seemed I also had to do as this man told me. I perched on the edge of the chair. My breath fluttered in my throat. Was my nightmare finally about to end? Was Christian going to pop out from somewhere and laugh at me for taking this romp seriously? My heart assured me it would be so even as my brain told me to be careful. Very careful.

"Shall I pour some wine?" Amy asked the man. He shook his head.

"No." I noticed his answer was abrupt, with no courtesy. Amy pouted and he inclined his head in her direction. "You may go now."

She walked away with only the tiniest of glances in my

direction. Suddenly, I wished she would stay. At least Amy was a known quantity, and it was obvious that she liked me. I was instinctively afraid of this unknown man.

"Dear Lady Kyle, I have waited such a long time for this evening. And now the time has arrived at last!" He steepled his fingers under his chin and smiled at me. "Now, I daresay you have many questions for me. Where would you like to begin?"

It was as if he had freed a gag from my tongue. Words poured out from my lips.

"Who are you? Where's Christian? What is this place? Where am I? I want to go home. Now." I stopped, panting slightly from the flood of words.

He inclined his head courteously and put his hand up, palm out. Instantly, I was dumb again. If I could have made a noise, I would have screamed in frustration.

"Just as I thought. There is, of course, much you wish to know. Now, as to who I am. My name is Soames. You may call me that, or you may address me as Mr. Soames. I am amenable to either. This place is a palace of pleasure for men who have far more money than is good for them. There's no point in telling you where you are, it's irrelevant. And Christian? I assume you mean Mr. Mountjoy?" I nodded. "Ah. By now, I imagine Mountjoy will be well on his way out of London." He made an elaborate show of consulting the watch that hung from his Albert chain. "I seem to recall him telling me that he was catching the 8:45 train down to Southampton. From there, he intends to take the ferry to France, eventually to make his way to Vienna. Why Vienna, I have no idea. I would have thought it a little too quiet for Mountjoy, but he clearly believes otherwise."

My lips stumbled over the questions that filled my

mouth. At that moment, only one thing seemed important. Christian had left me here? Run away and abandoned me in this terrible place?

"Why?" I said faintly. "Why has he gone? Without me?"

"Don't you understand yet?" Soames gave an almost fatherly smile. "He brought you here with the express purpose of leaving you with me. I gave him a great deal of money for the pleasure, I assure you. And I am delighted to see that it was money well spent."

My heart chilled. I understood now. Christian had abandoned me and run away. I had been kidnapped and was being held for ransom. Oh, Callum! I was so very sorry! I wanted to weep, but even that small solace was denied to me.

"My husband will pay you whatever you ask," I said stiffly. "He'll raise the money somehow to meet your price." I thought of lying on Callum's bed of gold and wanted to cry. How could I have done this to Callum? I was stupid and selfish.

Soames pursed his lips. I stared at him, trying to commit his features to memory. Callum would pay for my return, of course. But anything I could do to help him find this creature afterward and get his revenge, I would also do. He was clean-shaven. Brown hair, worn rather long and brushed back from his face. Age? Perhaps mid-forties. An easy face to disguise. But he would never be able to disguise his voice. It was deep and resonant. Deeply attractive. An opera singer's voice.

"Ah. I think, dear Lady Kyle, that you still do not quite understand. There is no question of a ransom. You are never going to see your husband again. In fact, once the first frenzy of activity of looking for you has died down and I can get you out of London safely, I doubt you will ever see

England again. I have a customer waiting for you, my dear. A very particular Parisian gentleman who has waited a long time for a woman who exactly fits his very discerning requirements. And now you are here, at last! What fun!" He clapped his hands with glee. Suddenly, his face became serious. "Much as I would love to get double the money for you, I don't think it would be at all wise."

"Callum will pay you," I repeated. Panic resonated in my voice and I took a deep breath to try and control it. "As long as I get back to him safely, he'll pay you."

"My dear Lady Kyle." Soames sounded deeply amused. "I had thought of a ransom, of course. A little more money —and easy money at that—is always most welcome. But then I changed my mind. I have heard a great deal about your husband's exploits in the Crimea. I understand he has a reputation as a gentleman of honor. One who will never give up if he considers the cause to be a just one. And what greater cause than having his beloved wife returned to him?"

I felt physically sick. I closed my eyes, torn between disbelief at my own stupidity and the pressing need to hold my nausea down. Not that I wouldn't have been happy to vomit all over Soames' beautiful furniture; I would. But I guessed in my present state my body would refuse to follow the most basic of instincts, and I thought that it might be only too likely that I could choke to death on my own bile. I swallowed and took a deep breath, speaking as calmly as I could.

"If Callum thinks I've just disappeared, he'll never rest until he finds me. You've made a terrible mistake, I promise you."

"What a clever girl you are! And such trust in your dear husband. But unfortunately, you don't know the whole story. When Lord Kyle comes home from his club, he will find a letter from you waiting for him. It will say that you could not face the boredom of returning to Glen Kyle. That becoming acquainted with Mountjoy again had made you long for the pleasures of the world you renounced. To cut it short, he will learn that you have decided to follow Mountjoy on his jaunts through Europe. You will help him live off his wits, etcetera, etcetera. I have many experts in my employ and one of them is a most expert forger who finds it easy to copy anybody's handwriting. I found myself in the fortunate position of having a note that you sent to Lady Margrave, excusing yourself from attending her rout. He assured me it contained enough to make the job an easy one."

Anger swelled and began to take the place of terror. Christian had done this to me. And to Callum. He had sold me. And I had thought he was our friend!

"Let me go," I said, and I was surprised by how calm I sounded. "You will regret it if you try and sell me. I promise you, your customer will not be happy with me. I'll make sure of that."

"Oh, but he will! I doubt there is another woman who is such a perfect match for his needs." Soames lifted his hands and began to tick points off on his fingers as he spoke. "Alain demanded a geisha. He has heard much of Japanese culture and is mad for it. Not just any geisha, however. He demanded a beautiful, cultured woman. Also, one who spoke perfect English. He himself is proud of his grasp of the English language. And this particular woman had to have one more quality. A unique one. She had to be able to play the part of both mistress and master, depending on his whim." I felt the blood leave my face as I understood. I glanced down at my shirt and trousers. If I had been able to,

I would have torn them off my body. Oh, Christian! What have you done to me? "You see, finally? I had virtually despaired of finding this ideal creature when dear Max Marchant whispered to me about an enchanting Japanese lady that Mountjoy had introduced to her, and how odd it was that a few weeks later she appeared to have become a he. I guessed Mountjoy's real purpose in showing you off to the guttersnipes of the East End was to attract my interest. Mountjoy is as trustworthy as a serpent. He is also a very old friend of mine. It took no time at all to persuade him to bring you to me."

"Bastard," I whispered. Soames raised his eyebrows and I wondered cynically if he thought I was talking about him or Christian.

"Good lord, such language from a lady! But then, you're not just any lady, are you? I've watched you, you know. I've seen you in the Alhambra and the Royal Opera House. Watched you conceal your boredom at fashionable soirees —and very well you did it, too. Have you ever thought of becoming an actress?—where I was a fellow guest of the great and the good. And I saw you help Mountjoy rob the poor fool who thought he was going to bugger you down an alleyway."

My lips moved, but no sound came out. I felt the last glimmer of hope curl and die in my heart. How long had Soames been watching me, waiting to pounce? And how could I never have noticed him? Finally, I managed to speak.

"Who are you?" I asked.

"Such perceptiveness! The ultimate question, of course. Any other woman would have continued to bleat on about how I would never get away with it. But you know I already have, don't you? As to who am I? Well, I think I may say without bragging that I am the greatest criminal mind in London. The police think me at least a dozen different people. I have stolen jewels from the necks of old and ugly women. Relieved banks of their hoarded gold. Blackmailed men without number, mainly those idiots who have enjoyed my hospitality here in my palace of pleasure and pain. And—I freely admit—kidnapped the odd heir to vast fortunes. Now, I know your next question! Why do I do it?"

He leaned forward and smiled warmly at me. I answered him at once.

"You do it because you can. Because it amuses you to get away with it. I suppose the money helps, but that's only a small part of it."

I had surprised him, I was bitterly pleased to see. The smile slipped for a moment, and I saw the utter coldness beneath.

"What a clever girl you are. I'm almost persuaded to keep you here for my own amusement. But no. A promise is a promise. You shall go to Paris to live a life of luxury as a pampered slave. A bird in a gilded cage."

His smile was back in place. A lock of hair fell over my face and I tried—and failed—to raise my hand to push it away. I thought of his words and almost smiled to myself. A slave? I had been a slave. I would not be a slave again. I knew that without any doubt at all. I glanced at his face and saw the tiniest flicker of—what? Doubt? Surprise? I changed the subject instinctively.

"What have you done to me?" I asked.

"I? I have done nothing at all to you. Mountjoy, though. Perhaps if we rephrased the question and asked what has he done to you, we might come to an answer."

He was watching me very carefully. I schooled my face

to remain passive and I saw yet again that glimmer of worry in his eyes.

"It was the flowers, wasn't it? My corsage." I glanced down at the carnations, so beautiful, so innocent, that Christian had fixed in my lapel. "I knew they smelled odd."

"Bravo!" Soames patted his hands together in exaggerated applause. "What a clever girl you are. I must take credit for a little of the deception. The liquid that Mountjoy poured on them is of my own devising. I have found it to be tremendously effective in subduing the most difficult of subjects. It allows the body to function, yet the mind to be bent entirely to the will of those around you. Far superior to chloroform, or anything else known to medical science."

He was preening, actually expecting me to be awed by his cleverness! I stared at him and he pouted sulkily.

"Ah, well. I suppose I could hardly expect you to find it amusing. Now, I think it is time you went to bed."

I had kept my head averted from my buttonhole while he was speaking, and tried to breathe as shallowly as I could. As Soames stood and walked toward me, I tensed away from him and I realized with a thrill of excitement that I had had actually been able to move of my own accord. I waited until he was bending over me, then jerked my head into his face as hard as I possibly could. My head was spinning with the pain of the blow, but I took a vicious satisfaction in seeing Soames reeling back, blood running from his nose.

I took my chance. I jerked to my feet and staggered toward the door as fast as I could move. My vision was swimming and my legs felt as if they had atrophied, but still I forced myself to lurch forward. But Soames was far quicker. His hands were around my waist before I could touch the door. He held me tightly, forcing my arms against my sides. I tried to kick him, and knew I had connected when I heard him shout angrily.

"You little bitch!" He breathed into my neck. I twisted my head and tried to bite his face. The last words I heard as I felt a violent pain at the back of my head were, "Such fun!"

TWENTY-FOUR

When the young moon is
Old, will you come to my own
Door and speak of love?

*W*hat a lovely day! It was the first time in all
the months we had spent in London that I
could remember the morning sun streaming through our
window. Normally, the best that I could hope to wake up to
was a thin, grey gloom that sunlight found it almost impossible to pierce. I was languid, and the bed was very comfortable. I could not feel Callum at my side and wondered if he
had risen early, enticed by the wonderful day outside.

I should, without any doubt, rouse myself and join him.
I yawned and tried to stretch and shook my head in confusion when I found that both my legs and arms were inca-
pable of being moved more than a few inches. I lifted my
head from the pillow and the movement triggered a
pounding headache, bad enough to make me groan out
loud. I flopped back on the bed and closed my eyes. I was
sure I could smell cigar smoke, but thought I must be

mistaken. Callum did not smoke. Was it a lingering odor from his clothes, left from last night's card game?

"You're awake at last. Come on, get some breakfast. I'll help you."

A woman's voice. I kept my eyes closed and the breath caught in my throat as my mind awoke fully and I remembered the final hours of last night before I had gone to sleep. But I hadn't just gone to sleep, had I? Soames had punched me hard enough on the back of my head to knock me unconscious. That was why I had such a terrible headache now. I felt so miserable, for a moment I wished he had hit me so hard I had never woken up. Oh, Callum! I was so very, very sorry. How did I come to be so foolish as to do this? Would he forgive me? For that matter, would I ever get the chance to ask for forgiveness? I stretched my eyes wide to force tears back.

"Come on, up with you. The coffee's getting cold."

Amy placed her long, thin cigar carefully on the edge of a dish full of potpourri on a bedside table.

"I don't want anything," I said pettishly. "Go away and leave me alone."

"If I were you I would eat and drink." Amy poured steaming coffee and held the cup close enough for me to smell the enticing aroma. "Come on, I'll help you sit up."

I wrenched my head to one side and tried to turn over. At once, I understood why I had not been able to stretch earlier. My hands were pinioned, perhaps six inches apart. I stared in disbelief at my wrists, manacled with steel clamps. The steel was padded and lined with red silk. From the center of the chain that held my wrists, a longer chain ran down the front of my body. I gave my ankles an experimental tug and found that they too were bound. I felt ill as I understood they were manacled to the chain that pinioned my wrists. I was trussed like a chicken ready for roasting.

Amy reached down and put her hand behind my back, forcing me to sit up.

"You must eat and drink." She held the coffee cup to my lips, but I turned my head away. "Stop being difficult. I tell you, you'll regret it if you don't."

"No, I won't," I said mulishly. "I'll starve to death before I allow myself to become a slave again."

Amy paused, mouthing the word "again" silently. She frowned at me and shook her head.

"You're a fool if you try." Her tone was crisp and unemotional. "If you persist in refusing to eat and drink, you will be force fed."

"You can't make me eat," I said, emphasizing each word.

"Of course we can. If you do not eat today, then tomorrow you will be force fed. Food will be mashed up into a pulp and placed in a rubber bag. A tube will lead from the bag. The tube will be pushed down your throat, directly into your stomach. While you are either held or chained down, your head will be forced back and held firmly in place so there is no obstruction. The bag will be squeezed until all the food has passed into your stomach. It is not pleasant. If you struggle, it will be painful. Painful for you, anyway. The person who is force feeding you will probably take great pleasure out of it."

I swallowed, already feeling the tube blocking my throat. But still I was defiant.

"You can't do that if I won't open my mouth," I said. I was annoyed to hear my voice was shaking.

"That is easily dealt with." Amy's tone was so unconcerned she might have been discussing the weather. "There are two ways of dealing with problem feeders. Firstly, somebody can pinch your nose so that you are forced to breathe through your mouth. If you still refuse to open your teeth, you will be hurt so badly that you scream out loud. At that point, the tube will be inserted. As Soames is anxious not to mark you in any way, it is more likely he will simply have someone hold your head still while he inserts a metal plate between your teeth. The plate is attached to a clamp that will be screwed open and left in place until the tube is inserted and the feeding finished."

She held the coffee cup up again. I stared at her face, trying to read her expression.

"How many times have you force fed prisoners?" I whispered.

"Many times," she said bluntly. "But rarely more than once each. Eat and drink. Be sensible."

Her voice did not change, but her eyes slid urgently toward the side of the room. As she lifted the coffee cup again, she winked, very quickly. I understood the hidden message at once. I wriggled and found if I hunched up with my knees drawn into my stomach I had a little movement. I took the cup off her clumsily and drank. It was clear to me that Soames—or somebody who would report every word to him—was watching us. Just as Auntie had watched us geisha, so many years ago in the Hidden World. The knowledge gave me the oddest sort of comfort. I had escaped from the Floating World. Somehow, I would escape from here.

I drank my coffee and managed to eat a slice of bread and butter I did not want. I sensed that Amy was relieved. Was she really on my side, I wondered? Could I trust her? I almost smiled as the thought passed through my mind. Did I have any choice in the matter? I knew I had been right about the spyhole when Soames pushed the door open the minute I had finished eating.

"Ah. Such a sensible girl. In view of the fact that you will eat and drink, one way or another, you might as well make it a pleasant experience. And how do you feel today?"

He ran his gaze down my naked body. I had an absurd impulse to try and cover my black moss with my chains, but instead sat upright with my hands loosely clasped in my lap. I may be Soames' prisoner, but never would I give him the satisfaction of thinking I was afraid of him.

"If you undo these chains and let me go, I will be a great deal better," I said coldly.

Soames' face creased into exaggerated lines of thought. "I see. And if I did that, would I have your word that you would not try and escape?"

"Of course." Hope lifted my spirits. I even managed to smile at him.

"Perhaps I will." I lifted my head hopefully. "But then again, perhaps not."

The bastard. He was teasing me, like a cruel man might dangle a piece of meat in front of a hungry dog, just out of reach.

"But if you are a very good girl, I might relent. Come here." He turned away and walked toward the window. I remained seated obstinately. Soames obviously registered the lack of movement as he called, "Amy. Do help our visitor to her feet."

Amy grabbed the manacles that ran between my hands and tugged me to my feet. The action looked brutal, but at the same time she supported me with her hand to my elbow and it was not painful. All the same, I took care to grunt, as if she had hurt me.

"Careful with the merchandise, Amy dear." Soames sounded bored. He did not turn as Amy pulled me to his side. "Now, Tara. Perhaps you might like to enjoy the view?"

He pulled the heavy lace curtain aside as he spoke. I took a deep breath as I saw the heavy, iron bars on the outside. I allowed my head to fall, even as I wondered if I might just be slim enough to squeeze through. He pushed my chin up and forced my head against the window pane, so that my cheek pressed against it.

"Now, dear. As you see, there are bars. We did once have a guest here who managed to force himself between them. A young boy, no doubt with all a boy's adventurous spirit. Alas, he had not taken a good look before he leaped, so to speak. You can see, I hope, that the wall is perfectly smooth. The brickwork is completely covered by stucco, with not a crack or an imperfection in it. Nor is there any drainpipe on this side of the building. And in case you were wondering, we are on the third floor. Our young guest would have found himself facing a very painful death if one of the servants had not happened to come in and help him back in before his grip gave way."

"In that case, it doesn't matter whether I'm chained or not. Take these chains off me," I muttered, my voice muffled where it pressed against the glass.

"I would. I really would. But only one thing militates against it. The fact that they cause you such distress."

I saw he was grinning as he let me go. He stood back a step and surveyed me critically. I knew then what a prize sheep or cow felt like at a livestock market, prodded and poked by a farmer who wanted to be sure he was going to get his money's worth. He walked around me, making little humming noises to himself.

"I'm sorry to disappoint you," I said curtly. "And your customer. In spite of all the rumors to the contrary, us Japanese women are made in exactly the same way as Western women. Perhaps I should tell you that when *gaijin* were rare in Japan, we used to think that all *gaijin* men had tails. That was a disappointment as well."

I thought I had gone too far for a moment. Soames paused in his inspection and then laughed out loud.

"I hoped I had found a very special prize in you, Tara. Now that we are better acquainted, I'm certain. I've telegraphed to Alain in Paris and I expect an answer shortly. The lazy creature rarely rises before noon, but I'm certain as soon as he gets my message he will be most excited. No doubt a little delay will only tantalize him further. I have no intention of letting you outside these four walls until the hue and cry over your disappearance has died down. Amy, take her away and help her wash. "

Amy tugged at my chain as if I was a performing bear and led me through a door opposite the bed. It contained a small bathroom, very luxuriously appointed. Amy ran a tap and picked up a flannel, lathering it with a cake of soap scented with carnations. No doubt Soames idea of a joke, I thought bitterly.

"I'll undo the lock that chains your arms to your ankles, if you promise to behave." She held the key in front of me.

I shrugged. "What option do I have?" I asked bitterly.

Amy undid my manacles and the chain fell to the floor with a clang. "Put your hands above your head," she instructed. I obeyed, and she leaned in close to soap me. If it hadn't been for the chains that held my wrists together, it would have reminded me of the bathhouse in Edo and being soaped by a maid.

"If you do as you're told, it will be better for you." Amy's whisper was so soft, I could almost have imagined it. "Turn around and put your arms down," she said in a normal tone. Now, I was sure. Amy had taken something of a fancy to me. Would she—could she—help me? I prayed so. She was the only chance I had.

"Amy, help me. My husband will pay you anything you want if you get me back to him."

I breathed the words into her hair as she leaned down to soap my belly and my black moss. My hopes sank as she helped me into the bathtub and turned on the shower without replying. It was only when the water began to hiss down noisily against the bath's surface that she spoke again very, very softly.

"Can't. Soames would find me and kill me. Just do as he says. Remember, he has eyes and ears everywhere."

She stepped back and held out a large bath towel silently.

I had no need to think over Amy's words. I did as I was told. I ate and drank whatever was put in front of me. I went to bed when instructed, although I slept little. I spent hours each day peering out the window but never saw a living soul. Even the birds seemed to avoid the house of pleasure. When I sensed—with the sixth sense that had been honed to perfection in the Green Tea House—that I was not being watched, I pressed every inch of the featureless door that led into my room, but I could never discover the mechanism that opened it. And when I wasn't doing that, I sat as comfortably as my chains would allow and meditated, allowing my thinking brain to sink into instinctual nothingness. I had escaped from slavery before. I had left the Floating World behind me. I had fled with Callum from captivity in Virginia. I had escaped from the prison of Chisaray Palace. I had done it three times in my life already. This time would be the fourth.

Soames regarded my calmness with apparent amusement. Yet, beneath his good humor, I sensed the beginning of puzzlement. Possibly, even, of worry.

"My dear, you really are a most exemplary guest. You do as you are told. You do not complain. I do hope you are not still hoping Lord Kyle will come to your rescue? I have heard that he has told his friends that the London air had taken its toll on your health and you had decided to return to Scotland early. Obviously, a sop to his pride. He could hardly tell the world that you had left him to racket around the world with a rake of an adventurer!"

He watched my face closely as he spoke. I smiled and was delighted to see a flicker of confusion in his expression.

"Callum plays his cards close to his chest," I said quietly. "That is why he is such an excellent gambler."

"I assure you, I am better," Soames snapped. I was right! He was angry. "No matter. The day is fast approaching when you leave for Paris. If your husband finds you there by some miracle, it doesn't matter to me. Like Mountjoy, I have become a little bored with London. Once you are gone, I shall close my Palace of Pain and reinvent myself far away."

I smiled and bowed my head politely as if his words didn't matter to me.

TWENTY-FIVE

Water flows through my
Fingers and leaves no trace. Just
As you also did

I was awoken by scuffling and laughter, quickly subdued, outside my door. My meditations had taken me to the innermost parts of myself. Whatever Soames did or did not do could have no impact on my essential being now. By giving me precious time to myself— a luxury I had not enjoyed for many years—Soames had unwittingly given me the greatest gift of all. My self-knowledge. And I knew now, deep in my soul, that the red thread of fate that connected me to Callum was not yet ready to be severed. I would be free of this place. Free of the threat of Alain, waiting for me in Paris. Free to think anew about my search for Kazhua. How it would happen, I had no idea. I just knew that it would.

The noises came to a halt outside my door. Above the men's laughter, I heard Amy, her voice unusually distressed.

"No, no. Gentlemen. Nothing of any interest for you

here, I assure you. Please, do come back downstairs. A number of my best girls are free and will be only too happy to entertain you in your private salon."

"Oh, Amy! You sound positively flustered! Not like you, old girl. Now then, are you going to show us what special find there is behind this door or do we break it down?"

I heard caws of drunken laughter from the men. If Amy answered, her voice was lost in their amusement.

"No? Right then! Stand well back!" The man's voice sank to a growl. I heard feet echo outside, and then the noise of a shoulder thudding against my door. And again. At the third attempt, the lock splintered and the door banged inward on its hinges.

The man who had battered it into submission fell into my bedroom. One of his friends hoisted him to his feet while the second turned up the gaslight from the dim flicker that was left burning all night, I assumed so that Soames could see me whenever he thought it necessary.

"Well now. Just look what we have here. Kept this well-hidden, haven't you? Speakee English?"

I blinked in the sudden light. The man who was speaking to me was youngish and fashionably dressed with a gold Albert stretching across his chest that would have vanished in seconds in Whitechapel. He leered at me and raised his eyebrows suggestively. For a foolish second, I thought about appealing to him to rescue me. Then I understood that the men—all three of them—must be customers of the Palace of Pain and I saved my breath. They might not be quite as dangerous as Soames, but they were here and he was not. But still, was this going to be my chance to escape? My heart thudded painfully in my chest. I kept a timid smile pinned to my face as I watched them, praying that they would find it amusing to take my chains off me. When—if—they did, I would try to slide between them and out the door. I had no idea where I would go once I was out, nor did I care. This was my chance. I would take it. But first, I had to lose those chains.

"She's promised to a friend of Soames. That's why she's kept up here." Amy's warning glance flashed quickly toward me and I turned my face from one man to the other, doing my best to look as if I hadn't understood a word they had said. I saw Amy close her eyes in relief and wondered if her expression was for her or me. Or perhaps both of us.

"Really? Well, in that case we'll be sure to be careful with her."

I sat up and allowed the bed covers to fall to my waist. I held out my manacled hands with as piteous an expression as I could manage. I heard all of the men suck in their breath.

"Oh, I say. Just look at that, Adrian." That from a fair-haired man with hair well slicked back with Macassar. "Ain't that something? All trussed up like a Christmas present. Or do I mean a Christmas turkey?"

"I think this must be our lucky day, boys." The first man —Adrian—grinned. I forced myself to stay very still; the tone of his voice had suddenly changed from amusement to lechery. "Amy, the keys."

He held out his hand to Amy, who shook her head. He frowned and clicked his fingers at his friends, nodding toward her. Before Amy could move, the other two had darted to her side. One put his arms around her neck and waist, pinioning her. The other began to pat her body, thoroughly enjoying himself. Finding the chatelaine at her belt, he delved in the little purse that hung from it and produced a bunch of keys with a cry of pleasure.

"Toss 'em over."

Adrian leaned over me, trying key after key in the lock that bound my hands to my ankle chain. I urged him on silently.

"There now!" He cawed triumphantly as the lock gave a click and the long chain that ran down my body came apart. I stretched luxuriantly, feeling the stiffness in my legs and back. In spite of the stiffness, I was all set to slide from the bed and make a run from it when Adrian's hand shot out and buried itself in my hair.

"Be careful with her! Soames will be very angry if you hurt her," Amy called out.

My eyes were watering too much from the pain in my scalp where it felt that my hair was being tugged out for me to see Amy. But the panic in her shrill voice was unmistakable.

"Ah. But Soames ain't here, is he? Besides, I know my old friend Soames. There might be a little unpleasantness, but nothing the right amount of gold can't put right. Up we come, my lovely. Boys, hang on to Amy. Who knows? I might find room for some pudding!"

All the men laughed loudly. Adrian leaned toward me and began to slide his hands beneath me. I waited until he was close and then threw the chain that still stretched between my wrists around his neck. The chains were not quite long enough for me to cross my hands for a better grip, but they were still long enough to give me the satisfaction of watching Adrian's face turn purple with shock and, I hoped, pain. His friends howled with laughter as I did my best to strangle him. It was almost worth my own pain when he jerked his arms up and forced my arms apart. He slapped me very hard and I flopped back against the pillow, my head ringing.

"Fucking bitch! Come here!" He was standing over me,

his eyes bulging and sweat dripping from his nose. I made a last ditch effort to scuttle across the bed, but hampered by my chains, I was too slow. He grabbed me by the hair again and pulled me across the bed until I was close to him.

"Go get her, Adrian!" Macassar shouted. His words were slurred, and I realized that they were all very drunk. "But leave a bit for the rest of us, old man."

Adrian grabbed my waist and hoisted me over his shoulder. The movement sent a wave of red agony through my shoulder. I had dislocated it while we were in the Crimea, and I wondered now if it had come out of its socket again. I screamed and bit Adrian's ear. Even through my pain, I was appalled when he laughed loudly.

"Go on, cunt. Have your bit of fun. I'm going to pay you back for it ten times over, just you wait."

He threw me onto the floor, hard enough to knock the breath out of me. The pain in my shoulder was joined by a terrible, deep ache in my back. He raised his foot, obviously with the intention of kicking my ribs, and in spite of my pain I tried to scrabble away from him.

The blow never landed.

"Gentlemen. Am I to assume that my hospitality downstairs wasn't sufficient for you? If so, I must apologize."

Soames. His voice as smooth as good chocolate, the tone almost amused. Yet it stopped Adrian with his foot in midair. I saw him lower it quickly. If I hadn't been experiencing such difficulty in breathing without causing myself even more pain, I would have taken the opportunity to bite his ankle.

"Soames." Adrian cleared his throat. "We didn't see you this evening. We thought you weren't here."

"Really? But as you see, I am." He bent down to my side and ran a finger around my shoulder. Even that light touch was excruciatingly painful. "How very remiss of Amy not to explain to you that Tara here is in the nature of a special order and not for public consumption."

Amy began to speak, but Soames lifted his hand and she fell silent at once.

"Sorry about that, old chap." Adrian's voice was gruff. Man-to-man amusement rang in his voice. "She did say something, but when we saw what a jewel you had tucked away up here, we didn't take a lot of notice." He fiddled with a sovereign case on his Albert chain. I was reminded of the case Christian had stolen from Jack and fury welled up in my throat, almost overwhelming my pain. "I'm sure a little donation to the house will cover any damage done?"

"I do believe you've dislocated her shoulder," Soames said. His voice was calm, neither angry nor surprised. Adrian shuffled, obviously relieved. "Now, Adrian. When you joined our little community here in the Palace of Pain, what was the one rule you were told was inviolable?"

Adrian cleared his throat and stared at his feet, like a schoolboy caught out in a prank. I writhed on the floor, trying to find some relief from my agony. Soames placed his hand on my shoulder and instinctively I tried to wriggle away from him. He raised his finger to me in warning and pressed the palm of his hand hard on the joint. There was an excruciating flash of pain so terrible that I lost consciousness for a moment. When I recovered, the pain had lessened so much that it was merely sore. I sighed deeply with relief.

"Yes, Adrian?" Satisfied with me, Soames stood up. He was much of a height to Adrian, but in spite of their physical similarity, he seemed to tower over the younger man.

"Ah. I believe we were told that we could play with the

girls as much as we liked, but we were never to cause lasting injury."

"Quite right!" Soames patted his palms together in a mockery of applause and then held out his hand. "Your sovereign case, Adrian. And any money you have in your pockets." Done with Adrian, he turned to the other men. They passed their money over to him as fast as if it was burning them. I sensed a flash of relief flicker between the three.

"Ah. All right and tight then, Soames. We'll be on our way."

"You're leaving so early in the night? Oh, I don't think so. Amy, escort our guests down to the Blue Room, if you please. Having taken so much money off them, I think it only fair they should get value for it."

Amy glanced at Soames and then, with a curiously defiant expression on her face, crossed the room and helped me climb back onto the bed. Only when she was sure I was comfortable did she turn around and walk to the door. She paused, her hands held out in invitation, and the three men walked past her, expectant smiles lighting up their faces.

"I think you'll find your shoulder is much better by morning. I can only apologize for the behavior of my guests." Soames bowed his head courteously. "After tonight, I very much doubt that they will ever wish to return to the Palace of Pain. A case of the biter bit, I think it's safe to say! I'm afraid I must put your manacles back in place. Your door will be replaced first thing in the morning."

I kept my face still. Had my chance come at last?

"Now naturally, you will be thinking that perhaps this will mean you can escape. Alas, my dear. I'm ahead of you there."

He pulled a handkerchief from his pocket and raised it toward his nose. But before it got to chest level, his hand whipped it across my face. I automatically drew in a breath of surprise and smelled the sweet, intensely alcoholic smell of chloroform. I had no doubt as to what it was. I had smelled it too often in the ward at the field hospital in the Crimea to be mistaken. I knew if I struggled, I would breathe deeper and it would take effect quicker. Instead, I forced my aching muscles to go rigid and then pretended to slump. My last conscious thought was bitter amusement that Soames was not in the least fooled. The handkerchief remained over my face until there was nothing but darkness around me.

I ached from head to foot when I awoke. My back and shoulder throbbed. My legs were stiff again from being bent by the manacles. And I felt nauseous and headachy from the effects of the chloroform.

"Drink this. Water will help."

Amy supported my neck and helped me take a sip. I stared at her, trying to work out what was strange about her. She smiled and I saw she was wearing makeup. It had been thickly applied, but it wasn't thick enough to disguise a black eye, nor the bruise on her cheek.

"Amy, what happened to you?" I whispered. She smiled and then winced as the movement caused her pain.

"You did." I realized suddenly that her normal stone face was expressive. She looked—and sounded—distressed.

"I mean, who hurt you? Soames?" I spoke softly. I was shocked when she laughed and answered me in a normal voice.

"It's all right. We can say what we like. He's not bothering to listen anymore. He's bored with you, and with the Palace of Pain as well. He's arranged for you to be transported to Paris the day after tomorrow. As far as he's concerned, you're history. Once you're out of the way, he's going to close this place down and disappear from London himself."

"I remember him saying that," I said. "What did he do to you? Why? It wasn't your fault those men barged in. You couldn't stop them."

"Unfortunately, Soames decided not to believe that." She fingered the bruise on her cheek and grimaced.

"I'm sorry," I said sincerely.

Amy stared at me for a second, and I could have sworn I saw tears in her eyes. "You really are, aren't you?" She sounded amazed. "Thank you for that. But a couple of bruises are nothing. Nothing at all compared to what happened. Do you know what that bastard did to me?" I shook my head, watching her. Feeling her pain. "As soon as I had left those idiots to the mercy of the girls in the Blue Room, he took me into one of the other private salons. There was a bachelor party underway. He opened the door and threw me to them."

I put my hand to my aching head. "I don't understand," I said. "I thought this place was all about men paying to have pain inflicted on them."

"That's because you only saw the main salon." She was smiling, but there was no amusement in it. "There are other rooms in the Palace of Pain. To be sure, many men come here because they enjoy having pain inflicted on them. But there are others who like to give pain rather than take it. That's what Adrian and his friends come here for. To hurt the girls Soames' provides for them. Only last night, they got something of a shock. The girls in the Blue Room are kept for very special customers. Those who find it exquisite to have the sort of pain that you can't even begin to imagine inflicted on them. Pain that makes what you saw in the main salon look like a Sunday school picnic. Soames was kind enough to tell me that when the girls had finished with them, he had them put in the carriage and thrown out naked in the middle of Piccadilly Circus, bound hand and foot and gagged. I doubt they would have been able to explain that away to their poor wives."

"I'm delighted to hear it. But what did he do to you?"

Amy held the cup to my lips and allowed me to drink before she answered.

"I told you. I was thrown to a bachelor party. Like Daniel to the lion, but I had no God to save me." She raised her head and I saw the shame and pain in her eyes. "They used me, Tara. All of them. They took great pleasure in me. In putting themselves into me, in any and all ways they could think of. Two, three of them at a time. I was passed around like the parcel in a child's game, with each one taking a piece of me. When I protested, they hit me. It's not the pain, I can live with that. The bruises will fade. But the memory of those bastards emptying themselves into me will stay with me forever. I can scrub myself until I'm raw, but I'll never get rid of their stench on me."

I remembered Lord Dai forcing himself upon me. Remembered the pain and the horror of being taken by an old man, a man I had come to hate. Remembered the agony when I thought he had caused me to miscarry. How much worse must it have been for poor Amy, who I guessed loved her own sex and would have viewed even being touched by a man with horror? A sudden memory of her stamping on the man's hand who had licked my boots gave me pause. She had ground her shoe into his bones with as much mercy as the men had shown her last night. And yet, if it hadn't been *me* he had been touching, would she have cared greatly?

"Oh, Amy. I am so sorry." I opened my arms as far as I could for the chains and held her close to me. For a second, she was rigid, and then she began to cry, very softly, like a child.

"He's going to take me with him," she said. "He says I'm too valuable to lose. He doesn't mean just that. I wouldn't care so much if he did. He's going to take me as his woman again and use me however he sees fit. I'm not going to let it happen, Tara. I'll kill myself first."

I rocked her back and forth, making soothing noises, just as if I was trying to comfort a child. Eventually, she stopped crying and sat up. Her face was a mess. Her makeup was streaked with her tears and it had caked around her mouth and chin.

"You're sure Soames isn't here?"

She frowned at my question, shrugging. "I'm positive. I saw him ride off in the carriage earlier and I haven't heard him come back. He's so pleased that all his plans are coming right, he's gloating over letting me know everything."

"If you're sure, let me go, then." Amy jerked back as if I had slapped her. I grabbed her wrists and held her tightly. She glanced down at my hands and her expression softened. "Nobody's going to know you helped me escape."

"I'm sorry. I can't do that." She smiled at me, her expression imploring me to understand. "If you got away, Soames would guess it was me who helped you. He'd hurt me until I told him the truth. And then I imagine he would kill me. Very slowly and very painfully. I expect I would welcome death when it finally came to me."

I swallowed in horror. Amy's calm acceptance of her fate appalled me and I spoke without thinking.

"You could get away," I urged. "Escape with me. Go somewhere he'd never find you."

"From Soames?" She shook her head in amazement. "You don't know him. He's rich and powerful. He has spies everywhere. There's nowhere I could run to in the whole world where he wouldn't find me. He's a monster."

"Callum—my husband—would protect you." I looked into her face, willing her to believe me. "I promise he would. If you take me to him, before Soames can leave London, Callum will make sure that he's caught. If nothing else can be proved against him, I'm willing to stand up in court and testify to what he's done to me. He can't hurt you if he's in prison."

"Of course he can." Amy looked at me as if I had run mad. "I told you, he has eyes and ears everywhere. His friends would find me. And they'd get you as well, no matter what your husband did to protect you."

"Then at least we'd suffer together!" I had no idea where the words came from, but as soon as I spoke, I knew it was the right thing to say. Amy stared at me, her lips parted.

"I love you, you know. As soon as I saw you walk in with Mountjoy, I felt as though I had been waiting for you all my life," she said softly. She stared at me hungrily as she spoke. I considered lying to her, but I couldn't bear to deceive her.

"I know," I said very gently. "I wish I could say I loved you as well, Amy. But I can't. At least, not how you want me to. If I could have you as a very dear friend, then that would make me very happy." I saw the light die in her eyes and grabbed for her hand. "Listen to me. Get us both out of here. If you do that, I promise Soames will never be able to hurt you again."

"I suppose we might be able to get away. Everything is in such confusion at the moment, it could be done." She shrugged. "But I tell you there's no point. Soames would find us. I know he would."

"Don't you see?" I pleaded. "That's his main weapon. He thinks you're so terrified of him, he can leave you on your own and you won't dare do anything. After what he did to you last night, don't you want some revenge?"

Amy raised her head and stared into space. "If I could kill the bastard in cold blood, it would give me great satisfaction to do it." She smiled coldly. "Assuming I could live to tell the tale, of course."

"I can't give Soames to you. Trust me, I would if I could!" I put my hands gently on each side of Amy's poor, bruised face, looking straight into her eyes. "But I can give you your freedom. Get away from here with me. Get me back to my husband. I promise you, he'll give you a new life. A new name, a new past to go with it. He and I will be the only ones who know who you are and where you've gone. You'll have enough money to do exactly as you like. And if that means turning the tables on Soames and getting your revenge on him, then that's up to you."

Even as I said the words, I couldn't help wondering if this was one miracle even Callum couldn't achieve. I squashed the doubt. He would do it. For me.

Amy was silent, pleating the bed covers between her fingers. I racked my brains for more arguments to convince her with, but found nothing. My hopes died. I sat back and gripped Amy's hand gently. Even knowing my own fate, I felt sorrow for her.

She looked at my face. Very slowly, she reached up and took my hands away from her cheeks, kissed my fingers gently, and reached into her pocket for her keyring. Her hand fumbled as she inserted the key into the lock and she almost dropped it on the floor. Retrieving it, she bent and undid the shackles around my ankles.

"Soames said he would be back after lunch." There was an expression in her eyes that I had never seen before. I stared at her and realized suddenly what it was. Hope. I knew then that I had won. I worried that one false word would make her change her mind, and I stared at her calmly, as if we were discussing nothing at all. Suddenly, she took a deep breath and nodded as if in answer to an unspoken question. "Dorcas is about your size. She's still asleep. I'll steal some of her clothes for you. Put them on and we'll walk out of here arm in arm."

There would be no second chance for us. I had to be sure she was right. I put my hand on her wrist and watched her face carefully.

"It can't be as easy as that," I protested. "Are you sure?"

"It always was," she said simply. "But I never understood that until now. All of us girls could walk out any time if we wanted to. If we dared. It's fear of Soames that keeps us here, just as much as if we were chained hand and foot like you are. I think I began to understand that when he insisted that you had to be kept chained all the time. He knew you weren't frightened of him, that no matter what he did to you or threatened you with, he would never make you fear him. I understand now that in the strangest way he is just a little bit afraid of you. That's why he's closing the Palace of Pain down as soon as you go. He can't shake the worry that somehow you'd come back and take your revenge on him."

I thought about what she was saying. The red thread of my fate had taken me to many strange places in my life. I had suffered much pain, been in much danger. But I had always survived. Perhaps Soames was right to fear me. I took a deep breath and stretched.

"In Japan, it is said that fear is only as deep as the mind allows. I don't fear Soames. He is no more than a man, no matter if he sees himself as a god. If you don't fear him, then he no longer has any power over you."

Amy put her arms around me and hugged me tightly. It hurt my shoulder, but I guessed she was also hurting her own bruised face, so I returned her embrace and we suffered the pain Soames had inflicted on us together.

TWENTY-SIX

Oceans rage and foam
Yet there is always safety
Upon the sea floor

*a*my and I walked out of the front door of the Palace of Pain. If anybody had seen us, they would have thought we were simply taking the air, we walked so calmly. In spite of outward appearances, my back rippled with expectation. As soon as my foot hit the garden path, I anticipated a shout, a hand on my shoulder dragging me back. But there was nothing. Sounding much braver than I felt, I encouraged Amy.

"You see? I told you. The only thing we had to fear was fear itself."

Amy said nothing, but nodded. Her hands were gripping her reticule so fiercely her knuckles protruded like white knobs. She wore a hat with a thick veil pulled over her face, I assumed to hide both her identity and her bruises.

"Nobody saw us go," she said when we were perhaps

fifty yards down the street. "I made sure of that. The rest of the girls are all sound asleep. They all had a busy night last night. The kitchen staff is busy. Soames and his henchmen are all out. He told me that he's already sold the house. That's where he's gone today, to make arrangements with his lawyer about signing the contract for the sale. You were to go to Paris soon." She laughed, but the sound had no humor in it at all. "Do you know, I've been his slave for nearly ten years and this is the first time he's ever told me anything? In fact, it's the first time he's ever left the house unguarded. Normally, there are a couple of big, strong thugs about the place to keep us girls in order. I think he must be so sure of himself that he thinks none of us would dare escape, even when we finally got the chance. If it hadn't been for you, I wouldn't have dared. I would have sat there behind an open door and waited for him to come back. And been pleased to see him when he did arrive. The bastard."

"Do the other girls know what's happening?" I was curious, but I also wanted to keep Amy talking. I sensed that left to herself there was still a strong chance that she would run back to her own prison. That to carry on obeying Soames would be easier than coping with freedom.

"They don't know anything. Soames has sold the house with all the contents. He intends to see you on your way, then he's simply going to disappear and take me with him. The girls will just wake up one morning and find they have nothing. Not so much as a roof over their heads."

"Bastard," I swore softly.

I heard the rumble of wheels on the cobbled street and we both froze. Amy put her hand on my arm and gripped hard.

"It's all right!" I sighed with relief. "It's a hansom cab. Just what we need. Here! Driver!" I put my hand up and waved. To my delight, the cab was empty and pulled over for us immediately.

Once we were seated, Amy shuffled over to me and grabbed my hand. She stared out of the window as our horse clopped briskly toward central London. I felt her fear.

"Did he never let you out?" I asked.

"Never. The Palace of Pain was my prison cell. He took me when I was barely more than a child. I had been begging on the streets, and he stopped in his carriage and spoke to me as if I was a grown up. I can remember it as if it was only yesterday. He asked me if I was hungry, if I had somewhere to sleep at night. I told him the truth. I hadn't had anything but bread and tea—and we made the tea leaves do until the water had no color in it when we poured it out—for the last month. I slept with my mother and my three brothers in a room we shared with another family in St. Giles, the nastiest slum in the whole of London town. He looked sorrowful for me and said that if I went with him, I would have as much food as I wanted and a room all of my own. Well, he wasn't lying about that, I suppose. I went with him without a second thought, and once he had cleaned me up, I was introduced to one of his clients. He took me every way it's possible for a man to take a girl. I cried all the next day. Soames came to visit me and told me—as if he was bestowing some great favor on me—that seeing as I had taken it hard, he would leave me for a day or two to recover. He did, but as soon as I stopped crying, there was another man, and then another. Every night. I got to the stage where it didn't matter anymore what they did to me. I just shut my mind off and waited until they had finished. Soames used me as well when he felt like it. But he was different. He was kind to me and told me what a good girl I was. How he was proud of me. And do you know, I believed him?" She laughed shortly. "I began to think of him as—not as my father exactly. I never knew him. Ma said he skipped out before I was born. But Soames became my protector. He made me feel that he would always be there for me. That he was the one person in the whole world who cared about me. He actually told me once that he was the only one who was allowed to hurt me now and do you know, I was grateful to him? I mean, how bloody pathetic can you get?"

"I understand," I said quietly. "I was a geisha in Japan. An old man paid a huge amount of money to deflower me when I was a child. I might have been allowed to go outside, but I was just as much a prisoner as you were."

Amy turned her head and stared at me. She had lifted her veil when we got into the cab and I saw a tear run down her face. She wiped it away as if she was ashamed of it.

"Perhaps you do understand, then. I used to think how good he was to me. Especially when he told me that I was being promoted. That I was no longer to service the clients. One of the clients had taken a fancy to the girl who had acted as hostess and had bought her out to be his mistress. Soames said I was to take her place. I leaped at the chance. All at once I had the chance to pay back the men who came to the palace to take their pleasure out of us girls. I persuaded Soames—not that it took much persuading—to encourage the ones who wanted to be hurt. There was money in it, I told him. And I was right. The harder we punished them, the sooner they came back. After a few months, the Punishment Room was taking more than the rest of the house put together. Soames was delighted. And so was I. I gloated over the idiots. Loved watching them having pain inflicted on them. Do you despise me, now that you know that?" she added abruptly.

"No." I didn't even have to think about it. How often had

I longed to take my revenge on Lord Dai? To stick his own dagger in his back when he was using me? Was I so different from Amy? I thought not. "But tell me the rest of it. What happened to make you realize that Soames didn't care about you? What made you hate him?"

"I noticed he wasn't taking me to his bed anywhere near as often as he used to. The other girls told me he had a new girl." Amy paused and drew a shuddering breath. I understood that the memory was still painful for her. "One who had just arrived and was about the age I was when he claimed me. I thought they were just jealous and I wouldn't listen to them. But one night, well, I suppose I was lonely. I decided I would go and surprise Soames. I did that all right. He had his new tart curled up at the side of him. She was even lying on my side of the bed. He didn't say a word to me. Just shouted for his thugs and told them to take me away and punish me for disturbing him. He shut the door in my face. Even then, I hadn't learned. I fawned round him, sure I could win him back. I suppose I did, after a fashion. He took me back to his bed, with *her* in it as well. After that, I finally worked out that he was the same as all the other men. They had no thoughts for me at all. They just wanted to use me. Just like Soames had all along. So I turned to one of the other girls for comfort and found it. And that was it for me. That was when I began to hate Soames, and he knew it. It seemed to amuse him. He balanced between encouraging me and hurting me. I never knew which mood he would be in. Each time he hurt me, I began to fear him a bit more. Each time he was kind to me, I worried what the punishment would be next time. Eventually, I got to the stage where if I saw his shadow, I started to tremble. At first, when he told me about his plans for the palace, I thought I was going to get away at last. I was over the moon. But then

I realized he was including me in his plans. At first, I was overjoyed. I hadn't learned my lesson even then. I thought it was because he really did care about me after all. But he soon destroyed that idea. I was far too valuable, far too well-trained to let slip away he told me. He intended to open another Palace of Pain, probably in Russia. He had heard that many of the aristocrats there appreciated that sort of thing. He would make another fortune, he gloated. I wanted to run away then, but I didn't dare. I knew he would find me and bring me back. Then you came along, and you were so courageous. I could see he was taken aback at first, and then after a while he began to worry about you. And I thought, if you could defy him, then perhaps there was a chance for me. And after he threw me to those pigs for them to play with me, I decided I didn't care. Even if I couldn't get away from him, I would help you escape."

"Why?" I asked gently.

"Weren't you listening to me?" Amy asked roughly. "I told you. Because I love you." She turned her head away so I couldn't see her expression. After a second, she added, "Besides, it was the only chance I was ever going to have to get my revenge on bastard Soames."

I wondered if she was trying to convince me or herself with her final words. I reached out and stroked her hair and put her head on my shoulder. I felt bitterly sorry for her. It seemed to me that of the two people she had ever loved, one of us had betrayed her. And I? I would do my best for her to find a future, but I could never return that love. Poor, poor Amy!

"It's all right." Her voice was muffled by my jacket. "I don't expect you to love me. It's enough that you've given me something I've never had before—a friend."

I stared straight ahead as the cab rattled on. My head

pounded. At the same time as I felt for Amy's anguish, I also knew that every turn of the wheels carried me toward Callum. And for that, my heart sang.

Amy sat up as we entered central London. She stared out of the window shyly, tugging my arm occasionally to ask where we were or what all the disruption was. I explained to her about Mr. Bazalgette's amazing plans for the new sewer system and she grunted.

"Bet it never gets as far as St. Giles and the other rookeries," she said cynically. "Do you know why London slums are called rookeries?" I shook my head. "It's because the posh folk reckon all us paupers are crammed in there like rooks in their nests. All noise and shit. All carrion together. They're not far from the truth either."

I had great difficulty getting her out of the cab as we reached our apartment. She shook her head, hanging on to the seat.

"Just leave me here," she said pathetically. "I don't want to meet your husband. We'll have to tell him I was part of keeping you prisoner. Besides, it's too grand in there for the likes of me."

I remembered the cool, detached Amy I had first met at the Palace of Pain and nearly wept as I wondered who had brought about this change in her, me or Soames? Looking at her terrified face, I made my mind up.

"Amy, get out of the cab and come with me. Now," I snapped at her brusquely, and she obeyed instinctively. The doorman was moving toward us, his face alight with surprise. I nodded at him. "Davis. Be so good as to pay the cabbie, please. And give him a good tip. He's come a long way."

"Lady Kyle! We thought you had gone back to Scotland. Is everything all right?"

"It is now." I smiled at him. "Is my husband in?"

"He is, ma'am. He came back not ten minutes ago."

I nodded my thanks and took Amy by the hand. She hunched as close to me as she could get and still walk and came with me like a lamb. Perhaps some of her terror passed into me. By the time we reached the door of our apartment, I was trembling. As far as I knew, Callum believed I had run off with Christian. And if that was the case, what sort of a welcome could I expect now, turning up out of the blue with a sadistic whore hanging on my arm? I took a deep breath and turned the door handle before I could hesitate, trusting the door would be open to me.

It was.

Callum rose as we walked in. His face was unshaven. He was hollow-eyed; if I asked him when he had last slept, I doubted he would be able to answer me. We stared at each other for a moment, his lips opening and closing but no sound at all coming from his throat. I kicked the door closed behind me, more to stop Amy bolting than anything else and walked toward him as bravely as I could.

"Callum." My voice was trembling so, his name sounded strange on my lips. I stared at him, waiting.

He was shaking his head, as if he doubted his own eyes. I could wait not a second longer. He didn't move as I walked up to him. It was only when I touched his face that he spoke. In Japanese. Then, my heart sang and I knew that I had been wrong to doubt him. That *he* had never doubted *me.*

"Tara-chan. It is you? What happened to you? Where have you been? Have you been hurt? How did you get here?" Then his hands were sliding all over me, touching and probing. I hissed with pain as his fingers found my poor shoulder and he stopped at once, staring at me as if he shared my hurt.

"It's nothing," I said. "Nothing at all. Oh, Callum. I'm back with you!" The tears came then. Callum put his arms around me and hugged me tightly. We rocked together silently until I managed to stop crying. I looked up at his dear face and saw the same expression I had once seen on a mother's face when her baby had been laid in her arms after a long, hard labor. Love and relief and joy all mingled together. "Nothing is going to part us again. Ever. If I have to walk on your shadow for the rest of my days, I'll do it happily."

"What happened to you?" Callum asked again. I began to answer him, then remembered Amy. I was almost surprised to see she was still there. I saw the expression of envy, so deep it was almost misery, on her face and I understood. She knew, finally, that she had lost me. And that I had found the person I loved. In the midst of my joy, my heart ached for her.

"Wait," I said urgently. "There's so much I need to tell you. But it can wait for a moment longer. Now, we have all the time in the world for ourselves." For Amy's benefit, I switched to English. "I don't know where to start." I watched Callum hungrily and he looked back at me with a face deep in wonder. "But before anything else, this is Amy. She helped me escape. Without her, you would never have seen me again."

Callum didn't hesitate. He let me go and walked over to Amy, his hand held out. I saw her through his eyes. The too-tightly fitting dress, cut to show off every inch of her slender figure. Makeup caked around her eyes and mouth. Shoes that had heels like spikes. And above all, the way she held herself. As if she expected him to raise his hand and strike her to the ground. He took her hand, and rather than shaking it, held it between both of his hands tightly.

"Amy. I'm forever in your debt. If you only knew the torment I've been going through, wondering what had happened to Tara. Nothing I can offer you could ever be enough, but at least tell me what you would like. Please."

I think it was the word "please" that broke through Amy's defenses. If Callum hadn't had hold of her hand, I was certain she would have crumpled to the floor. I spoke for her.

"At the moment, she needs somewhere where she'll be safe. Can she stay here with us?"

"Of course. I'll ring for the maid and get the spare bedroom ready." I felt Callum's shock, but he hid it manfully. "And I'll send Davis to tell Sergeant Lestrade you're here. He's had half the Metropolitan Police combing London for you."

Amy flinched at the mention of the police. She looked at me wildly, and I patted her arm.

"They're not going to know about you. I promise," I said soothingly. Callum stared silently from one to the other of us and I thought—not for the first time—what a good man he was. "Callum, I think Amy would like to lie down. The room can be made up later."

His face was bewildered as I steered Amy into the spare bedroom and drew the curtains. The bed was covered with a silk counterpane and she ran her fingers over it repeatedly.

"Do you want anything to eat or drink?" I asked. She shook her head and instead of replying turned away from me and buried her face in the pillow. I hesitated, and then left her alone.

"Tara." Callum could not contain himself. He was across

the room before I had taken a bare step. He wrapped his arms around me and I sank into his embrace. For a few moments, we had no need of words.

"It was Mountjoy, wasn't it?" Callum held me far enough away so that he could see my face. "I knew you could never have written that ridiculous note. At first, I thought it was some sort of joke. I waited until quite late, expecting you both to walk through the door, laughing at me. But when it got to midnight, I understood that wasn't going to happen. I called the police then, and they've been searching London for you ever since. And I've been going mad. What happened?"

I took a deep breath and told him. Everything. At first, I was worried he would be angry with me. He wasn't, but I could see that he was hurt.

"I had no idea you were so bored with life in London. Why didn't you tell me? I thought you were perfectly happy, gadding about without me. That's why I started going to the gambling houses, to give myself something to do to fill my time."

"I wasn't bored." I squeezed his hand, trying to find words to explain. "Or I suppose I was a bit, living the life of a society lady. We met the same people all the time. And none of them seemed to care about anything except the next dance or whether they were going to get an invitation to Lady Such-and-Such's rout. None of it meant anything to me. And I was desperately jealous that you and all the other men could get out of that circle. Do what you wanted to do. Go where you wanted. Whereas I was forbidden. Does that make any sense?"

"Knowing you as I do, yes. It makes perfect sense."

I smiled at him, grateful for his understanding. I left nothing out. I recalled meeting Max Marchant and getting the idea that I would be free if I posed as Mountjoy's boy. I took a deep breath before I told Callum about the night Mountjoy had robbed the gent who had taken me for a rent boy. He stared at me and shook his head.

"And you never said a word to me!" he marveled. "Never mind. Tell me how Mountjoy betrayed you in the end. Because I suppose he must have done."

"That he did," I said bleakly. I told him about the drugged flowers and how I had found myself in Soames' Palace of Pain. I had expected him to be furious, but he looked thoughtful.

"I've heard of that place. Some of the gentlemen tried to get me to go with them one evening. Said it was like nowhere else in London. I was going to say no anyway, but when they whispered about what went on there, I declined their kind offer very firmly." His face darkened. "Tara, this Soames character, did he force you to...to do anything against your will?"

"No," I said quickly. "He said I was a special order for a gentleman in Paris. I was going to be shipped out tomorrow. He kept me chained up." I held my hand up as I saw naked fury tighten Callum's face. "But the manacles were silk lined. I was fed and very well looked after. But if Amy hadn't been incredibly brave and helped me escape, I would have been drugged and ready to be shipped off to Paris by now. He kept her a prisoner as well. She'd been there since she was a child. She was totally under his spell, poor thing."

Before Callum could speak, there was a knock on the door and a man entered. Callum sprang to his feet and shook his hand.

"Sergeant Lestrade. Thank you for getting here so quickly."

I had expected a much older man, one wearing a

uniform. Sergeant Lestrade looked to be perhaps thirty and wore a sober suit. He held a trilby in his hands and looked at me with almost comical surprise.

Callum ushered him to a chair and I told my story yet again. Except this time I made no mention of Amy by name. When I finished, Lestrade was so excited he jumped to his feet and looked longingly at the door.

"Well, that's a tale and a half, Lady Kyle! But it all fits in with many another mystery we've been unable to solve. We've been looking for a kidnapper, and a jewel thief, and a bank robber, all along thinking they were different people. And now it seems they were one and the same man. I know of the Palace of Pain. It's out Epping way. We've had a close eye on it for nearly a year, but I could never manage to sneak a man inside to take a good look at what went on in there, and nobody ever complained, so we couldn't take any action. I just hope the bird hasn't flown before we get there now."

"I think Soames has probably gone by now," I said.

Lestrade frowned. "Well, we'll do our best. You would recognize him if you saw him again, Lady Kyle?"

"Most certainly." Even as I said it, I knew instinctively that Lestrade *was* too late. By the time his men arrived at the Palace of Pain, I was sure all they would find was a number of sleepy-eyed women. None of whom would ever admit to knowing Soames. I hoped I was wrong, but I doubted it.

"Well, we'll do our best to catch him, Lady Kyle, don't you doubt it. If we do get him, do you feel you could stand up in court and tell your story?"

"Yes," I said immediately. I saw Callum's concerned glance, but I shook my head at him. "If the chance comes,

I'll be more than happy to be the one that gets Soames all he deserves."

Lestrade left us shortly after. As if on cue, Amy came out of her bedroom and stood quietly, watching us.

"Amy. Please, do sit down." Callum waved her to a comfortable armchair. I could see she had recovered her normal elegant composure. She sat with all the grace of a cat curling up on a favorite lap. "You must know that I can never thank you enough for what you've done. You're an incredibly brave woman. I had already promised Lestrade reward money for anybody who led him to Tara. At the very least, will you accept that? And anything else that I can press on to you."

Amy glanced at me, and I nodded.

"Please?" I said.

She licked her lips and said nothing for a while. When she did speak, she took us both by surprise.

"I have always been very fond of animals. We never had pets in St. Giles. We couldn't afford to feed ourselves, never mind an animal. But there were always lots of stray dogs and cats about the place. Quite a few people kept rabbits. For eating, of course. I seem to remember there were even a couple of wild pigs until somebody caught them and ate them. I always had a way with the cats and dogs. They would never allow themselves to be petted by anybody except me." She paused, and Callum glanced at me with raised eyebrows. I shook my head. *Let her finish.* "What I would really like is to have a pet shop. One somewhere nice, where I would know that the people who bought my animals would look after them. I could have puppies and kittens. Posh ones. Kittens with blue eyes and brown faces and dogs with fancy sounding names. Perhaps fluffy-haired rabbits as well, as pets for the kiddies. Even a couple of little monkeys, for people who like that sort of thing. Parrots, as well. A few of them, so they would be company for each other. But on perches, not in cages. Never in cages. And all the right food for them, and collars and leashes and such."

Amy's mouth was a thin line. She stared at us stonily, daring us to laugh at her small ambition. Before I could answer her, Callum was on his feet and holding out his hand to her.

"It's yours. Everybody needs something to love," he added softly. Amy's lips quivered. He spoke quickly, pretending he hadn't noticed. "And you need somewhere to live. We must find you a good shop, in the right area. One with an apartment upstairs so you can lock your own front door at night."

I had to ask. "Amy, are you sure you want to stay in London? What if Soames comes back?"

"I'm not frightened of him anymore," she said simply. "My life is my own again now. And if he finds me, I would tell him that. He thrives on fear. If he knew I didn't care about him one way or the other, I would have no attraction for him anymore. Besides which, I intend to make sure I'm safe. I'm going to buy myself a wedding band from a pawn shop and I'll tell all my new neighbors how my man was killed serving in the army in India. Get them feeling sorry for me, like. Whenever I meet the bobby on the beat, I'll invite him in for a cup of tea. Ask after his wife and family. Make myself known, if you get me."

I did. I walked across the rug and embraced Amy. I was proud to call her my friend, and I told her so.

TWENTY-SEVEN

Do you see? If we
Walk closely together, then
Our shadows are one

*I*t wasn't raining. In fact, the weather was warm and sunny. Alfie had his head on my thigh, and I shifted, trying to get comfortable. He moved reluctantly and gave a great, doggy sigh. When I ignored that, he raised his head and made a soft, questioning noise deep in his throat.

"Later, Alfie. I don't feel like going for a walk just yet."

The deerhound scrutinized me sorrowfully. I avoided his reproachful gaze. We would go for a walk. But not just yet. I was waiting for something. I had no idea what it was, but the foreknowledge of something about to happen had been with me from the moment I awoke. I smiled to myself and put my hands on my belly in great content. My baby had quickened a few weeks before, and now I took great delight in every movement, even the unexpected kicks that made me gasp. He—for I was sure it was going to be a man-child—was vigorous. Almost nothing could give me greater pleasure. Nothing, except to have Kazhua back in my life. But this time, I deliberately pushed the hope that my new baby was an omen, forecasting her return, away from my thoughts. Perhaps I was catching Callum's superstition, but after the loss of my last baby I forced myself to wish for nothing but the birth of a healthy child.

Every day that I awoke was happiness. We were back in Glen Kyle, in the Highlands of Scotland. Home, at last. Although I could not forget the terrible time I had spent in the Palace of Pain, it was beginning to feel more like a nightmare than something that had actually happened.

As I had predicted, by the time Sergeant Lestrade got his men to Epping, it was as if Soames had never been there. His entire haul was a bunch of bewildered tarts and equipment that had him scratching his head as he tried to work out what it was used for. Lestrade assured us that Soames would be found and brought to justice. I doubted it. Poor Amy finally decided to take the money that Callum pressed on her. She would find her own shop, she said. Callum, bless him, had simply accepted her words and had discreetly left the room for us to say our goodbyes.

"You will be all right?" I asked foolishly.

"I think so," Amy said very seriously. "I told you, I'm going to make myself a well-known and respected member of the community." Her lips twisted briefly as she spoke the word "respected." "And I intend to buy a very large dog. Not to sell in the shop, but for myself. I'm going to train him to be suspicious of anybody who looks at me the wrong way. He can sleep at the side of my bed. If Soames or any of his men try to get to me, they're going to get a very nasty shock. I'll be well protected, don't you worry."

She grinned and gave me a brief kiss before she walked away. She paused at the door and smiled at me.

"Take care yourself, *Tomo*," she said, and then she was gone.

Today, for some reason, the memories were especially vivid. I shook my head, intent on flinging them away.

"Lady Kyle."

Lost in my thoughts, I had not heard the door open. I smiled at Donald, Callum's Estate Manager. Before we had gone to war in the Crimea, I had been sure that Donald not only disliked me, but that he also disapproved of Callum's choice of wife. Perhaps I had been wrong, or perhaps it was the knowledge that Kyle was about to have an heir, but since our return from London, Donald had so far forgotten himself that he even smiled at me occasionally.

"Hello, Donald. What is it? Callum's not here at the moment. Did you want him?"

"No." Donald had forgotten to use my title. That was unheard of. I sat up, staring at him with interest. "It was you I wanted, ma'am. You have visitors. Would you like me to show them in?"

"Who is it?" I was intrigued. Normally, the maid would come and announce visitors, all of whom were known to our staff. Everybody in the house from the scullery maid to Donald himself had relatives working in other houses in Kyle. Everybody knew each other. What was so unusual about these visitors that Donald had chosen to ask if I wanted to see them? He stared at me, his mouth pursed like a button that had been sewn on to his face.

"The lady said she would prefer to introduce herself, ma'am." Why, I wondered, was he staring at me so intently? I put my feet down from the sofa. Alfie seemed to have caught Donald's uncertainty. He was wagging his tail and at the same time muttering, deep in his throat. I stilled him with my hand and nodded at Donald.

"I see," I said, although I didn't see at all. "Please, show them in, Donald."

I knew her at once.

She walked toward me in front of a tall, handsome Japanese man. From his bearing and the rich subtlety of his robes, I guessed he was a nobleman. The thought flickered through my mind, *Not Danjuro, then.* Another Japanese woman stood respectfully at his side, with her eyes lowered politely. But I spared them all just the one glance. I had eyes for nobody except my daughter.

My Kazhua.

Oh, but she was so beautiful! She had Simon's eyes, a true and lovely green. And I could see her father in her auburn hair and widow's peak. But her skin tone was mine, and the way her cheekbones curved like a curlew's wing. I put my hand to my throat, as if I could force out the words that lingered there.

Kazhua stared at me, and then slid to the floor with all the elegance of a piece of silk folding. She prostrated herself full length, so I could barely hear her voice.

"*Anata ni oaidekite kouei desu, Terue-san.*" *I am honored to meet you, Terue-san.*

I sank to my knees beside my daughter and raised her up. We stared at each other silently. Finally, I found my voice and my manners together and managed to croak,

"*Meiyo wa watashi, musumedesu.*" *The honor is mine, daughter.*

Her lovely lips trembled into a smile and I began to laugh and cry at the same time. I ran my fingertips over her face, hardly able to believe that this vision before me was flesh and blood.

"Mother?" she whispered. She spoke in English, and it was just one small shock on top of the greater one. I responded instinctively in English.

"Kazhua. Oh, Kazhua. My daughter. Every day since I had to leave you, I've dreamed of meeting you again. And now that you're here, I can't bring myself to believe it."

We stared at each other, and then Kazhua put her arms around me and we embraced, both of us shuddering with tears. I had no idea how long we stayed locked together, but finally I heard Callum's voice and his hands were helping me to my feet. I saw Kazhua glance at my thickening waist, and suddenly I was deeply embarrassed. Then I saw the joy in her eyes and my own happiness was complete and utter.

We sat together on the sofa, our arms wrapped around each other. Alfie, catching the mood, ran around the room barking loudly until Callum threatened to throw him out unless he shut up. Then he sat and wagged his plumed tail so briskly it scratched on the floor and made everybody laugh. I couldn't take my gaze off Kazhua. How, I wondered, had I managed to live all this time without her at my side?

We had so much to say to each other, but first I had one question above all else to ask.

"Do you hate me, daughter? I would have given my life not to have left you behind, but it would have been useless. If I had stayed, all three of us—you, your father, and me— would have been put to death."

"I know," she said simply. "I got your letter, eventually. Not long before I escaped from the yakuza Akira and left for America with Danjuro." I glanced at her male companion and raised my eyebrows in curiosity. Kazhua shook her head. "Mother, this is Lord Shimazu. He is my sponsor for the kabuki. And my friend." Shimazu bowed to me courteously. Kazhua then bowed her head courteously at the woman who had not yet spoken. "This is Mineko. She was my younger sister in the Hidden House, and now she acts in the kabuki with me."

Pride welled in my heart and tears came again. My daughter—just as I had—had broken with tradition. She and her friend both acted in the kabuki. I wondered if I would ever have the words to tell her how proud of her I was. Suddenly, I remembered my manners.

"Please, allow me to introduce my husband. Callum, Lord Kyle."

Callum rose and bowed, very correctly. Equally formally he murmured his pleasure at our visitors' presence. In perfect Japanese. I smiled at him proudly.

"This must all seem so strange to you, Kazhua," I apologized. Kazhua laughed and shook her head and I stared at her in astonishment.

"Not at all. I know far more about you than you think. When I ran away from Edo with Danjuro, we ended up in America. I acted in the kabuki with him for a while, but we grew apart and went our separate ways." She frowned and I raised my eyebrows at her. She met my eyes and I read the message there clearly. We would speak about all that later. "I first met Shimazu-san on board a ship, on our way to America. Then the red thread of our fates led us to each other again in America, just as I always knew that one day my red thread would find the mother I had lost. You were always in my thoughts." She smiled at me. I saw her beautiful face through a haze of joyful tears. "We landed in San Francisco. A friend there helped me discover that a Japanese lady had arrived there with her American husband at about the time I was born. She gave me this, and

I knew it was you and my father." Kazhua held out a scrap of pasteboard to me. I shook my head in disbelief as I recognized it as the photograph Simon and I had had taken just before we left San Francisco. Or Yerba Buena, as it had been called then. My hand trembled as I handed it back to Kazhua. "My friend found out that you had both moved on to Virginia from San Francisco. Shimazu-chan went with me to Virginia, to High Grove Plantation. I hoped I would find you there. We didn't find you, or my father, but we did find my uncle William." Her face was suddenly full of wonder. "In the space of a minute, I went from having nobody to finding I had a family. He told us all about how my father had died, searching for me in Edo. That made me very sad, but also very proud. He also told me how Callum-san had helped free many slaves, and how you had helped him escape in the end. I knew then that I was proud of both my parents, and also my new father."

"But how did you find us here? Scotland is a long way from Virginia." I leaned forward in my eagerness to hear her words.

"William sent us to talk to Reverend Smallbone. He knew your history, Callum-san."

Callum smiled and shook his head. "Callum is quite good enough, Kazhua," he said.

She smiled back at him before she spoke again. "He told us that you had both escaped to Canada but that Callum's home was here, in Scotland. He said that you talked to him often about how you missed Glen Kyle."

"We went to Edo to find you," I interrupted. Suddenly, it seemed very important that Kazhua should know that we had tried, and failed, to find her. "I think you couldn't have been gone more than a few months, perhaps a year. We met Akira." Kazhua shuddered. I nodded my understanding.

"Eventually, we found out that you had escaped to America. I cursed all the gods when I thought that I had been there myself for so long. I couldn't believe that fate had been so cruel to us."

Kazhua looked at me with wonder in her eyes. "It's worse than you know. I went back to Edo," she said. "It must have been quite soon after you had left, but nobody told me that somebody had been searching for me. I had no idea."

"I'm not surprised about that," I explained. "We took great care to make sure nobody realized we were interested in you. We were worried it would awaken memories that were best left undisturbed, for all our sakes."

We both shook our heads in disbelief at the ways our paths had crossed, but always a fraction too late.

"Akira's dead," Kazhua said. She nodded at Mineko. "He had taken poor Mineko as his concubine. She nearly died herself when rival yakuza set fire to his house. There was a terrible battle. He is dead," she added, as if I had doubted it. "I saw him die."

"Good," I said simply. I felt no remorse at my words. "He was a terrible man, but I think he would rather have died than lived without you, Kazhua."

We were all silent for a moment. Then Alfie, becoming bored, scratched vigorously behind his ear and broke the tension and we all laughed.

"Can you stay?" I asked shyly. "All of you. Stay here, I mean. Or must you go back to America soon?"

Kazhua turned her head to glance at her nobleman. He shrugged and smiled. Kazhua's gaze went to Mineko, who grinned.

"If you are happy to have us here, we can stay." She smiled radiantly. "We must go to London eventually. Mineko and I are going to act in the theater there. We have a contract to perform in *Twelfth Night* at the Theater Royal, on Drury Lane. We must be there by Christmas."

She stopped, staring at me as I gasped in disbelief.

"I've seen *Twelfth Night*. At the Theater Royal." I shook my head. "Of course. You and Mineko are going to play Viola and Sebastian, aren't you?" I began to smile. The red thread of fate again. How could I ever have doubted that we would find each other?

"We are. And after that, we may decide to open a kabuki in London. Who knows, you may yet get tired of having me so close!" I shook my head and mouthed *never* silently. We smiled at each other. "There is a long, long story to tell you, Mother. And I know there is so much more I need to hear from you. But there is plenty of time. I would be very happy if we could stay with you, at least until my little brother is born."

We all sat quietly for a long time. There would be need for words, lots and lots of words, later. But for now, it was enough that the red thread of fate had finally led me to my daughter.

I had no idea I was crying until Kazhua mopped away my tears with her sleeve.

Callum put his arm around me, and I smiled tenderly at Kazhua.

"We have found each other at last, daughter. I always knew that one day our fates would lead us to each other again." I glanced up at Callum and saw great joy in his expression. I understood at once that I spoke for us both. "Nothing will ever part us again. Even if we are half a world away from each other, we will always be united in our hearts and minds. The world is ours, Kazhua. And now that we are together we have all the time there is left to us in this world."

The happiness that was in all our hearts overwhelmed the need for mere words. We sat silently. I watched as Kazhua lifted her hand and looked wonderingly at her smallest finger. I had no need to look at my own hand. I felt the red thread of my fate tug gently but insistently as it ran toward her. To my daughter.

THANK YOU!

We hope you enjoyed *This World is Ours*. Make sure you never miss a new release by subscribing to our mailing list. http://redempresspublishing.com/subscribe/

ABOUT THE AUTHOR

 India Millar started her career in heavy industry at British Gas and ended it in the rarefied atmosphere of the British Library. She now lives on Spain's glorious Costa Blanca North in an entirely male dominated household comprised of her husband, a dog, and a cat. In addition to historical romances, India also writes popular guides to living in Spain under a different name.

Website: www.indiamillar.co.uk

ABOUT THE PUBLISHER

VISIT OUR WEBSITE
TO SEE ALL OF OUR HIGH QUALITY BOOKS:

http://www.redempresspublishing.com

Quality trade paperbacks, downloads, audio books, and books in foreign languages in genres such as historical, romance, mystery, and fantasy.

Made in the USA
Middletown, DE
18 December 2023

46068441R00215